Michael Jecks is the author of the bestselling Knights Templar series, comprising thirty-two novels starring Baldwin de Furnshill. *Blood of the Innocents* is the final chapter in the Hundred Years' War trilogy that started with *Fields of Glory*, followed by *Blood on the Sand*. A regular speaker at library and literary events, he is a past Chairman of the Crime Writers' Association and a Fellow of the Royal Literary Fund at Exeter University. Michael lives with his wife, children and dogs in northern Dartmoor.

To find out more visit his website: www.michaeljecks.com, follow him on twitter @MichaelJecks, or find him on facebook: www.facebook.com/Michael.Jecks.author

MICHAEL JECKS

BLOOD OF THE INNOCENTS

**SIMON &
SCHUSTER**

London · New York · Sydney · Toronto · New Delhi

A CBS COMPANY

First published in Great Britain by Simon & Schuster UK Ltd, 2016
A CBS COMPANY

1 3 5 7 9 10 8 6 4 2

Simon & Schuster UK Ltd
1st Floor
222 Gray's Inn Road
London WC1X 8HB

www.simonandschuster.co.uk

Simon & Schuster Australia, Sydney
Simon & Schuster India, New Delhi

A CIP catalogue record for this book
is available from the British Library

Trade Paperback ISBN: 978-1-4711-4997-9
eBook ISBN: 978-1-4711-4999-3

Typeset in the UK by M Rules
Printed and bound by CPI Group (UK) Ltd, Croydon, CR0 4YY

Simon & Schuster UK Ltd are committed to sourcing paper
that is made from wood grown in sustainable forests and support the Forest
Stewardship Council, the leading international forest certification organisation.
Our books displaying the FSC logo are printed on FSC certified paper.

This book is dedicated to
Beryl Joan Jecks
22nd March 1929 – 4th October 2015
a perfect mother

And

Andrew Setchell
6th July 1961 – 4th February 2016
a perfect friend

Both are hugely missed

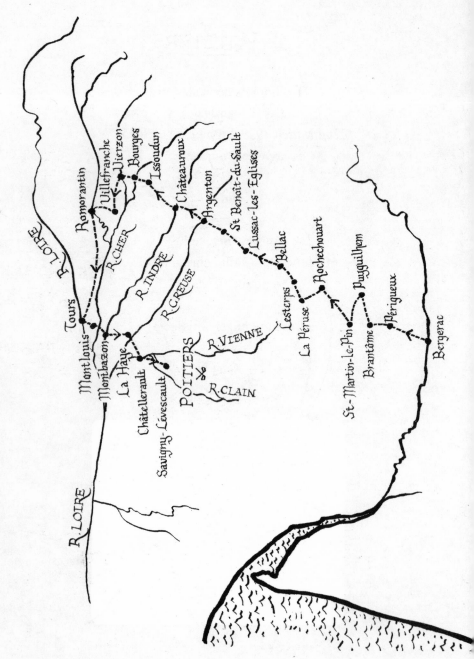

ENGLISH LINE OF MARCH

R. LOIRE

R. LOIRE

Romorantin

Villefranche

Vierzon

Bourges

Issoudun

R. CHER

R. INDRE

Châteauroux

Argenton

St Benoît-du-Sault

Lussac-les-Eglises

R. C. REUSE

Tours

Montlouis

Montbazon

La Haye

Châtellerault

Savigny-Lévescault

POITIERS

R. VIENNE

R. CLAIN

Bellac

Lesterps

La Péruse

Rochechouart

Puyguilhem

St-Martin-le-Pin

Brantôme

Périgueux

Bergerac

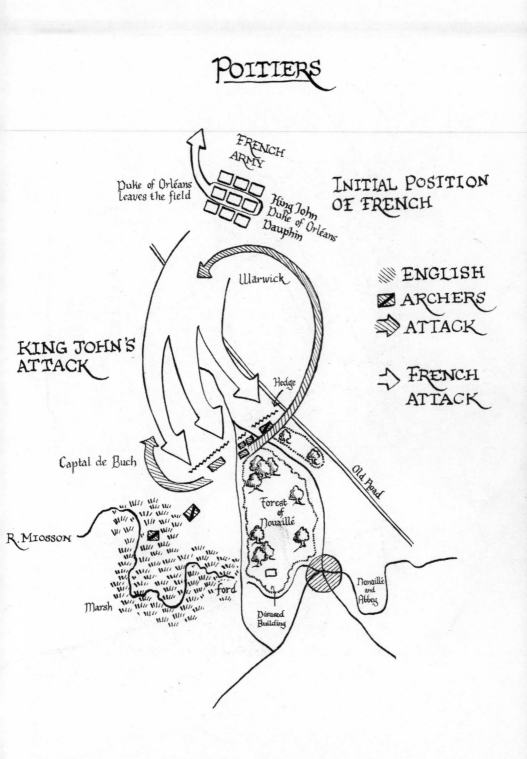

POITIERS

FRENCH
ARMY

Duke of Orléans
leaves the field

King John
Duke of Orléans
Dauphin

INITIAL POSITION
OF FRENCH

Warwick

KING JOHN'S
ATTACK

Hedge

Captal de Buch

R. MIOSSON

Forest
of
Nouaillé

Old Road

Marsh

ford

Disused
Building

Nouaillé
and
Abbey

ENGLISH

ARCHERS

ATTACK

FRENCH
ATTACK

CAST OF CHARACTERS

King John	the King of France
The Dauphin	the heir to the King of France
King Charles	the devious and political King of Navarre
Thomas de Ladit	priest and Chancellor to the King of Navarre
Arnaud	servant in the pay of King Charles
Bernard	brother to Arnaud and also King Charles's servant
Sir John de Sully	knight bannaret and loyal servant of the Prince of Wales
Grandarse	the centener of a hundred men under Sir John
John Hawkwood	a vintener in Grandarse's command, before known as John of Essex
Members of Vintaine	Clip
	Dogbreath
	Gilles
	Nick
	Pierre and Felix, aka Père et Fils
	Baz
	Imbert
	Robin

Berenger Fripper	an old soldier, now leader of a mercenary company
Will	Berenger's second in command in the company of mercenaries
Simon of Shoreditch	vintener in Berenger's company
Peter of Reading	vintener in Berenger's company
Companions of Berenger's	Saul of Plymouth, originally from Berenger's mercenary band
	Loys, a younger member of Berenger's force
	Fulk, a powerful Swiss warrior who joined Berenger
Archibald	a 'gynour' who commands a number of 'gonnes'
Ed	assistant to Archibald
Béatrice	a French orphan who accompanies Archibald and Ed
Denisot	the Bayle of Domps
Gaillarde	wife to Denisot
Ethor	steward to the priory near Domps
Alazaïs	widow in Uzerche
Perrin and Charlot	sons of Alazaïs
Abbot Andry	the Abbot of St Jacques

PROLOGUE

Rouen, Tuesday 5 April 1356

The screams rose, rough and agonised on the warm afternoon air as the cleaver rose again, and the crowds watching shivered, appalled, as the executioner prepared to bring the blade down once more.

Grasping his heavy weapon, the man looked as though he was in a hellish nightmare, his soul already held firmly in the devil's talons. His eyes were wide and raw-rimmed, and the cleaver trembled in his drunken grip. He was no torturer: he was a forger, and inexperienced at this butchery. Yet he had been offered a royal pardon if he would perform this task: killing four men. His life in exchange for four. It had seemed an easy arrangement.

But he was made for less stern work. He would spew if that appalling shrieking of agony and terror didn't stop soon.

He brought the blade down yet again, and a little puff of blood rose, droplets hitting his face and making him blink as his victim wailed with a voice made raw and harsh. Colin Doublet's Adam's apple had been slammed three times into the executioner's block already as the cleaver had missed its mark. The forger wrestled with the weapon. It had become stuck in Colin's neck, gripped by a vertebra, and the bile rose as he jerked it this way and that. He hefted it again, bringing it down, his eyes closed to block the hideous sight.

Thomas de Ladit, tireless servant of King Charles, ordained priest and Chancellor to the King of Navarre, watched with revulsion. What, he reflected bitterly, was Colin's crime, exactly? Only that he was the devoted servant to King Charles of Navarre. For that he was being slowly cut to pieces by this slaughterman. Death by a hundred cuts. And after him it would be the turn of the three noblemen.

Thomas peered up at the wagon where the King of France, John II, stood with a cup of wine, laughing. His friends joined in the merriment, but not his son the Dauphin. The heir to the throne was grim with fury. His friends and allies were being hacked to death, but protesting was futile. His father had given his command and issued the death sentence. Nothing could be done to save them. Thomas bowed his head, his face guarded by the cowl of his priest's robe.

He wished he could shut out the screams as easily as he could shut out the sight.

The day had begun so well, too.

King Charles of Navarre was short but, as Thomas knew, although God had seen fit to reduce his height, He had given the King the strength of character, the will and determination, of an Emperor. That was why the King of France could not tolerate him. That was why he must be subdued: because Charles of Navarre had the charisma and guile of a ruler, while King John II had nothing. He was a brute, who blustered and threatened like a tavern bully.

Except today the company would learn that the French King was not so gullible as they had thought.

Thomas de Ladit stood at the rear of the great hall and observed as the servants moved among the guests. Charles himself sat at the right hand of the Dauphin, and the two men chatted quietly, laughing much, as the council ate. Navarre's wit and charm were two of his great strengths, but Thomas knew that his sense of humour concealed a penetrating intellect. He may not be a great warrior or war leader, but he was shrewd, bold and intensely astute when it came to guessing what lay in another man's mind.

A figure moved past him, breaking his train of thought. Thomas threw a glance at the man and saw Colin Doublet, esquire to King Charles. He was no threat. The esquire nodded to Thomas as he passed carrying a heavy plate to the King and Dauphin, bowing low as he proffered the meats laid out so temptingly. Thomas's mouth watered at the smells and sights in the hall, but he would eat later. His duty was to remain here, to watch for danger and to be on hand in case his Lord needed his counsel. Discussions would continue during the meal here at Rouen's great castle. The men about the table were the leading nobles of Normandy, and there was much to discuss.

The aristocracy of France had been divided in recent years. There were those who continued to support King John, but more and more were turning to Charles of Navarre, King John's own son-in-law.

Charles had a strong claim to the throne, in fact it was considered stronger than King John's by many. John himself was growing irrational in the face of his financial and military woes. When he deprived Navarre of Angoulême and gave it to his favourite, the Lords and Barons saw that he could as easily deprive them of their property. For Charles of Navarre it was a humiliation too far, and led to him seeking an association with the English. Thomas de Ladit knew that Charles was keeping that route open to himself. The English King was content to split France in two and share the spoils with Charles, removing King John. He did not realise that Charles wanted to remove John so that he could take the whole realm. Most were dull enough to swallow Charles's flattery at face value. Very few were bright enough to see his true aims. Certainly not King John!

Even the Dauphin, Prince of France and Duke of Normandy, was becoming more closely allied with Charles of Navarre. It was not surprising. The Dauphin wanted to be popular, to rule with the approval of his Lords; it was too late for King John to achieve that, but with King Charles of Navarre aiding him, the Dauphin could hope that a little of the Navarrese charisma would redound to his credit. He was keen enough, if not terribly bright.

Much had already been agreed. Soon, when their meal was finished, other, more parochial, affairs would be talked over. First, these nasty stories of kidnaps from the villages about here. Children were being taken from their beds at night, it was said. The peasants were complaining about it, although the dullards probably cared little. Those taken were little girls mostly, and fathers never minded losing one of them. The brats were only additional mouths, when all was said and done, and expensive when they came of age and a dowry must be found. Besides, peasants rutted in the mud and filth and often gave rise to unexpected offspring. They could not truly care for all their brats, any more than a bitch for her pups when they were weaned. Still, it was curious that nobody seemed to know who was responsible. There were tales that the children were killed, not ransomed. If not for money, why take them? Whatever the reason, the Dauphin was keen to learn who was responsible. He had mentioned that he wanted to talk about the kidnappings later this afternoon when they reconvened and ...

There was a rattling sound from somewhere and Thomas frowned, glancing about him. Black-haired Bernard was over at the northern wall, but he seemed to have heard nothing. The young, fair servant, Arnaud, was at his side, but he stood smiling to himself as usual, as if listening to a tune no one else could hear. Little ever seemed to unsettle him. Still, Thomas was concerned. An esquire, Martin de Rouen, stood listening intently but made no move and Thomas gradually began to relax.

This meal was a reward for those who were loyal and he didn't want anything to spoil the effect. He and King Charles had discussed the seating in detail for days before this banquet. The Compte d'Harcourt should be closer to the Dauphin, rewarded for his loyalty during the recent attempts to remove King John and replace him with his more malleable son; the Lord of Graville could be a little further away, but not so far as to be insulting; Guillaume de Mainemares should be slightly further away ...

Arnaud frowned. He glanced at Bernard, then shot a look at Martin, and suddenly Thomas could hear it too. The noise was growing. Thomas felt his face take on an unaccustomed frown. Everything had been planned to the minutest detail, and yet some fool was destroying the ambience of this gathering. Someone in the kitchen, no doubt, was clattering about with the pans. Although, and now his frown grew with his rising alarm, that did not sound like the coppers and pans from the kitchen. It was surely the sound of armour.

He began to step forward, but before he could take more than a half-step there was a thunderous crash as the door to the tower was flung wide, and there was a sudden roar as a party of men-at-arms rushed inside, men with swords already in their hands.

Those sitting at the great tables leaped to their feet, clumsily grabbing for swords and knives as they rose. Thomas himself was unarmed, but he saw Colin drop his platter and move to the side of his King even as Thomas saw the figure stalking into the hall, his brutish face lowered truculently, his prognathous jaw moving with rage, his eyes almost hidden beneath his heavy brows. His face was the same colour as his red hair as he moved into the middle of the chamber, glaring about him.

'Put down your weapons, unless you want to be accused of treason!' he roared.

Thomas felt his stomach tighten. He shivered and shrank back into the shadows of a pillar. The King's brother, the Duke d'Orléans, was there, as was Anjou and Arnoul d'Audrehem, the Marshal of France. To have such men, and a small army of a hundred or more men-at-arms, spoke of a coming disaster.

It was the Marshal who spoke now. He stood with the Duke d'Orléans at the King's side, his sword aloft. 'You heard your King! Put down your weapons. Anyone who moves shall die!'

There was silence in the room. Thomas saw Harcourt gently push his sword back in his scabbard and take his hand from the hilt, others among the diners released their weapons, hands open in demonstration of compliance, although there was no diminution of tension.

'You fucking traitor!' King John hissed. He moved to King Charles, who still sat in his seat, unmoving, but deathly pale. Thomas felt his heart lurch at the sight. It was known, and laughed about behind the King's back, that John was no warrior, but his temper was legendary. He could kill when he was in a black mood like this. He could even kill Charles, his son-in-law. 'You plot to have me killed? You deserve to die!'

Colin Doublet sprang forward at that, pulling his dagger free, but before he could strike, two of the King's men-at-arms grabbed him. One brought his sword's pommel down hard onto his head, and Colin's legs buckled as the dagger fell from his grasp.

The Dauphin peered haughtily at his father. He dared to speak with disdain. 'What's the meaning of this? What are you doing here? My Lord, these men are my guests, they are safe here, under my roof.'

The King ignored him. 'Take that scum out of my sight!' he bellowed, and King Charles was hauled to his feet and dragged towards the doors, his esquire behind him.

It was the signal for the rest of the room. Men slipped past the King's guards and ran for the doors. Thomas stood long enough to see Harcourt shoved back against a wall, a sword at his throat, Graville was beaten to the ground and kicked until he was silent, while a servant who tried to protect him was knocked senseless.

He had seen enough. Thomas de Ladit slipped through the door behind him and made his way down the spiral staircase inside the tower. At the bottom there was a door to the inner court, and he made his way through that to the outer. Soon he was in the streets of Rouen.

There was a scream, and then there came the sound of running feet and shouting. Quickly he pulled into a doorway. Soon Arnaud and Bernard appeared, Arnaud still wearing that stupid smile on his face as though this was all some game, while Bernard held the single-minded glower of a man who would stop at nothing. Thomas beckoned them. They joined him in his dark doorway, and soon a group of men-at-arms hurtled past.

'We must escape,' Bernard said.

'We will,' Thomas said, 'but first we must see what happens

to King Charles and the others. We must bear witness, both for King Charles's allies here and in England, but also for Navarre. I will not leave until I know what is to happen to them.'

Thus it was that Thomas de Ladit heard the sentence of imprisonment in the Louvre for his master and King, and that he was witness to the execution of the others.

And thus it was that he swore vengeance on the King of France for that injustice. He looked up at the King of France again, and momentarily he caught the eye of the Dauphin. The King's son stared at him, and Thomas could have sworn that there was a fleeting smile on his face, as though the Prince was already planning his father's demise for this insult.

Later, at the Champ-du-Pardon, when the four had finally been silenced, Thomas did not wait to watch as they were wrapped in chains and hanged from the gibbet, their heads spiked on lances overlooking Rouen from the execution hill. He met Arnaud and Bernard, and together with them made his way south, hoping to find a Navarrese stronghold where he could be safe. Behind him, the forger knelt, shaking like a man with an ague, staring at his hands, while the headless bodies of the Compte d'Harcourt, the Lord de Graville and Guillaume de Mainemares were hauled up to join Colin's.

'We will be avenged, my King,' Thomas swore under his breath as he walked away. 'I swear it.'

CHAPTER ONE

Bordeaux, Tuesday 5 July

The body was near the common sewer, at the back of the rows of poor timber and mud cottages that lined the roads here south of the river in the suburbs of the English town of Bordeaux. At first Ed thought it was an obscene painting on the wall of a cottage. Then he saw the hair move in the breeze.

It was a small figure, with hair the colour of dirty straw, limbs like fragile sticks, wearing a thin shift that had been ripped aside, the legs forced apart, the arms outstretched like the crucifixion paintings he had seen on church walls, although this was no painting.

When Ed first caught sight of her, he stopped and stood still, the alarm ringing in his head as though a tocsin was tolling just for him. These were dangerous parts. Men would kill to steal shoes or an empty purse, anything for the price of a whore in the stews or a jug of ale in a tavern. Ed had been a soldier, and he knew when to keep quiet. He carefully moved back into the shadow at the corner of a wall, cautiously looking all around him.

No, even in the gathering gloom of twilight the body didn't scare him. Rather it was the men who could do this to a little girl that alarmed him. They would do worse to him.

Ed had seen death in many forms for a man of only three-and-twenty; he had grown habituated to it. When he was seven years old and the French attacked their city, he had seen his father slain and his mother raped and murdered the same day. Five years afterwards, seeking revenge, he had joined the English host and travelled with the King to France for the astonishing chevauchée that ended in the magnificent achievement that was Crécy and the capture of Calais. That campaign was such a glorious success that men still spoke of it in hushed, reverential tones even now, but all he saw was still more butchery – men, women and children – until death itself had become a commonplace.

And then, a scant couple of years later, when he was back in England, he had seen God's judgement. Like a disciplinarian parent who gives a beating after a treat so that his children will not grow up believing that they are entitled to constant rewards, it seemed He was demonstrating that the English might be granted a glorious victory, but there would inevitably be a reckoning. That was when the Great Pestilence had swept up from France and settled in England, taking one life in every two, so it seemed, before it disappeared.

This body was not like any of those others.

He stared at her for a long time before stepping forward cautiously. That was when he noticed the other man, the man who rocked on his haunches and moaned to himself, his head in his hands. He was almost hidden behind a cart and the detritus of the road, crouched low.

10

Ed thought he was weeping at first, and that this must be a friend, or perhaps the father of the dead figure. He looked at the girl again: at the tousled hair, the eyes wide and staring as if in unimaginable pain, the mouth stuffed with shreds of linen to gag her, the hands pinned to the wall by large-headed nails, the smears of blood at her thighs where the skirts of her tunic had been ripped away. Ed had thought she was dead, but then he heard a shrill, muffled squeal. She was alive, but gagged. He felt a thrill of rage clot his heart as he saw the feebly moving leg, the head shaking with panic. The man must surely go and wrest her from her bonds, he thought. Why didn't he hurry?

He was about to go to help the man, when the fellow stood, glanced about him, gave a stunted cry, and then hurried forward. Ed saw the flash of steel, and the girl's torment was ended.

Ed couldn't help his cry of shock. The man turned and saw him. Ed saw dark hair, wide eyes, a mouth like a gash in his beard, and then he was bolting away like a greyhound with a broken paw, low, hunched in anguish, lurching, but moving swiftly, while Ed hurried to the girl.

Her eyes were clear and gazed into his as though he was a thousand miles away. She was only a child.

'Why?' Ed demanded of the fleeing man, and then he grabbed at his horn and blew three blasts to call for help.

As he allowed his horn to fall to his side again, the sound of laughter came to Ed on the wind. It chilled his blood.

It sounded like the giggling of a demon.

The town shone like a small ochre jewel in the early evening light, glowing with a golden fire where the sun's low light struck the pale stones of the church and walls. It sat in the curve of the river as snug and comfortable as a puppy in its basket, the trees of the forest standing behind as if sheltering it, while the rocky outcrops falling down to the river served as a warning to all who might dare consider an attack.

Those little cliffs would deter all but the most determined, but the long approach through the forest was dangerous too. The citizens had manufactured defences: pits, trenches lined with spikes, spring-traps to shatter the leg of a man or horse, trip-wires that would release swinging spiked balls of steel to crush a man's skull. The inventiveness of peasants and castellans alike was a constant, unpleasant source of surprise to the men on their horses.

There was a bridge over the river. It was wood, with a stone tower at this side to protect it, and someone had set a chain across the road as night fell.

The leader of the small band narrowed his eyes. His sight was failing, but he could make out the line of the bridge's supports, the great wooden planks that criss-crossed the void and held up the roadway.

It was the cause of the town's prosperity, that bridge. They had sweated to build it; they had saved and expended their treasure; they had maintained it at still more cost, but this little bridge in the Limousin was worth all the money and more, because every traveller crossing it, whether heading east or west, must pay for the privilege. If the townspeople had been wise, they would have destroyed that bridge. But few men were keen to destroy the source of their own wealth. Packhorses, carts, wagons and individual travellers would pay much to pass over it, because it was the only crossing for many miles.

That bridge was the reason why these men had come here.

Throughout France the people lived in terror. Since the disaster of Crécy and the loss of Calais the country had trembled. Outlaws and mercenaries took advantage of the void left by so many dead noblemen and men-at-arms who would have enforced the law. These routiers, the dregs of the cess-pits and gutters of Gascony, Flanders, the Holy Roman Empire and beyond, set out on their own campaigns of murder and looting. The English who had remained in France after fighting for their King were used to slaughter. They preferred to remain here and take what they wanted by force of arms, rather than return to their lives as peasants in England. It was easier, and life was sweet.

So the English and their mercenaries waxed while the peasants on whom they preyed waned.

Berenger cared nothing. He had hoped for a life of ease and peace, but it was shattered, and he blamed God – and France. His life had ended just as he thought he could hang up his sword forever. The French could rot.

But that bridge: control that, and a man would own the tolls paid to cross the river.

Berenger Fripper and his men were keen to have those tolls.

As Archibald carefully stirred the mixture, he thought about the opportunities he was missing. There were times when he wondered whether he still suited this work.

There was no doubt that war was a younger man's business. For a fellow like him, a man in his middle years, the days of rising early, riding to battle and carousing with comrades afterwards were long gone, not that many would want to join him. When he caught sight of himself in a mirror, he was surprised by the sight of the man looking back at him: his hair was pale and thin, his beard full and mostly grey, his blue eyes hidden beneath his bushy brows, and surrounded by so many wrinkles it seemed a miracle that the man was still living. It seemed but a blink of his eye since he was an eager monk, but that was many years ago. Archibald glanced down at his body as he stirred. He wore his customary leather coif, and a loose lace flicked across

his face in the breeze that passed through the workshop. He had a
kerchief about his throat, and a thick sleeveless leather jack with
a linen chemise beneath, all pocked and blackened with sooty
marks, and below that was his heavy leather apron, like a smith's
in that it was discoloured all over with black scorch marks and
occasional holes. Looking at himself, he shook his head. His
paunch was grown greatly in the last two years. Life here was too
easy. He would find it hard to go to war again.

'Master, how is it?'

'It goes well enough,' Archibald said, concentrating on turning the paddle and keeping the mixture moving gently. Mixing
dry powders like this was always slightly nerve-wracking. He
must not make the concoction get warm, but always be gentle.

Ed crossed the floor. Archibald raised an eyebrow as he
stood staring down at the large bowl. 'What is it?'

Ed stared at the mixture doubtfully. 'Have you added all
the—'

'If you think you can do better, you should set up your own
house and find your own customers,' Archibald said evenly.
'Until then, you should recall who it was that taught you all
you know.' He peered closer at Ed. 'What is it? Something has
alarmed you.'

He knew Ed like his own flesh and blood. The lad was usually relaxed and unemotional, but today he was on edge.

It was almost ten years ago that he had first met Ed. Then the
boy had been a gangling brat, little able to feed himself, nervous
and wary in the presence of men. Archibald had taken him in
and adopted him, and since then he had come to appreciate the
lad. Ed had a quick mind, a sharp wit and was utterly devoted
to Archibald and Béatrice, the young woman whom they had
discovered on the march to Crécy, and who had remained with
the army for the following year. Archibald had often wondered

whether the two would find love or tenderness in each other's arms, but so far his hopes had been dashed. Béatrice and the Donkey (an affectionate nickname given to Ed by the rest of that first vintaine) appeared to be as fond of each other as any brother and sister, but no more. Béatrice felt the full weight of her extra four or five years, and Ed was content to take his few pennies to the whores in the stews when he needed to indulge his natural desires.

'Aye, you taught me all you could,' Ed said. 'Do you think that passing on information is like other gifts? Once you have given it, it is no longer yours?'

'What is that supposed to mean?' Archibald demanded, still stirring gently. 'And don't try to change the subject. What has upset you, boy? I know you well enough. You've a face like an alewife who's just found her beer's turned to piss.'

Ed gave a smile. 'No secrets from you, eh, Gynour?'

'I doubt you could manage it.'

'I saw a man murder a little girl today. A black-haired, black-bearded man. He had nailed her to a wall like a crucifixion and raped her, poor child.'

Archibald winced. 'There are many demons in this world. Did you recognise him?'

'No, but I'd know this man again, I think.'

Ed returned to his table, cutting a loaf in half and scooping out the creamy-coloured crumb.

'Did you report it?'

'No. I blew my horn for the hue and cry, but left them to it.'

'Good.' Neither Ed nor Archibald was sure of the customs of this town, but in England reporting a murder would entail being amerced, held over by payment of a surety until the coroner could investigate, and neither had any intention of waiting here for some King's officer to decide to amble over. Ed didn't want to have to pay a fine, but more to the point, he didn't want to end up as a suspect. All too often a foreign first finder could become the first – and only – suspect.

Ed worked on two more loaves, and then crossed to the pot set over the fire. He ladled two good scoops of pottage into the makeshift trenchers. Setting them on the table, he pulled his spoon out from under his shirt and took the thong from over his head. 'Food, old man,' he called, then, 'Béatrice!'

Archibald set his mixing bowl aside. It was difficult to grind the mixture. Usually men would add the brimstone, sal petrae and charcoal into their wooden pestles and cautiously crush them into powder. Recently Archibald had been pounding the individual components and then mixing the three together, but he was thinking that he may leave it to Béatrice in future. She had the woman's touch. In any case, he wasn't sure yet that it was a more efficient means of making his black powder. He walked to the table, wiping grimy hands on his apron, and was pulling the stool from under the table when Béatrice walked in.

The French woman was tall, as elegant and slender as a birch, with all the associated strength. Archibald had first encountered her when the vintener in Grandarse's company had asked him to look after the two. Then she had been thin and drawn, driven by her fear of her countrymen. Her family had been destroyed when her father had been executed, she had told him once, and she joined with the English because she thought she had little choice. Now she had grown into an attractive woman.

Archibald closed his eyes as she sat, and spoke a few brief words in thanks for the food in front of them. When he reopened his eyes he frowned.

'What is in this?' he asked, peering into the trencher.

'Ramsons, peas, some beans and plenty of good water from further up the river,' Ed said. His face lightened momentarily.

'Something wrong?'

'I was just thinking. I heard some news today,' Ed said. He and Archibald exchanged a glance. Mention of young girls being raped would upset Béatrice, and neither wished to offend or upset her.

'Well? What of it?'

'There is to be another raid under the Prince. He is to take an army into France again.'

'Where this time? Last year he ravaged the whole of the south as far as Narbonne. Where does he intend to attack this time?'

'Oh, it must have slipped his mind to tell me!' Ed said sarcastically. 'How would I know? Do you think he would ask me for my advice before setting off?'

'I had hoped you could learn a little more, certainly.'

'I did.' Ed smiled slowly as he chewed a hunk of bread. 'I spoke to Sir John de Sully's esquire. He told me that the army will need serpentine and a Master Gynour ... but in their absence, he will be content to have you go with him.'

CHAPTER TWO

It was midnight. Berenger sniffed the air. There was a chill that seemed to impregnate a man's skin, seeping in like oil into a cloth until it had laid hold of a man's bones. He stood, studying the town's bulk in the distance, his cloak wrapped tight about him, a figure of deeper darkness in the gloom of night.

It was called Uzerche, he had learned. They had found a young goatherd in the hills before the town, and he had been eager to help them. In exchange they had swiftly ended his troubles with a knife. Berenger had seen to it that it was swift. There had already been too much suffering in this sorry land.

The men were rested. It was time.

Berenger signalled with his hand to his sergeant, Will, who called out quietly, and the men climbed to their feet. Will was tall and elegant. Many thought him effete, with his bright, little-boy-blue eyes and wistful grin under his unkempt thatch of fair hair. Women adored him, and men sneered at him, until they saw him fighting. He was as brave and heedless of danger as a berserker in battle.

The horses and ponies were left with the boys, and the whole party of almost a hundred men formed a column and began to tramp onwards.

There were few lights. At this time of night in a small town, there would be some watchmen, but the larger part of the citizens would be asleep. The curfew would be in place, and all fires damped and smothered while the people slumbered. It was the ideal time for the assault.

They were at the bridge. Four men with scaling ladders went to the tower. There was one figure at the wall, but as he peered down, Will pointed him out. Will's man Alex loosed his arrow, striking the sentry in the head at the same time as two others hit him in the breast and throat. He was dead before he could cry out. Berenger had feared that the noise of the arrows slamming into his mail would itself wake the garrison, yet there was no sound from inside.

The four men were followed by another four, and soon Berenger heard the cry of an owl on the evening air, and knew that the tower was theirs.

More men, more ladders, now crossing the bridge to the main town beyond.

There were sentinels on the walls, but as the English quietly scrambled up the rungs, it became clear that the guards were dozing. Not one cried out in alarm.

To his left, Will led one group; further on, Simon was first to breast the wall with another section; beyond him Peter: all of them courageous and bold leaders, each with their own contingent of twenty men. With men like this it was hard to fail.

Berenger's men bore their scaling ladder to the wall and leaned it quietly. He was beaten to the rungs by Loys, who sprang up it with the agility of a monkey. Berenger felt the familiar excitement roiling in his belly as he set his foot to the first rung.

There was no fear, such as he had known when he was new to his business, only a firm determination to win the town. He hurried up the ladder to the battlements and climbed over, landing quietly on the packed stones of the inner walkway. There, he stood gazing about him.

Two guards had been dispatched by Simon on the walkway, both dying where they slept. Loys was stabbing them again, just to be certain. One looked as though he was still sleeping, but he had been stabbed by three of Simon's men already, none wishing to risk his waking, and now Loys opened his throat from ear to ear, grinning all the while as if in imitation of the appalling wound.

Already the English were scattering. Some went left with Peter, to the nearer guard tower. More pulled a ladder up after them and lowered it inside the town before making their way down and quietly scurrying to the gates. Berenger followed them, and nodded to Will.

Seeing Berenger's approval, Will hissed to the others, and Simon with three of his men set themselves at the massive baulks of timber holding the gates. They slid back into their sockets in the walls, and willing hands hauled at the gates, pulling them wide. With a groan from the iron hinges, the gates were drawn inwards, and the men began to cheer. With whoops of glee the remaining routiers burst in through the gates with an infernal clamour. Their boots thundered like waves crashing heavily on a shingle shore, but then their bellows and howls were overwhelmed by the cries of dismay from the population.

Their attack was a surprise. Men and women who had been slumbering in their beds were woken to the shrieks of their neighbours, to the sound of doors being smashed with axes and great hammers, the timbers broken and rent asunder, and blood-crazed English fighters leaping over them to ransack, rape and kill.

Berenger saw his men pelting up the main street and stood watching. His heart once would have felt pity, but not now. These people were the cause of his emptiness inside. Their terror fed his vengeful nature. He felt like a demon watching sinners herded to pits of flames. There was no compassion – only urgency to get this over with.

In the roadway up ahead he saw a tavern. His blood craved wine and he crossed to it. On either side the houses were broken open and men poured into them. He heard a scream, a rising ululation of terror, and as he glanced up he saw a figure fly through a window. It span, emitting a mewling noise, and in its wake he heard a cry like the last horrified squeal of a soul in torment. Looking up, he saw a woman with long, dark hair, her mouth wide, her eyes staring at her child as it hurtled to the ground. Her face was jerked from the window, and he saw her no more, although her screaming continued.

The child was only perhaps one year old. Its neck was broken now, and its struggle for life was over. Berenger stared at it for a moment. He wanted to feel something, to have some sorrow for the life ended, but there was nothing. His heart was as empty as an up-ended jug. No: a broken jug. His heart was shattered and broken. It could no longer contain anything like mercy.

There was only one creature for which he could feel sadness, and that was himself. He had already lost everything he loved or valued.

Wednesday 6 July

On the first day after their assault, Berenger held court in the market square. Some fires still raged over to the east of the town, but Berenger had ordered that the houses near them should be torn down, and while the populace whimpered and wrung their hands, his men eagerly despoiled the buildings and then used some of their scarce resources of serpentine powder to detonate them. One of his men was struck by a flying splinter two feet long, and all but cut in half, but he was the only fatality.

Berenger had breakfasted in a tavern with a flagon of wine and bread. He had taken the house of a widow, but her cold anger made him prefer to eat elsewhere. Her name was Alazaïs, and he liked her slanted eyes and the fixed resentment in them, but he had not raped her or tried to take her with subterfuge. His attraction to her lay in the location of her house: nothing more.

His men had pushed, cajoled or bullied all the townspeople to the square, and now held them back with lance-staves or shields as he trudged past them along the cleared corridor, his jug and goblet in his hands, still chewing. At the far end of the square stood a wagon, and Berenger drank more wine as he peered at the boxes set like steps beside it, before climbing up and surveying the scene before him.

The townsfolk were a poor lot. Behind the fence of lances they stood downcast, many of the women standing a little apart from their men, shivering, blood marking their skirts just as the shame marked their souls. Three women had been segregated: one stood and tried to scream, but her voice was broken after the horrors of the night; two others sat on the cobbles and wailed, one with her arms tightly wrapped around herself as though she was a ball of wool and feared she might unravel entirely.

Berenger let his eyes pass over the rest of the town. Men and husbands stood despondent, their hands resting on women and children, not daring to meet his or any of his men's eyes; some gazed about them defiantly or with contempt in their eyes. One of the priests glowered like a boy thrashed unfairly, while some had their faces in their hands. Boys and men had pulled hoods or hats over their features to hide from the stares of the soldiers.

'People of Uzerche,' Berenger said. 'I am named Berenger Fripper. I am the captain of this company. We are not your enemies. We are your friends. We are not here to rob and harm you, but to *protect* you. There are many fellows about the roads and woods who would destroy your town for the pleasure of it. We are not like them. Think of us as your guardians.'

He could taste that word. It had the flavour, sharp and unsavoury, of copper. Once, he would have scorned such a speech, but then life had been different. He could see Will below him at the wall of the nearest building, eating an apple while he watched the crowd with amusement.

Berenger looked out over the people again. 'Your King cannot help you. Your Lord is dead and his son is a child still. There is no one else who can serve you and your interests. We are here to protect the bridge and ensure the safety of all the citizens here. We shall stay here a little while. I am sure you will want to support us in our efforts.'

'We don't need protection!' an old man said.

Will motioned with his chin and the nearest soldier to the fellow reached for him, but Berenger gave a curt command and the man fell back again.

'You may not realise you need protection, but we have a clearer idea of the risks you run here. We can guard you and the bridge so that you come to no harm.'

The eyes stared up at him, dulled with the horrors of the last few hours. Through the watches of the night, these people had been beaten and robbed, their daughters and women raped and many slain.

Berenger forced a smile to his lips. It felt like a sneer. 'We look forward to a peaceful stay with you while we look after you all.'

'You are sent from the Devil himself!'

This was from another voice. Berenger scoured the crowd and finally saw who had spoken: the town's priest. He stood, bent with a crook back, his hand gripping a staff. He must have been in his late sixties from the look of his sunken cheeks, sallow complexion and washed-out blue eyes. Beside him another man in clerical garb tried to shush him, but seeing Berenger staring down at them, the cleric was still with fear.

'You think so?' Berenger said. 'If you were more holy, perhaps your town would have been saved. Perhaps, old fool, if you were more pious you could have saved people from the plague when that coursed through these lands and destroyed all that was beautiful and worthy. But you were no doubt suckling on the tits of your personal whore when good men and women and boys saw their loved ones die slowly and horribly!'

'I have no whore! I am a man of God!'

'You are a man. No better and no worse than any other. God has forsaken us all. We are here to wallow in our shame and guilt, while the good people we knew are taken.' In his mind's eye he saw her again: Marguerite. His resolve was stiffened.

'You are a heretic! You will burn in—'

Berenger pointed at him. 'Did you see all the people who died when the plague came here? Did you lose all those you loved? *We* did! Did you see the suppurating buboes, see the women and children coughing and succumbing to that horror? *I* did! Do you *dare* to tell me that God was responsible for that, because if you do, I'll swear on the Devil that no God who could do that was a God of love or mercy, and I'll curse you to the Devil if you dare naysay it!'

The priest opened his mouth, but the guard had heard enough. He lifted his lance and thrust once, hard, hitting the priest in the face with the butt-end. The priest's mouth was ripped open, and a spray of blood appeared as he was thrown backwards. His companion gave a yelp and bent to him, helping him sit up again.

'Does anyone else have any questions?' Berenger demanded. He poured from his jug and gulped the wine. It was good. The wine hit his belly like a burning torch striking dry thatch: he could feel the flames licking upwards through his entire body. He made his way down the rickety steps and drained the wine. The cleric was helping the priest to his feet.

'What shall we do with them?' Will asked, indicating the crowd.

'You can send them all to Hell for all I care,' Berenger said. He wiped his mouth on the back of his hand and peered round at them as he refilled his goblet.

Yes. Wine was good. It filled the space where love had once thrilled him, and numbed the senses that had known happiness, removing those memories that otherwise would have softened him to the suffering of others. It removed the sight of the dead. All those whom he had known and loved, all those with whom he had fought, and whose faces invaded his every dream.

He didn't want to feel their pain. He didn't want to feel anything.

CHAPTER THREE

In his rented lodgings in Bordeaux, Sir John de Sully issued his commands with a light heart.

He had been a fighter all his life, and had been luckier than most. Born in 1281, he was already seventy-five years old, but his enthusiasm and zest for life were undimmed. He had the conviction that God must soon want to take him, but if that were the case, he intended to make best use of the time he had left. There was no point being alive and spending all one's time preparing for death: better to act as though each day was your last and behave gloriously, honourably and generously as a knight should.

'It is confirmed?' he said.

'The Prince has ordered the muster, Sir John. He will leave today for La Réole. We are to join him as soon as we are ready.'

'He has paid us?' The Prince was a good lord who believed in rewarding his men, but even he could occasionally forget to reimburse his knights for their efforts.

'Yes.'

'Good!' His broad smile was proof of Sir John's relief. 'Then buy what we are likely to need for the journey, and get a saddle-maker to look at my second-best. I think that the cantle may be damaged. Then we will need to let the men know.'

'I already have. The centeners are outside.'

'Good. Bring them in.'

Sir John sat on his chair and eyed the two as they entered. One, Grandarse, was a vast figure who seemed to fill the room on his own. While his esquire, Richard Bakere, beckoned the steward to fetch wine for them all, Grandarse walked to the fire in the middle of the floor and cast an appraising eye over the sideboard, the display of pewter and silver, and the tapestries hanging on the walls.

'You can't have them, Grandarse.'

The centener grinned broadly. 'Aye, well, I'll take them when you've no further use for them.'

'Why? To sell so you can fill your belly? In God's name, man, you're already the weight of four soldiers! Your paunch is the size of a calf as it is!'

'This body is honed and trained for your honour, Sir John. I only eat that I might give you better service, and increase your glory,' Grandarse said seriously, patting his belly. His blue eyes twinkled.

Sir John shook his head, studying him reflectively. 'You're looking old, Grandarse. Are you sure this isn't going to be too much for you?'

'I'm twenty years younger than you, Sir John, so perhaps you'd like to go take a holiday from war yourself?'

'Aye, go swyve a goat,' the knight chuckled. 'I have plenty of fights left in me if the Good Lord leaves me a little more time.'

'Aye, and so have I,' Grandarse said. He took the mazer proffered by the steward and peered into it suspiciously. Taking a long pull of wine, he smacked his lips appreciatively. 'If you have a little more of this to bring to battle, I'll be happy to be at your side.'

Sir John stood. The other centener, a serious, staid man called Henry, drank more sparingly. He had hooded eyes and a manner of leaning forward and staring without blinking that was unsettling, but for all that Sir John knew him to be loyal, shrewd, and a man whose archers would follow him to the Devil and back.

'We will need to provision the men and stock up on all items for the campaign,' Sir John said, and walked to the table near the door to his solar, where they discussed food, equipment and recruiting.

'We have too few men just now,' Sir John said after a while.

'We'll manage. With the Prince leading us,' Grandarse said, 'we can match any army the French can throw at us.'

'That is all true. However, I want more men,' Sir John said.

'Aye,' Grandarse sighed. More men would mean depleting his profits. He was paid to recruit men, and if he chose to collect a smaller force, he could slip the remainder of the money into his purse after paying them. 'If you are sure, sir.'

'I am. You have a few days. Soon we shall move to a forward encampment. We will be travelling to La Réole.'

The two centeners nodded. All levity was gone now.

'The Prince has told me of the battle plan,' Sir John said. 'The Duke of Lancaster is to sail for Brittany in a few days. Our King had a powerful ally in Charles of Navarre, and the Duke sails to protect some of Charles's territory, to take the pressure off his people. He has been imprisoned, because it is said he was plotting to have King John captured and assassinated.'

'Was he plotting that?' Grandarse asked.

'It's said he planned to act as regent controlling the King's son, the Dauphin, as they call him. Whether it's true or not,

I've no idea,' the knight said. 'All that matters is that, since the announcement of this scheming, all have turned against him. The Dauphin, who was his greatest friend and ally, now lays siege to Navarre's men at Évreux. The Duke intends to raise that siege. He will attack in the north and sow distress. At the same time, we shall advance as soon as we are ready, and create a great confusion in the hearts of Frenchmen: should they attack us in the south, or should they concentrate their efforts on Lancaster's men? And while they wonder, a third blow will be struck, for King Edward is determined to attack in Flanders. He intends to join with Lancaster and take command of a great army that will threaten Paris. All the while, we shall ride northwards sowing dissension and misery as we come, ready to fall on the rear of the French as they meet with King Edward and Lancaster!'

Grandarse gave a low growl. 'That is news to my liking.'

'We will also be in charge of some gonnes,' Sir John added.

'Shite,' Grandarse muttered. Henry made no comment but the tightening of his lips indicated his displeasure.

'I know. I don't like it myself,' Sir John said. He drained his cup and waved the steward over with the jug. 'But the fact is, the King and his son like them. They scare me, but by God, they scare the enemy more. We are to bring Archibald Tanner with us once more. He will be responsible for the gonnes and powder.'

There were many more items to discuss: numbers of arrow sheaves, bow staves, strings, how many spares of each, how many wagons and carts would be needed to transport so much, and how many wagons and oxen devoted to carry the gonnes and powders.

'We will not have a huge army this time, but there will soon be so many men hunting for oxen and packhorses that we'll be fighting for fewer and fewer before we know it. You'll need to get on with things. And find more men.'

'How long do we have?' Henry asked.

'A matter of days. Perhaps a little more, but expect less rather than more.'

Grandarse hoicked his belt upwards as he considered this. 'I have John of Essex, although now he prefers to be called John Hawkwood – I'll be buggered if I'll call him that. Still, he's good at organising things generally. I'll leave them to sort out the majority of the carts and wagons for my centaine. If there's any spare, Henry, I'll tell you. What else?'

'We will need to have some wine and ale for the first weeks, until we get to forage for what we need.'

'Aye.'

'And men. You need more men, don't forget.'

'Aye.'

'Why do you look so despondent now, Grandarse?' Henry demanded after the silence had dragged. 'I've never seen you look so akin to a whipped hound before!'

'I was just thinking, with a number of new men, it'll be a tough job to teach them how to march and fight in one month. It's a shame we don't have Berenger with us. He was always good for beating the dullards into shape, as well as sorting the planning and provisioning.'

Denisot, the Bayle of Domps, was eating his breakfast when Poton arrived. At first the bayle thought that he could discount the tale as the ramblings of an old drunkard.

Poton was well known for drinking too much and brawling with men much younger than himself. Usually, Denisot knew, the fellow would pick a fight with a man much more competent than he, and would end up nursing a battered and bruised face while grumpily denying responsibility. Denisot would listen and, after a suitable pause for reflection, impose a fine.

This was different. The news that Poton brought of an unknown girl's body hanging in the woods was enough to make Denisot set aside his meal and listen carefully. Denisot was a thin man in his mid-thirties, with an overlarge nose that he pointed like a hawk's beak. His eyes were dark, and perpetually narrowed when speaking, as though he was straining to remember his companion's name. Some thought it was a device he nurtured, hoping always to unsettle those who would try to conceal information from him, for Denisot was responsible for the law in this poor, troubled land.

'Where was this body?'

'In the trees at the bend in the road, just before the old fish ponds,' the man said.

Poton stood with his hat in his hands, resentful at the attention he was being given. He was a bent old man, one of the last of his family of free men, but still forced to slave for the seigneur. All men must labour, as Denisot knew, but not all appreciated the laws that demanded so much. Poton was one of those who could remember the last uprising here, when men had been forced to rebel through hunger and poverty. When a man saw his wife and children die of starvation while the fruits of all their efforts went to feed the knights and men-at-arms who infested the lands about, it was hardly surprising that the fellow would snatch up a weapon. But the fights were short-lived. Since their enemies had suits of armour and better, sharper weapons, the contests ended all too swiftly.

'And she was hanging, you say?'

'She was nailed to a thick board, with iron nails in her palms and elbows. They had bound her elbows, too, with thick hempen cords.'

'Rope as well?'

'Yes, Bayle. The nails were poor, with small heads.

Perhaps the man who did this thought they would rip from her flesh.'

Denisot nodded. The rope meant the child would be forced to endure her death agonies: they would support her weight and she would have no opportunity for escape.

'You didn't cut her down? She might yet be alive,' Denisot said, to take his mind away from that thought.

Poton clenched his jaw. 'Her eyes were already gone, and peck-marks showed where the carrion birds had feasted. If she had breath in her body, the crows and ravens would not have gone near her. You think it possible she was alive? Maybe you know more than me, but I've seen sheep and cattle with their bodies eaten like that, and never once were they alive still.'

'I see. Well! You will have to take me to her. It is late. We should go in the morning.'

The old peasant inclined his head and turned to leave, but Denisot called him back. 'Before you go,' he said, 'were there any signs of men about the road and tree? You saw nothing of soldiers?'

'I didn't look. I saw her body there, and hurried away.'

'And you saw no evidence of an army?'

'I saw no English,' Poton said, meeting his eyes at last and grimly holding his gaze. It was Denisot who looked away.

He drank the last of his goblet of wine, stood, and said, 'Return at dawn. You must take me there.'

Poton nodded. He had no desire to see that corpse again tonight. Tomorrow would be too soon. Later, when talking of the body with friends, he would tell how the girl swung in the tree with every little soughing breeze, but he never mentioned how the fingers seemed to move as the board twisted gently, the rope cracking and squeaking like the doors to Hell, nor how it looked as if the child's hands were beckoning the peasant to join her.

*

Denisot rode on his pony while Poton ambled at his side. It was a dark day with great, blue-black, angry clouds overhead. Their journey was rich with the scent of soil and the thick, cloying odour of rotting leaves, but the humidity was building all the way, and Denisot was soon aware of the sweat trickling down his back in the thundery air. They had little light, but their journey was not long, and they reached the body within the hour.

Denisot stopped his pony beneath the figure. Just then a gust of wind rattled the branches of the trees nearby, and the plank turned until the eyeless, ravaged face of the girl seemed to stare at him. The movement made crows feasting on her face leap into the air, their feathers rustling like the winding-sheets of a long-dead army, their raucous cries the taunts and jeers of devils on the wind.

She was hanging from a wooden cross-piece that dangled by a rope thrown over a limb high on the tree, and tied off nearby. Her body was slumped like a crooked crucifix in the lower branches of the tree, her head bent, her arms stretched to either side and up, her body dangling unsupported.

'Dear God!' Denisot muttered, and crossed himself. 'Untie the rope,' he called. 'Let us free this poor chit.'

The rope ran from the limb to a smaller oak nearby. It had been tied securely, and with the weight of the body, Poton could not release the knot. He had a little knife in a sheath at his waist, and set it to the rope. It parted with a ripping sound as the fibres were sheared. Denisot climbed from his horse to see the body fall to the ground.

The girl had fallen face-down, and Denisot pulled the plank over, hauling the body with it.

'Do you recognise the child?' Denisot asked.

Poton shrugged emphatically. 'I've never seen her before.'

'Nor I,' Denisot murmured.

Once she had been a pretty little thing. Her hair was that red-gold that catches the sun with sparkles of fire, and it was thick and curled madly over her shoulders. She would have been three and a half, perhaps four feet tall in life, but the horrible damage done to her had left her looking shrunken and shrivelled.

Close to, her injuries were enough to make even the bayle gag. There were long scrapes where her flesh had been torn away. Her chin was raw to the bone, and her elbows too. Each injury had been expanded by the pecking beaks of the crows and ravens, but the initial scars were still just visible.

'What happened to her, eh?' Poton asked.

'I think she was dragged here behind a horse,' Denisot guessed. 'That's why she has lost so much flesh. Look, there are still pebbles and gravel in the wounds.'

Poton peered more closely, nodding, while Denisot studied the body carefully, trying to prevent his stomach's rebellion.

'She was only eleven or twelve, I would say,' he reflected.

'Who could have done such a thing to her?'

'And *why*?'

'I expect she was raped.'

He began to study the roadway, looking for evidence of large groups of men, but the roadway was well used. After the dry spell of the last few weeks there was no mud to be churned, only dry soil. He could tell nothing from the ground about here.

Poton stood by the corpse while Denisot continued his futile search for signs of the men who had committed this crime. There were plenty of powerful men in the area who could afford to have annoying peasants removed, but this was baffling. A knight or nobleman would take a man's head off without thinking, while a servant might stab in the back on his master's command, but to drag a child like this for some distance and rape her, then kill her in this most horrific manner, crucifying her, that spoke of unthinking brutality beyond anything Denisot had seen.

The two lifted the body onto the back of his pony, using the trailing rope to secure the figure in place, and started to trudge homewards.

As they walked, Denisot could not help but look at the body slumped over the pony's back. She was so young, so small. The sight of her little body made an unfamiliar anger kindle in his belly.

He wanted to avenge her, but there was little he could do. The kingdom was being torn apart by ravenous brutes: English, Guyennois, Flemings – there were all too many who would come here to steal, rape and murder.

What could a provincial official like him do against so many?

CHAPTER FOUR

Grandarse passed by the busy street smiling beatifically at the passers-by. His purse was deliciously heavy on his belt, and he had it bound at his side, where it rattled most intriguingly as he walked. Men eyed his purse more than they eyed his face. Not that it surprised him. Beneath his genial exterior, the portly man was fully aware of everyone about him.

Rather than his usual leather jerkin and stained old coif, Grandarse wore a rich cotte with long sleeves and a heavy cloak trimmed with fur. A thick, felt hat set the seal on the image he wanted to portray. He knew that these streets were dangerous. There were few enough cities in all Christendom that were safe. Thieves, cut-purses, club-men of all forms roamed the darker alleys in search of prey, and Grandarse was the ideal target for them.

He heard a step or two behind him as he entered an alley between two towering buildings. Making his way along it, he heard the soft footsteps following him. Many people would see a man with a belly as gross as Grandarse's and assume he was an easy gull. Only a merchant would be so fat, and merchants rarely wanted to risk their own safety when confronted by a bold fellow with a knife. In the dark of an alleyway, a gleaming dagger's edge would be enough to scare a rich man into handing over his wealth. It wouldn't take much, not with a grossly fat merchant. And any cut-purse could content himself with the reflection that a man that rich must have used coercion or usury to acquire his wealth. He deserved to be divested of his money.

Grandarse suddenly put on a spurt of speed. His boots slapped into the puddles and ordure that lay on the alley's floor, and then he whirled about and pulled back his cloak to show his sword.

Two men behind him hesitated and exchanged a look as he shed a little of his smile on them. 'You want something?' he asked cheerily.

'Your purse. Just untie it and throw it to us,' one of the men said. He was younger, from the look of him, and had an oval face with a narrow chin. He wore a green linen shirt and a dark coat. A hood over his head left his face in the dark, but Grandarse could see that his eyes flitted about the alley nervously. This boy was concerned that there might be a trick of some sort, but was not sure what form it might take.

'What, this purse? You want to take coins from me?'

'Just untie it and hurry up,' the other said. He was built more heavily that the first, and had thick, greying hair held long. His clothes were worn, but neatly patched. Grandarse was certain he was a sailor who had fled his ship. Few soldiers could sew that well. Looking at them, they could be father and son. They were, he decided.

'I'll give you one each, and if you refuse, you will regret it all your lives,' he said.

'Untie the purse,' the first said. His attention was focused on that leather bag as though it held inside all the secrets of eternal life and alchemy mixed.

'Ah, I cannot,' Grandarse said, drawing his sword regretfully. 'But I will still give you your coins. You deserve your reward.'

He stepped forward as the two blows were struck.

'You didn't hit them too hard, did you?' he asked of his accomplices. The two would-be robbers lay on the ground, the older snoring gently. 'He sounds like a puppy after taking the teat, that one,' he said, prodding the man with his boot.

Dogbreath and John of Essex glared at him.

'Why, you think we'd bilk you of your fee?' Dogbreath said.

He was a scrawny man with grey hair that matched his face. His voice was a whine that put Grandarse in mind of a nail running down a slate. He shivered. The man looked like a cur that had been kicked beyond submission and into rabid fury.

'I have no doubt you'd do that if you thought you could get away with it,' Grandarse said. He grinned. 'But you know you wouldn't, so you won't, will you? Now, take these two scrotes back to the camp and get them ready. Hopefully they'll still be able to walk after a while.'

'Oh, aye. I'll get them to dance for me if I like,' Dogbreath muttered. He flourished his own knife. 'I can tickle them up in a . . .'

'Just help them up and get them back to camp,' Grandarse said. He glowered at Dogbreath, then at the other man. 'What are you grinning at?'

'Nothing, Centener.'

'Good. Then wipe that smirk off your face and get these shites back to camp.'

That evening Grandarse stood out in the drizzle and surveyed his new recruits.

He never thought he would say it, but he was for once glad to have Clip and Dogbreath in his centaine. Clip was the same wizened little fellow, with that whine of dissatisfaction still nailed to his voice. Dogbreath was a scowling man with the complexion of someone who had been locked in a cell for too many years. Apart from that, the two had always been remarkable in that they were so similar, and yet had never fraternised during previous campaigns. However, now that they were the only two members whom Grandarse knew from past battles, he would have to rely on them more. Jack Fletcher, Matt and Geoff were all gone.

However, here he had his newest recruits lined up to inspect. It was not a sight to inspire a man.

'You are now lucky men,' he roared. 'I have saved you from a life of brief pleasures and swift justice. All of you, every one, is a miserable shit who deserves to find a berth in the gaols of a dozen kingdoms, but I am giving you a chance of glory. Real glory! Your names will live forever, like Arthur and his knights!'

'Who are—' one man started. He was taller, a serious-looking, fair-haired man, but even as he spoke, Dogbreath appeared before him, grinning wickedly.

'What's your name?'

'Er . . . Baz, I—'

'Do you like taking a shit in the morning?' he asked.

'I . . . er . . .' It occurred to the fellow that there was potentially no good answer.

'Because if you like them so much, and you don't want to listen to the centener there, then there's always a job needs doing. Either digging a new pit or moving the shit from a full one,' Dogbreath said nastily. 'Sometimes, if you're careless, you can fall in. And drown. Think of that!' He licked his lips, displaying his foul gums and, from the expression on the young recruit's face, exhaling. Dogbreath was well named, and it was rumoured that the air from his mouth was more noxious and poisonous than that which regularly emanated from his arse. No one who had smelled either would want to repeat the experience.

Grandarse looked at John of Essex, or John *Hawkwood*, he reminded himself. Hawkwood was chewing on a piece of dried meat, eyeing the men without enthusiasm.

'I know,' Grandarse said, 'that you have had experience of the bow, and I can tell that a fair number of you have skills with knife or sword. Who has fought for the King before?'

He stared at a tall, lean man with mousy hair. This fellow had given his name as Robin of London, and from his build he had never suffered from hunger. He looked like many a poacher, in Grandarse's experience. 'You've been a fighter, haven't you?'

Robin cast an eye along the others in the line with him and shook his head. 'I know nothing about fighting, me. I'm just a trader in cloths. I was caught and brung 'ere without knowing what was goin' on.'

'Really?' Grandarse walked closer and peered at him. The man's accent was like none he had heard before. It sounded like a mixture, as if the man was trying to sound like a fellow from Suffolk. He took hold of Robin's hands and studied his right hand. He saw that there were calluses on the first three fingers. On the left, there was a ridge of scarred skin on the side of the forefinger's knuckle. Robin's whole story, he decided, was a fabrication. It was common enough for men to avoid service by lying. 'You're an archer,' he said. 'Good. You can show us what you're like.'

'I'm no good with a bow,' Robin said with his voice low and angry. He had given up the pretence and now sounded like a natural-born Londoner.

Grandarse stared at him. 'You'll be a fucking star with a bow with all that hard skin, lad,' he said. 'Or I'll have to peel it off your fingers with a knife. Understand me?'

'Yes.'

'Yes, *Centener*!'

Robin stared at him with real hatred. 'Yes, Centener.' In his voice it sounded like a curse.

'Good!' Grandarse said, clapping his hands and rubbing them together. 'Now, who else have we got here?'

There was the father and son from Bordeaux who stood and shuffled unhappily. After questioning them when they had recovered from their headaches, Grandarse had learned that the father's name was Pierre and his son was Felix. They declared that they were in Bordeaux for the market and had fallen on hard times when they had been robbed, but Grandarse could tell from the look in their eyes that there was more to them than that. He was sure that they had some experience of fighting, although both denied it, and the boy had the marks of shackles on his wrists and ankles. When Grandarse looked at them, both looked resigned to their fate. When he questioned them, they soon admitted that the boy had been accused of a felony and would have been hanged, but he had been offered the chance to join the Prince's army in return for a pardon. Grandarse told himself to keep an eye on them.

Behind them was a taller man with lowered brows and suspicious, deep-set eyes. He had a beard and hair that was as black as a Celt's.

Grandarse pointed at him. 'What's your name?'

'Imbert.'

'Have you used a bow?'

'Sometimes.'

The man looked away as though that was the end of his

interview, and Grandarse sighed to himself, walking along the rest of the line of recruits. Dogbreath gave him a sneering smile; beside him Clip ducked his head in imitation of respect, and looked up at him with wary suspicion. Beyond them were another pair: one a short, grinning fellow of perhaps five-and-twenty, and a taller, slimmer, more serious fellow who listened carefully and with apparent concern.

'Who are you?'

The shorter man was almost as fat as Grandarse himself, and his smile was as expansive as the sky. 'I am called Gilles, Centener,' he said. 'I know I'll be good here.'

'Why are you here?' Grandarse asked.

'Well, I've heard how much money others have made from the raids. I lived in a small vill in Oxfordshire, you see, and I thought I might as well come see the world, make some money, save a bit for when I settle down.'

Grandarse looked him up and down. The lad was well dressed, with soft woollen hosen, a shirt of fine muslin, his cotte hardy cut from strong but soft linen. 'You're the son of a rich man,' he said.

'Nay, only a hardworking freeman.'

'Then you robbed him, eh? If not, someone else. Keep an eye on your purses, boys, while this one's around. Who are you?'

This to the last recruit, a grinning, wiry fellow with black hair and clear, grey eyes. 'I'm Nick, Centener.'

'God's ballocks, but was there ever such a collection of short-arsed, fat little wastrels gathered all together in one place,' Grandarse wondered aloud as if astonished that he could have collected so many. He walked back to the top of the line shaking his head.

In among the fifteen men he had collected there were

probably more gaolbirds than free men, but then that was the way of things when a man went to the town to recruit. Most of those who would put their name forward would do so in the hope of earning a pardon, or of winning some kind of renown and being given their freedom. In the case of these men, none had volunteered. Grandarse had captured them with Dogbreath and Clip, and they were reluctant fighters at best, although all would appreciate their pay when they could pocket it.

'Well?' he said later, when he was sitting with his feet towards the fire, his fist gripping a large jug of cider. 'What do you think of them, Essex?'

'I think they'd sooner stab your paunch than your enemy's,' Hawkwood said.

'You could be right there.'

'And if you want my advice—'

'I've been at this job a while, boy,' Grandarse growled.

'Of course,' Hawkwood said, and closed his mouth, staring into the fire.

'Well?'

'Oh, I wouldn't wish to insult you. You know your job as well as any, after all,' Hawkwood added.

Grandarse squirmed a little. 'Aye. True enough,' he said at last. 'But I need to know if you're the right sort of material, too. So, what were you thinking?'

Hawkwood threw him a look. 'First, I think you should use my name.'

'John?'

'Hawkwood. Remember that name, Grandarse. It'll be famous one day.'

'And I'll be the King's sergeant in charge of the royal whores! Well?'

'If I were you, I'd have some men keep an eye for a group of five to ten men trying to escape the camp.'

'Ballocks! You're probably right.'

Thomas de Ladit had run from the terror of the north and sought peace down here, far away from the King's men, only to throw himself into this lunacy. He could have wept from frustration and fear as he helped the old priest away from the square.

There were many there who knew their priest, but no one moved to help the two as they hobbled down the lane.

'No, no, not here. Take me to the physician,' the priest mumbled through broken teeth and mashed lips.

'Père Albert, you need to rest. Let me take you to your bed and then I'll send a boy to bring a physician.'

The priest looked down at his hands as though confused. 'My staff! In the name of all that is holy, I left my staff in the square when that godless, murderous swine hit me. He's lucky I'm not ten years younger! I'd break his face for him!' He looked up at Thomas with quick decisiveness. 'Take me to the physician, and then take the road south. There's nothing for you here, Thomas. This is not your battle. Go south and seek your Lord's lands. You should be safe in Navarre.'

'What of you? You have shown me kindness these last weeks.'

'I will live unless I die, and if I die, I will die cursing these heathens to Hell and back until they all know the terror that everlasting damnation can bring,' Père Albert said, as firmly as his ravaged mouth would allow.

'Let me take you home.'

The priest stopped and gripped his arm fiercely. 'Those men do not care whether we live or die, Thomas. These people here are my people. I have lived here with them all my life. They look up to me. You have no place here, though. You must take yourself away. If they ever learn you are the Chancellor of King Charles of Navarre, you will be captured and held until they can force a ransom from someone. And if they get nothing, they will torture you to death for the fun of it! You have heard what these men are like. Mercenaries who would cut off your fingers to take your rings. They have no feelings for other human beings. All they care about is gold and silver. You have to flee.'

Thomas stared at him. He wanted to say, 'Flee? Flee where?' After all, he was one of the few men who knew the truth about the negotiations Charles of Navarre had held with the English, offering to split France between them both, half to King Edward, half to Charles.

The old priest continued, 'I should take the road west, head towards Périgueux first, then south by degrees. If you go to the English at Bordeaux, you may be able to find a ship to take you to Galicia and avoid the mountains. The English are friends to your King, are they not?'

Thomas de Ladit gave a brief laugh but there was no humour in it. 'They were.'

'Why, surely they are still allies?'

'My Lord is a very competent politician. He has always used his position to gain power. At first, he thought that he could win back lands by intrigue. When King John took away his territories to reward others, my Lord fought back as he could. He made friends at court, he courted the Dauphin and finally he sent for help from the English. But when his threats worked, he turned against the English. They are in Normandy now, but if they have learned the truth about his duplicity, I think that they would be very keen to speak with me.'

'Then all the more reason to head south as speedily as you may. Escape while you can! Find yourself a place of sanctuary.'

'There is no sanctuary for me,' Thomas said, and he felt as though his heart would break as he admitted it to himself.

Clip snored and mumbled, then rolled over. A tree root stuck in his back and he moved away, trying to get comfortable. It wasn't easy. He had slept on sandy beaches, he had slept on ploughed fields, he had slept on roadways, but he had always found it difficult to sleep where there were too many roots.

He'd picked this spot because it looked so soft and inviting, and safe underneath the oak, too. But no matter where he tried to go, this patch of grass concealed lumps and bumps that would have tested a drunken man-at-arms in full armour. Clip had no chance. He opened his eyes and was about to sit up when he saw a large shape against the sky.

It was a man, moving carefully and silently between the various recumbent figures on the ground. As Clip watched, he saw the man lift his leg high in an elaborate step over one fellow, then pause and rest when another nearby grunted and muttered in his sleep.

Where are you going? Clip wondered. He considered calling out, but then thought better of it as he recognised that it was Imbert. Imbert was a big man, and he was close enough to reach Clip and clobber him before any of the others had woken. Clip quickly closed his eyes in case Imbert should see a glint in the dark.

Thus it was that when there was a sudden movement, a thud like a lead maul striking a log, and a soft sound like a body collapsing gently, aided by a man's supportive hands, Clip saw none of it. When he opened his eyes, there was no sign of Imbert. However, there was a louder snore from the direction in which he had been walking. Clip sat up, peering in that direction. He saw a new body lying on the grass with no blanket. When he glanced about him, he saw Imbert's blanket where he had settled, supposedly for the night. Grandarse was apparently asleep some yards away, farting and chuckling in a dream, while the others seemed to be content too. Only one man seemed to be awake. When Clip glanced over at Robin, he was sure he caught a brief glimpse, as though an eye had been open and watching him.

CHAPTER FIVE

Thursday 7 July

Denisot was home before the second hour of the morning after speaking with the priest, and pursed his lips when he saw the familiar figure waiting for him.

Ethor was built like the prior's barns: massively. He had shoulders that would have suited a bull for power, and his forehead was as heavy as a destrier's. But his long features were not unkind. He had a mass of unruly brown hair, and sharp little dark eyes, almost hidden beneath his thick brows. His moustache and beard were extravagant, a cause for annoyance with the prior he served as steward, but he refused to allow the barber near his cheeks. So, since the prior knew him to be shrewd and competent at resolving disputes between the ecclesiastical community and the people of Domps, he was permitted to keep his beard.

Denisot and he were often forced to confer. Usually a visit from Ethor presaged a call from the priory to explain some infringement of the rules, but at least, as Denisot told himself,

Ethor was reasonable. They were often able to negotiate together without having to involve the prior's court.

However, Denisot had enough to deal with today with the crucified body without having more troubles thrown in his direction. He hoped this was a simple matter.

'My friend,' he said as Ethor approached. 'I am glad to see you.'

'You soon won't be,' Ethor said. 'I have no good news.'

'Nor have I,' Denisot said. 'I am in the troubling situation of having discovered a dead body.'

'You will soon have many more,' Ethor said uncompromisingly.

Denisot frowned at that. He led the way to a bench at the side of his house, from where he could see the roadway. 'Will you eat a little bread and cheese with me?'

Ethor nodded and Denisot bellowed for food and drink; while they waited, Denisot spoke of the body Poton had shown him.

'Crucified? In God's name, that is the work of the Devil!'

'Or his agents on Earth,' Denisot agreed heavily.

'And what have you done about it?' Ethor said.

'I took her to the church and she lies there now. This afternoon we shall call the villagers together to discuss the matter.'

'I may be able to help you,' Ethor said.

'How so?'

'There are messages coming from Uzerche. The town is taken by the English.'

Denisot was generally careful to avoid curses, but he felt himself close to a profanity at that news. 'This is certain? I had not heard of any raids being launched in our direction.'

'You know how the English are. They will send out small parties to try their fortune,' Ethor growled. 'They roam over a wide area plundering the peasants. I dare say a small group rode up past us a few days ago scouting out the land for their main body, found your girl and killed her.'

Denisot's wife, Gaillarde, appeared in the doorway, a servant boy following her with trenchers of cheese and a board holding a one-day-old loaf. She herself carried a jug of wine and two mazers and set them down on the bench near Ethor. She pointedly ignored her husband, pouring for Ethor and leaving Denisot's cup empty. Her job done, she left the men and went back inside.

'You been stabbing your lance in another woman?' Ethor asked, his brows lowered so his eyes were almost entirely hidden as he gazed after her.

'You think I have time? That harpy would probably be glad if I did. She would really have something to complain about.'

Ethor laughed. 'I've seen your maid, Denisot. You mean to tell me you haven't been asking her to serve your pork sword?'

Denisot's face darkened. 'Gaillarde would know in a trice if I dared.'

'Where is she? I'll try my own luck with her.'

'You think my wife would allow her to come and tempt us with her charms? Suzette will be indoors cleaning or something, while Gaillarde forces the boy to come and serve guests or their master,' Denisot said bitterly.

Ethor chuckled. 'I see: she has you fixed. She has Suzette hidden away, and keeps you away from her at all hours. So, what's the matter with her, then?'

Denisot gave an emphatic shrug. 'She's a woman. When I have learned what makes her unhappy, I will sell the cure and become as rich as a cardinal.'

Ethor chuckled and poured wine for Denisot.

Denisot took the mazer from him and the two sipped. Then Denisot set his cup aside. 'Very well. What have you heard?'

'The town was attacked in the night. All guards were slain where they stood, the gates were opened and the English went through the town like plums through a hound. They've burned and slaughtered all in their path, I hear.'

'What will they do now?'

'You know what the English are like,' Ethor said. 'They'll ravage the place and then go on to the next. There's no telling where they'll try next, but I fear that it could be in our direction. We should prepare ourselves.'

Denisot nodded grimly and sipped his wine. 'The meeting with the villagers is even more vital now. We have to prepare ourselves for attack.'

Later, when Denisot stood before the rest of the men of the village, he had to bellow at the top of his voice to kill off the hubbub. He was at the door to the village church, the body of the dead girl on the ground before him. It had been decided that the interior of the church would not provide enough space for all to view the body.

'We can be sure that the English have been here,' he said. 'They have taken Uzerche, and we know that they came past us, for why else would we have this poor child found in this state?'

'She was crucified,' the priest said, shaking his head and crossing himself several times. 'It is an abhorrent crime, to kill a child in this manner. To taint the image of the death of Christ!'

'It's a pretty foul way to kill whether it's in the style of the Son of God or anyone else,' Nicolas said. The peasant had a round, ruddy face with heavy jowls. He drew down the corners of his fleshy mouth and rubbed his fingers on his leather jerkin with loathing. 'The man who could do this does not deserve to be protected by the law. He should be pulled through the streets to the top of the hill and broken on the wheel.'

'Who knows this girl?' Denisot said sharply. He had seen enough meetings degenerate into squabbles and arguments. With the news of Uzerche, he was keen to get the matter of the body put away so that the men could all return to the more important matter of the town's survival.

'I have not seen her,' the priest said, shaking his head as he studied the body.

'Someone must know her!' Denisot declared, raising his voice and glaring about him. 'Come, does no one recall seeing her on the road? At market?'

'Perhaps,' Ethor said, 'she was found miles away by the English. They are all murderers and thieves, those routiers. Perhaps they discovered her at the side of the road twenty miles away and took her as a marching wife? It is the sort of thing they do.'

'You think mercenaries would take a child like this for their beds?' Denisot said. 'I have heard that they kill without thinking, but if they were to take a wife they would surely have a grown woman who could march with them?'

'No one here recognises her,' Nicolas said. 'She will have to be buried in a pauper's grave. So, what of the English?'

'We should at least ask in neighbouring towns whether anyone has gone missing,' Denisot said. 'Perhaps we ought to send to Chamberet – or to Sussac?'

There was a grumbling from the villagers, but when the priest stood and agreed with him, the disgruntled noise settled down. However, when it came to finding a man to take the message, the others all looked down or away.

Denisot sighed. 'I shall go, then.'

As soon as that was announced, business moved on swiftly to the threat of mercenaries and Englishmen. 'Has anybody heard anything since Uzerche was taken?'

'I heard from old Remon that the day before yesterday he saw horses with thirty or more men in armour,' Talebot said. He was a perpetually anxious-looking man, tall and grey-featured even after hours labouring in the sun. He had never recovered from the loss of his wife and two sons in the plague, and now his eyes squinted permanently as though he was still peering at the world from behind a veil of tears.

'Remon?' Denisot said.

He was reminded that Remon lived far to the south, perhaps a quarter of the way to Uzerche itself, almost six miles on the road to Chamberet. He had a small patch of land with a cottage, and held it as a free man. His wife was feared in every market, where her ability to negotiate discounts made her despised by all sellers, but Remon was amiable enough.

Talebot nodded as others spoke about old Remon. 'Yes, he saw them, he says, about the last hours of daylight. They were riding incautiously, looking about them. He had no idea who they might be, but he hid himself just in case.'

'They had no children such as this with them?' Denisot said.

'Not that Remon told me, but he wouldn't have spent long looking,' Talebot said. 'They must have been English. If he had got too close, they would have murdered him, just as they kill all others.'

Denisot felt a flame of anger. 'They are only men,' he said. 'No better nor worse than us!'

'But they have the weapons,' Talebot said.

CHAPTER SIX

Friday 8 July

Berenger was up early that morning. He rose quietly, as was his wont, and made his way out from the building where he had established his command centre, a widow's house just off the square near the middle of the town.

He had no fears of the townspeople here; he had no fear of anyone living. No weapon could hurt him. Weapons were only a means to end his suffering in this miserable world. With a sword at his side and his padded coat with hardened leather breastplate, he felt as safe as he would anywhere in the world.

But the dead: the dead were different. In his dreams he saw them again, all those whose lives he had ended or seen ended. Young boys slain because they tried to protect their father's farm; a young girl decapitated because a jumpy member of Berenger's company had caught a fleeting glimpse of a moving figure and thought it was a man trying to kill him. All those dead; all the mutilated. They came to him at night. It was only the wine that protected him from them. And from *her*. From the memory of his wife.

There was a woman's body in the corner of a building, and he slowed slightly as he took in the sight of her torn skirts, bared breast and spread legs. Another woman dead. Too many were dying. Men in mercenary companies did not join because they were kind or gentle, and those in the towns where they stayed did not feel warmth and comradeship towards those who raped their wives and daughters and left them for dead. He lengthened his stride as he approached the gate, and hardly slowed as he mounted the stairs to the walkway.

'You can go,' he said to the yawning guard.

A young fighter, Loys had joined the English in Guyenne. He had shown himself to be hardy, but he was not the brightest of the men, in Berenger's opinion, and his pale, thin face was growing haggard. English and Low Countries fighters laughed at his pale hair, gangling limbs and credulity, and he had often been the butt of their malicious jokes.

Loys nodded gratefully and stretched his back, then spread his hands. Long hours gripping his spear shaft had turned his fingers into claws. He jerked his head over the surrounding landscape. 'Nothing moving there, Frip.'

'Thanks. Go and sleep.'

The man turned and lumbered down the stone steps, leaving Berenger alone over the gate. From here he could see the bridge clearly, the small stone tower defending the approach standing a little more than a bowshot away over the river. It was the river that defined this little town. It had slashed through the ground here like a surgeon's knife, although not so neatly. Here, about Uzerche, it had gouged a long finger from the land pointing northwards, with the bridge at the tip of the fingernail.

Although the weather had been mild, the river was still full and its thunder and roar could be heard from almost everywhere in the town.

Beyond the tower, trees broke the line of the landscape as it rolled away. Berenger stood at the town's gate, and behind him the town rose on tier upon tier of rock, with wealthy houses bearing turrets and castellations like so many castles. This place was wealthy, and much of the wealth came from that little timber bridge.

'Frip?'

He turned to see his second-in-command, Will. The fair-haired Englishman came up the stairs in a rush and stood staring about him. 'A fine morning.'

'No trouble?'

'A couple of my boys got frisky with a young maid, but she wasn't badly injured,' Will said easily. 'I had her sent home.'

'Did you check to see she was safe?'

'Why would I? She was only a French maid.'

'Not the woman who lies dead not a bowshot from here, then?'

'I don't think so.'

'You should keep your men under tighter control,' Berenger snapped. His head felt heavy, and the thoughts moved sluggishly in his mind. 'We don't want the townspeople to rise against us.'

'They'll regret it if they do, won't they?' Will said. 'We have men enough and weapons to keep them all down.'

'Perhaps. But it would be better if we didn't have to. If we stick to keeping them safe from robbers and thieves, we can stay here for a long time and enjoy some peace ourselves.'

'Perhaps,' Will said. He was smiling again. 'But too much peace will make the men sloppy and lazy.'

Berenger wanted to argue. There had been a time ten years

before when he would have made it a point to correct Will. It was futile to inflict more violence and suffering on a town than was entirely necessary; the consequence would be revolt and the need to use even more force to quash it. Berenger had no compunction about using violence on those who tried to thwart him, but he deprecated using it unnecessarily.

'The men need their releases, Frip. You know that as well as any.'

Berenger stared away, over the landscape. His back was injured, his face bore a ragged scar, his shoulder had a hideous star-shaped wound where a bolt had passed through him. Yes, he had endured enough of battle to know that men must have their relaxation. Soldiers needed women for sex and comfort, just as they needed their wine and ale. And the latter inspired a desire for the former.

But that was not enough to justify further destruction for no reason.

'If you find another man raping a woman in the town, you will have him handed over to the woman's family for them to take their revenge according to the customs of the land,' he said. 'I won't have our position here threatened by one or two men's greed.'

'You may find that the men are not satisfied with that.'

'Then they can see me. They know where I am.'

Berenger felt his back stiffen as he turned back to stare at the view again. Below him, some trees waved in the faint breeze. A cool air, filled with the scent of fish and refuse, rose from the river below, and he sniffed it like a hound tasting the odour of a hart in the wind. For a moment his memories faded and he could feel only the satisfaction of emptiness. No pain, no joy, only a calmness. He closed his eyes. At any moment he expected to hear Will draw his sword, and then he knew that he would feel that one stab and at last find the embrace of eternity. It would bring peace at last.

He longed for that blow.

When he heard Will turn and leave the wall, he felt desolation to be still alive.

CHAPTER SEVEN

Thomas de Ladit was exhausted when he finally walked into Thiviers. It was a small town, with buildings of a pale, yellowish grey that seemed to glow from within when the sun struck them. It had a wall, but that would be but little defence against determined men such as those who had carried the walls at Uzerche, Thomas was sure. But for now, he did not care. All he wanted was a bed for the night and some peace.

He found a small hostelry which offered reasonable rates for an evening, and as the curfew was rung, he lay back on a soft mattress, sharing it with a large, grunting peasant whose dialect was so harsh and obscure, Thomas found it hard to comprehend more than one word in every three. Perhaps that was partially caused by the wine he had drunk with his simple meal of pottage and bread. This being a Friday, he eschewed the offered meats with a frown of disapproval.

For a long time he lay staring up at the ceiling. This was surely the worst year of his life. He had lost his master, he had lost his own possessions in that mad, panicked rush from Rouen, when he and two servants had run from the disaster that had overrun the rest of the King of Navarre's household.

The three had kept moving. At first Thomas had wanted to rush from one safe town to another in King Charles's estates, but Bernard had persuaded him that any manors and castles that Thomas knew of, King John would also know well. They would be the places where the French officers would go first to confiscate Charles's lands and revenues. The three would be safer if they kept to small villages and farmsteads.

Thomas did not like Bernard. The man was uncouth and smelled. And whenever they went to a tavern or inn, he seemed to stare at the young women and children of the area with a great intensity. All in all, it was a good thing when Thomas and the two were separated some miles west of Chartres.

It had been an unseasonably chilly evening, and the three had settled down to a doze near a fire, when a whole group of men bearing torches appeared and tried to capture them. Arnaud and Bernard had instantly awoken and fled northwards, while Thomas managed to slip away quietly into a small copse. When day broke, he took himself east, and by degrees he trudged more and more south until he ended up in Uzerche with the good Père who had taken him in and fed him until he was fit once more.

Now he must make his way southwards and reach Navarre. There, as the Chancellor of the small kingdom at the other side of the Pyrenees, back in Pamplona, he would be safe. The French would find it difficult to break through the protective mountains.

He stretched, feeling the tenderness in his feet turn to heat. Although he had travelled far and wide with his King, that had been mostly on horseback and over a considerable time. These last weeks had tested his poor body more than he could have imagined. It had seemed so easy at first, just slogging onwards without thinking, but since his halt at Uzerche the miles had felt harder and harder, as though he was constantly being drawn back to the north. He was just not as young as once he had been.

With luck it wouldn't be too much longer. He would make his way to the coast, pick up a ship and leave France. If he could, he would never return.

Rolling over, he closed his eyes and was soon asleep.

When Grandarse saw him later that day, Archibald was almost finished. He had already cleaned and greased the two ribaulde-quins, his latest pride and joy. These were three-barrelled gonnes with small calibres, set on small carriages like hand-carts. They were no good at any range, but as enemies came closer, their fire was devastating.

He patted the barrel of his great gonne, like a master petting his hound, as Grandarse approached.

'If you put on more of a paunch, you won't be able to find a belt to encompass your girth,' Archibald said. He pulled off his coif and rubbed his shaven head with his cloth before pulling the coif back on.

'There are times when I dislike you.'

'Rare enough, I trust,' Archibald grinned.

'Yes. Usually I detest you,' Grandarse growled.

'That's good, then,' Archibald said. He studied the centener. 'What is it? You look like you bit into a raisin and found it was a sloe.'

'You don't have eighty-two men and only three vinteners.'

'You have eighty-two men? You only need four vinteners, then. You can see to the last.'

Grandarse snorted. 'I'm centener, and I'm paid for five vin-taines. I need a good man to bring the rabble together in the last group. I can control one, but I need another man. I wondered whether you could leave the gonnes to Ed and Béatrice, and maybe . . .'

'No.'

'It would only be until we could find someone else.'

'You think I could control your archers? Man, I couldn't even string one of those things. Better that you find someone who can inspire their confidence; they're all terrified of me. They think I'm associated with the devil. My powder alarms them all, the superstitious fools!'

'Who else can I ask?' Grandarse demanded petulantly. 'I need another man.'

'Merge the men. Make four of the five and look to the fourth vintaine yourself.'

'But . . .'

'You need to find a way to do it,' Archibald said. 'I have enough on my plate already. That is your job.'

Grandarse left Archibald in a dispirited mood and made his way down to the butts where the men were practising.

'Well?' he asked Hawkwood. 'How are they doing?'

'Mostly hopeless, except as a barrier between real archers and an attacking enemy. Watch!'

Grandarse did. The men had been drawing bows for almost an hour of the sun now, and he could see that six of them were unused to such efforts. They held one arm straight and tried to pull the bow with the right. One almost hit the wicker quiver resting on the ground before him. Two seemed competent with lighter bows, but four could not hold the bow still, and Grandarse groaned to see how the arrow-heads wavered and wobbled before the command to 'Loose!' When the arrows flew, he winced to see how they sprang forward, some flying high over the targets, others burying themselves in the grass, while most passed between. The butts were almost all unmarked. Only a couple of archers had succeeded in hitting them.

'I'm surprised at you, Robin,' he called.

Robin's missiles were dotted about the butts. Not one had hit the boards where he was supposed to aim.

'I told you I was no good.'

'I don't fucking believe you.'

Robin shrugged. He leaned on his bow, unperturbed by the accusation. 'I don't think I give a shit what you believe.'

Grandarse smiled. 'Perhaps a lashing will make you care a little more? I want you to loose six more arrows at the butt, and if you don't hit with all of them, I'll have you flogged. Does that help with your keenness?'

He motioned to the boy with the arrows, who scampered forward with a handful and dropped them into the wicker quiver before Robin. The tall man gazed at Grandarse speculatively. There was a coldness in his eyes that quite surprised Grandarse. It didn't worry him unduly – he was more than accustomed to threats, whether implicit or explicit, and he was comfortable with his ability to protect himself – but it was a surprise. Insubordination in the face of a threat of flogging was a new experience to him.

Robin took up an arrow. He weighed it in his hand and turned away to face the butts, the bow loose in his left hand, standing relaxed.

'Watch this,' Grandarse breathed to Hawkwood.

Robin picked up five more arrows and held them loosely between the fingers of his left hand. The sixth he nocked and then he stood quietly, the bow easy in his hand, drawing the string a mere hand's breadth, then relaxing, allowing the string to return while never letting go; pulling and releasing the string as though testing the tension and the bow's movement.

Then he suddenly moved. He lifted both hands over his head like a man stretching, then brought both hands down, keeping his left arm straight, while crooking his right until the string touched his cheek, his fingers at his ear, and released; he did so again, seemingly without hesitation, the bow rising and falling, and when the arrow was in the right line, it was loosed; again, again, again.

Grandarse puffed out his cheeks as he took in the sight of five arrows, each perfectly stabbing the bull's-eye of each of the nearer five targets. Robin had shown off, taking the butts of the other archers near him.

'Keep still, Grandarse,' Hawkwood hissed.

It was only then that Grandarse realised the archer was staring down the shaft of the sixth and last arrow, and it was pointing straight at his face. He felt his buttocks clench. Not from fear: he had faced enemy arrows and lances all his adult life; but there was something about the sight of the eye behind that weapon that brought home to him how fleeting was his life.

'You loose that arrow and you'll be dead before Grandarse,' Hawkwood said. He was moving away from Grandarse, circling round. Grandarse saw that he had drawn his dagger and was already holding it by the tip, ready to hurl it.

'I don't appreciate being threatened,' Robin said.

'Get used to it. This is an army,' Grandarse said.

'I still don't like it.'

'You want to go?'

'No,' Robin said. 'I'm here because you forced me. I didn't want to join this army but now I'm here, I might as well make some money.'

'And it'll be good for you. You want money? Stay with me and Sir John de Sully and you'll make enough to buy a tavern if you want. But if you point that at me any longer, you little shit, I'll cut your head off and piss down your throat.'

'I do want to make money,' Robin said, 'and I'll be a good fighter. I just don't like you threatening me.'

He span about, making Hawkwood duck in sudden alarm, and then the arrow was flying towards the butts. It didn't split the arrow already resting there, but from where Grandarse was standing it was a close thing. Robin stared at the target for a moment, then patted the bow stave as though congratulating it. When he walked away, still gripping the bow, no one contested his passage.

Hawkwood puffed out his lips in a silent whistle, and he heard Grandarse's quiet 'God's fucking ballocks', but for once didn't feel the urge to comment.

Gaillarde wept. She often wept. There was little else for her. Her anger and bitterness kept her alive. Her womb was as shrivelled as an ancient prune, and all the love she had in her was long gone.

Sometimes she thought she ought to leave her husband and join a convent. There was the little sisterhood over to the north. Since the pestilence that community had been keen to recruit ever more women, and age was no barrier. For nuns, an older novice was attractive. She would be less likely to be afflicted with the natural urges of others. A young girl could be tempted at all hours, but a woman who had conceived and given birth already was more stable and reliable, less prone to silly infatuations.

But she didn't want to go. She just wanted her husband to confess and go to the priest for absolution. If only he could see the harm he was doing.

'Mistress?'

That little slut with the wayward eye, Suzette, could infuse even the most innocent-seeming question with a depth of contempt. She treated Gaillarde with cold scorn whenever she could. It was clear that Denisot had taken to her bed rather than sleep with Gaillarde. Consorting with the housemaid! It was shameful in any man, but in a bayle, a man who should be beyond reproach, it was a disgrace. He brought shame to them all.

'What?'

'Do you want me to press the bedclothes?'

Gaillarde wanted to slap her face, but that would only show that the girl had got to her again. She was always like that, asking silly questions that were, or should be, unnecessary. 'Yes.'

The girl went away, and Gaillarde fell back onto her stool. Her mind was empty of all thoughts. She was merely a husk of a human. This is what her husband had done to her. She was no woman. A woman had purpose; a woman had children and must raise them. Her husband's manifest infidelities and deceits had taken her life's meaning from her.

She hated him.

A pint and a half of wine down, Berenger was feeling mellow when the men appeared. It made him grumpy to be called from his table at the inn.

The English had swarmed all over the land in recent years. Ten years ago the King's host had met the French army at Crécy and slaughtered thousands of the French nobles. In the intervening years more and more battles had shown that the English had little to fear when facing a French force, and when the Prince brought his men and marched across the country, they didn't simply trample the crops, they devastated the land. Theirs was not a kindly war, it was *dampnum*, warfare by terror. The army marched across a wide front, up to thirty miles wide, and burned and looted every town, every village, every farmstead, even every cottage in their path. It was the Prince's intention to prove to the peasants that they could not rely on King John to come and save them. He wanted to make them so petrified of the English that they would willingly come into the peace of the English King, a warrior who could defend them.

If a man had marched across Berenger's lands, threatening all he held dear, he would immediately have grabbed a spear and sword and gone to join whichever force was gathering to kill the invaders. A fruitless, pointless act perhaps, but at least it had the merit of demonstrating courage.

There had been cases over the years of French towns and villages trying to stand and fight the English. Of course, it was invariably a poor show. The English men-at-arms looked on such rabble as fine sport, in the same way that they would view foxes or boar as enormous fun, running them down with ease. If a force looked threatening, the archers would soften them up first, and then the men in steel would charge in to continue the killing.

But at least those men died with defiance in their hearts. This group was somehow horrible. It was degrading. These men came from this area, yet they were keen to join the forces laying waste to their lands. They were little better than traitors.

It was a group of six men. Three were boys, perhaps each eleven years old, although one looked nearer eight or nine. Berenger stared at them without blinking for a long while. His own boy would be their age, if he had lived. But there was no point remembering those happier days: his wife, her son whom Berenger adopted, their own natural child. All were gone, swept away by the plague.

He gulped more wine. The boys could work. There was always a need for grooms, lads to hold the horses in a fight, more to bring arrows to the archers, even for sturdy fellows to carry goods on the march. They could be useful.

The other three, they were more interesting. One was a

youngish lad with fair hair, slender about the hips but with broad shoulders, who ducked his head and peered up at Berenger from below his brows, head hunched over. He looked like a kicked puppy. With him was an older, dark, wild-looking bearded man with a 'Fuck you' look in his eyes. There was no fear or submission in this one. He held Berenger's gaze for a long time, dark eyes narrowing in his round face as though he was measuring Berenger more than Berenger measured him.

Finally there was a man who stood a short distance apart. He was taller, well built and fair-haired, but with an expression of mild amusement in his blue eyes. When he met Berenger's look, there was no challenge in him, only a quizzical air of enquiry.

'Where are you from?' he asked the third man.

'I come from a small town in the Free Cantons, not far from Morgarten,' the blond man said. 'I am called Fulk.'

'Can you fight?'

'I fight with axe, sword and spear. If you have an enemy far away, I can use a crossbow.'

'What of you?' Berenger asked the black-haired man.

This one seemed to consider. 'I am called Bernard. My brother Arnaud here and me, we're used to fighting with swords.'

'Where are you from?'

'We come from Rouen. We were in the service of Charles of Navarre, but he was captured by King John, and three of the noblemen of Normandy were slaughtered by order of the King, so we chose to leave.'

'You are welcome,' Berenger said. He turned to Will. 'See to it that they are given a good billet.'

'I'll take them into my own vintaine,' Will said. 'They'll soon learn with my men.'

Berenger nodded. It was of little importance to him. He turned and returned to the inn – he wanted more wine.

CHAPTER EIGHT

Monday 18 July

As Grandarse walked the feelings of disgust and concern mingled with the proprietorial pride that he always had on looking at a new company.

The army was arrayed ready to ride. Older warriors stood by their mounts, their weapons slung over shoulders or hanging from sheaths. Their heavier items lay on the ground. Newer recruits tried to look bold and experienced by holding on to their weaponry; older hands saved their arms from exhaustion.

They would learn, Grandarse reflected, just as he had himself all those years ago.

The English host had many components. Dukes and other noblemen would bring their own men with them, both horsemen and archers. There was a matter of honour, and besides, all had signed contracts stating how many men they would be able to field when called by their King. Knights had a scale of responsibility. Sir John de Sully, for example, was senior, he was a knight banneret, and was responsible for bringing his own force of two hundred. Each hundred was separated into five vintaines, each of twenty men, in theory. The fact was, there were never enough men to fill the ranks.

Grandarse joined Hawkwood and looked up, pulling a grimace. 'It'll be raining before noon, I reckon.'

'Perhaps. Who will you put in charge of the new vintaine?'

They discussed the group amiably. John Hawkwood was the son of a tanner, and had enjoyed a lucrative career in the last ten years since going to war. He had first met Grandarse during the siege of Calais, but since then he had taken up the life of a soldier with enthusiasm. He had fought with the King's men during recent campaigns, finishing up with the Prince of Wales's chevauchée last year. On that raid the English had devastated the country from Arouille to Toulouse and Narbonne, and returned with so many valuables that finding sufficient wagons and horses or oxen to draw them had been a serious problem. A vastly larger French army had been discovered, but as the smaller English force approached, the French retreated, refusing to give battle.

'You will want someone who understands archery,' Hawkwood said.

'Who, then?'

Hawkwood frowned as he considered the men in the vintaine. 'Dogbreath is good in a hand-to-hand fight,' he said.

Grandarse gave a hollow laugh. 'Him?'

John had to admit Grandarse's response was fair. Dogbreath's skills with bow and arrow were invariably forgotten in the heat of battle. It only took a moment for him to throw caution to the winds and hurl himself at an enemy. A commander had to be more cool-headed, especially since Dogbreath could as easily hurl himself at another member of his own army as on one of the enemy.

'How about Robin of London? He seems level-headed enough.'

'I don't know. Until I see him in a fight I can't be sure about him. He certainly has the skills of an archer. I don't know that I've seen a more accurate fellow, but for all that he's come from London for some reason, and I would be happier if I knew what that reason was.'

'Yes.'

'If only we had someone like Jack Fletcher again.'

'He didn't come?'

'Dead. The pestilence, like so many.'

They discussed the strengths and weaknesses of each of the men in the group. By common agreement, there were three that they would not consider, but at last they had little alternative.

'What of the two?'

Grandarse threw him a bitter glance. 'What, you'd have the youngster? Or the older one who's more like an outlaw than a member of the Prince's army?'

'Well, they both showed initiative.'

Grandarse pulled his mouth down while he considered the father and son who had tried to rob him in the alley. In his eyes, Heaven was near Durham, and the farther from that city a man was born, the more feeble he grew, both in brains and in brawn. 'I don't like them.'

'Well, there's always Clip,' John said.

'Now you're pulling my tarse!'

The blast of horns brought them both back to the matter in hand.

Sir John de Sully was mounted on his favourite heavy palfrey. He wore his armour and a heavy coat of plates, his bascinet held in the crook of his elbow. Turning in his saddle, he caught sight of Grandarse and nodded to him and Hawkwood before surveying the ranks of archers seated more or less comfortably on their ponies and scruffy rounseys. Two of the less fortunate were sitting, legs dangling, on mangy donkeys, while the boys who would have to hold the mounts or fetch and carry, bringing arrows and bowstrings to the men in battle, waited wearily, yawning or resting their backs against trees or leaning on horses with their eyes closed.

Lazy bratchets, Grandarse thought to himself. Some of them were eleven or older, but they still tried to sleep at every opportunity. He'd have to beat one or two to inspire the rest to work properly.

The horns blew again, and at last Grandarse saw the fists raised and punched forward in command to march. He shifted in his saddle and glanced at Hawkwood.

'Well, John. I hope you're ready. We're off to war again soon.'

'Bergerac first, and then, give it another two, maybe three weeks and we'll be off,' Hawkwood agreed. There was a suppressed excitement about him.

He'll make a good captain one day, Grandarse thought to himself, but then the centaine was moving, and he succumbed to the rolling gait of his horse. When he rode on long distances he often found that his mind would empty. It was different when he was in the middle of dangerous territory. On those occasions he would recall every blade of grass, every twig; but on days like this, passing through quiet lands with no danger threatening, he could travel twenty or thirty miles and not recall a single foot of his journey.

His last thought, before he allowed his mind to enter that quiet void of introspection, was that he wished he had some of the old team back here. To have Jack and Fripper around would make his job a great deal easier.

Jack was dead. If only he could learn where Fripper was, he would be happier.

Wednesday 20 July

Berenger knew something was wrong as he walked along the streets. He saw a pair of his men, and they nodded, but their eyes were hooded and they averted their gaze, talking loudly, like criminals about to be taken by the watch. He knew that look – he had worn it often enough himself.

He had been at a tavern for his lunch, and his pot of thick pottage with herbs and rabbit had been washed down with a quart of good local wine. It had made him feel comfortable and slightly dizzy after the ale before lunch, but his mind was as clear as a crystal as he strode out and down the street, thinking idly of his wife. She died so young. So terribly young.

There were two men on the left at the street's corner ahead. Another man lounged on the right side, his hat half over his face. Something made him lurch up and lift his hat, and then he stared in Berenger's direction.

Berenger recognised all three of them as men from Will's vintaine. They were loyal to his subordinate, Berenger knew, but they were also mercenaries. They would fight for whoever offered them the most money. Berenger stooped, tying the laces on his boot while he considered. He could return to the tavern, perhaps, or seek support from other men, but where would he find a man he could trust? Better to brazen it out, or fight and accept the consequences.

He stood upright again, rolling slightly, listening carefully to all sounds. The street was ominously silent, but that meant he could hear that no one was following him now. There was no subtle, quiet footfall behind him as he made his way up the alley. He took off his hat as he went, wiping a fine dew of sweat from his brow, and then dropping his hat. Staring at it stupidly like a drunk, he chuckled to himself, then picked it up in his left hand and dusted it off by slapping it against his right forearm. He was almost at the two men now, and he smiled broadly at them.

They grinned back, but he could see the tension in their eyes. Exchanging a glance, he saw one look over the way to the third fellow and heard the man step forward quietly. Berenger was still slapping his hat against his arm, but now his dagger was already unsheathed, concealed by his hat.

The first man didn't realise. They had all fallen for his ploy of pretending to be drunk, and now the farthest to his left was moving forward to take hold of Berenger's arm. Once he had grabbed hold of Berenger, his companion would whip out a knife and stab him, or perhaps both of them would grasp an arm each and the third would take the opportunity to slip a dagger between his shoulders. They would want to give him a quick death. He hadn't been a bad leader, luckily.

But he was a bad enemy.

His knife was ready and his mind was clear. Berenger had been a warrior and fighter for longer than these three put together, and he was prepared. With the cold reasoning of the professional he analysed his enemies, evaluated the worst threats, and then acted.

He stepped sharply to the side, and the momentum of the first man spitted him on Berenger's blade. It sank into his belly. Berenger twisted his hand viciously, then slashed it right, the blade ripping through the man's gut and pulling a coil of viscera with it. The man opened his mouth to scream, but no sound came. Instead he grabbed at his bowels as though to shove them back into the gaping hole in his flesh. Berenger continued to turn, whipping his blade across the face of the second fellow, who shrieked as the edge took his cheek. It tore through his skin, smashing his teeth, and Berenger moved, punching with his fist until the cross slammed into the man's nose and eye. He screamed and fell, his hands to his face, even as Berenger continued his turn, trying to whirl to catch the third man, but he knew he was too late.

There was a raking, dragging sensation at his flank, under his arm, and he felt the tearing as muscles were sliced. He felt something rip, a skittering over his ribs, and then his dagger was back and he could jerk his body away. The third man stepped back quickly, alarmed.

'What, boy, suddenly scared to fight a man?' Berenger spat.

The fellow had a long knife in his hand. So that was what had sheared through his jacket and muscles. Berenger let his sword waver, then the point dropped. He still gripped his hat in his hand, and now he fanned his face with it. It was hard not to pant, and he felt weary – but not so weary that he couldn't see the man's eyes suddenly narrow.

Quick as an adder, the fellow lashed out with his knife, dropping his body in the thrust, but Berenger shoved his hat forward. The blade sliced through it, and Berenger yanked it to the side, feeling the blade cut into the flesh under his wrist, before thrusting with his long knife. It sank into the boy's throat, just above the 'V' of his collar bone. There was a quiver of ecstatic agony as the blade passed through his windpipe and throat, coming to rest on his spine. Berenger could feel it catch on bone.

Berenger stared into his eyes, seeing the realisation that he was stabbed sink in. The lad's knife clattered on the floor, and Berenger saw the shocked mournfulness in his eyes at the feel of the chilly steel deep in his body, then Berenger wrenched his blade free. The flesh sucked at the metal as though reluctant to relinquish its hold. It would have been easier if Berenger had turned it, ripping apart the body from within, but that would have given the lad a quick death, and he was in no mind to give him that. Instead he withdrew the steel cleanly and straight and watched as the blood began to gush from the fellow's mouth and nostrils, his hands clutching at his throat, his heels hammering on the ground as he drowned in his own blood.

Berenger studied the three, panting, his knife still in his hand. He felt no elation at his success, only a numbing dullness that sapped his energy. It was all he could do not to drop his dagger.

His hat was ruined. After being stabbed and used as a shield to defend himself against the last man's knife, it was a ravaged mess.

The second man was still alive. He sat on his rump, his hands to his ruined mouth, staring at Berenger, then down at his comrades. The first was not dead yet, but he had a cold blueness about his lips, and a grey cast to his face. Berenger knew that he would soon die: he sat with his back to a wall, still gripping his bowels in both hands, weeping weakly. He had vomited, and there was blood all down his breast.

'They're both dead already,' Berenger said. 'Do you want to die too?'

The fellow shook his head. Berenger remembered his face. He was called Owen, a young fighter from Warwickshire, he seemed to remember. A sudden lancing pain struck him under his arm, and he rested the tip of his dagger on Owen's breast. 'Why?'

Owen tried to speak, but as soon as he tried to enunciate a word, a spray of blood erupted from the side of his cheek. He bowed his head and sobbed as Berenger pushed slightly with his blade. 'Speak!'

'Vill . . . 'e – cold us . . .'

'Will told you to do it?'

The man nodded, his eyes closed. He was a mercenary. The punishment for a rebel was clear enough. Berenger need only shove his sword down hard, and the third of the assassins would be dead. He stood, studying the fellow for a moment or two, but then stepped back and left the lad there, in the dirt of the road, soaking up the blood of his companions as they slowly sagged. By the time Berenger turned and stalked off up the hill, both were dead, and only Owen remained, still sobbing, hunched over in his relief and shame.

Berenger made his way to his house and entered with a careful tread. His back and flank were giving him hell, and he made his way to the large seat at his table with the caution of a man who fears that the slightest mistake could make his heart spring from his breast or his brain roll from his skull.

The widow whose house he had commandeered had slightly slanted eyes in a narrow face with high cheekbones, and auburn hair that strayed permanently from her tight-fitting coif. She looked anxious, as well she might, since she had two sons, one of six years and one of ten, but no man to look after her. Apparently he had died in a fever two summers before, and she had been content to live alone, to the scandal of her neighbours, no doubt. So, while she resented Berenger's arrival, she did understand that he protected her.

Several of his men had tried to take the house and her virtue, but Berenger had drawn a line. Although he had already commanded that the women of the town were to be safe from rape, he did not suffer from false hopes. Some of the men were incapable of restraint. He made sure it was known that this woman and her children were under his personal protection. Any man giving them any cause for complaint would answer to him directly. Berenger was the commander of mercenaries. His men would all want to avoid his displeasure.

'Wine?' she asked now.

Berenger stared at her. He slumped into the seat with a low grunt of pain. 'Yes.'

She frowned at him, but then tilted her head and went to fetch a jug and mazer. It was a good cup, with silver chasing around the lip of a sycamore bowl, and she filled it, watching him all the while. Berenger took it up, but already there was a coldness in his breast and the hand holding the cup shook so much that wine was spilled over the table and his lap. He took the cup in his other hand and tried to sip, but the shaking was like an ague.

Alazaïs curled her lip, assuming him to be drunk, and took up a napkin to wipe the wine from the table. She passed it to him to clean his own lap, and when she took the cloth back from him, she saw the blood. 'You are injured!'

'I'll be fine,' he said.

She set her jaw, staring at him for a moment like a woman looking at a little unruly boy, and then left the room. In a little while she returned with a tall, lugubrious man with black moustache and beard and the rich clothing of a professional.

'Who are you?' Berenger managed. He had to grit his teeth to stop them from chattering.

'I am a surgeon and apothecary. I have skill with wounds. Let me see yours, and I will be able to reassure this good woman that you will soon be dead and out of her house.'

'The pox on you!'

'Very likely. Now, where were you stabbed?'

Berenger lifted his arm and let the doctor peer at his wound.

'Oh, I will have to deny her the pleasure of my reassurance,' the doctor said. 'Sadly, I think you will live.'

CHAPTER NINE

Berenger was sore and enfeebled when the doctor was finished. 'Are you trying to kill me or save me?' he demanded at one point when the pain grew too acute. Alazaïs brought warmed water and plenty of towels, and Berenger mumbled his thanks to her, studying his tormenter balefully before sucking down a pint of wine to try to deaden the pain in his flank.

The blade had missed its mark in that vicious little fight. It had been aimed at the hollow of his armpit, where it could achieve a swift death, tearing through his lungs and even into his heart, but the suddenness of his response had thrown his attacker's aim off, and the blade had slipped over his ribs, slicing through muscles and skin. It was sore, and would remain so for a while.

The physician, who was called Antoine, whistled when Berenger's jacket and bloody chemise were removed. 'You are used to pain, I see,' he said, studying the various scars that marred his back.

'I'm a warrior,' Berenger snarled.

'It is a bad injury, but you will mend, God willing. The wound is long, but not deep. You are lucky.'

'You say you can heal me?'

'I see no reason to think you will not be fit again. So long as you do nothing that could strain the muscle for a few days.'

After long experience, Berenger was glad. He considered that the physician was as good as his word. Berenger felt as well patched and mended as he had after any encounter with a medical man after a battle.

'Do not work that arm too much. You will tear open the wound again,' Antoine said as he applied a sweet-smelling salve to a strip of muslin. Berenger couldn't place the odour: it was something like honey and herbs, with an aromatic background, a little like strong rose water. 'You must rest it and try not to exert yourself for two weeks at least.'

'I will be sure to be careful,' Berenger said with a wince. 'But you may have noticed that I am a mercenary commander.'

'Yes. And you were attacked by others from your band. That appears curious to me. Perhaps I am old-fashioned, but I had expected that your soldiers would be loyal to you. It seems the stories of your men are true.'

'What stories?' He picked up the mazer of wine.

'People have often noted that those who seek only money are less consistent in their loyalty than those who fight for their honour and the glory of their masters.'

Berenger slammed the mazer down on the table. 'You should be more careful with your words, potion-peddler! You think I'm without honour? I've fought for my King wherever I've been sent! I've been scorched, stabbed, cut and beaten in his service, and you dare say I'm less loyal than others?'

'I made no comment about you. But it is clear that your men do not treat you with affection.'

'You have no idea how they are. Most are good, loyal, decent men.'

'But these few were not?' Antoine said with a sneer on his lips.

'They will none of them try to hurt me again.'

'You killed them all?' This was from Alazaïs. She looked on with apparent calm, but in her eyes there was alarm.

'You need not worry. Two are slain, the third has an injury that he will not forget in a hurry.'

'So you slaughtered them. How will their companions react to that?' the physician asked. He had pushed all his tools and potions into a large, soft leather bag. He drew the strings tight about the neck to seal it and stood. 'Do you think they will respond to you with friendliness or suspicion? They will expect you to distrust them, I dare say. Any action of yours will be measured in their eyes as to whether it shows you to be bitter or angry with them. I do not envy you your position.'

'I will be fine,' Berenger said.

He stood and winced, swaying a little, like a willow when the wind blows hard.

'Sit!' Alazaïs commanded. 'If you try to do anything now, you will hurt yourself even more.'

There was a look of such genuine concern in her eyes that Berenger felt warmed for a moment. Then he realised that her fear was for herself. She was a woman, after all. In Berenger she had a new protector: if his men killed him, she would have no one.

'I have to see the men,' Berenger said. He did not mean to sound so harsh.

'Why?' asked the physician with scarcely concealed distaste. 'So that they can make sure of killing you this time? First, you need to sleep. Then I should search for friends in your band. You will need them all the more, the next time someone tries to kill you.'

Thursday 21 July

Grandarse was up before the dawn that morning. He had a habit of early rising that had never been broken. However, today he was unrested. He had not slept well.

The previous evening he had spoken to Sir John, and had suggested taking his men away from the rest of the gathering army and making their way eastward. It would help to meld the team, help him to spot the weaker men, and get them a little more fit as they marched. Besides, there was a need for reconnaissance. Scouts were being sent off north and east in case of French forces gathering. It would make sense to have a force of archers sent in support of them, so that the scouts could ride back with news of their enemies.

'Lazy fuckwits,' he muttered to himself as he made his way from one snoring line of men to another, kicking each ankle and boot as he went. He wanted them up and ready.

His centaine was sprawled haphazardly in a malodorous collection near the embers of a series of campfires. Most of the men were no trouble and were already moving and collecting their belongings in the gathering light. These were not Grandarse's concern. His mind was fixed on the vintaine of newer men.

All the centaine had enjoyed a good meal last evening. It was needed. After several nights of camping out in the open, there had been an increase in tension among the men. Occasionally fighting broke out between members of the different vintaines. That was all to the good, usually. Grandarse was more than happy to see truculent archers of his coming to blows with men from other companies. Commonly he would be able to make a profit, running a purse for whichever may be the winner. However just now he was not sure which of the men would go too far and which could be controlled. Better by far to give them another occupation.

Now, marching with his men, he studied the little vintaine once more.

Few of them had the look of experienced fighters. Imbert may have fought often enough, but he didn't move or look like an archer. No, if Grandarse had to guess, he was one of that growing number of outlaws that had infested poor England since the pestilence struck down so many. Men suddenly decided their oaths and their honour mattered little. They tried to demand more money for themselves, they insulted their masters and caused untold trouble wherever they went.

Robin was clearly an archer. His skill was undoubted, and his calm, confident demeanour was impressive. Grandarse had watched, and whenever there was bickering or snapping among the men of the vintaine, the others looked to Robin to smooth over the ruffled feathers. There was little doubt that he was the only man competent to lead the others.

Later yesterday, after the priests had come to give the men their Mass, Sir John de Sully had appeared again, walking quietly through the men. 'Grandarse, a word,' he said.

'Sir John?'

'Tomorrow, when you go, keep on to La Réole. That is where the Prince is to form his forward headquarters. Wait for us there. The Prince will want to finish the basic training of new recruits, test their skills and have a final test of the equipment and stores, before he moves off with the army.'

'Very good. It's about time. The men will get restless else.'

'We're waiting for reinforcements first,' Sir John said. 'In the meantime, I've heard a few comments about some of your men.'

Shite, Grandarse thought. *Which prick has fucked around this time?* 'Really? What sort of comments?'

'The usual. Complaints that you have some men who were not willing and eager to serve the King.'

'I find that hard to believe,' Grandarse said, thinking, *I'll kick those bastards' arses into next week if I find out who it was.*

'Do you?' Sir John said, and gave him a look in which suspicion was mixed with amusement. 'If I believed that, I would have to believe you had lost your skill as a soldier, Grandarse. What do you think of your men?'

'They're all keen and eager. They're like the mastiffs straining at their leashes when they can see the bull to bait,' Grandarse lied.

'What of the new men? You have two vintaines without a vintener, I believe? One has little in it apart from recent recruits.'

'Yes. I tried to foist them on to John of Essex, but he wouldn't have it.'

'That's the man calls himself Hawkwood now?'

'Yes. But I won't dignify him to that degree. He came from Essex. It's a good enough name.'

'Is there no one in those vintaines who shows skill with a bow and who can teach the others?'

Grandarse hesitated, then, reluctantly, 'There is one. He calls himself Robin of London.'

'And he is good with bow and arrow?'

'He could hit an eagle's eye at a hundred yards.'

'I doubt it. Has he experience of leadership?'

'Not that he's told me, no.'

'Perhaps he will suffice, even so. Give him command of his vintaine, make it clear he is subordinate to all other vinteners, and we shall see what happens. I trust you can command the other vintaine?'

'Aye.'

'After all, from counting the men in your centaine, there seems to be few enough.'

'Oh, I think that you must have miscounted, Sir John, I—'

'Don't test my patience, Grandarse. We've known each other far too long for that,' Sir John said. He peered up at the sky, then about him. 'You'll make your profit on this ride. But don't leave the men in your command feeling deserted. You take on the command of the spare vintaine. There will be all too little time to train the men after we reach Bergerac. I think that the Prince is determined to advance as soon as he may, and that will mean that we will have only a little time to train the men there.'

'How long will we have, do you think?'

'A matter of a couple of weeks or so. No longer. You will need to get the men used to marching and fighting in the time we have left.'

'Not long enough.'

'You will have to make it so.'

'Aye. Well, I'll do all I can.' He turned a shrewd eye to the knight. 'So, Sir John: this chevauchée. Is it to aim for the north, then?'

'As I told you before, the army is to ride north and bring *dampnum* to the peasants and townsfolk in our path,' Sir John said. 'We have the objective of riding to meet with King Edward's army near Flanders or the Duke's forces in Brittany. I don't know which the Prince's advisers will suggest as the more important of the two.'

'Aye. That pleases me well. There are good pickings about the towns and cities north of us, and no one has riffled through them before.'

'We will be passing through the richest lands in France, and you will have many opportunities to enrich yourself. Especially when we come to blows with the French. Catch yourself a count or a duke and you will never have to fight again.'

Grandarse patted his stomach. 'I would have to catch a right rich knight to keep this in shape!'

Aye, Sir John had been cheerful enough on hearing Grandarse's words, but there was a look in his eye that Grandarse didn't like. It was the look of a man who was unsure of the next few weeks.

Denisot could not leave immediately. There were too many duties for a bayle even in a small community like Domps, and it was a week before he could pack a pair of satchels with some bread and cold meats and prepare to leave.

He walked back into the house and saw his maid, Suzette, who smiled and lowered her head when he asked where his wife was. Suzette's eyes flickered once towards the door out to the dairy, and Denisot grunted to himself. She knew he was in a hurry to be off.

She gave him a wink, and he felt it like a kiss, before she turned and made her way out to the front. Perhaps Gaillarde was right. It may be better were he to dispense with her. She was a sore temptation, and no man could bear such a temptation for long without succumbing. But she was also pretty, a breath of fresh air in a household that had grown ever more troublesome in recent months.

'How long will you be?' Gaillarde demanded when he found her skimming cream from a wide, flat dish.

'As quick as I can be. A day to ride there and discuss, and then home, if I'm lucky.' He didn't add that, if he was really lucky, he would be forced to wait and talk to a family suddenly deprived of a young daughter, and perhaps spend a night in a tavern with happy, cheerful bawds and harlots who could tease him to pleasures that the priest would abhor and which his wife was determined to refuse him.

'One day? You'll be home tonight.'

'Unless something happens. If I learn something, I may have to stay away for a day, I suppose. And if the mercenaries are about—'

'What, you think you are likely to be attacked?' she said scathingly, looking him up and down.

'English mercenaries don't care who they kill,' he said.

'Be quick, then,' she said, turning back to her cream.

Even her farewells sounded like scoldings. Denisot turned on his heel and returned to his horse. As he passed Suzette, he was tempted to grab her and kiss her goodbye. Any contact with a woman was appealing. But the moment passed and he continued out to his mount.

That day Berenger was at the town square early in the afternoon.

There was a group of his men over at the tavern near the church, and a second, louder, mob were gambling over fighting cocks. The cheering and jeering of the men grew with the sound of the battle, yet Berenger could still hear the rustling of feathers clearly over the men egging them on. The clucking and squawking of the birds rose and rose, until there was a flurry and a series of cries from the audience as one bird died.

Walking to the tavern, Berenger sat at a bench and waited to be served. When the anxious storeowner appeared, Berenger ordered a jug of wine and waited. Several of the men inside glanced at him affecting disinterest, but he could tell that several were surprised to see him there. News must travel fast, he thought. They must have assumed he was more badly injured than was the case.

Loys was sitting on his own at another table, his head hunched. Berenger guessed that he had been the target of another humorous sally that left him looking a fool. On a whim, Berenger beckoned him. He was one of the few men in the band whom Berenger thought would be on his side. When his wine arrived, he ordered a second cup.

Will appeared in the square while Berenger was pouring the two cups, and on seeing Berenger, the vintener made his way directly to him. He saw the second cup and would have taken it, but Berenger pointedly lifted it and passed it to Loys.

Will's eyes narrowed slightly at this affront. Then: 'Frip, I heard you'd been attacked. I'm shocked, really shocked. Who could have done such a thing?'

'Haven't you had the bodies lifted already? I left one alive to tell the tale as best he could, but the others are dead,' Berenger said shortly. 'Who put them up to it, I wonder?'

'Put them up to it?' Will said. 'What makes you think that?'

'If you're going to lie, you can at least try to lie convincingly,' Berenger said. 'They were all from your vintaine, Will. They were your men through and through. What did you bribe them? A sack of gold from my stores, or just all the wine they could drink?'

'These are dangerous accusations,' Will said.

'No. The danger was in setting your men on to me.'

'So you say,' Will said laconically. 'Well, I deny it. So what now? Will you instruct a pleader to come and present your case?'

'I have my pleader already,' Berenger said, pulling his sword from its scabbard and placing it on the bench beside him. Loys stared from Berenger to his sword, and then at Will.

'You have a weapon, and you would unsheathe it here? I

think you made a rule that all the men in the band should beware any such actions on pain of death. Do you think yourself above the law, Frip?'

'I accuse you of mutiny. You egged on three men to waylay me and try to have me killed.'

'Yes. I did.'

'You don't even deny it?'

'Why should I? I have the whole company behind me, old man.' The contempt in his voice dripped like acid. 'Did you think I would make my move without thinking it through? The men have been less than delighted with your rules and restrictions for weeks now, and the more you drink, the less happy they are. Now there is news of a new chevauchée, the men are anxious.'

'What new chevauchée?'

'You see, Frip? You don't pay attention. There are stories that the Prince is at Bergerac and gathering his forces. But we don't know which direction he'll take. Perhaps he'll come up here and we will be able to join him? It would be good to be a part of another chevauchée if it's as profitable as last year's.'

Berenger stared at him. He had heard of the previous year's raid. Prince Edward had taken a small army across to Toulouse and beyond. Men were still talking about the gold, silver, silks and ransoms the participants had won. 'You think Prince Edward would accept you and your rabble? I've fought with the Prince and his father.'

'Yes, you have told us before. But the men agree with me. It's time for a new leader.'

'That would be you, I suppose?'

'If you like, we can hold an election now.'

Berenger shook his head slowly. There was no point. With so many men from his company all about him and listening, it was clear Will was confident of his position. Berenger had failed in the first requirement of a leader: he had not kept enough men close to him. He picked up the cup of wine with a peculiar feeling that this was a dream and must soon end, although he had no idea how.

'The final straw was ordering that the men couldn't take any of the women they wanted here. There were several had an eye on the widow in your house, and the idea that you wouldn't share her upset them.'

'She is to be left alone.'

'She will have many friends tonight.' Will sucked at his teeth. 'Perhaps if you hurry, you can enjoy her one last time, eh?'

CHAPTER TEN

Berenger stared, but then stood, gripping his sword. Will smiled easily, and three other men rose from their tables.

'Feel lucky, Frip?' Will said.

Berenger cursed him and set off to return to Alazaïs's house. He must return before she was attacked. As he went, he became aware that Loys was at his side. 'Leave me, boy! I am dead already,' he said. 'Go back to Will and you will be safe for now, but leave the company as soon as you can.'

'I'll stay with you. You are my commander. I won't stay with Will.'

'It is your choice then,' Berenger said. He felt oddly comforted by the fact that one man would stay by his side. They were at the top of the street where the house stood, and as he peered along it, he could hear laughter and the sound of splintering wood. He ran, his sword grasped firmly in his fist, and pelted in at the front door, his back and torn flank shrieking with agony. There came a scream, and as he entered, he saw five men in the passageway. He threw himself on those nearest him.

Their attention was fixed on the door to the steps that led upstairs to the bedchambers. They were alternately beating upon it with their fists and tugging at the timbers. One had a sword out and was trying to lever the door open at the risk of ruining his blade.

The first died before he knew he was being attacked. Berenger's sword slid under his ribs, and then he wrenched it as he pulled it free, and the corridor was filled with the smell of blood and shit as the man gave a sharp gasp and fell. Beside him was a bearded man with brown hair under his cap, and he gaped to see his companion collapse, but then he thrust himself away as Berenger's blade slipped near his throat.

Berenger had drawn his long knife as well, and thrust with that at the bearded man, who ducked behind the man with the sword. Berenger's knife caught that man's throat, opening his neck. A fine spray of red misted the corridor and then a gush of thick blood pumped over Berenger and the others. He felt the warmth on his face and breast, and as he took the fight to the next man, he felt only elation. Fighting and killing made him feel alive. He stabbed and thrust, and Loys joined him. In the narrowing corridor, their opponents were hampered. While Loys and Berenger pushed them back, these others could not fight. They were drunk on Alazaïs's wine, and had not expected to be attacked. Soon another man was screaming on the floor, his hamstrings cut and a pool of blood spreading from a wound in his leg. He tripped one of the remaining two men, and Berenger stabbed quickly, his sword entering the man's skull just over his ear. Then there was only the bearded man left. He was still tugging at the door.

Berenger moved closer to kill him, but as he did so, the door finally gave way and Alazaïs appeared in it, a war hammer with a protruding spike in her hands. She tried to swing it at the man's head, but he moved underneath it and caught her hand, turning, so that she was pulled between him and Berenger. She was held there, two steps up the staircase, gripped by his left arm about her waist, and he wrenched the war hammer from her hand with ease, smiling.

'What do you want, Fripper? Want her dead? Keep on coming. I'll put a spike in her head that'll stop her heart in a second. Want that?'

'Let her go and I'll let *you* go.'

'Right, I can trust your word, can I?' the man sneered. He deliberately moved his hand from her waist to her breast and clutched it. Alazaïs's face went cold and grey at his touch. 'Good feel, this. She has a nice body. I can share her, if you want a go too. But I expect you've already enjoyed her, eh?'

Berenger felt her despair and horror like a physical pain in his chest. The mercenary had begun to pull Alazaïs up the rest of the stairs with him, keeping her before him like a shield. There was nothing Berenger could do to prevent him. Berenger was tired already, and his back felt as though his injury had been ripped wide again, but he dare not put his sword down. He didn't want to see Alazaïs made to suffer more than she already had. She stared at him with a brittle expression of fear, overwhelmed by the horror of what lay in store for her.

'You know you can trust me,' Berenger said. 'I have been in charge of the company for the last seven months. You know me. If I give my word, you know I can be trusted.'

'Men break their oaths when it comes to their women.' The man kept on going up the stairs, pulling Alazaïs with him.

Berenger walked up, holding his gaze as he went.

'Keep back! You come too close and she'll get a pain in her head that won't go away!'

Berenger kicked out and hooked his ankle behind Alazaïs's

knee. She collapsed suddenly like a pole-axed horse, and although the mercenary swung his hammer, it was too late. She was too low and falling down the stairs, knocking Berenger from his feet.

The mercenary swore, turned and fled up the stairs.

'My *children*!' Alazaïs wailed.

Berenger sprang over her clumsily and hurried up the stairs. There was a corner at the top, and he took that warily, anxiously jerking his head around it, hoping not to receive a death-blow from the hammer, but the man wasn't there. He was already at the far end of the room, and now he had his knife out and held it to the throat of Alazaïs's oldest son, Perrin. The ten-year-old was shivering and crying, but every time he tried to wipe his eyes, the man holding him smacked his hand away.

The sight of the lad's terror and the mercenary's harsh response was enough to make the blood burn like acid in Berenger's heart. He gritted his teeth.

Loys was behind him. Berenger took some comfort from that as he waved his sword's point and edged around the room.

'Come closer, and I'll stick the bratchet!'

'You hurt him and you won't leave this room alive,' Berenger said. He was sweating now. If only there was a jug of wine somewhere near. He could do with a long draught. But if he did, he would be still more incapable of freeing the boy. He had to get the boy.

There was a sudden clamour from the hall below. Berenger heard Will's voice calling up the stairs. 'Frip? Don't try to take my head off. I'm here to help. Belot, don't do anything. I'm coming up with an idea that may help us all.'

His face appeared at the top of the stairs, and he gave a momentary frown to see how the boy was gripped. 'Belot, let the boy go, in Christ's name! What's he done to you?'

'Soon as I do, Fripper's going to use his sword. He's blaming me for all this, and it's not even my fault!' the man called Belot said.

'Let him go!' Will said.

Reluctantly, Belot stared from Berenger to Will, and then shrugged and took his knife away. At the same he gave the boy a shove that propelled him towards Berenger, who only just moved his blade away in time.

'Are you well, boy?' he asked gruffly.

'Yes, master.' The lad was as terrified by Berenger as he was by Belot. All he knew was that these mercenaries had appeared almost two weeks ago, and now they were fighting. He was petrified.

'Good.' Looking up, Berenger saw Will walk to his man and drop a gauntleted fist onto his shoulder. Berenger pushed the boy gently towards the stairs and his mother.

'Let it go, Frip. Let Belot here alone. You have been with the company for long enough. There are two options here: I can have you killed, which would be easy enough, but messy; you have already killed two yesterday, half-crippled another, and killed three more today.'

'Four today.'

'Four? In God's name, it had seemed so straightforward to remove you! You see? So, I think the second approach would be easier. Either submit to me and agree to serve again as a vintener, or leave with my blessing. You can go anywhere you want, with your horse and some food to take with you. Which will it be?

'Take the woman, take her children too. You can go with them wherever you want, if you don't want to remain a part of the company. But you won't return.'

'You mean this? You will allow us to leave?'

Will shrugged. 'Come, let us get some food and wine. You and I have been allies for long enough.'

'We were,' Berenger said warily, but he allowed Will to persuade him. He had little choice. Will had the entire force at his command, so it seemed. At least Will did not try to suggest that they had been friends.

He followed Will down the stairs. Alazaïs and her two sons followed. Berenger could hear that Perrin and Charlot, his younger brother, were both snivelling, but at least they weren't complaining. That much sense had been battered into their heads, apparently, since the arrival of the English.

English! Only a quarter of the men were truly English. As for the rest, the majority were adventurers from every corner of France and the Holy Roman Empire. There was even that wiry man who claimed to come from a land with high mountains near Morgarten. He had the calmest blue eyes Berenger had ever seen, but there was a coldness about him that didn't allow for companionability or friendship. In any case, the land he described didn't sound convincing to Berenger. Mountains that were capped with snow all year round, high cliffs and plunging valleys. Fulk claimed that his father had helped destroy a French army some years ago, but that sounded unlikely to Berenger too.

All he knew was, men whom he could trust were rare. It was not like the glory days when he had been a centener in King Edward III's army when they won their glorious victory.

At the bottom of the stairs, Will led the way out into the open. Alazaïs would have remained in her house, but Berenger took her hand and led her from her home. 'Stay here and I cannot protect you, or your sons,' he said. She nodded and brought her boys with her.

For some moments, Berenger stood in the doorway, waiting. Outside almost all the company had gathered, and he had a quick certainty that they were there to see to his end. He expected to be grabbed and dragged away to a gallows, there to be hanged. It was the normal way for those who broke the unwritten rules of the company: a death, swift and sure.

But Berenger had broken no rules. His failure lay in imposing rules on the men that they had decided to reject. They were not here on a war footing, but were enjoying the spoils of their victory over the town. They wanted to enjoy it still more. For that reason they had agreed to depose Berenger.

'Well?' he demanded.

There was a shuffling and some of the men looked away. Loys was at his side, and as Berenger looked about the rest of the men, he saw Fulk peering at him. His eyes were the colour of the sky reflected on a calm lake in midsummer, a deep blue that was almost indigo. Fulk stepped forward. As always, he carried a long-handled halberd with a blade on one side, a spike at the top and a hammer on the reverse. It was his weapon of choice, and having seen how he could wield it, Berenger knew how fearsome it could be.

'What?' he said.

The Swiss grinned, then shrugged and set his head to one side. He was blond and handsome in his confidence. 'You would give up the command without fighting? You would walk away from us, your company? All to protect this woman?'

'If I was to fight Will, who would support me?' Berenger looked about the men of the crowd, and felt a perverse pleasure to see how the men averted their eyes from him. It was an affirmation of sorts. The other new man, Arnaud, held his gaze and smiled as if confused, but his brother, Bernard, glowered like an angry bear. At least his decision was proved right. Only Saul of Plymouth held his gaze without wavering.

'You would do this?' Fulk pressed.

'For her and her children, yes,' Berenger said, his attention pulled back to the Swiss.

In the crowd, Saul hawked and spat, then picked up his pack and walked towards Berenger.

'What do you want?' Berenger said.

Saul was shorter than Berenger, and had a face that looked like old leather, with wrinkles on top of wrinkles. His hair was faded, and receded badly from his brow, leaving a round patch of fluff. He met Berenger's gaze now with a steady certainty. 'God love you, Frip, you're a man of pride and honour, but you're only one against all the company. You need at least one man to stand with you. Mind you, if they attack us now, boy, we're fucked,' he said.

Berenger's stern expression cracked. 'Thank you.'

'Keep your sword at the ready,' Saul said, and stood at his side.

CHAPTER ELEVEN

It had been a good afternoon for Denisot.

He had ridden at a careful pace, filled with the constant fear that he might be being watched as he travelled along the road beneath the trees. Their branches towered overhead and met, creating a tunnel that smelled of loam and rich soil. Occasionally he caught a whiff of fox spray, but apart from that there was nothing. He half-expected to detect the rank odour of stale sweat and the damp smell of horses which had slept out of doors for too long, and to hear the jingle of harnesses and clatter of weapons as a mercenary band bore down on him; but there was nothing and he arrived safely.

The town of Chamberet was far enough from his home for the people to be interested in his tale. Here he was not merely an official put in place by a nobleman to collect taxes and enforce the peace, but a slightly exotic stranger from a foreign town, an alien. While most of the populace had heard rumours of what had happened at Uzerche, he was the first to bring definite news of the atrocities that the capture of the town had entailed. After all, a crucifixion was not common. Murders tended to be committed with a knife, especially when the victim was a raped child. It must surely have been committed by those terrible sons of the Devil, the English. They were all vicious and perverted.

He had met with his counterpart and then the priest, and held meetings with some of the people of the town, and on all sides he received eager attention, but it was not until late in the afternoon that he met a grizzled innkeeper with a face marked with as many red lines as a surgeon's map of a body and a nose that was the colour and size of an overripe plum, who frowned at the description of the body and then gave a contemplative nod.

'I know the girl you mean, I think. She was here a while ago. Over a week, I think. Not a local girl. I never saw her before, anyway. She didn't seem all there, if you know what I mean. Her brain was addled.'

'In what way?' Denisot said.

'Oh, you know the sort. Wide-eyed and empty-brained. You would have found space for a quart of ale in her skull. She came here and spent the evening sitting by the fire and flinching whenever anyone stepped near her. She didn't even have the price of a warm drink on her. No idea about how to get by.'

'Did no one speak to her?'

'Like I said, she jumped like a started squirrel when anyone stepped close to her. No one tried to speak to her. It was embarrassing.' He wiped his face on his apron, transferring charcoal smuts along with his sweat.

Denisot was coming to dislike the man. 'What was her name?'

'I don't know. Alicia or something.'

'Did she say where she came from?'

'Like I said, she wasn't very talkative, but I got the impression she came up from the south. And you say she's dead?'

'Yes. I think the English dragged her behind their horses and then crucified her after they were done with their pleasures.'

'An evil death.'

Denisot could not disagree with that. There were worse ways to die, of course. He had seen a few of them. Before long he would see more.

When Will offered them wine, Berenger and his companions followed him down the hill to the inn, where a table was cleared for them, the landlord twittering and chirping like a sparrow as the men swept the cups and trenchers onto the floor, evicting three travellers who had been enjoying their meal in order to make space for Berenger and Will. Saul and Loys sat on a bench, while Alazaïs and her children stood nearby, like peasants accused of theft before a bayle.

When they were seated, Will poured Berenger a cup of wine and leaned forward, his elbows on the table. 'So, Frip, what now?'

'You said I can leave?' Berenger ignored the cup. He felt as though the Devil was tempting him to drink.

'With your wench and her boys, if you must. If I am unreasonable towards you, it'll only make the others think again about having me as their leader. I don't need that sort of trouble. Better for me – and you too, incidentally – if you merely ride off and leave us to our own devices.'

'You will not try to attack us as we go?'

'You will have a free hand. I only want to see you go. You haven't been a bad leader, Frip, but you drink too much. You can't be trusted. If you would only have a monk's allowance you would be all right, but with your consumption you're growing irrational. It's no good for us.'

'Have you seen how ineffectual I am in a fight? Ask your friend Owen,' Berenger said.

'I never said a word about your fighting ability, Frip. Only your ability to plan, to think rationally. You should have known better than to threaten to hang the men for taking a wench or two. What does it matter what they do to the women?'

'The plan was to take the town and hold it. You terrorise all the people of the town, and they will despair. If they despair, they will lose their fear because if existence itself is a torment, they have nothing to lose by death. If you assault their women, you will bring them to revolt even more swiftly. We agreed that.'

'And you drank too much when you got here and became illogical. I couldn't discuss it with you. Well, there we are. You cannot remain as commander, and I think you are right not to stay under my command. I think you could be a sore difficulty to the men, were you to remain here. Better that you seek your fortune with another company.'

'I created this company,' Berenger said.

'You honed it, yes. But there was a company before you, and there will be another after you. Under me.'

Will's eyes glittered and he didn't blink. That was a classic proof of his intent. When he grew serious and stared fixedly, a man could be certain that he was in earnest.

'You can take your horse, a single pack, your sword and belongings. Any friends going with you will have the same courtesy extended. I'm not being generous. This is natural self-interest. If the others think I am unfair or unreasonable, they will seek to replace me as well. So, better by far that you take what is mostly yours. You will have food, too, and water. But beyond that, you take nothing.'

Berenger considered him. If Will intended to kill him, a second abortive attempt in the village would destroy his chances of leading the company. But if he allowed Berenger to ride away, the others would accept that. Berenger would have left the band. If he stayed, Berenger would never have allowed a rival to survive. He would be a constant source of trouble. Others in the company might decide that he was a better leader and hasten the new captain's end, if it meant bringing back the previous commander. Berenger was uncomfortably sure that Will would feel the same. 'What of the widow?'

'If she goes with you, she can take her dress and shoes. If she remains, she can keep her house. I am sure she will soon find a man to replace you,' Will said, and cast her a smile.

'She will need a mount, as will her boys.'

'Don't test me too far. If you want her and she wants you, you can go together, alive. I am not denuding the company of mounts, though. She stays and keeps her property, or goes and leaves all behind. It's her choice.'

Berenger looked at her and saw her irresolution. 'If you stay, you know what will happen.'

She nodded. 'I will go with you.'

Will left them in the tavern soon afterwards. Berenger waited, an itching in his back telling him that many men from the company were watching him. He could sense their eyes, the compulsive urge to grab a bow, a sword, a dagger, and set about him, but none of them did. Perhaps it was the last vestige of their respect for him that held them back. He didn't know, but at this moment he was grateful.

He glanced at Alazaïs. She had the haunted look of a hart held at bay while the hunters draw their bows, but her eyes held his firmly. It was clear enough that here there was no safety for

her or her children. She would be better off for a while, until her
new lover grew dissatisfied or bored, and then she would lose
her house and belongings. She knew that. Better to make a clean
break and leave with Berenger.

Loys and Saul were agreed too. Their contracts with the
company were void. There was nothing here for them either.
They would remain with Berenger.

The innkeeper wanted to charge a high fee for their drinks
and beds for the night, but Saul spoke to him. Later Saul would
only say that he 'haggled' with the fellow, but from that moment
on, whenever the innkeeper appeared in the chamber, he was
careful to avoid approaching within two yards of Saul.

At the back of the inn was a door to a room used as a kitchen,
while beyond there was a large communal room for travellers with a huge palliasse. It smelled of fresh herbs, and there
was meadowsweet strewn over the blankets, but Berenger was
unpleasantly convinced that he would wake itching and irritable
after ten minutes' dozing on it. Loys and Saul bedded down in
one corner of the sleeping chamber, with Alazaïs and her children at the farther side of the palliasse. Berenger had insisted
on the men taking watches through the night, and himself stood
the first, standing at the inn's entrance and watching as the sky
darkened.

In the town all was quiet. Berenger stood guard in his
fashion, leaning on a polearm while staring up at the sky.
Occasionally clouds drifted past, as silent and apparently insub-
stantial as ghosts on the wind, but he knew that they must be
dense and heavy, for when they passed over the moon they
enshadowed the whole of the town. It was as though a man
had set a shield before a candle. Berenger was not particularly
afflicted with superstition, but he could remember when he was
younger, he had seen a cloud pass over the moon and become

convinced that the end of the world was to come. Ever since, he felt a vague frisson of unease when he saw the view dimmed in this way.

He had intended to show this to his sons, but he had never had the chance.

Struck with a sudden melancholy, he felt a sob forming in his breast and it was all he could do to swallow it back. He struck angrily at the moisture in his eyes, wiping it away. His boy was dead, and his wife and her son too. His old life was gone, and there was nothing he could do to bring it back.

He heard the door behind him open. Saul and Loys had demanded that they should share the guard duty with Berenger, and he assumed one of them was entering, mistrusting him and thinking that he allowed them to oversleep without calling them to their duty. If it were not for the dampness still in his eyes, he would have turned and told them to return to their beds a while longer, but then he smelled her fragrance, a mixture of rose water and musk. It was a scent he had snuffed many times in the last few days, one that had twisted the knife in his heart. There were memories attached to that perfume.

'I couldn't sleep. Can I join you here?'

She spoke quietly, so as not to wake the household, and he was grateful that she showed due concern for others. After all, she was the widow of a wealthy man, and as such she was used to giving commands and not considering the effect on other people. A waft of her perfume reached his nostrils and he was assailed by a desire to hold her. Nothing more, just to hold her and bury his nostrils in her hair and breathe her in, as though he could inhale enough purity to wipe away his memories of the last ten years. Except he couldn't. Those memories were lodged in his brain as firmly as the nails in a church door.

In truth, he was unsure of his feelings for her. He felt anxious in her presence, but it wasn't the fear of a youth for appearing foolish, it was as though she held the key to a door he dare not open. Or reopen.

God's cods, he needed a pot of wine!

'I don't want to be distracted,' he said. Peering at her now, in the dark, her face was a mask of shadows. She could be smiling at him, laughing at his absurdly childish behaviour, or glaring, readying a knife to gut him.

'You really think he could attack us here? He said we could leave.'

There was no humour or contempt in her tone. He could only hear fretfulness. 'He's a lying son of a whore,' he said. 'I wouldn't trust him further than I could piss, and that's not far.'

'He stopped that man from harming my son,' she said softly, her voice almost a sigh.

'Aye. But I'm not sure he would want all the company to see one of his men killing a boy just to irritate me. If he had, some more would have rallied to my side, and that could have pre-cipitated a confrontation. As it is, this way he removes me, he gets to steal all you own, and keeps most of my wealth as well. His only fear is that I might return to take back what is mine and yours.'

'That is why you keep a watch all night?'

'That is why.'

'You saved me and my boys. I am grateful.'

She said nothing more. With a quiet susurration of linen, she quietly moved back to the room where her boys slept.

Berenger stared out at the shadowed street. No movement, no glint of steel nor spark from a flint. Perhaps she was right to question his insistence on keeping watch: perhaps Will had no further interest in Berenger or the woman; he had won all he wanted.

But while Berenger wanted to believe that, there was a strong conviction that Will would not want to leave a potential rival leader in place, especially since he had already tried to assassinate him. Will would not understand that a man could willingly forget an insult like that. In truth, Berenger wasn't sure he could. Yet now, in the cold and dark of a Limousin night, he was happy to forgive both assaults and leave Uzerche with his life and soul intact.

Grandarse rode gloomily on his pony while his men trudged along in the rain that sheeted down. His men looked and sounded even less happy. The moans and complaints continued all through the day.

Clip's whine rose over the other voices.

'Why are we sent off so soon? Everyone else has warm, dry beds this night. Us? We're going to be walking on until we have to stop or drown!'

'We'll be allowed to stop soon,' a voice called back. Grandarse thought it might be the new man called Gilles. He sounded less cheery now.

'You think so?' Clip complained. 'You don't know much about soldiering, do you? They'll march us all the way to this town, then turn us round to march back. We'll get no rest. And when we think it can't get any worse, they'll throw us all into a battle that will kill off half of us. That's how we fight in this army. By walking wherever we're told, and then by dying there. They'll see us all killed. You mark my words!'

Grandarse smiled but he was not happy. He had held that short conversation with Archibald ten or more days ago, which had left him disgruntled and irritable. Archibald had suggested he should seek Berenger to help with the new recruits.

'Yes, just go and find Frip,' he muttered to himself now.

'That'll be easy, with a country the size of France. I'll only have to stop at the next village and ask and they'll be sure to know. A miserable-looking old git with scars and a frowning eye. Easy.'

But there was a thought in the back of his mind: if Fripper was still alive, and there was no certainty of the fact, then it was at least very likely that he wouldn't be too far away. These were hard days, and a man would avoid the main centres of French authority. He would not approach near to Paris on his own, nor would he try to travel to the south since the Prince's rampage all the way from Bordeaux to Narbonne last year. That would be suicidal, for the French there would have all-too-clear memories of the atrocities caused by the English.

Which left him with the question, where would Berenger have gone, if he was still alive? He was not in Calais, and surely if he was in the English territories of Guyenne or Aquitaine, he would have offered himself to the Prince when he heard there was to be a fresh campaign? Unless he was already engaged to fight for another knight or baron, of course. Or had joined another band.

It was of no interest just now. Grandarse snorted to himself. He had gone to find Robin and told him the news that Robin was to be the vintener of his band.

'You must be desperate.'

'I am.'

'I will take on the men, if you are sure, but I'll want the pay of a vintener.'

'You will have it, of course.'

'I will,' Robin said, staring at him in that unsettling way of his, head thrust forward, slightly tilted, so that it was his left eye that focused on Grandarse.

'You will have Imbert and the others, and . . .'

'You do realise three have tried to escape already?'

'Eh? What?'

'Imbert and the father and son from Bordeaux have all tried to escape. First time was on the very night you brought 'em in.'

'You stopped them?'

'I gave Imbert a tap on the 'ead and the other two seemed to realise that any enemy out there was much less scary than me. Then the two tried again the night after. I had to hit Pierre quite hard to make him understand I was serious.'

'Why?'

Robin looked away. Part of him wanted to explain: that he was once a reputable man-at-arms and archer, a man who had been respected and valued by his master, Sir Reynald, until that master had died in the pitched battle off the coast of Flanders at the place they called Sluys. Robin had been there, but could do nothing to rescue his master when he fell into the water, the blood bubbling and seething all about him as Robin saw his face disappear from sight. The weight of his chain mail and steel bascinet were enough to drag him down.

Lady Marjorie had never forgiven him. Robin was banned from the house. His belongings, such as they were, were thrown after him as he left the manor that last time. It was the beginning of his wanderings. He had become an outcast.

And then there was the disaster. The fight in an ale house, both men drunk, both keen to eradicate the assumed insult, both swinging fists and then knives, the wash of blood over his face, the shock as he realised what he had done. Then the headlong rush to the church, grasping the altar-cloth and waiting until the coroner arrived and permitted him to abjure the realm. There was nothing else for him. So he came here, and was given a chance to redeem himself.

This, he felt, was his chance to establish himself again, to become accepted. At first he had been reluctant, but when he saw Imbert trying to escape on that first night, he had felt a sudden rage that anyone could think to flee while his companions were still there, and had struck the man down. Only later did he realise that he could have escaped himself. And by then it was too late. He was committed to the vintaine.

'I wish I fuckin' knew,' he said.

CHAPTER TWELVE

Friday 22 July

Berenger turned in his saddle and peered back.

This morning they had set off as soon as Will had allowed the gates to be opened, although Will had insisted on their breaking their fast first. 'It is only fair,' he said when Berenger demurred. 'Eat before a journey. You always used to insist on that yourself.'

It was true. He had forgotten that in the last wandering years. It was hard to remember all he had once known. This morning he had a headache. He had woken with a cup still in his hand, the wine tipped over his lap and the floor. After Alazaïs had gone to her bed he had been unsettled enough to want more to drink, and had sated his thirst over the hours, forgetting to rouse Loys and Saul to take over the guard duty. If one of his own sentinels had behaved like that, the man would have been flogged for such dereliction. Saul walked in and saw him, but wisely chose to say nothing, and Berenger had sat silently as they chewed through a hard farmer's loaf and grey cheese.

Will had not objected to Alazaïs and the children going to the church to pray before they set off. 'Be sure to confess to all your incontinent behaviour and thoughts of lascivious couplings with me and my men!' Will had laughed. Alazaïs had reddened in embarrassment and fury, and Berenger had walked with her to the church as though protecting her from further shame. However, he would not enter. She must walk inside with her boys, leaving Berenger at the door.

Now she looked up at him. 'Why did you not come into the church to pray with me?'

'What? Oh, I have no faith.'

'You are a heretic?' she exclaimed.

'That is a lie put about by our enemies. Just because I'm English does not make me a bad Christian,' he said.

'But you say you have no faith?'

'You weren't there when the plague struck,' he said. 'I don't believe God could have served us with that disaster without malice. He must hate us. He hates me.'

She made a hurried Sign of the Cross. 'You think you are cursed?'

'I *know* I am cursed. I *think* I am hated by God. How could he take everything from me unless he detests me?'

'He took so much?'

Berenger wasn't paying attention. 'It is this land, I think. It is so drenched and beslubbered in blood, it is a miracle that anything can grow. All man's vices and lusts are concentrated here. No matter whether it's the greed of the nobles or the avarice of the merchants or the lusts of the common folk, it is all here on display and accepted. Look at Uzerche, your town. It holds so much wealth that it attracted men like ...'

'Men like you,' Alazaïs said.

'Yes. But I didn't plan to destroy. I was hoping we might

take the town and live there for a while,' Berenger said. His head was hurting, and the brightness of the sun was no assistance. 'I thought we could live with the town, like a nobleman in a castle, and all might benefit.'

'How would the free townsfolk benefit from you ordering their lives and stealing their money?'

Berenger pulled a grimace and looked away. 'I didn't want the men to go raping for no purpose. I didn't want men and women to be killed out of hand every day. Only a few at first so that the populace would come to accept the new rule of law. But the men were unused to living in a town at peace. That was the trouble.'

'The town's men were slaughtered because they tried to defend their women and children! You call that "the trouble"!'

'You don't understand. That is the point of an attack. The first assault is violent, so that all will bow to the new order. After that, we could grow more beneficent and help people. But only when they grew to trust us.'

'I think if you have men who are used to plunder and murder, they would find it difficult to become used to the idea of living in peace with the people they have subdued.'

'Perhaps,' Berenger said. He pulled out a wineskin and began to drink. It soothed the acid in his stomach, but did nothing for the acid eating at his soul.

After sending Suzette to fetch bread, Gaillarde wept. Denisot had not come home last night. He had said he would, but he hadn't. Again. He was staying there in the town, enjoying himself with harlots and drinking himself to oblivion.

She wanted her husband back; she wanted her *life* back. Once, ten years before, they had been happy. As bayle, Denisot was tax collector, adjudicator, peace-maker and thief-taker.

They always had enough money, and the birth of their two children had left them fulfilled. Gaillarde had been so full of love, she had thought her heart must break when she looked at her children and husband. Denisot had been gentle, kindly, loving. Or so it had seemed. He had the duty of keeping the town peaceful and making sure that even the loudest disputes between man and wife were kept quiet. Yet now he could not even make peace in his own house. She wished he could. She was lonely, so lonely.

But the life they had enjoyed was gone. It had been snatched from them when God took Pons and Fabrisse. The memory of her children was as hard and cold as a dagger to the heart.

When the pestilence arrived here nine years ago, it ravaged the land. Men and women lost parents, children and spouses, in a sudden attack that scarred all those left alive. In one village six miles to the east, Gaillarde had heard that only one child survived of the whole population, while in the priory itself more than half the monks died. Those remaining could scarcely cope with the services and their other duties. And those left behind were not necessarily the better men, she knew. It sometimes seemed to her that all the kinder, good men were killed. Perhaps, as some said, the disease came to take away the best and sweetest, leaving the Devil's for whenever he would come to take them.

But no, she could not believe that. There were too many good men who had lived, while quite a few whom she would be surprised to be allowed even to approach the gates of Heaven had been taken away. It was, as the priest said afterwards, as he sat on the wall outside the church with tears streaming down both cheeks, utterly inexplicable. God's will was not to be denied, but men could not expect to understand his every whim. That priest had disappeared a few months after the last of the dead had been buried. She thought his mind had been broken as well as his heart.

No man should have to live through that. The priest had been in despair after having to bury so many, but they were only *people*. They weren't his own flesh, his own blood. Gaillarde had lost everything. Her little children were taken from her, and for that she bore a terrible hatred. She knew the new priest was right to defend God, standing before the congregation and explaining that it was the evil of men and women that had caused the visitation of this terror on the people, but Gaillarde could not believe that. Why would He take away her boy and tiny girl from her?

She knew God was forgiving. She knew He was kindness and love. So their children could not have been taken from her by Him. Gaillarde had come to the conclusion that it was not Him, but Denisot who was to blame.

At first, when her children had died, she had blamed herself. So many did. It was natural for a parent to accept all responsibility. She had not done enough. Somehow, she should have been able to protect them from the foul miasma that physicians said brought the pestilence. She was like all other parents: they needed to have someone to blame.

Gaillarde was no philosopher, but for her it was natural to seek the guilty. It was unsatisfying to accuse a foul air that moved from one to another as if on the whim of some Devil. There was no body to punch, no form to detest. But then, when she spoke to the new, young priest, and he advised her to consider her own life, and how God might have been punishing her, Gaillarde could not understand. She could not escape the fact that her own life had been filled with piety and honour, and she had not been guilty of any offence against God, not that she knew of. And that confused her for a long time.

But then, when after four years she could not fall pregnant again, she began to look at Denisot askance. She reviewed his life, and found many aspects wanting. Perhaps he was having affairs; perhaps he was frequenting the whores when he went to Limoges and elsewhere; perhaps he was stealing taxes from the people. Tax collectors were always said to be thieves with their fingers in the cash boxes. Perhaps it was nothing *she* had done; what if Denisot himself was guilty of crimes.

That would mean *he* had killed their children, that *he* had made her womb dry and shrivel.

She allowed him into their bed, but when he approached her, she froze at his touch. She could not help it.

He was a lonely man, yes. He had lost his children. But his crimes had made him. And his offences meant that his wife was being punished too.

And now? Now she hated him.

The road was long and winding, and Denisot grew warm in the hot sun. He fanned himself, and wished he had brought more water, but a short while later he found a small stream at the side of the road and dismounted to refill his leather flask. His horse was keen too, and Denisot let him drink his fill before they continued.

He had come to learn all he could about the dead girl, and to see for himself what the risks were from the English devils at Uzerche, but there was no sign of pillaging about here. The farms stood in their fields, the peasants worked as labourers will anywhere, and Denisot found himself submitting to the soporific effect of the sun and his plodding pony. He had been led to believe that if there was a threat of Englishmen, the land for miles would be laid waste. The English devils tended to ride on a broad front, so that they could wage war over the widest area.

Only when they had need of haste would they resort to riding in a narrow column. Fields would be burned, houses too, and bodies would lie strewn about, men, women and children, lying in a mess of blood. The savagery of the English was shocking. They were like ravening wolves launching themselves on an unsuspecting world.

Yet here all was calm, all was secure and peaceful. He found his eyes were closing as he nodded with the horse's movement.

He came to with a jerk. There were three riders ahead of him, and they were approaching at speed, throwing up a cloud of dust from the dry surface. Denisot caught his breath and stared about him. Fool! He had been idly dreaming while the road had taken him to a dreadful place at which to meet brigands. Although a short way ahead there was a wood that came down to the road, where he sat now there was no escape. The way here was passing through a cutting where a hill had been carved away for the road. On his left a rocky cliff loomed fifteen feet overhead, while on his right the ground fell away into a river valley. There was no way of escape, other than to turn and ride back the way he had come and hope that he might outride these men.

But even as he had the thought, he saw that the riders were reining in and dismounting. Two of them hurried up in among the trees, while one took their mounts away, up the hill behind the trees. Surely that was a boy, Denisot thought. The other two appeared to be carrying crossbows and full quivers, he thought, and as he watched they merged in amidst the ferns and undergrowth. Soon there was no sign that anyone had been there. The dust on the air drifted away, and all was as peaceful and calm as it had been moments before.

Denisot sat anxiously on his horse, unsure how to proceed. If he continued, the men with the crossbows might attack him.

He had no defence against crossbows. He had a sword in his scabbard, but while it was a good weapon that had once been his father's, it was less than useless against men such as these – for he had no doubt that these must be English murderers set on robbing the next merchant to pass.

He was coming to the conclusion that his best option would be to return and fetch help in the form of officers, when he saw more dust on the air. It looked like a small party of men riding towards him. Two, no, three of them. And with them were others on foot, all advancing towards the men who had taken up positions in the trees beside the road.

Denisot felt the breath thicken in his lungs. Time seemed to slow, and he stared in horror as the men in the trees knelt with their bows spanned and ready. He saw a man bend and fix a bolt into the channel before resting the stock over his shoulder and taking aim. The travellers would be killed.

They had stopped. Perhaps they had seen the men lying in wait. A stray sound had betrayed the men, maybe? One of the riders dismounted, and his place was taken by another. They were so far away that they were mere figures in the distance, but Denisot could make out the fact that two of the walkers were smaller than the others. He thought they could be children.

He could think of nothing to do that would save them. He had no choice: surely he must flee. He could at least save himself and make his way back to Domps, and there he could alert the town. He could . . .

A voice came to him, clear on the warm air. It was the voice of a young boy. For just a moment he thought it was Pons, his Pons. In his mind's eye at that moment he saw his own dear son in the road.

He would not run. He had only the one honourable option.

Without further consideration, he slapped his mount with his hand, then again, and raked his spurs down the brute's flanks. The beast began to edge forward, and then when he jabbed his heels again, the horse began to canter and then gallop. Denisot tore off his hat and waved it urgently, whooping as loudly as he could. He passed around a bend, where the bowmen were hidden, and then he was riding straight at them, and to his horror he saw the nearer man turn and take deliberate aim. He saw the bolt fly, and his eyes widened in horror at the thought of the iron-tipped quarrel striking him, and ducked hurriedly. Feeling the change in his position, the horse pulled away to the right, and the missile flew past safely.

The man was hauling the bowstring up to the nut again, and Denisot felt a quickening terror. He was so close now, he could not see how he could escape a second bolt, but then he realised that there were not only the two men he had seen on the road: at least seven were in among the trees, all with bows, and all glaring now at him.

He was level with the trees now, and heard another quarrel hiss past his head, and then he was past them, and tearing on down the road towards the little group he had seen.

CHAPTER THIRTEEN

Thomas de Ladit, his feet sore, stumbled on, convinced that he would never make it to Bordeaux.

This country was obnoxious to him. It had all the perils of damnation, as far as he was concerned. The roads were dreadful, the inn he had stayed in last night had been deplorable – he was sure that the itching about his legs was from fleas – and there were rumours of the English massing ready to attack.

He had stayed almost a week in Thiviers, and then made his way to Périgueux, thinking that he would learn the best route to Bordeaux from there, but on his way he had been set upon and beaten by some scruffy peasants. They hadn't bothered to rob him, luckily, but they had left him feeling very battered and bruised, and he had needed to rest at the next village he came to. Now, a week later, he was determined just to escape this country and find his way homewards again.

Normandy had been such a delightful place to live while King Charles was there with the Dauphin, so it was a great shock to come down here to the warmer climates and learn that the peasants had no idea of the common civilities for a man of his importance. Not that he could even remonstrate with them. He dare not announce to the world who he was.

The officer in Périgueux to whom he had reported the bullies who beat him so on the road outside the town seemed to think that it was more the fault of Thomas, as an outsider, than the peasants themselves. There was a distinct impression given that Thomas should have moved out of their way when they approached him. Foreigners had little right to use the same road as those who lived and laboured in the area.

He walked on, limping from a badly stubbed big toe on his left foot, and thus it was he didn't realise his danger until it was too late.

'Morning, Master,' Hawkwood said.

Hearing Hawkwood's laugh, Thomas turned to flee, but his legs would not move fast enough. Before he could take more than three paces, a lance-butt struck the back of his head and he was down like a stunned rabbit in the middle of the roadway.

Laughing men surrounded him on horseback, and he snatched up a handful of the gritty soil, thinking he could fling it in their faces. This was not *right*!

Thomas de Ladit was an important man in the service of the King of Navarre, in God's name. These men should bow to him and beg his forgiveness, not assault him as though he was some kind of felon.

He climbed to his feet, glaring at the men all around. That they were outlaws was his first thought, but then, as he took in their weapons and the wolfish smile on their leader's rotund face, he let the soil slip from his fingers.

These weren't *French* bandits. These were much worse: they were *English*.

*

Berenger had to nag her for a quarter-mile before she agreed.

'Come, madam, you are exhausted. I can see that.'

'You have saved my life already. I will walk,' she said. 'Charlot, be quiet!'

The boy pulled a face in response. He and his older brother had been singing and playing as they went, both relieved to be safe from the mercenaries and full of high spirits to be setting off on an adventure.

'Charlot!'

He evaded the hand that tried to smack his ear and darted away, laughing.

'You can set your jaw like a mule if you want, madam,' Berenger said as she glared after her son, 'but I know women. You will only demand that I buy you new shoes in the next town, and that would be additional expense. Besides, it is demeaning for me to ride while you suffer on the ground. Any man would think that I was a mean fellow. They might take me for a priest!'

'I think the danger worth risking,' she said.

'Why, is my saddle not of sufficient quality for you?' he said. 'Come, widow, please. If you will not ride, I will walk in any case. There is no joy in riding when I can see you limping with sore feet. Please, I entreat you!'

She turned her head and would have ignored him, but he swung his leg over his mount's rump and walked beside her.

When he had her attention, he lifted his brows and made his face to go round-eyed with feigned shock. 'Good widow, look what I have discovered! A horse without a rider! Do you think there could be a rider without a horse nearby? Perhaps if you were to climb into the saddle, you may espy the poor rider. No doubt he allowed himself to be bucked from his seat by the violence of the beast's gait. Or by the stubbornness of a mule in the near vicinity?'

So saying, he draped the reins over her shoulder and walked on, casting a glance back at her as he went.

She relented.

'Aha! I see you can smile, in any case,' he said delightedly, and she gave a little gasp of amused exasperation. He grinned. 'Come! Let me help you.'

She took the offer of his linked hands, and he helped her up. She took the reins and smiled down at him with a cocked eyebrow. 'You help a lady very prettily,' she said.

He felt his smile dim. 'I have not had the opportunity too often in recent years,' he admitted, and then turned away.

Loys said, 'What's that?' and Berenger's joy was turned to sourness and evil.

He saw the dust of the road at first, and then there was the clattering of hoofs and, in the midst of it, he saw a terrified-looking rider pelting along without regard to the large stones of the road or the risks of a broken neck. His eyesight was not good, but he was sure that there was a solitary rider. No other men appeared to be near him.

Saul suddenly bellowed, 'Men in the woods! *Ambush! Ambush!*' and turned his beast to the edge of the roadway. Loys was about to follow him when there was a flash of sun on polished steel, and men stepped from the cover of the trees letting loose their quarrels. The heavy bolts flew past quickly, whistling, and Berenger saw the cloud of dust as the horse ahead of them went sprawling, fatally wounded. Next he saw the bolt that struck Loys, catching him at the left shoulder and spinning him around on his horse. He had scarcely time to kick his feet free of the stirrups before he slammed into the surface of the road. Berenger was about to go to his aid when he realised that the boys and Alazaïs were all in the open, easy targets. He turned to them just in time to see the bolt that hit Alazaïs between her breasts.

He heard nothing, and for a moment his life paused. There was a roaring in his ears, as though he was listening to the sea in a storm, and his arms hung slackly as he watched her. Her eyes were fixed on his as her hands rose as if to pull the bolt from her breast. Then her back bent and she leaned over the cantle, her chin dropping. He shouted '*No!*' but she began to slide out of the saddle as he watched.

The bolt had hit her in the middle of her ribcage, and the shock had probably stopped her heart in that instant, for even as she slipped from her mount, Berenger saw that her eyes were already empty, as though she had been a corpse for hours already. The horse reared, alarmed to feel that something was wrong with his rider, and that was enough to throw her from him, crashing down into the road.

'*No!*' Berenger shouted again, and with that shout he felt his heart shatter into tiny fragments. His life was ended once more.

Berenger's cry was a shriek from the pits of his soul, and he drew his sword. He ran towards the source of the bolts that whizzed and hissed past him. Many appeared to be flying, but he was unhurt. There was a deep, guttural roar from behind him, and Berenger saw that Saul was standing at the side of Alazaïs. At his feet were the bodies of the two boys. They had run to their mother when she fell, and bolts had passed through both thin little figures. Saul, the great seaman and fighter who had been in Berenger's company for all the last three years and had taken over a vintaine when Berenger himself was elected leader seven months ago, was beside himself with mingled rage and despair. As Berenger watched, Saul took a grip of his sword in his right hand, a war-axe in his left, and suddenly bolted for the trees. Berenger joined him, his head down and his arms pumping as he moved, avoiding a straight line and jigging like a fly as he covered the ground.

On the way he passed the man who had ridden towards them. The man was lying on the ground, trapped with one leg under his dead horse. Berenger almost stabbed him. It was an automatic reaction – in a battle a sensible man never left a potential enemy behind him – but the man had something in his eyes when Berenger approached, an anger, but not directed at Berenger. Besides, if he was an enemy, why had the men in the trees loosed their bows at him?

An arrow pierced the air by his head and Berenger continued, pounding through the dust, on and on, until he was in among the trees. Saul was over on his right, and as Berenger spotted him, he saw Saul strike with his axe, spin and stab with the sword, and then crouch as a bolt flew past him, then he was back, the axe whirling.

Berenger ran on, and saw a man rise in front of him, crossbow on his shoulder, already aiming at Berenger. It was one of Will's men, he saw, and he tried to move faster, but he knew he would be too late. There were seven or eight yards between them and Berenger couldn't cover the distance in time to save himself.

Then the bow was knocked up and away, and the bolt flew harmlessly into the sky. Berenger roared with relief and rage, and then saw Fulk. The great Swiss had his halberd in his fist, and as the crossbow was loosed safely into the air, the savage blade of the polearm hooked back and opened the archer's throat from side to side in one easy slash. The man collapsed, his hands to his throat, as Fulk leaned round the tree and nodded to Berenger.

Fulk was the last man Berenger expected to find fighting on his side. He had never shown any signs of friendship towards him, except for the brief conversation in farewell the day before.

Even as the thought passed through his mind, Berenger realised Fulk had disappeared into the undergrowth, only to appear at another tree farther up the hill. Berenger saw his fearsome weapon flash with a red, oily gleam, and another man was jerked into the open, his head impaled on the spike. Fulk had to fight to retrieve his weapon from the man's body.

Berenger ran on among the trees. He could hear Saul screaming as he found another man, and then Berenger found himself confronting a youth. It was Alain of Chartres. The fellow had been in Will's vintaine for the last year, and was determined always to advance himself. Berenger felt the rage building in his breast until it felt as though he must scorch his flesh with the heat of his fury. He flew at the lad, beating at him with his sword in the most unscientific manner, until Alain had his back to a tree and could only duck and block Berenger's blows with terror in his eyes, whimpering as death approached.

With a quick blow from above, then a flick of his wrist and a stab that tore the stitching at his flank, Berenger attacked inside Alain's defence and his sword-point entered Alain's shoulder, cutting through the flesh and gristle of the socket and shearing the bone. The lad gave a high, keening shriek and his sword fell to the ground. Berenger stepped on it, and placed his sword at Alain's throat, ready for the final blow, but then a thought occurred to him, and instead he whacked the solid pommel on the boy's head. The lad's eyes rolled up and he fell on his face into a mass of brambles.

There were brambles everywhere here in the woods. They caught and snagged on Berenger's hosen as he made his way through the undergrowth towards the last men of the ambush. Two were fighting Saul, and Berenger joined the battle, dispatching his foe with three quick slashes; Saul had dropped his sword somewhere, and now he flew in close with his axe, the head flashing in the sunlight. The man he fought had a grin on his face at first, thinking a man with a sword could easily keep an axeman at bay, but gradually it came to him that this axeman was more than competent at parrying and blocking, and all the while Saul was pushing him back, his weapon glittering as it moved faster and faster.

'End it,' Berenger snapped.

Saul said nothing, but the next blow took off the man's hand and wrist, still clutching his sword. The man gaped, clutching at his stump with his good hand, and had time to look at Saul with shock before the axe fell once more and his head rolled in the dirt.

The battle was over.

Berenger stood panting in the sunlight that filtered through the trees. He realised that he had a cut on his left forearm, and another in his left hip, but worse by far was his back, where his efforts had ripped the physician Antoine's careful efforts.

Saul had taken a stab to his back, but it was not deep. He also had a jagged cut over his left ear, but he would survive that, just as he had survived so many other wounds in the past. However, Berenger was concerned when he saw Loys. The bolt had entered below his collarbone. It was a vicious-looking bolt with a heavy head and wooden section. The wood had splintered when it hit Loys, and bits and pieces of wood were all about the main head. It looked much worse than it truly was, however. When Berenger moved it, he soon realised that the head was not barbed, and he could remove it easily while Loys lay at the roadside. Fulk looked at the injury carefully, then walked away. He soon returned with moss with which he packed the wound, while Loys winced and looked away, his face grey with pain.

When he was done, Fulk gave Loys a flask with some drink

in it, which Loys sipped while Fulk went to Alazaïs's body. He grabbed at her skirts and, before Berenger could remonstrate, the Swiss had cut away a long strip. He helped Loys sit up, groaning and muttering about 'Damned Swiss tarse fiddlers', before he wrapped the linen over and about Loy's breast, holding the pad of moss in place.

Berenger left him to his ministrations and went back to Alazaïs's body. She lay on her side, one leg drawn up as though she was sleeping. In her face there was the serenity he had noticed before, a calmness and inner beauty that even death could not efface. It made him feel humble just to see it, as though seeing this woman with all the trials and problems of life shorn away was itself a gift. Only a short distance from her lay her two boys. Their blood had pooled and run together, so that it was now mingled as it congealed.

'I will make him pay for this,' Berenger said. 'I swear to you, Alazaïs, he will pay.'

He rose and walked to the horse lying in the roadway. The rider was still trapped, and Berenger had to strain, sitting on his rump and pushing with his feet, to roll the horse's corpse enough to release the fellow.

'I owe you my life,' he said. It was a foolish comment, perhaps, but with those words he felt the weight of obligation land on his shoulders.

'I wouldn't see an ambush against a traveller,' Denisot said. He had dragged his leg from beneath the horse and now sat massaging it. It was not broken, fortunately, but it would be many weeks before he could walk without a severe limp.

'My name is Berenger Fripper.'

'Denisot, the Bayle of Domps,' Denisot said. He peered at Berenger with careful interest. The man was clearly English, and

Denisot knew that meant he was likely one of the hated murderers who infested this poor land. 'Who were they?' he asked, indicating the bodies in the woods.

'Men who wanted me dead, sent by a traitor,' Berenger said. He rose and walked back to the woods, seeking the youth.

The boy still lay in the brambles, and Berenger tipped a flask of water over his head before Alain stirred, muzzily staring about him, then moaning and whimpering as his ruined shoulder moved.

'You know me, boy,' Berenger said. He squatted on his haunches before the fellow as he tried to sit upright, moaning and weeping at the pain from his shoulder. 'You know I keep my word.'

'Yes.'

'Who am I?'

'The captain, sir.'

'Stop your moaning or I'll put a stop to it forever. Answer me and you may be allowed to live.'

'Yes, sir.'

'Who ordered you to ambush us today?'

'You know who.'

Berenger picked up a stick and prodded it at the boy's shoulder. 'I asked you a question. Be honest and frank and I'll be merciful,' he said as Alain screamed and tried to knock the stick away. His effort pressed the stick's point into his wound and widened the lips of the gash. Alain screamed all the louder.

'Who?'

'Will! It was Will!' Alain sobbed, his left hand at his ruined shoulder. He looked up at Berenger with a gleam of hatred. 'He told us to come out here and kill you all. He said to kill the bitch and her pups first. He said that a whore like that wasn't worth the price of a bolt, but that we should kill her and her pups so you would see you'd lost everything. He said you should feel the pain of loss before you died.'

'You killed her to punish me,' Berenger breathed.

Fulk had joined them and now stood at Berenger's shoulder with Saul. 'That is what I heard Will order,' he agreed. 'Will wanted the men to lie in wait and kill the woman and her children while you looked on, then kill you.'

'Why did you decide to stop them?'

'He ordered me. I was sent with the others to waylay you. I didn't like the idea. What, attack you just because you wanted to leave?'

'I left because I wanted to impose discipline.'

'*Ja.* You are a commander. A commander must always impose discipline. It is a part of your job to enforce it and see that all men obey. I would not argue with your position.'

Saul was eyeing him doubtfully. 'You didn't elect to join us when we left.'

'I saw no need to. It was when I heard that there was to be an attack on you that I decided to leave the company. If the company wants to punish a bad commander, I'm happy with that. But I am Swiss. I believe in holding a court and discussing a man's crimes before all the men, and then punishing him before them.' He shrugged. There was contempt in his voice as he continued. 'To tell a man he is free to go, and then attack him on the road like a common outlaw, that is not the action of an honourable man. I will have nothing to do with a commander who proposes that.'

Berenger was content with his words. 'I am glad you decided to help us. If it weren't for you and that man there, we would be dead now.'

'What will you do now?'

'What can I do? I have no company: none of us do. I have to find a new life.'

Denisot limped to join them. He stood gazing down at the youth. 'Was this one of the ambushers?'

Fulk nodded and kicked the lad. He screamed briefly, clutching at his cods with his left hand, vomiting into the bushes at his side. 'What shall we do with him?'

Berenger pulled out his knife. There was a dull ache behind his eyes and he wanted desperately to have a drink. The shaking in his hand shocked him. It made the blade of his knife move wildly as he stood there. Then he looked about him, feeling lost and empty inside. Bodies lay all over this wood. Up there was the man he had killed first. There was the man he had seen Fulk kill with a slash to the throat. Further on, he saw a splash of red on an oak where the man had lost his hand, and back there, on the road, Alazaïs and her children lay in the dirt. A short gust of wind brought the smell to him, the odour of battle. It tasted of blood and smelled of tin and shit, and the feel of it in his nostrils made Berenger shiver like a horse on a battlefield.

Fulk found their horses farther up the hill. They were clumped together in a huddle as though fearful of their welcome. Two were missing, he reckoned. 'Probably the two who were guarding them took to their heels when they saw how the fight was going,' he said. 'I daresay they've made it all the way back to Uzerche by now.'

This boy wasn't responsible for their deaths, and he could serve a useful purpose still. 'Give him a horse and send him back with a message: "This is what happens when you try to fight real men. I'll return for a reckoning soon." Take that, and take it swiftly. This man here is the bayle of a town near here. If he finds you on the road you will be declared outlaw and beheaded.'

'You'd let him go?' Denisot said with surprise.

'What good will his death serve? At least this way, Will knows that I am alive. It will make him fear my revenge.'

Saul said, 'I'd cut his balls off first.'

'Leave him. He's already useless. He'll never be a fighter again, not with that arm. He'll be lucky if it's not amputated in a week, or it goes septic and kills him. He's nothing.'

'But you'll return to take revenge on Will?' Fulk said.

'In time. Not until I've healed and I know what is happening with the men,' Berenger said. He moved his arm experimentally and winced. His back felt soaked in blood and he knew he must have his wounds seen to again.

They gave a mount to Alain and sent him on his way, but the other horses they decided to take with them to the abbey. They would be able to use them as remounts, or perhaps sell them if they grew desperate.

'I shall go with you,' Fulk said. 'I have no wish to return to Will's company. He would not be grateful for my part today.'

'First, Master Fripper will need to find a physician,' Denisot said. He wanted to see these men taken into Domps and captured, so that they could pay for the death of the girl found by Poton, and for all the other crimes committed by the English, but there was something about them that made him feel unsure. If he had all the men of Domps summoned to arrest them, he suspected that many would die. Better by far to take them somewhere and see them healed and sent on their way.

'I can help you,' he said. With those words he sealed his fate.

Will was furious when Alain returned. The horse-minders were never seen again after the attempted ambush. They had made off when they saw how the battle was developing, terrified of reporting their failure to their new commander, but Alain rode back to Uzerche, lurching in the saddle, and was there before the curfew bell was tolled. He found Will at a bar with two town whores sharing his drinks, one sitting on his lap, a second beside him on the bench. The first had untied his braies and was playing with his tarse, her hand inside his hosen while she kissed him amorously.

'They escaped?' Will repeated, averting his face so her kiss missed his lips and instead smeared down his cheek. She chuckled deep in her throat and moved her hand more energetically.

'The woman and her brats were killed, but someone rode up and warned the captain. He was able to turn the attack to his own advantage,' Alain said nervously, watching the woman. His arm was thrust into a strap of leather while the company's physician, who was a good barber but not so competent with the tools of a healer, hovered nearby, waiting to get the lad to a table and look at his injury. Alain was faintly yellow about the face now, and sweating with the pain of his wound.

'They had surprise, they had accurate weapons: they should have been able to destroy Berenger's little group in one loosing of bolts with or without a man giving them warning!'

'After he warned them of the ambush, Fulk turned against us. He was with them,' the boy said.

'Fulk? That goat-swyving son of a Swiss peasant! I should have realised he'd go and do something like that!' Will stood, the whore falling from his lap to the floor with an indignant squeak. 'You tell me that prickle helped Fripper to escape?'

'Who gives a shit for him?' the whore said, climbing to her feet. 'He's gone, but I'm here.'

'You stupid bitch, do you think he'll just go? We killed the woman he wanted. He may be drink-addled and foolish, but he won't let that stop him. He will see me taking her life as a grave insult. With that to spur him, as well as me taking leadership of the company, he will seek revenge.'

'What can one man do against your army?' the woman on the bench asked. She had her blouse open, and her full breasts were on display. She moved a hand over her nipple in blatant invitation when she saw Will look at her.

'Little enough,' Will said. He wetted his lips as she moved her attention to her other breast.

'He's only one man. You have a hundred at your back. He's nothing.'

'True. Did he say anything else?'

'He told me to hurry. The man who warned him of the ambush, he was there. Fripper said he was a bailiff to a town near here.'

'Did he say where?'

'No. But he said that you should beware. He said, "This is what happens when you try to fight real men. I'll be back for a reckoning soon."'

Will chuckled then. 'I look forward to it!'

CHAPTER FOURTEEN

'We should go to Limoges,' Denisot declared.

'Fuck your mother!' Fulk declared. 'You think we want to put our heads on the block for the headsman's sword? If we go there, we will be killed for sure.'

'Where else can we go? You need a physician,' Denisot said, looking at Loys and Berenger.

'We will not go to Limoges. Is there nowhere else?' Berenger asked.

Eventually, on the recommendation of Denisot, they decided to make their way to the Abbaye de St Jacques. It was a small abbey some fifteen miles east of Limoges, Denisot explained, and from what he had heard, they had an expert infirmarer.

'What will they make of us there?' Saul demanded.

Denisot held out his hands expressively. 'Look at your comrades, my friend. Will they survive if you do not get them to a physician soon? Your younger companion has a hole in his breast that could go foul at any time; your leader has a terrible injury in his flank and back, and you yourself have injuries that should be seen to.'

'There must be other physicians.'

'Not many. The best is a man in Uzerche. You want to return there?'

'He's right,' Berenger said. 'We cannot go back, and we have to travel to Guyenne, in any case. This abbey will not be far from our path. I don't want to go south in case we meet up with some of Will's men.'

Loys gave a low whimper of pain. That settled the matter.

Berenger felt sickly. He was cold even in the sunlight, and his back was appallingly painful. Fulk had a look at it, and said that there was plenty of watery blood and a little weak pus, but nothing to worry about. Still, with the chill in his bones and the shaking, as well as his desperate need for a cup of strong wine, Berenger felt nearer death than life. However, he would not leave Alazaïs and her two boys to the attention of crows and wild dogs. He insisted that they should all be loaded onto the spare horses and taken to the nearest church.

It delayed them, but Denisot brought them to a small church in a village some miles from Chamberet, where the priest was known to him. When they clattered to a halt before his church, the father was working in a small vegetable patch at the side of the cemetery. He straightened and leaned on his spade, watching the men as Denisot called to him and explained what had happened. After a brief discussion the priest agreed to accept the mother and her sons. He was happy to accept Denisot's word as bayle that they were Christian, and Fulk carried the three little bundles into the church with Saul.

'I will look after them,' the priest said.

Berenger looked into his eyes. He felt no gratitude, only a fierce, feverish rage at the world for allowing Will to destroy

Alazaïs. 'Do so! They were dear to me. I will return to see that you have treated them well, and it will go evilly for you if you have abused them!'

The priest stared up at him. 'I will pray for you too.'

Berenger spat at the ground. It was tempting to pull out his dagger and mark the man's face for his effrontery, but before he could match action to thought, Fulk returned and mounted his horse between them.

Suddenly Berenger felt an unaccountable misery. It struck him that he would never see Alazaïs again and it was his own fault. This was not the responsibility of others: this was his, and he must bear it for the rest of his days. She was dead because he had taken his company of men to her town. He had invested Will with rank in the company, and that error of judgement had allowed Will to take over the men. It was his arrogance and attempt to enrich himself that had directly led to Alazaïs's death. He had not molested her, let alone raped her, for there had been something about her that kept him away, a warmth in her soul that looked almost angelic, and which it would have been heresy to harm. It could perhaps have soothed his soul, had he grown to know her better. Only that morning he had seen a different side to her character as she smiled at him in genuine gratitude when he offered her his horse.

And now she was dead, and that smile had died with her.

All because of him.

Saturday 23 July

The two English centaines had stopped for the night, and were draped over the side of a hill like a badly laid table-cloth. Camp fires were already burning and the faces of the vintaine were lit with a healthy golden glow as they waited for their pottage to warm through.

Robin approached with the weight of command lying on him like an ingot of lead.

It was a relief to see that the men looked more comfortable with each other than they had. When they had set off, Clip and Dogbreath looked on him accusingly as though suspecting him of being a spy for Sir John. The two appeared to have formed an unholy alliance: the two experienced members of the vintaine against all others. Robin would have to try to do something to meld them and the other members. He would have considered making them both sergeants under him, each responsible for eight of the men, but that would lead to additional friction, he was sure. Neither man would be ideal. Both were too self-obsessed and keen on their own safety to be reliable commanders of others.

Pierre and Felix, the father and son, didn't look up as he took his seat. Imbert gave him a sidelong glance: he suspected that Robin was the cause of his headache and foiled escape. The father and son seemed to think that they were safe so long as they avoided his gaze. That was fine by Robin. Clip was picking at his teeth with a sharpened stick while eyeing the rest of the vintaine with mixed contempt and disdain.

'All I was saying was,' Dogbreath said, 'if you want to see how to lead men, you only have to look to Sir John.'

'What is this?' Robin asked.

'Imbert was saying he didn't understand why half the men here were fighting for a cause they don't understand,' Dogbreath said. He snorted contemptuously.

Clip sneered and threw his stick away. 'It's not fair on us. The knights get all the rewards, and we just get to slog our way through the mud and get gutted on a field.'

'You haven't yet,' Gilles said, smiling. He looked like a twenty-year-old, always cheerful and happy as though this was just a great adventure he was embarked on. 'You told me you have been fighting for most of your life, and look at you! Not even a scratch.'

'He has scratches, but only where the women fought him off,' Dogbreath muttered.

'Fought me off? They wouldn't want to. Not when they see the size of my oak,' Clip said.

Felix leaned forward and picked up Clip's discarded stick. 'You dropped your oak,' he said mildly. His father guffawed with laughter, soon joined by Gilles and Nick.

'Swyve a goat!' Clip swore, scowling at them all. He turned to Felix. 'You haven't any tarse to speak of. When you've proved yourself in a battle, then you can take the piss. Until then, remember who's the most experienced fighter in this vintaine.'

Gilles chuckled. 'You mean Robin?'

Robin smiled to himself.

Clip shook his head. His voice, usually so whining, took on a self-satisfied tone. 'You think you're so clever, but I warn you, you'll all get killed. The knights won't give a shit for any of you. They'll trample you into the dirt, just like the French did to their men at Crécy. They rode them down and killed them because they couldn't fight our arrow-storm, and when it suits our lot, they'll do the same.'

'You talk nonsense, Clip,' Robin said.

'Oh yeah? How many battles have you fought in, then?'

'I couldn't count.'

'I can, though, and I've been in more than all this lot put together!' Clip sat back, contentedly, snorting his derision.

'I fought at Espagnols-sur-Mer,' Robin said reflectively. 'And I was at the siege of Calais, and I fought in many of the chevauchées in the early years of the war. So I have some experience. More than that, I can use a bow, so I think I am superior to you.'

'You reckon you can beat me in a trial with bows and arrows?' Clip said.

'Any day.'

Imbert eyed him. 'That would be a trial worth watching.'

Robin met his look but before he could comment, Dogbreath nodded his head towards Grandarse. 'What did the man tell the centener?'

They had captured several peasants and merchants in the last few days, but none who had the inbuilt arrogance of the man limping along behind Hawkwood's vintaine. His name, they soon learned, was Thomas de Ladit, but that told none of them much. However, Grandarse had refused to let them hurt him. There was something about his demeanour that spoke of wealth and position, and to Grandarse that meant he could be worth money.

'Nothing. Only that he was travelling to Bordeaux.'

'I think I ought to speak to him,' Dogbreath said.

'He is not to be hurt. Grandarse thinks he could be useful.'

'I wouldn't hurt him. Just let him *think* he could be hurt,' Dogbreath said.

It was at best twenty miles to the abbey, heading both west and north, but that was as the raven flew. In reality the road climbed and turned, taking them over small ridges and hills between the trees, and at each high point Berenger stopped and gazed back the way they had come, fearing to see a cloud of dust that might indicate pursuit. When darkness fell, they encamped in woods near a river and munched on some bread and cold meats before settling for the night. At dawn, they continued west and north.

Denisot watched the men with a feeling of distinct

nervousness. The men were quiet, and for the most part their journey was silent but for the clattering of hoofs on stones, yet Denisot was anxious. These were clearly trained mercenaries, and any Frenchman would be fearful of them. These were the very men who slit the throats of Frenchmen and women, and who threw children onto fires. They had ravaged all the way from Burgundy across the south of France, and up to the north. They were fearful of no man, and many believed that they were the personification of evil, and worshipped the Devil.

Surely it was men such as these who were the murderers of the poor child crucified in the woods? The girl with the wide eyes and supposedly empty brain called 'Alicia' who had been seen in Chamberet. These fellows were capable of any crime. Perhaps they would kill Denisot before they even reached the abbey? But that was not likely. Of them all, only Fulk appeared to be fit and well. The others were all nursing injuries of a greater or lesser form. Besides, while it was plain enough that these men were trained and expert killers, from the result of the little battle he had seen on the road, he did not get the impression that they were indiscriminate. And the anger came from their apparent betrayal by another man, and the murder of the woman and her children. They seemed unlikely murderers and rapists of a little girl.

There was another reason why he felt safer with them. He had saved their lives once already, and they did not know the way to the abbey.

They needed him.

It was late when Abbot Andry was, much to his surprise, called to the gates. The porter was usually more than capable of issuing such support as was necessary when travellers knocked on his doors, and it was with a degree of curiosity that the Abbot left his chamber and crossed the court to the main gates.

'He says he is scared by the sight of them,' the lay-brother sent to fetch him hissed as they went.

'Scared, hmm?' the Abbot repeated. 'And why should that be, eh?'

At three-and-sixty, Abbot Andry had survived the trials of the last decade and more without obvious suffering. He was stooped, it was true, but his eyesight was still clear enough in full daylight, and although he looked thin and ill-fed, that was the result of his habit of eating sparingly. His knees bore the calluses of the religious life, and his joints ached more during Matins through the long winter nights than once they had, but he was hearty enough, which was more than could be said of so many of his friends.

The men at his gate were clearly men of war. There was one fellow at the front who looked like any other, but the others were all clearly soldiers, from the range of weapons they bore to their toughened leather braces and mail.

'God give you peace,' he said. 'You are welcome here, my friends. Can we offer you any – hmm – assistance?'

'If you would allow us inside, my Lord Abbot, we would be grateful for an evening under a roof. My name is Berenger Fripper, and we travel across to our folk in Guyenne, if we can. We are injured. An ambush by felons.'

'You intend to travel without harming any of my compatriots? I wouldn't wish to heal your injuries and make you whole again, if you then wish to go and kill my people,' the Abbot said.

'I swear on the Gospels that we have no intention to do harm to any on our way,' Berenger said. 'There are some who may intend harm to us, but if we fight them it will be more in defence.'

The Abbot studied him for a long moment, considering. He nodded to himself, shot a look towards his porter, and beckoned.

'Give me the key. See, Master Fripper? I trust you to the extent of opening the gate myself, so that if you harm any, you will harm me first, eh? There! It is done. Enter, my sons, and peace be with you while you remain in my protection.'

'I am grateful,' Berenger said. As he reached the Abbot, he bent his knee and kissed the Abbot's ring. 'I have no wish to harm you or any of your folk, I swear.'

Rising again, he grunted with the pain of his back. The Abbot peered closer and saw the stain of blood. 'My friend, you have a grievous injury. What is this?'

'We were waylaid,' Berenger said. 'Like I said, felons assailed us on our way here.'

'Was this an attack in response to your own assault, I wonder, hmm?' the Abbot said. He gazed searchingly at Berenger as though seeking an answer in the lines of his face. 'But it matters not. My abbey is fortunate to have an Infirmarer who is as keen to help the English as he is our own folk. I hope you will find healing here.'

'I am truly grateful,' Berenger said with a careful bow.

'You are unwell, my son,' the Abbot noted. It was hard not to see how the man suffered. He shook like a poplar in a wind, and his face was a yellowish-grey. There was an unwholesome sheen to it, as though he was sweating.

'I feel the pain of my wounds, but I am also very thirsty.'

'I see.' The Abbot turned and began to walk back to his chamber, beckoning the lay-brother. 'You will go to the infirmary and inform Brother Nicholas that he has patients. Tell him to come and fetch them as soon as he may, and then run to the vintner and ask for wine for our guests. Swiftly, now! Run as fast as the wind itself!'

'Abbot, again, I am grateful,' Berenger called. 'God bring you joy and peace.'

The Abbot turned to face him. There was a steely glitter in his eyes. 'I will pray for you all, because that is my duty, but I will take no pleasure in it. I would have all of you healthy and well again, hmm, but only so that you are soon well enough to continue on your way. I know what sort of men you are. Do you think your kind bring joy? No, you may keep your gratitude and your money. I would have neither. My fear is that you will bring harm to our community here.'

'If harm follows us, it was not brought by us,' Berenger said. He swallowed and tottered until Denisot went to his side and held his arm. 'We have been attacked and those with us were slain. A woman and her sons. All killed for no reason.'

'No reason? Perhaps they were killed in order to make a point, a point only you could understand. In any case, it is not my concern. We will do all we can to help cure you and to make your recovery as swift as we know how.'

There was a tiny crackle. Robin heard it, but didn't move. He remained rolled up in his blanket as though asleep, but his ears were suddenly attuned. It was the sort of quiet noise made by a man trying to move with extreme caution so as not to be heard. It was the sound of an assassin.

He had expected this. Ever since that first night, when he had heard Imbert rise and try to make his way off, he had known that Imbert would come for him. It was plain enough in Imbert's face whenever the man looked at him. He had been ready and waiting for the last few days, but the fact was that even a man fearful of attack must sleep. Robin had been on edge, prepared, sleeping only fitfully, every night since he had hit Imbert, but now exhaustion had caught up with him. There was no reserve on which he could call.

There was an instant's panic, but he knew that it was already too late to protect himself. In that fleeting moment he reviewed rolling away, somehow pulling his knife from its sheath, grabbing a rock, a tree-limb, anything, to defend himself. But all the while his brain was telling him that he couldn't move in time. He had time to open an eye, to turn his head, but his arms and legs were sluggish from sleep, and the chance of escape was remote.

'Do it, you prick!' he muttered, levering himself up on hands and knees, and then he heard the thud and he was slammed against the ground with a vast weight on his back.

'You all right?' he heard Dogbreath say.

With some effort, Robin fought his way from beneath the comatose figure. It was Imbert, who lay with his mouth slackly open. For the second time in a few weeks he had been knocked cold.

'I saw you the other night,' Clip said. He was standing at Dogbreath's side.

'God preserve you, Clip,' Robin managed. He eased himself upward. As he glanced about him, he saw that Pierre and Felix were both awake. He wondered if they would have tried to help him. Nick, beside them, looked more than half-asleep still.

'Couldn't see the new vintener murdered, could we?' Clip said with that horrible smile of his that was so like a leer. 'Can you imagine what Grandarse'd do if that happened? He might make *me* vintener. I don't want that.' He cast a glance at Imbert, who was stirring, and gave him a vicious kick in the stomach. 'He'd have had us all digging the shit out of the latrines just so he could order us to fill them in again, too. I don't like digging the shit out. I've done that before when he was pissed with me.'

'Tie him up,' Robin said. 'He'll be flogged in the morning.'

'Flogged? It's not enough,' Dogbreath said. 'If I see him try something like that again, I'll skin the fucker myself and nail his hide to a church door.' He kicked Imbert again. 'Clip and me'll keep an eye on him for you, Vintener. He won't try it again, 'less he wants to learn what real pain is.'

Sunday 24 July

Dogbreath woke before the dawn. He had always woken early, and today was just another day, so far as he was concerned.

He was glad that he'd seen Imbert and saved Robin from injury. In Dogbreath's experience, when a vintener or sergeant was killed in his sleep, other men in the vintaine were likely to be punished, whether or not they had anything to do with the attack. Besides, he was growing to like Robin. The man had a quiet confidence about him that inspired trust, and there were not that many people whom Dogbreath had met who had similarly made him feel a kind of loyalty to them. Mostly he found that he was treated with contempt bordering on loathing, and he reciprocated. It was rare for him to feel anything other than hatred, but Robin made him feel wanted, and he wanted to reciprocate.

When he had been younger, his parents owned and ran an alehouse near Chepe Street in London, but when some drinkers became rowdy one night, his father was killed in the ensuing brawl. Dogbreath and his mother kept the place going, but as money grew tighter and tighter, gradually the customers came to see his mother as an additional resource. At last, when Dogbreath was fourteen, he was taunted by children in the street calling out that his mother was a whore and he was a bastard. When he returned, angry and bitter, he found his mother drunk in the main chamber, while two men watched a companion serving her. It was enough. He took up his pack with his spare shirt, a bowl and a spoon, and left the alehouse. His mother didn't even notice as he walked from the door.

He had never returned. Instead, he had gone to the port where he found a ship willing to take him on as a cabin boy. That had been a hard upbringing, and he had learned to loathe sailors and the sea before long, but it had given him a core of determination and self-confidence the first time he drew his knife on another man and forced him away. Few had tried to molest him at night after they saw the old sailor's injury. Dogbreath had nearly taken his eye that night. It was the first time he had lost his temper, and the power and energy it gave him had excited and terrified him in equal measure. Not now, though. Now he relished the loss of all control as he threw himself into battle. Without that release, he sometimes thought he must explode, like one of Archibald's gonnes when the spark caught the vent.

What he would do were there no more battles to fight, he did not know. He walked to fetch water, and on his way back from the stream, he caught sight of Thomas de Ladit, who sat huddled at a tree's base, bound hand and foot.

The prisoner had been interrogated when they caught him, but he had refused to answer many of their questions. He was clearly nervous, but he appeared keen to be taken to their captain. All the men knew that rich men were anxious to be caught and keen to be taken to a commander who could accept a ransom and protect their hostage. This fellow looked like a man of that kind, and more than one of the men was growing restless. After all, although Hawkwood had claimed the right to hold Thomas under his protection, and said he wanted the man undamaged when they returned to the main column, many of the men would be happy to tickle him up a bit if they could win even a small ransom. They weren't here to enjoy the views; most wanted money.

Dogbreath himself felt sure that Thomas had money or

information that could be useful. He squatted in front of Thomas and nudged his foot with his dagger's blade. 'Wake!'

Thomas came to blearily. He had walked far yesterday before these murderous club-men caught him, and afterwards they had made him continue with them, no matter how much he complained about his poor feet. He fell once. Afterwards he was warned in no uncertain terms that if he were to fall again, they would not stop, but would drag him on with them. He had kept on his feet. Waking was no pleasure.

'What?' he said as he recognised one of his persecutors from the day before. His eyes moved to the dagger held negligently in Dogbreath's hand. 'What will you do with me?'

'I don't want to do anything to you,' Dogbreath smiled. He balanced his weapon in his hand. 'I do want to hear all you can tell me about the places you've come from, the money you've seen, the money buried for safety . . .'

'I can't tell you anything!'

'What of your own money?'

'I have nothing. My master is arrested,' Thomas said without thinking.

'So you have no value to us.' Dogbreath shook his head in mock sadness, and then flicked his blade up. It span and he caught it by the tip as though about to hurl it at Thomas, who cringed at the sight.

'Don't!'

'What can you tell me? Do you have money? Did you see any on your travels?'

'No, they took it all. The soldiers.'

Dogbreath shrugged. 'Did you meet with many soldiers? There were no French soldiers on the roads or in the towns as you passed?'

'Only a few, and only in the towns,' Thomas said. He was

desperate to show himself keen to help now, his eyes fixed fearfully on the knife. 'They were trying to reinforce the walls at Périgueux, and at Thiviers they were training the apprentices and peasants in how to fight. But there were no soldiers in the countryside. I saw no sign of an army or of any muster.'

Dogbreath nodded. 'They have heard of our approach, then?'

Thomas allowed a little asperity to enter his voice. 'Yes, since your army is already so close.'

'We're still many miles from the towns.'

'Yes, but the men who took Uzerche have already terrorised the countryside. I left because I am not French. I am servant to the King of Navarre, as I said yesterday, and your ally, so . . .'

'You say that the English are near? Where? Is it very close? I hadn't heard that other men were sent to scout.'

'Scout? No, they took the town four weeks ago.'

Dogbreath's face took on a terrifying aspect. He hated to think men could make fun of him. 'You're pulling my tarse, you fucking goat-fiddler! You're telling me that there was a town captured a month ago? Our army was still in Bordeaux then. You're lying to me and . . .'

'No, no! I swear it! I'm an ally of the English. You have to take me to your commander, and let me explain. I keep *telling* you: I'm a friend! The men climbed over the walls at night, and by daybreak they had the whole place. It was taken almost without an injury. And their leader, he said that he was there to protect us all. Not that the townsfolk believed him. The priest, my friend, was beaten almost to death,' he saw no reason not to embellish a little, 'and I only escaped by the grace of God. Their leader was a terrible, fierce man.'

'What did they call themselves, this gang?'

'It was a company of men. More than a hundred, although

not so many as two hundred. Their leader was a man called Berenger Fripper, but . . .'

'*What?* Say that name again!'

In Uzerche, many of the mercenaries were growing bored with such diversions as were available. While the town itself had a good store of wine and beer, and provisions of all kinds sufficient to keep the men fed for some weeks, Will knew that their attractions would soon pall. There were women, but these were themselves a problem.

Some of the younger members of the company had early on formed friendships with the girls about the town, but others took their women without wooing. It was starting to lead to more and more fractious relations. The townsmen were determined to protect the honour of their wives, sisters and daughters, and more and more often men from the company were coming to blows with them. One member of the company had been found stabbed and beaten to death in a gutter, and Will had the men from the nearest house dragged into the street. Two were clubbed to a bloody mess in front of their women and the rest of the home-owners, the sound of thudding clubs dulled by the screams and wails of the wives and daughters watching. Both took a long time to die.

To try to maintain the peace, in recent days Will had sent all the vinteners out with their men. He recalled Berenger saying that a good commander would always keep his men busy, and the best activity for a fighter was to learn all he could about the territory on which he may have to fight. Besides, Will wanted them to scout for potential plunder. Merchants and others must want to use the bridge, and they would be called upon to pay for the privilege, but in the meantime it would be good to increase the mercenaries' purses by finding travellers and charging 'tolls' for the use of the roads.

'Simon, take your men south and then sweep around to the west,' he said. He still had Simon and Peter as commanders of vintaines, but he had yet to replace Berenger. Several of his men had been slaughtered during the failed attempts to kill Berenger. It would take Will some time to find more men who were capable of fighting efficiently, but he would. For now, Simon and Peter would have to take on the duties of command. 'If you find a large body against you, don't offer a battle, but come back here.'

'Why, don't you think we could kill any French cockroaches who try to deny us our road?' Simon said. He was a sandy-haired man of eight-and-twenty, who had already been a warrior for fourteen years. He stood an inch shorter than Will, but his shoulders were almost as broad as his height. He had a strongly muscled left arm, but two fingers on his right were gone: cut off in a battle.

'I have every faith in you,' Will said. 'But if you don't come and warn us of a large force gathering, I'll personally cut your ballocks off. Take what you can that's easy, but if there's a risk to the town, come here and help us defend it.'

Simon sneered, but finally agreed and left to give his men their orders.

'What of me?' Peter asked.

'Take your fellows up to the north. There's a town up there called Chamberet. See whether there's anything worth taking. If you have any trouble, burn the place.'

There was no fanfare. That sort of pretentiousness was not the Prince's way. He was happy with the regalia of his rank, but he didn't flaunt it unnecessarily. Just now he wore a suit of armour that gleamed in the sunlight, but he was bareheaded. With him were the commanders of his army: Oxford, Warwick, Suffolk, all of them veterans of the Scottish wars as well as numerous chevauchées in France both here to the south and along the north. With them were the centeners, and one or two of the senior vinteners who had ambled over to listen.

Sir John stood and watched the Prince and his entourage march forward to the middle of the square. All the commanders of the army were gathered there, and their cheers rose as their commander took his place in the centre. He lifted his hands, grinning, palms out in a gesture of silence, and waited until the noise died down.

'Captains, I thank you for attending to me. Can you all hear me? My Lords, knights, men-at-arms, we have been wasting away here for too long, I fear. Here at Bergerac we have been kept comfortably, but I think that now we are come into August it is perhaps time to make a move. Do you agree?'

There was a low growl of assent from the men listening, and the Prince bared his teeth. He was a good-looking man, Edward of Woodstock. Tall, fair-haired, with a moustache and beard neatly trimmed in preparation for the campaign, he looked every part the young warlord preparing for action.

'My friends, for we are all friends here, I do not march into France from any desire to harm people, but purely to bring order into the world. If a tyrant can steal a throne that is not rightfully his, which kingdom will be safe? It is not to be borne that a man can steal a kingdom. I will not permit it. I will lead you into France, where we shall, with God's good grace, meet with this John who calls himself King, and there we shall beat him so thoroughly that he will be forced to surrender his crown to us. God will smile upon our deeds, for God knows that the crown is rightfully mine in line from my father. It was his mother who was sister to the French King, and were she not most cruelly robbed of her inheritance by the Valois and his kin, she would have seen the crown passed to her son, my father by right of descent. But no! This false John sought to enrich himself, as did his predecessor. Now he must be shaking in his cordovan leather boots! No matter how expensive and well made his boots, they will not serve to help him! Unless he wishes to turn and flee in them!'

Prince Edward stopped and peered at the men about him as a ripple of laughter ran around them.

'I see bold Englishmen here surrounding me. I see courageous knights and squires who have fought and struggled with me over many years. We are grown in power and might since my first battles here. Now we make up the strongest army in Christendom, because we fight with God on our side, and against Him, none may succeed.

'We came here to Bergerac because I wanted to leave my options open to the last. From here we could advance in any direction. However, there is only one direction that makes sense. That is in the direction where the false French King lies quaking at our advance. My friends, we shall attack to the north.'

There was a roar then, of men bellowing their approval and excitement. Steel gauntlets clattered against steel breastplates, sword and dagger pommels hammered on shields, and from hundreds of throats there were cheers.

The Prince held up his hand for silence. 'Friends, I fear that there are concerns that the Duke of Armagnac might take it into his head to enter our lands and attack Bordeaux. We cannot afford to risk that. So I will send back three thousand men. It is a hard decision, but we shall have enough men to ensure our victory even with fewer than ten thousand. Unless the French can field thirty thousand against us, I fear the battles will all be a little too easy for us to win!'

There was a louder cheer then. He continued, 'This is the best way to end the wars. We have been fighting for many years already. Now, we may bring it to an end at last. My father has tried to bring about the key battle with the French army for some twenty years already. Now we have a possibility of success. Not only do we savage the peasants in a war of *dampnum*, bringing the taste of horror and defeat to the people of the lands so that all may see that their King cannot succeed even to protect the most lowly in his realm, we also ride through some of the French King's most valuable lands. With our ride, we shall destroy the lands on which he depends for his taxes. Without his taxes, he must suffer.'

Again he paused and eyed his audience. Then a grin broke over his face. It was the sheer joy of the pirate. 'And that of which we shall deprive him, we may take home. If you have a wife, a sweetheart, or even a mother – not you, Jed, I know you could not have one!' he said, pointing to a young squire to the right, who instantly coloured with embarrassment. 'Any person you love and whom you would have love you, for them you will bring the wealth of this land. We will visit Limoges, Châteauroux, Bourges, and on up to Chârtres, all of them vastly wealthy towns, and we shall take them all and despoil them of their wealth. Any abbots, any merchants, any knights or noblemen whom we can capture, we shall hold to ransom, as is the custom, and you will all benefit! There is no reason why we should not make money from their errors, after all!'

A loud cry of delight greeted this announcement, and he gave that piratical grin once more. He took a moment to glance at the men at his side, and then gazed about his commanders once more. Sir John felt sure that he had been about to say something else, and had decided that this was not the time. It made him wonder what the Prince could have been considering.

'So, my friends, now is the time to prepare. We have need of all equipment to be ready for our departure in two days. I want the wagons loaded and prepared, carts filled, arrow sheaves loaded and ready for immediate use. Check the bow staves, check the strings, you who are responsible for the archers. Gynours, make sure your gonnes are loaded carefully against any sudden downpours. Ensure that the powder is secured against the damp. And above all, ensure that your men are ready. We march in two days!'

CHAPTER FIFTEEN

Sir John de Sully left the Prince and men-at-arms cheering in the square with a thrilling in his veins that he recognised so well. It would not be long before he was fighting again. He had a sudden vision of flames and blood, steel and flesh, and he stopped in the road.

'Sir John?' Richard Bakere said solicitously. His squire had been with him for more years than he could remember. Once he had offered to knight Richard, but his squire refused the suggestion. He was content to serve.

'I'm well enough,' Sir John said.

'You look as though you are in pain.'

'No. It's just a twinge in my hand,' Sir John lied. He saw Richard nod. After all, his master was in his middle seventies. He was entitled to some infirmities.

'May I fetch you a cloak or something?'

'I'm not unwell. I just get these pains sometimes,' Sir John said. The sharp pain from a tendon stretched too far was the least of his grievances.

They continued on their way, stepping about the piles of manure and broken trash that lay in the streets until they were back at Sir John's rented home. There they found two men waiting.

'Grandarse? What is it?' Sir John said.

'We've just returned, Sir John. We captured a fellow named Thomas de Ladit. He was keen to talk. He said he was in Uzerche, a town north of here, and it was taken by a company of mercenaries. Their leader, he said, was a man called Berenger Fripper.'

'You are sure of this?' Sir John said.

Grandarse elbowed Dogbreath, who sullenly nodded. 'That's what he said. Said Fripper was at this town. Didn't sound like Fripper, though. Threatening the people and all.'

'What do you think, Grandarse?'

The centener glanced at Dogbreath. 'I don't think another man would take Frip's name. This must be him. But not only him: he has a company with him.'

'We have need of more men,' Sir John said. 'Go to Uzerche and see if you can find Fripper.'

'There is more, Sir John. This prisoner, he claims he is Chancellor to the King of Navarre.'

'What is he doing here, then?'

Grandarse pulled a face. 'I think you need to talk to him about that.'

'Very well, I shall. But for now, bring me Fripper, Grandarse. You'll need to take at least forty men, but be quick and return soon. We will march before the end of the week.'

Monday 25 July

'I need to get up,' Berenger declared on the third day.

'That's good, my friend. If you need to be up and out and

about, you carry on. It'll save me a lot of work, if you go out into the world first.'

'I will be well enough to travel?'

'No. You will be dead in a week. So travel far and fast. Let some other poor physician take over your ravaged, wretched body, so that I may sleep for a week and make sure that the abbey doesn't suffer the expense of any more herbs and medicaments.'

'I feel greatly improved.'

'You are.'

Nicholas, the Brother Infirmarer, was a man of about thirty years with a long, dark-complexioned face and laughing eyes. He stood half a head shorter than Berenger, but gave the impression of great strength. At his waist was a rosary, and Berenger caught sight of a golden crucifix, but then he concentrated on the man's face as Nicholas continued, 'But if you leave this chamber and go gallivanting about the country, you will soon be dead. Your wound is not dangerous yet. It is not festering. Given time, it will heal. However, if you insist on leaving the safety of the abbey, I will wager a fair sum that you will pass through dangerous lands. Places where miasma lurks. Perhaps a swamp with malaria. Your wounds will become befouled, septic, and you will die. On the other hand, there is also the other possibility, which is that local people who have heard of you will come here to kill you out of hand. So, you can take your pick, I suppose.'

'You know how to make a man feel comforted.'

'Yes, well, that is a skill I have developed,' the Infirmarer said. He probed, making Berenger hiss.

'If you want to kill me, stab me, damn your soul! There's no need for this slow, damned torture!'

'Ah, so the English soldiers are not fearless and incapable of feeling pain,' the monk said mildly, frowning as he pulled at

159

another loose flap of skin, sealing the injury. 'The rumours are false, clearly. You are not a race of superior men.'

'We have courage and determination enough,' Berenger said. He winced at a fresh prod.

'Keep still. I may be a mere mediocre medical man, but I like to have compliant patients when I sew them up. A man with all your injuries should appreciate a physician's skills. You have made use of them often enough.'

'Did you learn your bedside manner here, or did some demon teach you?' Berenger growled.

'It was naturally a demon. Where else would a man like me learn such skills?'

Tuesday 2 August

It was already eleven days since Denisot should have returned. In all that time there was nothing to say what had happened to him. He had left her and ridden off, and Gaillarde had waited, expecting daily some hint of news, but nothing came.

For the first week her rage knew no bounds. There was a strumpet in the tavern who had caught his eye. Who could say but that he had not run away with a whore? She had teased him and wriggled her backside at him. He was foolish enough, and so driven by his lusts that a wench with a large bust could tempt him all too easily.

What they would live on, she had no idea, she thought as she shouted at Suzette for her slowness. The foolish chit was growing pale and restless while Denisot was away. Perhaps she was pining for him? Gaillarde had always suspected that the two were enjoying each other's bodies whenever she wasn't looking. It was the way of men like him.

He should be back by now.

There was a deepening fury in her. It was building with every passing day, until today it suddenly dissipated while she was in the market. She came across three men talking about an attack down south of Chamberet. A party had been ambushed, and bodies were discovered by the roadside. News had been slow to arrive, because there were constant rumours of English fighters riding about the area, but a pair of enterprising sergeants had ridden along the road towards Domps, and there they found a dead horse and a number of dead men. They brought the saddle and bridle back with them, and Gaillarde stared at them with a face made wooden with shock. She could hear a loud whistling in her ears, and she had to shake her head, trying to make sense of the man's words.

'Denisot is fine. He cannot be hurt,' she said several times. 'That sounds like his horse, and I know that saddle and bridle. I helped him buy them. But he cannot be injured.'

Their faces were grim and sympathetic, but she ignored them. She was as sure as she could be that her husband was unhurt. He may be imperfect, and he might have been responsible for the deaths of their children, but he was surely not dead.

No. He could not be dead. She walked home with a curious, light feeling in her legs and body, and the whistling sound would not leave her. He was alive. Of course he was alive. And when he came back eventually, she would make him regret ever thinking of staying away so long.

And then, as she closed the door behind her at her home, she suddenly realised she had left all her purchases at the market, and burst into sobs that tore at her soul.

Berenger learned to be quiet in his reflections in the presence of the amiable and loquacious brother. The Abbot himself, Berenger soon realised, was sure to hear anything that he discussed with the Infirmarer.

Not that there was much to hear, he thought. The men all came to see him during the day, but he sent them away when their eyes showed their concern. He wanted no sympathy or meaningless words. His back was afire, and he wanted them to leave him.

Now Denisot visited to see how he progressed, his face grave but not twisted with compassion. It gave Berenger a feeling of satisfaction to see one man at least who didn't shower him with platitudes.

'I'm well enough. There is nothing wrong with me just now that a good pint of red wine wouldn't improve.'

'The Infirmarer has left orders that you are not to be given strong drink. He said that it might inflame your passions and lead to arguments and violence that may break the mending flesh of your flank and back.'

'Oh, did he?' Berenger said, but just now the pain in his back was such that he could do no more than move a little before the stiffness and pain forced him to stop and let the breath hiss between his teeth. 'That mendacious, unctuous . . .'

'Talking about me again, my friend?' the Infirmarer called. He was tending to another injured patient, a boy who had fallen into a mill and crushed his arm. It had been set as best the Infirmarer could manage, but the fellow would never hold a bow or a sword, he said. It would be withered forever.

'Master Fripper, I have to leave,' Denisot said.

'We need you to help us. I thought you would remain with us on the way to the coast.'

'As to that, just keep travelling west, and then south. But I have a wife who will wonder what has happened to me. One or two days away was to be expected,' he lied, 'but to be away for this long will leave her sorely concerned. I must get back.'

'Very well. If you must,' Berenger said. He gritted his teeth. The desire for a jug of strong wine was almost overwhelming. He had a cold sweat at his brow, and he felt as though insects were crawling under his skin. 'You have my gratitude, in any case. You have saved my life, and I do not forget a debt.'

'It was nothing. You owe me nothing. I am glad to have helped you, that is all.'

'Well, if there is ever anything you need, find me. I will help as I may.'

Denisot chewed at his lip. 'There is one thing. When I met you on the road, I was seeking information about a murder. A girl was killed. Only a youngster, perhaps ten or eleven years old, with fair hair, curly, worn quite long. She may have been named Alicia.'

Berenger considered. 'She wore no coif?'

'Perhaps. She had been raped when I found her, and dragged for miles from the look of her wounds. Did you see anything of a girl like her?'

'Not that I recall.'

'She was left dead. They crucified her and lifted her into a tree, whoever killed her. Was that something that your company might do?'

'I will not lie: some of the men could have done that. I did not. When I had to kill a man, it was with a knife or sword. If it was a military punishment, I would allow a flogging or a hanging, but I've never seen an Englishman kill a man by crucifixion, let alone a child. If I found a man who raped children and tortured them by those means, I would see to it that he did not last in my army.'

Denisot frowned. 'This man who tried to kill you. Would he be capable of that kind of brutality?'

'There is little I would not think him capable of,' Berenger said heavily.

Denisot nodded. He eyed Berenger seriously. He would be glad to be away from these mercenaries, but he could understand how men might become loyal to this vintener. 'Farewell, Master Fripper. Travel carefully.'

'Aye, well, Godspeed, my friend.' Berenger stared after him when Denisot walked from the room. He would miss the Frenchman with the serious eyes.

Thursday 4 August

Although he had expected a painful reaction when he returned from his wanderings with the mercenaries, even Denisot was surprised by the depth of Gaillarde's rage after his two day journey home.

'You didn't even think about me, did you?' she screamed.

He ducked as a pot narrowly missed his head and smashed in a cloud of red dust against the wall. 'Woman! Gaillarde, what are you doing?'

'You promised me one day, that you'd be back that same night. One night I could bear, but you were away for almost two weeks! How does that make a woman feel, do you think? Was there no messenger you could send? Did you not think or care what I might be thinking, stuck here in this vile pit? You have no feeling for me at all. You are an uncaring man! You only ever think about your job and your—'

'*Woman*—'

'What, does the word scare you? Your *whores*! There, I've said it! You've been away with them for the last week, and now you deign to return to me and your home, now you're weary and full of the pox or some other disease from the bitches you've covered!'

'I've not been with any women!'

But his protestations were pointless, as he knew they would be. He tried to explain about the attack on Berenger and the others, but she paid him no heed, just went on screeching at him. There was no talking to her when she was in this kind of mood, which was why it was ever more tempting to go away on business and leave her, each time for longer and longer. The return was always more painful than the last, but at least he had some freedom and peace of mind while he was away.

He walked from the house and out to the roadway, so he didn't see her face crumple and hear her passionate weeping.

At the end of his street was the little wine shop run by Pathau, the man from Limoges who had turned up one year with a cask of wine and gradually made himself indispensable to the people of Domps. As Denisot took his seat on a stool in the sun, Pathau appeared with a cup and jug of wine, a large man with an enormous paunch and florid features hidden behind a bushy, gingerish, grizzled beard. He had a ragged cloth tucked into a cord bound about his waist to serve as a cleaning cloth, apron and face cloth. He threw a glance towards Denisot's house before pouring. 'She's not happy, then.'

'Gaillarde grows concerned when I go away,' Denisot explained. He nodded to the wife of the smith, who stalked along in a hurry as always. She would be in a hurry on the day she died, he thought.

'So I heard,' Pathau said.

'She is lonely.'

'Yes. I heard her. I think everyone this side of Chamberet heard her.'

'Really?'

'If you are going to try to have a discussion with her in that mood,' Pathau began, but then set himself to sucking at his teeth. It was not his place to advise a man on how to control his wife.

'I am sorry. She just flies into a passion sometimes.'

'She must be told to keep the peace,' Pathau said. It was the duty of all to see that the people in the village didn't break the King's Peace.

Denisot nodded. 'What would you do?'

Pathau drew down the edges of his mouth into a characteristic grimace as he shrugged. 'Me? I'd take her outside, tie her to a tree and whip her until she agreed to see reason. You can't let a woman take control of everything.'

Denisot made no comment. Pathau was besotted with his wife and would not raise his voice to her, let alone a whip. Denisot was not so fortunate. He had been happily married with his wife for the first years, until the plague struck. After that, all marital harmony was destroyed. He was too fond of her still – or his memory of how she had once been – to inflict that kind of punishment on her. However, if he was not careful, others in the village might decide to take charge.

He didn't hear the feet pattering up the street until the urchin was standing panting before him.

'What?' he snapped.

'Bayle Denisot, please! You must come!'

He rolled his eyes heavenwards. 'What is it now?'

'Murder, Bayle! There's been a murder!'

Back in the house, Gaillarde spat, 'Get out!' to Suzette before rushing upstairs to her bedchamber, where she flung herself onto the bed and sobbed as though her heart would burst.

He was uncaring! A thoughtless, feckless man with the brains of a flea! He didn't care about her at all. She had been so upset for the last days, thinking him dead, and now he suddenly returns with a casual comment about helping some injured men, and not a thought for what she must have been thinking!

She hated him. She loathed the ground he walked on. He was dim, a cods-for-brains lummox with the attention of a sparrow when it came to her feelings. She detested him.

It would be so much easier if she didn't care.

The child's body was not a pair of miles from the village, the poor, frail little body half concealed in the trees to the east of the road to Chamberet. This was not the same as the murder of the first, though. Alicia had been dragged some distance before she was tied and nailed to her plank of wood. This child had not been dragged anywhere, but from the blood at her thighs, she had suffered the same indignities of rape before death.

'Someone nailed her to that board and lifted her into the trees,' said Gobert Piquier.

Gobert was a barrel-chested farmer of two-and-forty with a square face and the clearest blue eyes Denisot had ever seen. It was his son who had summoned Denisot from the tavern, and who now stood sawing at the rope that held the small body aloft with a knife that was in sore need of sharpening, while his father clutched the small figure in his arms. Denisot was touched to see that the old farmer had tears running down his cheeks. At last the final cord gave way and Gobert took her full weight. 'Poor little thing.'

'How long has she been up here?' Denisot wondered to himself.

'I was here two days ago, and she wasn't here then,' Gobert said with certainty. 'She has not decayed much. With the warm weather, I would have expected her to have rotted more than this if she had been here more than three days.'

'Yes. That is reasonable. When you were last here, did you see anyone about?'

'No. But I wasn't looking. There were men up here, though, I

167

remember. Some English devils, I think. They rode through from the Chamberet road.'

'When?'

'Yesterday they passed my house. I don't think they saw me.'

'Are there any reports of them killing others like this?'

'Not that I've heard.'

Denisot considered. Perhaps they had passed through. He had heard that such men would often ride out with scouting parties, and return later to despoil those places that looked most likely to hold a large amount of booty. He left the body and began to cast about.

There had been rain the day before yesterday. A party of riders might have left traces of their passage in the drying mud.

He did not have to look far.

A matter of only twenty yards from the roadside he found a place where the vegetation had been trampled into the mire by a number of horses, and then he found a little area where the grasses were flat. It was only six feet by five at the widest. Someone could have lain here. Denisot closed his eyes. He could easily imagine a man tempting a maid to join him here on a blanket, but a child? It made him feel sick to think that a man could catch a girl and rape her, but he knew such horrors, and worse, were a commonplace where mercenaries took hold of the land.

Denisot crouched and stared at the ground, as though it could tell him of the horror of that child's last moments. The terror of being captured and brought here, to be held down and entered by all the men of the party, raped multiple times, and then not even given the dignity of being left alone to huddle and try to find some comfort, but to be nailed to a cross-bar and then hauled up into the trees to die slowly, dangling. Perhaps she was already dead. He hoped so, he prayed so, but Denisot doubted it. Such men did not care for their victims. They enjoyed watching their suffering, like men who enjoyed the bear baiting or who went to watch dogs fighting. This was another form of amusement. The men who did this to her would have enjoyed watching as her last moments passed by.

The men who did this deserved to die in a similar manner.

Thomas de Ladit was content at last. His feet were healing with the new boots that Sir John had provided, and the thicker cloak and new tunic were much to his liking. It was more in keeping with his importance in Navarre, he felt.

There was much that he had been forced to explain when Sir John interrogated him. Why he was here, why he had left Uzerche, what had happened in Normandy when the French King broke into his own son's hall and arrested all the men there.

'What was the atmosphere between the King and the Dauphin when King John took Navarre and executed the others?' Sir John asked.

'It was not good.'

'And yet the Dauphin is said to be marching against us with his father?'

'Of course he is! He is the heir to the throne of France! He would hardly leave the kingdom in peril because of a quarrel with his father. I think your sovereigns have had arguments with their children over the years! Even in Navarre we heard tales of your King's father, Edward II and his bitter disputes with his own father. Yet both would don armour to protect their lands.'

'That is true,' Sir John said. 'Then the rift between the two is healed?'

'I think not. But they will seek to preserve the throne no matter what their personal feelings.'

'And your master?'

'He is held imprisoned unjustly,' Thomas said stoutly.

'You think he was innocent of all the offences laid at his door? He attempted to ally himself with us to bring about the end of the reign of King John,' Sir John observed.

'He never meant to.'

'What does that mean?'

Thomas was flustered. He had not intended to let slip the fact that Navarre had deviously used the English as bargaining chips in his negotiations with the French. 'I . . . I mean he was forced into seeking an accommodation with your King because he could see no future with the King of France. King John is always too indecisive, and when he does make a decision it is invariably ill-considered and foolish.'

'I see,' Sir John said, but there was a steely glint in his eye as he absorbed this.

Thomas was unpleasantly sure that he had not pulled the wool over the knight's eyes. He only hoped that he would not be witness to this knight meeting his master any time soon.

CHAPTER SIXTEEN

There was an all-pervading stench of burned wood and thatch as Grandarse rode into the hamlet that afternoon.

He did not need to give orders. Clip and Dogbreath were already scurrying on foot towards the main door of the wreckage. Once this would have been an important property, with many buildings. Now it was a devastated mess, with half-butchered cattle lying rotting on the ground.

'Anything you can find,' Grandarse bellowed as his men scattered in among the barns and sheds.

It was a shame to see a place so devastated. Once this would have been a thriving little hamlet with enough space for three or four families. Since the plague had arrived many similar farms had been left abandoned to rot as survivors of the pestilence fled, but this place had been burned and sacked by men who delighted in horror.

'How many?' he asked as Clip came back.

'Ach, seven all told, men and lads.'

'Women?'

'One old crone, but no others.'

'All taken, then?'

'Or escaped. But if they escaped, why were the menfolk all slaughtered?' Clip said. He shook his head. 'It's not the way Frip used to behave.'

'He didn't join in with the sack of towns in those days,' Grandarse agreed, 'but a man changes in ten years. Besides, this could have been another group. There's nothing to say that it was Frip who commanded this.'

'No.'

Grandarse and the men had already covered fifteen miles that morning. He had them dismount and feed and water their horses, sending Clip and Dogbreath to scout about the place while the others had some bread and meats.

'Why us?' Clip whined.

'Because you're the least valuable,' Hawkwood called from his vintaine.

'You think that's funny?' Clip scowled.

'Yes!' Hawkwood said, while the men around him laughed.

'You wouldn't cope without me and him,' Clip sneered.

'How could we?' Hawkwood said. 'We shall just have to muddle on through, if you are killed.'

'Us? We won't be alone.' Clip shook his head as he returned to his accustomed prediction. 'We'll all be killed, you wait and see. You can chuckle now, but soon you'll be begging for your mothers to come and save you. We'll all die on this campaign. What, with the whole might of the French army here to avenge what we did to them at Crécy and Calais? They'll trample us into the mud, Vintener, you mark my words. Into the mud.'

Grandarse grunted, hoicked his belt up and spat accurately into the fire. 'But not before you've gone and found 'em, eh? Go on, bugger off, Clip, you lazy git.'

'Just make sure that there's some food kept by for them as do all the work,' Clip said.

'Work?' Hawkwood said with apparent surprise.

'Aye, well, you wouldn't recognise it if it bit your arse,' Clip said, leading his pony away. 'It's just lucky some are more dedicated than you.'

Denisot was back in the village late in the afternoon. He went to his house, carefully avoiding Suzette in case his wife should get the wrong idea, and packed a small bag. Outside he saw a young churl playing with a hoop and sent him, with the promise of a coin, to fetch Ethor. Then he went to his wife. He found her at the back, feeding grain to the chickens.

'I don't want you to go,' she said when she heard he must leave once more.

'This is a dead child, woman,' he said. 'I must take a cart to fetch her so that she can be buried as a child should be.'

'Why you? You have only just returned to me!' she said.

He saw the brittle despair in her eyes. 'I am the bayle, Gaillarde. What would you have me do? If it were our child . . .'

He had said the wrong thing, he realised immediately.

'Our child? We have no children, do we?' she said, her voice a wail. 'They are dead already, and we shall never have another!'

'Gaillarde, my love!'

'You are going to seek a woman!'

'Wife, why would I? I love only you,' he protested. 'We are both sad, since Pons and Fabrisse died, but we are still alive. We have to be strong for their memory.'

'You mean that?'

He took her shoulders in his hands and stared into her eyes. Deep within them he saw the fear and doubt. He could see it with ease. It was like peering into a mirror of his soul.

'Woman, I care about children. This girl is the second I have found raped and murdered. These children could have been ours, if Pons and Fabrisse were still alive. I want to do all I can to help find the murderers, but if you want, I will remain here.'

'You would send another?'

'Yes. If it will help you, if it will help remind us both of how we were before God took our children.'

She sniffed and rubbed her nose with the heel of her hand. 'Go, Denisot, but return soon.'

'I will, my love, my wife. I will.'

They smiled at each other, and then Gaillarde pushed him away with a fleeting return of her irritation. 'Go! You want to demand that I burst into tears, you layabout?'

He laughed, and walked away.

Friday 5 August

Denisot and Ethor had spent Thursday night at the site. First they had retrieved the girl's body with as much care as Denisot could bring, and placed her gently on the cart's bed. The girl was younger than Alicia, Denisot guessed. He covered her with a blanket and glanced about him, feeling weary. There was still nothing. Just a mass of flattened grasses and the impressions of boots in the mud. Later, while he lay rolled in blanket and cloak, he found he had to wipe the tears from his eyes. It was a lonely place for a young woman to die.

That morning they had another look about the area.

'The man who could do this should be stopped before he can hurt another,' Ethor said. 'If he's found, you won't need to convene a court, Denisot.'

'I wouldn't want to. He must be driven by the Devil to do things like this,' Denisot said.

They soon had the cart rattling back towards their town, the body covered by a blanket. Denisot and his friend maintained an uncomfortable silence on the way. Ethor had never married, but he knew of Denisot's sadness at losing his own children, and could see how Denisot's eyes kept returning to the figure under the covering. He could imagine how Denisot felt, on finding these two victims. No father liked to think of the death of his own children, but to be confronted with the deaths of others must make the loss of his own uniquely terrible and hard to bear.

Both men were so fully involved in their own thoughts that they did not hear the rattle of hoofs and clinking of harness over the rumble and thud of the cart's wheels until it was too late.

'Hoi! Stop, if you don't want to be speared like a hog!'

The town was large, and the walls stood out clearly in the early light as the mists rose and smoke drifted from a hundred chimneys.

Grandarse shifted uncomfortably. He hadn't slept well the previous night, and he felt unrefreshed and irritable as he glared along the river towards the town. 'What's it called, you say?'

Hawkwood peered at the town from narrowed eyes. 'Brive, they said, I think.'

Grandarse nodded. The two shepherds had been easy targets. Although they were not wealthy in terms of money, a shepherd, he had learned over the years, could be a useful source of local information. 'It's not the place Frip's supposed to be.'

'I was going to ask for more information about that, but they died,' Hawkwood said. His tone was neutral, but there was a glint of anger in his eyes. He had given instructions not to kill the two until he had checked their stories, but Imbert had ignored his commands. One day, he thought, there would be a reckoning with Imbert.

'Did they say where Uzerche lay?' Grandarse said.

'To the north, they thought. Up along that road.'

Grandarse nodded. There was a river at this side of the town, and beyond he could see the road winding northwards. They would have to pass over the bridge, then go on, past the town while remaining in arrow- and bolt-shot of the town, until they could pass beyond and continue.

Hawkwood voiced his concerns. 'The river is fast enough to ensure we would need a bridge, but if we keep to the road they could destroy the bridge before we reach it, and even then they'd keep up a sharp practice against us with their bows as we passed by.'

'Aye,' Grandarse agreed.

'Do you want to wait until dark?'

'No. But we won't cross here. Let us ride on to the next bridge or ford. It will hold us up a little, but better that than losing half our men unnecessarily.'

When Denisot looked up, there were fifteen all told, all mounted on sturdy, powerful ponies and rounseys, and all wearing mail or thick, stiffened leather, with steel bascinets to protect their heads. Most gripped long spears, while three held maces and one last carried a whip. He cracked it in the air occasionally, as though wishing he had a back to lash.

Before Denisot and Ethor could think of bolting, they were encircled, with a sparkling ring of steel threatening their breasts. Both held their hands up, glaring at the mercenaries all about them.

The man who had spoken was in his middle twenties, and had a squint in his left eye. His hair was a pale, mousy colour, and he had a thin beard of wispy gingerish hair. His face looked as though he would smile a lot, but now he glowered as he peered at the two. 'What is in the cart?'

Denisot felt an unaccountable anger building. 'You are English? Then you will probably know already what is in there.'

'What do you mean?'

'What is your name?'

The young mercenary's horse moved skittishly beneath him as he grinned. 'You are bold enough! Still, I am content to exchange names. I am called Peter of Reading, and now, I ask that you return the compliment. What is your name?'

'I am the Bayle of Domps, and I am named Denisot.'

'Well, Bayle Denisot, what are you doing down here?'

'I am here investigating a murder, and I will search for the murderer, no matter where he is.'

'What murder?'

Denisot said nothing, but grasped the corner of the blanket and flung it away. The girl's face was suddenly revealed.

'Look! A child! Raped, and then nailed to a board and hung in the trees to die. Look at her! This is what men like you do in this country every day!'

Peter glanced about him at the other faces. These were battle-hardened men. Denisot saw little shock or horror. Rather, there was interest in the faces peering down at the little figure.

'Where did you find her?'

'She was in the woods a league south of here,' Denisot said. 'It was reported to me and I came to find her so that we can find her murderer if possible.'

'You will have to look carefully,' one man called. 'There are enough bodies already lying about the countryside, and many murderers.'

'I will look very carefully,' Denisot said scornfully. 'And I will not hesitate to bring the criminals to justice.'

'You think to threaten us?' Peter of Reading said.

'I know what sort of men you are. You do not make me

fearful. But no man with a soul would want to support or protect this kind of murderer. A man who rapes and then murders by crucifixion in imitation of the death of Christ, is a man who will bring all his comrades to Hell with him, for surely he is the Devil himself.'

Peter kicked his horse and his lance-point came closer and closer to Denisot. 'Don't forget what sort of man you are threatening, bailiff,' he said as the tip touched Denisot's stomach. Denisot could feel the sharp point pressing at his skin, and he steeled himself to stand still, even if he must be injured or slain. He was quite certain, seeing the look in Peter's eyes, that he would be stabbed for sure if he tried to turn and run, but he felt no fear. He would go to Heaven, with luck, and there be reunited with his children. Soon his wife would join him, and his struggles would be over. In Heaven, all would be happiness and love. What was there here for him? He felt a slight rip at his belly, a jerk so infinitesimal it was almost unnoticeable, but he noticed it as the material of his jack gave way and then his shirt too. He could feel the oily menace of the metal against his flesh now and, looking up into Peter's face, he was sure that the mercenary was about to thrust it home.

Then a horse broke wind. The routiers all about burst out with guffaws of laughter. As if it had all been an elaborate joke, Peter lifted his lance away and set it at the rest, chuckling. 'You have a bold spirit, bailiff, aye, I'll give you that! You are bold and prepared to stand your ground. I salute you! But don't go threatening any of my companions, eh? You may find other men in my company are less amiable than me!'

'Others are easier, too.'

'You've met some of us?'

'I've met Berenger and his companions.'

Peter's face changed. His laughter was stilled and he peered closely. 'I'd heard he escaped. That's good. Do you know if he is safe?'

'I left him so. He is being looked after by the monks of St Jacques,' Denisot said without thinking.

'Where is that?'

'Many miles from here.'

Peter gave another laugh. 'He was a friend of mine, bailiff. I won't seek to hurt him. As proof, I won't even ask where the monastery is. But you should be careful in your dealings about here. Watch out for my companions. As I said, not all are as friendly as me.'

So saying, he gave a sharp whistle, and the array of lances was lifted away. The riders turned their mounts and set off up the road again, riding at a gentle canter, keeping a loose formation of riders side-by-side in pairs.

Ethor took a deep breath.

'We've been friends a long time, you and me, Denisot. Let me just tell you, if you ever try to accuse a vintaine of mercenaries of something like that again, you will die.'

'I didn't think.'

'Because if you ever do that again, I'll throttle you myself!'

CHAPTER SEVENTEEN

Saturday 6 August

Berenger was quick to heal. At the end of the first week his back had been a mass of scabs; already now the flesh had healed well, and the Infirmarer declared himself delighted with the quality of his handiwork when he prodded and poked, before bending to the altar and giving thanks for his success, while his rosary and golden crucifix rattled and tapped at the side of Berenger's cot.

The healing chamber was like a chapel. Each bed was positioned carefully to give a clear view of the altar with the crucifix, for naturally it was the prayers and the nearness of the holy altar that cured men of their ills here.

It was hard to like a man whose sole interest in life appeared to be making his wounds still more painful, but Berenger appreciated the depth of his knowledge, and grew to look forward to his visits. The Infirmarer had a caustic wit and an unsympathetic manner.

'Ouch! That hurts!' Berenger said.

'You haven't lost your sense of feeling then.'

'What do you do when you have no patients to hurt? Go and find a baby to torture?'

'No. That would involve travelling. I find it easier to hurt little puppies and kittens.'

'You are a sick man, Infirmarer.'

'So my patients tell me.'

Loys recovered more slowly. Some splinters of wood were left when the bolt was removed, and there came a day when the Infirmarer discovered a thick, green pus leaking from behind the clot, and Loys became feverish, giggling, and then shouting like a drunkard.

Suddenly the Infirmary was invaded by assistants to the Infirmarer. One brought a charcoal brazier and lit it, while others brought cloths and hot water. Berenger watched as they used a scorched knife to reopen the wound. Then a hot brand was used to sear the wound while Loys arched his back in agony, the pain so intense he could make no sound. When the Infirmarer finally settled back, there was sweat running down his face.

He left the room and returned a little later with a skin of wine and some cups. He poured for Berenger and Saul and another for himself, and then drank deeply. 'There are some parts of this work I hate.'

'You did well,' Berenger said grudgingly.

'I hope I cleaned the wound sufficiently.' He glanced towards Loys. 'I fear that the boy is weak. The next day will tell us whether our prayers have been answered.'

'You can only do your best. Is there more wine?'

The Infirmarer nodded and passed the jug. Berenger poured a large cup and drank deeply. It was a powerful wine and he could feel his troubles lifting. It brought an atmosphere with it, an odour and sense of sunshine and happiness. With another draught he could almost remember her face, the little figure held so gently in her arms, the warmth and pain of such a strong affection in his heart. The world had been a jolly, kindly place then, ten years ago.

But the world had changed, and he had changed with it.

The Infirmarer saw the change in his expression. 'Do you want to talk about it, my friend?'

'What?' Berenger said. 'There's nothing to discuss.'

The Infirmarer glanced at Saul, who sat on the next cot watching Berenger warily. He looked back at Berenger and said softly, 'One day you will want to talk to a friend. When you are ready, I am happy to listen. And if I am not, there is always another who will.'

'Who would listen to an old soldier's story?'

The Infirmarer nodded towards the altar. 'I think you know who will listen, my friend.'

'*Him?* He never listened to me before when I was a religious man and only sought to help others. Why would He help me now?' Berenger said.

Sunday 7 August

They had been riding for too long. Peter was weary after his long reconnaissance, and as he came round the last curve in the road, he was thinking only of the wine and the women who were waiting back in Uzerche. Will and the other members of the company would be having a marvellous time there, drinking their way through the barrels in the storehouses during the day and spending their evenings whoring, while Peter and his men were riding all about the area ensuring that they were safe from attack.

It was enough. He had ridden hard and there was little enough to show for it. A cart with a box of furs taken from two merchants riding to market, some food and plate from a small manor. It was not enough to justify the length of their journey.

'We'll return today,' he said to Ulric, a glowering Saxon with a scar that ran from his right temple to his chin.

'About focking time,' Ulric said in his thick accent. 'I want to get to a seat that does not rock under me all the day long.'

'We'll get back as soon as we can,' Peter said. He rose in his saddle and was about to call to the rest of the men, when one of his scouts came back at a fast trot.

'There's a town ahead.'

Peter spurred his mount and rode up to where the second scout sat on his mount staring ahead. 'Well?'

The scout pointed. Peter saw a thin smear of smoke against the sky. 'We will ride on. I want to know what size that place is before we return,' he said.

What was it that bayle had said? He was the Bayle of Domps, he said, didn't he? Perhaps this was his town, then. It meant nothing to Peter, although if there was an abbey nearby, perhaps this was where Fripper had gone when he escaped the ambush. That would interest Will.

Monday 8 August

Clip was riding before the column with a growing sense of grievance.

He should be back with the main army, not prancing around in the wrong direction like this, making his way through a thick forest. There were others who could be easily used for this kind of service, but no, it was him again, sent on a daft mission, in a direction where there were no decent manors to plunder, no monasteries, no nunneries, no rich merchants to deprive of their furs and gold. It was a waste of time. And meantime the army would have packed up and started to advance, if all he had heard was right. The men who were still with Sir John had opportunities to enrich themselves, to find wine and ale, to drink and whore and enjoy themselves . . . and he was here, scouting before Grandarse with Dogbreath, riding at the arrow's tip with forty men behind him. He was the man in danger if they met the enemy, as usual.

'How much further do you think it is?' Dogbreath asked again.

'How the fuck should I know?' Clip snapped. 'It's just another town on this bleeding river. They all look the same to me. Who gives a shit about one more? Fucking Fripper, if he's there, could have picked a better place. Why'd he come here? What's the point of taking a town so far from anywhere? He could have stayed nearer Calais or gone south towards Bordeaux, but no, if the story's right, he came all the way to this, the arse-end of the world. I don't see it. I think we're wasting our time.'

'You don't think he's there?'

'No. What, a little town around here? What sort of money can he win here? There's nothing. I think that merchant, or whatever he was, was lying. He wanted to keep his head on his shoulders so he told Sir John a tale that would keep him alive.'

Dogbreath scowled. 'I'll tickle him up with my dagger next time I see him, then.'

'You do that. Meantime, I'll . . .' He stopped, staring ahead, and his head dropped onto his chest as he peered fixedly.

Dogbreath sniggered. 'It was a bird, Clip.'

His companion said nothing, but jerked his hand quickly to indicate silence, never once ceasing in his careful study of the road ahead. 'Riders. Lots of them,' he said, whirling his horse's head about and cantering back.

'Grandarse, there are men coming. Possibly two vintaines-worth, possibly more.'

'You say so?' Grandarse glanced over Clip at the road ahead. 'I can't see anything.'

'The road turns in among those trees. I saw three flashes of reflected sun. When I looked, I could see shapes passing between the trees. I counted fifteen between one pair of trunks. I reckon they were men on horseback. Riding double file, that means thirty men. Could be I'm wrong. But if I'm right . . .'

Grandarse nodded. 'Enough!' He had never known Clip to make a mistake when scouting. It was why he was used so often. That and the fact that his whining grated on a man's nerves after a few miles. Grandarse looked about him quickly. To his left the road fell down among the trees. It was a shallow incline, but enough.

The Centener turned to his men. 'Hawkwood, take yours down there into the trees, dismount, and keep them aiming up here towards the roadway. We don't have men the other side of the road, so any target is yours. Understand? Have the men string their bows, and be quick, but wait for my command. If there's any trouble, take the rearmost first. Understand? Good. The rest of you, with me! Clip and Dogbreath, you too.'

In a few moments, the road was empty. Grandarse and the other men remained on their horses, while Hawkwood's men crouched or stood behind trees, arrows nocked and ready. They did not have long to wait.

There was an arrogance about the men riding towards them, as though they owned these woods, this road, and the whole of the land all about. It was enough to make Grandarse grimace. If any of his men were to behave so foolishly, they would deserve to be captured or slain. He lifted his hand. Hawkwood was staring at him, his own hand raised. As the first of the horsemen passed Hawkwood, Grandarse studied them carefully. There was no emblem on the men's surcoats, no flag or banner to declare their allegiance. These fellows were outlaws, or he was an earl. He felt his belly clenching with the promise of battle and gripped his reins more tightly in his left hand, readying himself. Then, when the foremost riders were level with him, he dropped his hand.

There was a slew of arrows, a hissing terror that slammed into the horsemen from their flank, and he roared to his men as he slammed his spurs into the horse's flanks, feeling the jolt as the brute was startled from his temporary torpor, muscles hurling Grandarse forward.

Shrieks, cries, bellows of defiance and alarm, and the column of men was thrown into confusion, but even as Grandarse burst from the woods he saw that they were recovering. There were some fools at the back who tried to ride to safety, but they were swiftly picked off by Robin and Imbert. Grandarse could see the commander of the little party, a sandy-haired man who bellowed at his men like a drunken ale-wife, trying to rally them. Older heads than his were already dropping from their mounts and attempting to string their bows; a few saw Grandarse and his companions and drew swords or grabbed lances to defend themselves, but Grandarse ignored them.

Bellowing, '*Hold!*' at the top of his voice, Grandarse rode straight for the sandy-haired man. The fellow turned and saw his danger too late. He tried to spur away, but Grandarse's horse rode hard into his flank, the stallion raised his head a moment before slamming into the other with his breast, and there was an audible crack. Rider and horse were thrown to the ground, both sliding on the gravel, the man's leg beneath the horse, trapping him.

'Put down your weapons!' Grandarse roared. 'All of you! Any man who clings to his sword will have his arm cut from his body! If you try to attack me or my men, you will be killed immediately!'

'Who are you?' a man called suspiciously.

Grandarse smiled evilly. 'I'm the man who's going to be your centener as soon as you join the army of the Prince of Wales.'

'Prince of Wales?' More than one of the men took on anxious expressions, as men will who realise that their past might be about to catch up with them. Some looked warily back the way they had come, as though estimating the distance to safety. The sight of the bodies of those who had already tried to flee was a sobering sight.

'Any man who doesn't want to serve his Prince can explain to him why that is,' Grandarse said comfortably. 'Who are you, and where are you from?'

The man whom he had barged to the ground remained there, yelping as his rounsey jerked and rolled upright, clambering to its feet. The fellow maintained his grip on the reins and tried to haul himself up, but gave a loud groan and collapsed as his leg gave way. He sat gaping at his twisted leg in disbelief.

'You! What's your name?' Grandarse demanded. He had to repeat the question three times before the man seemed to hear.

'Simon of Shoreditch,' he managed. His face was pale, and now was growing green. 'I am the captain. Shit, my leg, I—'

'You'll need a man to set it,' Grandarse said dismissively as Simon's eyes rolled up into his head and he toppled sideways. 'Perhaps now would be a good idea.'

'I had been told that you were healing, but I am pleased to see you so much improved.'

Berenger stopped and turned to face the Abbot. He had been walking in the orchard, enjoying the tranquillity. All was warm and clean here, with only the humid odour of soil and grass heating in the sun. The orchard felt as comforting as a secure room with a hot fire and a hound basking in the warmth. He almost expected to feel a rumble of contentment through his feet, as if the land itself was enjoying it.

'I am glad to see you, my Lord Abbot.'

'And I you.' The Abbot fell into step beside Berenger, and the two walked in companionable silence for a space.

'I used to think all smells had a sharpness to them,' Berenger said at last, quietly.

'Yes?'

'I have fought too many battles. I thought everything smelled of blood and steel and burned houses, but here I am learning that there are still pleasant experiences – the world can continue without death.'

'You have been a warrior for long?'

'I started when I was a boy, fighting in Scotland. When the King came to France, it was natural that I should join him.'

'But you have suffered much, eh?'

'I have been injured. I've been struck by quarrels, stabbed, slashed, beaten . . . I have endured.'

'Not only in battle.'

Berenger shook his head, but didn't speak. That pain of his loss was still too raw.

The Abbot bent his head as he walked, staring at the small flowers in among the grasses. 'I was here when the great pestilence appeared. Ten years ago, almost. It's shocking, isn't it, how so much has changed since then. We all suffered greatly, of course. When it hit us, I think there were some fifty men working here. We had the choir, of course, but there were all the lay-brothers too, and of all of us, only five survived. One tenth only.'

'Who else lived?'

'There was me, the Brother Infirmarer, the Salsarius and one of the lay-brothers who was responsible for the mill. It was a grave position to be in, for of course we could not maintain the estates afterwards. The villagers on whom we depended were themselves sorely depleted, and just holding services for the dead was a dreadful responsibility and took so much of our time. It was truly appalling. But you know that, of course.'

'Yes.'

'Where were you when you experienced it?'

Berenger shook his head, then: 'In Calais.'

'Alone?'

'I was afterwards.' Suddenly Berenger was aware of a thickness in his throat. He had to swallow before he could add: 'And ever since.'

Grandarse glanced at Hawkwood as the vintaines rounded up their new recruits into a shuffling, embittered group. Hawkwood was watching the prisoners, but he was most carefully eyeing a younger fellow who had the sallow, anxious look of a man who was never too sure where his next meal would come from.

Hawkwood called Dogbreath over. 'Take him,' he said.

The youngster was clearly terrified to have been singled out. Dogbreath and Clip had to grab his arms and physically yank him from among his companions.

'What are you doing? What do you want with me?'

Dogbreath chuckled hoarsely in the back of his throat, while Clip shoved him to the road's edge and then down in among the trees.

'What? What did I do? You're going to kill me, aren't you? Why? What have I done?'

'Shut up,' Clip said. 'You were in the wrong place, that's all. It's just bad luck. Tough. Get used to it.'

'What are you going to do to me?'

Dogbreath smiled evilly. 'We're going to have some fun, that's what!'

The boy looked as though he was about to faint. There was a rising hubbub behind them from the road, where some of the other men were protesting at the way their young comrade had been taken away. Clip pushed the lad again and this time he caught his foot on a root and went sprawling, smashing his face on a fallen bough. He pushed himself up on all fours, and Clip kicked him hard in the flank. The lad gave a wailing gasp and collapsed, wheezing.

'Listen, Prickle,' Clip said quietly. 'We want to know some things about you and your mates. If you answer honestly and quickly, you may live. But every time I think you're lying, my friend here is going to encourage you with his dagger. Understand?'

'I don't know anything! You need to ask Simon. He knows what's happening and things. I don't, Will never tells us anything!' He had rolled back to sit and now stared at them with wide, fearful eyes.

'Who's Will?' Clip asked.

'He's the leader of our company. When he kicked out the old drunk, he was elected.'

Clip shook his head. 'I don't understand you,' he said, and kicked again.

The lad curled into a ball, whining with a high keening as he cupped his ballocks, rocking back and forth.

'I told you, I want the truth and that quickly. Who is this Will?'

'He's just the leader of our company, like I said.'

'How long's he been there?'

'Since Fripper was kicked out. Two weeks since, I think. I don't know!'

'Fripper?' Dogbreath snarled. 'Who?'

'Fripper! He was our captain, but he was drunk and Will kicked him out. I don't know more than that!'

'This Fripper – was he so tall?' Clip asked, holding his hand out. 'Big scar over his face like this?' He matched gesture to words, indicating a line across his brow, nose, down across his cheek to his jaw.

'Yes, yes, that's him.'

'What happened to him?' Dogbreath demanded.

Clip saw him fingering his dagger. Both knew the most common manner in which a captain would lose his command. 'Did this Will kill him?'

'No! He was allowed to go. He had friends with him, and they left.'

Clip shot a look at Dogbreath. Dogbreath nodded slowly, and said, 'That was it? This Will just let him go? Doesn't sound like any leader I've known.'

'He didn't mean to,' the lad said tearfully. He curled into still more of a ball as though, if he could, he would have pushed himself into the soil and away from the two. 'He had his men try to ambush Fripper, but Fripper saw them and killed them all before they could hurt him.'

'Not such a drunk, then,' Clip said.

'I suppose.'

'Were you there to help kill him?'

'No! I was back at the town, waiting with the others.'

'So you knew he was going to be attacked?'

The boy's mouth moved, but while his eyes went from one to the other, guessing at the answer they wanted to hear, no sound came.

'You didn't think to warn him, did you?' Dogbreath hissed.

'He was a commander! What else would he think would

happen? It's the way of things! I didn't do it, though. I wasn't there!'

Clip bared his teeth in a snarl, then lunged down, grabbed the squawking lad by the jerkin, and pulled him to his feet.

'Come, boy. If we're going to get anywhere tonight, we'll need you ready to march.'

'You let them go?' Will demanded. He stood and began to pace the room. 'They could have taken you straight to Fripper and let us catch him! In Christ's name, do you not realise what an opportunity you've let fall through your fingers? Are you so moon-struck you didn't see how important these two men were?'

Peter watched him with his thumbs stuck in his belt, sucking at his teeth while his commander ranted.

Will was a brave man, but his temper could always get the better of him when he thought his own will was being thwarted. Like many who were unsure of their own competence, he would deride the opinions of others when they disagreed with his own. He disliked any problems or interruptions, especially if he felt that they affected his reputation. He was very fond of his reputation.

When Will had first made moves to remove Berenger, it had been enormously popular with the men. On a show of hands in the tavern among Will's men, there were none who disputed his main contention that Berenger was old and past it. No one who saw his red-rimmed eyes and smelled his acrid breath in the morning could have doubted that. He was growing ridiculous, and no company of fighters could rely on a man who was thought ridiculous by his own fellows. A mercenary army was effective only for so long as the commander was trusted by his men. If he became unpredictable or capricious, the men would lose faith in his ability to win them plunder. Usually the exit for such a man was a rope or a knife. After all, effective discipline was a key requirement of a commander. Without that, mutiny was natural. Not that it was called mutiny. It was the natural order of men, that the strongest would take over for as long as he was strongest.

With Will, the men had put in place a man whom all admired. He had been brave in battle, bold and most important, very lucky. All the targets which engaged his interest had fallen to him. His one failing recently had been the matter of the execution of his predecessor. He had tried, but both attempts had failed. First the attack in town, and then the ambush that had succeeded in killing the woman and her children, leaving a dangerous man in search of revenge. Now Peter had lost the opportunity of finding Fripper when all he had to do was bring this peasant to him.

Peter eased his shoulders as Will ranted. He had plenty of time. After all, Peter was in a strong position. Many of Will's men had been in his vintaine, and they mostly died in the costly attempts to kill Berenger. Now he relied on Simon and three others to maintain his position. His own power within the Company was reduced.

'Have you finished yet?' Peter asked.

'Don't you speak to me like that!'

'I'll speak how I like,' Peter said. There was a touch of ice in his voice now. He would not bow to Will here in the hall. He would show respect before the rest of the company, as was natural for discipline, but in private there was no need. As mercenaries they were equals; no, Peter had more men than Will now. He was superior in force. He walked to the table and poured himself a mazer of wine.

Will was filled with rage. 'You come here and tell me you've allowed the link to Fripper to slip through your fingers and expect me to be pleased?'

'Yes, because if you listen, I can tell you where Berenger is.'

CHAPTER EIGHTEEN

Tuesday 9 August

Berenger felt more comfortable. He tried to put all thoughts of his family from his mind, and instead found himself thinking more and more about the men he had once known.

It was easy to recall men like Geoff, and Jack, and the others in his vintaine. Those had, mostly, been happy days. He had been a respected commander of men, for the most part. Even when he had suffered, such as when he had been sent up to the northern borders to help fight the Scottish, and had received the wound about his face as a result, he had been proud to be among friends. Or that was how he remembered his time.

Of course, many of them had died while he was with them, suffering from an array of stab wounds, cuts, crossbow bolts, even shards of flying metal when gonnes exploded catastrophically, the whirling slivers of metal cutting men's bodies in half, severing limbs and leaving a hideous trail in their wake, like a lunatic's demented visions of Hell.

But those days had been better than more recent ones.

There was a curious sense of freedom to be released from Uzerche. He did, in truth, feel recovered from the bleak misery that had settled on him after his final eviction as leader. The memory of Alazaïs lying in the roadway, her two boys at her side, was enough to make him want to weep still, but now her face was fading in his memory. Hers was only one of a number of faces he could remember. There was a woman he had found at the roadside while slogging eastwards during the Crécy campaign, a matron in a doorway in a tiny hamlet near Paris, a young woman still clutching her beheaded infant at a vill on the march from Crécy to Calais.

In those years there had been so many deaths, so many horrors. He could not comprehend the full magnitude of the disaster that had befallen the land. He had a strange feeling that not one death among all of them had been unique. They had been nothing more than discrete fractions, small parts of the whole swathe of deaths that had encompassed France before, during and after the horror of the pestilence. Alazaïs's death was no more singular in its way than any number of killings in the last few years.

For the first time, Berenger began to see the wars and his involvement in them less as little distinct moments of time, and more as a continuously flowing river of events, with each battle, each rape, each murder little more than curvetting ripples and currents. Each individual, each separate, but nevertheless a part of the flow. Stopping the death and killing would be like damming a great river. It was impossible.

A sudden vista of dead faces sprang into his mind. Men, women, children, lying on the ground like a carpet of corpses, a tapestry woven from misery. Most he recognised. Men whose lives he had ended with his blades or arrows, women whom he had seen dying at the hands of his companions, some of them staring at him now as though pleading for his aid. He had not been able to save them, and even now, although he offered up prayers for their souls, he knew it was not enough. He had done too much harm in his life to be able to make reparation now. There was nothing he could do.

'How could any man or woman want to bring a child to life?' he wondered. How indeed. To bring life into the midst of all this destruction and horror seemed perverse. There was no sense in it. No, if he could have his life again, he would avoid bloodshed. He would rest his bones in a quiet valley like this.

Perhaps he should be a monk, he pondered. A man dedicated to the souls of the toilers; a man who would forsake the world and spend his time in prayer and contemplation. That was an appealing idea now. In the past he had never desired more than a home with a child or two to carry on his name, a good woman who would see to it that his table was full, that his guests would always be welcomed, and that his bed was warm at night. Those dreams seemed so immature and pathetic now. Better by far to fight with the Heavenly Host against evil.

Fulk was sitting at the gate on a bench positioned so that travellers could rest their weary legs. He looked up as Berenger approached. 'Evening, Fripper.'

Berenger nodded and gratefully accepted the jug of ale Fulk passed him. He drank well, but not too deeply; he did not feel the need of intoxication, only a natural thirst.

'The back, it is healing?' Fulk asked.

'Yes. I am much mended, my friend.'

'It is good. Perhaps soon we shall leave this place.'

'I am content here.'

'It is good. But that only means it will be a sore temptation for companies of routiers or others.'

'With God's grace we can hope they will miss this place,' Berenger said. 'We can hope that the abbey will escape. What would an army do in this direction? It is far from Bordeaux.'

'There is talk of the English coming this way.'

Berenger gave a quick frown. 'What would they come up here for?'

'I don't know. Perhaps it is Will and the company?'

'Perhaps.'

Suddenly all the ease which Berenger had felt settling on him in the last hours were gone. He took up Fulk's jug and drank again.

Wednesday 10 August

Early the next morning the Infirmarer discovered Berenger lying on the floor near his bed, a pool of vomit close by his head.

'Get off me!' Berenger said, waving at him in a futile gesture of dismissal.

'You need help to get up,' the Infirmarer said calmly. 'And you must do so as quickly as you may, or else I shall call the Abbot. If you are well enough to drink so much that you become this oafish, you are clearly well able to leave our gates and find your way to a tavern somewhere so that you can indulge your gluttonous whims to your heart's content.'

'I'm no glutton! I'm a routier! I'm guilty of things you cannot comprehend: a commander of routiers.'

'Yes, however, there are none here with you. So for now, you are a drunk.'

'Not drunk. I wish I was. Can't you just leave me alone?'

'I need you back in your bed. You defile the chamber. I will have to clean up all this.'

'Piss on you!'

The Infirmarer was a patient man. He often had cause to be, but there were times when his stores of goodwill to others ran a little dry, and this was one of those occasions. Berenger had drunk more than his share of wine every day, and to be in this stinking state, he must have taken an excess. He had brought nothing with him, so the only source for him was somewhere within the abbey. He grasped Berenger's arms and hoisted him up, being careful not to harm his wounds, and placed him on his palliasse once more.

'What was the cause of this?'

Berenger blinked at him. 'What do you mean? I drank a little, that is all.'

'It is morning, Master. You have been drinking all night.'

'It helps. I could not sleep.'

'Why not?'

'What does it matter? It helps.'

'Is it your own acts of cruelty that keep you awake?'

The Infirmarer watched him closely as he asked his questions. He had seen others who had been distraught by their own actions in battle, who had relived each bloody sword-cut into another's face or body every night for their rest of their lives. It did not matter whether it was a man fighting to defend himself in the line of battle, or whether it was a man taking revenge for an insult, often it was the mere fact of surviving that led a man to question his place in the world.

'Not my cruelty, no. I can hardly remember them all,' Berenger said with a twisted grin.

'Then what ails you?'

'You cannot understand.'

'Then it is a woman,' the Infirmarer said.

Berenger said nothing, but his eyes fell to studying the floor.

'Who was she?'

'She was my wife,' Berenger said, and suddenly the tears began to flow. He dashed them away angrily.

'What happened to her?'

'The *pestilence* came. That's what happened. It took her, just as it took my son. I was happy for the first time in many years, and after Calais I settled with her in the town. King Edward was generous with the houses and plots in Calais, and I took one. I married. But we knew only a year of joy, before the pestilence took her son. She was already large with our child when he died, I think that made her ill. She had the baby too early and he died, and a little while later, she died too. I think from a broken heart. And I wanted to. I really wanted to die. But I couldn't. I didn't.'

'You cannot take your own life. No man can choose when his life will end. Only God can decide that.'

'I'm not strong enough to kill myself or I would have done, many times over the years. If God had any compassion He would have taken me by now.'

'So, what will you do? Continue drinking until you have dis-solved your brain? Are you so determined to die?'

'It is all those I've seen dead. They come to me at night and torment me!'

'Perhaps it is your feeling of guilt that brings them to your mind?'

Berenger gave him a look of disgust. 'You think I am evil because I've been a soldier? I've known loss too! I lost my wife and sons, damn you!'

'And they would be happy to see you like this? Self-destructive and selfish to the suffering of all others?'

'My wife would understand.'

'Why should she? She would not understand your behaviour any more than I can.'

'She understands me, damn you! She too comes to me in my sleep.'

'Perhaps. Her shade may come to try to persuade you to divert yourself from your actions.'

'No,' Berenger said. And his voice continued with a sob of self-pity. 'I know why she comes: she comes to remind me I promised to look after her. I promised to love her and protect her!' He covered his face in his hands. 'I failed. I failed her when she needed me!'

'Master, she would not wish to see you sad. It has been many years since her death, has it not?'

'It doesn't matter. Ten years, twenty – what do years mean?'

'They mean life and death. You have life. You should make better use of it.'

'I have no life. Since she died, I have nothing.'

'She would be angry to hear you say that. She has gone on to join with the Heavenly Father and life eternal, and you will join her one day, if you are worthy; but continue on this path of dissolution and death, and you will not see her again,' the Infirmarer said sharply.

'I would join with her today if I could,' Berenger said. His head hung, and his eyes filled with tears that brimmed and ran down his cheeks.

'You may not, my son. You know that.' The Infirmarer saw Saul and Fulk appear in the doorway and he waved them away impatiently. 'That is not in your hands to decide.'

'Yes. But this world is unwholesome to me. I could give it up in a moment.'

'You said she comes back to remind you that you should have protected her. Do you blame yourself for her death?'

'Blame myself? No, I blame all France. It was French people who brought the pestilence to Calais. It's all because of France that she is dead. I *curse* the land!'

'You blame the country?'

'I detest this land. I despise it. If I had the power, I would destroy it all in fire and then sink it beneath the waves.'

'What of the people?'

Berenger looked up at him. The tears were still running, but his eyes were cold and unwavering as he said, 'Without my Marguerite, I care nothing for any of them!'

'No? So you put all blame and responsibility on her shoulders?' the Infirmarer said. 'You blame your dead wife for all? You deny your own responsibility for your situation?'

Berenger opened his mouth, but the Infirmarer cut over him before he could speak.

'You have a responsibility to live your life as she would like to see you. You believe she would want to know that you were nothing more than a routier and club-man who enjoyed destroying other lives for no reason? I think her memory deserves better than that. Don't you?'

Thursday 11 August

The Abbot visited Berenger in the infirmary in the afternoon before Vespers and stood over him as he lay on his belly, while the Infirmarer washed his back and dressed it.

'You seem to have made a remarkable recovery,' he observed. 'In a few more days, you'll be perfectly healed, eh?'

'I am vastly grateful to you and your good Infirmarer for all the care you have taken of me and the others,' Berenger said. His mouth was dry again, and he longed to reach for the skin of wine he had installed under the palliasse, but it would be hard to reach it while the Infirmarer was working on his wound.

'We are happy to have been of some help to you. However, I think that the time approaches when you must leave.'

Berenger felt as though he had been bludgeoned. 'Leave?'

It was like falling into a deep well. His stomach lurched, his head whirled, and he had to fight the urge to spew. He knew that one day he would have to leave the abbey, but he had not thought it would be quite so soon. Of course, it made sense, but it was a daunting prospect. He and the others had many miles to cover, all the way to the coast and Guyenne, and their little band could be set upon by any local Lord or group of disaffected soldiers. With a journey of over a hundred sweltering miles to travel, it was unlikely that they would all make it. It was unlikely *any* would make it.

The Infirmarer rested his hand on Berenger's back, as if he understood Berenger's thoughts. Berenger lifted himself onto his forearms and then elbows, grunting with the effort.

'Not until you are perfectly hale and hearty, of course,' the Abbot said. 'But there is no place in a monastery like ours for men who are so worldly as you and your men. You are, when all is said and done, fighters. We have need of peace here in our cloister. I will not throw you from our doors, but you must pre-pare for the day when you will leave us.'

'I do understand. And again, I am glad of the help you have been able to give us. When you wish us to go, we will.'

The Abbot gave a quiet smile. 'That is good. Well, I am sure that some exercise would do you good, too. If the Infirmarer will let you know when you are, in his opinion, fit enough you may take horses and ride about the area. I will let the stablemen know that you are to be helped to saddle and prepare.'

Berenger swung his legs down to sit on the edge of his cot. It was tiring, but he was feeling the strength return to his flank and back. The Infirmarer had told him that the worst of his injuries were to the skin, rather than to the muscles. Although he had felt, so he thought, the muscles rip, the actual damage was lessened because the weapon had been clean and sharp. He lifted his arm experimentally, licking his lips. They felt very dry.

'My friend, some days ago we walked in the orchard. Perhaps you would accompany me again?' the Abbot said.

'Aye, with pleasure,' Berenger said. He pulled his shirt over his head and stood, reaching down for his wine skin.

'You are thirsty?'

Berenger heard the note of quiet discontent in his voice. He hesitated, and then left the skin where it was. 'A little.' He looked at the Abbot, whose eyes were narrowed as if testing Berenger. 'I don't need it.'

'I am glad. It is a crutch for the weak, my friend. You don't need it.'

Berenger could have laughed aloud at that. He felt the need of it all the more after the Abbot's words about leaving.

It had been a long, hard journey to this, the third crucifixion, and Denisot was glad to be returning, even with an uncertain welcome from his wife. He was not so badly delayed as the last time with Fripper and his men. Perhaps she may even be glad to see him again so soon.

A third child; a third family deprived; a third young life ended in rape, torture and horror. There were no words to describe his hatred of the man responsible. Such a man was a demon. He was like a rabid dog. Denisot would have no compunction in putting him down. Such a man was a danger to the whole community: he would find this man and kill him.

He had heard of this one from a goatherd. The old man, Ponton, lived most of his life far from the town, walking with his animals over the hills and staying out with them for days at a time. He had heard the slaying and led Denisot and Ethor back to the place where it had happened.

'There was a shouting and laughing. It was the laughing got to me,' Ponton said, staring about him. A lanky fellow, with skin the colour of walnut, wiry and skinny, he looked as though his body had no fat in it, like a man who had fasted for a month. He could hear them down in the valley. Horses and men, the noise of their passage loud in the cool evening air. 'Sound passes a long way at that time of evening,' he said.

'What did you see?'

Ponton spoke slowly and deliberately, as a man will who rarely speaks to others. Every word was considered, weighed, and spoken when he was sure it held the correct meaning.

'I was up at the pasture last evening. When I heard the noise, I went to the trees and peered through them. There was a force of English in the woods below me. Through the trees I saw them. They had stopped at the house of Jean Rives.'

Denisot nodded. A peasant who farmed a few sheep and pigs, Jean was in his middle thirties, and had a daughter and wife who tended to the house, the garden, and spent most of their time making quarrels with each other as daughters and mothers will.

'I saw one grab at the girl. She screamed, Jean came out with a stick to protect her, and a man ran him through with a lance. The girl screamed again as he died. Then they found her mother and raped them both. The house was set afire, and then they threw the mother inside. I could hear her die. It was piteous.'

'The girl?'

'They left and rode away, leaving her behind. She was on the ground. I saw her through the trees. I was going to help her, but before I could reach her, I saw a man appear. He was one of the English, I think. He pulled a board from the house, and then he struck the child across the face until she was silent. I saw him nail her hands to the board, then he took her again.'

'You mean he raped her once her hands were nailed to the wood?'

'Yes. Then he hoisted her up on the plank with a rope, and

tied her off, up there in the trees. He settled down and waited while she cried out for help.'

His old eyes filled with tears and he averted his gaze. 'I didn't ought to have left my goats alone, but I couldn't leave these poor souls here without telling anyone.'

Ethor was staring about him with a look of extreme melancholy. 'How many were they, Ponton?'

'At least five. Beyond that, I don't know.'

'The man who came back and did this,' Denisot said, pointing to the girl's body. They had cut her down, but she was dead and cool to the touch. 'Was he one of the first five?'

'Who else could he have been?'

'I just wanted to make sure,' Denisot said. He shook his head. Jean Rives was dead, only a matter of feet from his threshold. He lay before it, an expression of pained surprise on his face. Behind him, the cottage was a blackened shell. The timbers had burned through and collapsed, and one section of wall had already fallen. Inside was the blackened figure of the mother, curled into a foetal ball. Ethor and Denisot carefully noted the damage done to the three before loading them all onto the back of the cart they had brought for this purpose.

Ethor wrote down the details on a sheet of parchment. 'We have to make sure that we don't miss anything out,' he grumbled. 'My memory's not as good as it was.'

Denisot nodded. It made sense, but as they set off to return home, Ponton striding up the hill to his goats on his long legs, he felt overwhelmed. 'What can we achieve?'

'We can try to have this man found and executed,' Ethor said.

'Whoever he is, do you think we shall have an opportunity to do anything?' Denisot asked. 'Look at us, two officials who should be representing our Lords here, and yet the English can ride everywhere. We cannot even raise a force to stop them.'

'Have you tried to?'

'What would be the point? People are too fearful of the English. They won't want to join us to remove them from Uzerche. Why would they? They know that if they were to leave their homes and go to help the people in the town, they would leave their own wives and children unprotected. And many would die against the English. We know the truth of them. They are ruthless and invincible. If they can kill off most of the noble-men of France in a battle, what would they do to unprotected, untrained levies from Domps? They could wipe out all the males in the town without breaking into a sweat.'

'I think you do some of our neighbours a disservice.'

'Which?' Denisot enquired wryly.

They had rounded one side of a hill as he spoke, and now he looked ahead over the trees towards their homes. Denisot felt the blood drain from his face. Suddenly he felt his legs quiver as though he might topple. 'Ethor, what is that?'

'Good God in Heaven, Denisot! I hope it's not what I think it is!'

The two men stopped to stare. There, ahead of them, where their town should be, was an enormous blue-black cloud. It rose high over the trees, like a thunderhead, but there was no other cloud in the sky.

'It's the Devil's sign,' Denisot said. He felt as though his heart had already broken in anticipation.

CHAPTER NINETEEN

The Abbot was quietly reflective as they walked. Then he took a deep breath.

'Master Fripper, I have discussed you with the good Brother Infirmarer. We were both concerned for you, for the injury done to your back was as nothing to the injury you had suffered inside. You were being eaten alive by your demons. And you had many. I think you are almost healed body and soul.'

'I do feel well,' Berenger admitted.

'And it is good to see you so recovered. You spoke of the shade of your wife visiting you. Does she still, eh?'

'Often. Only when I see her I do not feel the horror and hatred for the world that once I did.'

'I am glad to hear it. Perhaps she is prepared to let you go. You . . . you have cried out in your sleep. Other people, I think, have come to disturb your rest. Do they still?'

Berenger did not meet his eyes. 'I do not see them now. At night, many of them will return to me.'

'My friend, I believe that you have a demon inside you. He

was strong, and he knew how to push you to do his bidding. He knew how to make you angry, and how to keep you on edge so that you were capable of the worst excesses.'

'He was most competent, then.'

'You must not listen to him. He weakens. If you continue to fight him, you will prevail. In future, promise me that you will try to seek the best in all men.'

'I will do my best. My last talk with the Infirmarer persuaded me of that. I shall do my best to do that and remember my wife and how she would like me to behave and think.'

'Good. Where will you go?'

'I was thinking of heading west and finding my way to the English towns in Guyenne.'

'That is good, but the roads are dangerous. There are bands of club-men, outlaws and murderous English. Still, you and your men can defend yourselves against outlaws on the road.'

'Perhaps so.'

'I have heard rumours that the English are moving. They appeared outside Périgueux and tormented the poor townspeople there for some days. Where they are now, God Himself alone knows. You must be careful. The roads are not safe. The English attack everyone, and may not recognise you as their own; the locals will certainly kill you if they realise you are English.'

'I thank you for your kind warning.'

'Do not forget: although you may see off your devil, there are many others with their own demons. Even among the local population. There are rumours near here of a man who rapes children and crucifies them.'

Berenger shook his head. 'I recall Bayle Denisot speaking of that.'

'It brings a new horror to our poor land.'

Berenger nodded, but in his mind he saw Will again, and

wondered what horrors the company was inflicting on the locals of Uzerche and beyond.

Peter strode along the town's main street and eyed the buildings. Already mercenaries were making their way from the houses and out into the streets. A wailing procession of younger women had already been gathered, their hands bound securely with ropes that were tied to saddles, while the older ones knelt in the dirt and smothered their faces and hair in dust in their despair.

This was an unnecessary distraction, Peter thought. The town had done nothing to him or Will, but Will was determined to punish the place just because the bailiff had been the man who had saved Berenger from death. And now they had lost Simon's vintaine too. It had clearly unsettled Will, as though he was aware that events were gathering momentum against him.

'Burn it all!' Will bellowed from the other side of a small square.

'What purpose will it serve?' David asked Peter. He was a thick-set man with long black hair that looked out of place against his dark complexion. His shoulders were as broad as an ox's, and he looked vicious and cruel, but Peter knew that he had personally saved three children from death this morning. Other men had found them cowering under a table in a house, and were about to spit them all, when David saw to it that they were released. Hopefully they had made it from the town, but Peter doubted it somehow. In any case, they were not his responsibility.

'Purpose? None. He just wants to make an impression. He's a weak man. I've seen others like him. Not a thought for strategy, only a series of tactics. He's not bright enough to plan a campaign.'

'Dull fucker,' David said.

'Yes. But right now, he has the command.'

'Right now, yes. But I think if it was put to the vote, you'd probably have the majority.'

'Perhaps. But I'm not putting my head in that sack, thanks. Besides, what's the point? Will is determined to find Fripper and kill him. And if I was to put money on that fight, I wouldn't expect Will to win.'

Friday 12 August

It was a beautiful, clear morning filled with the scent of roses and incense from the church when Berenger walked out into the garden from the infirmary. He had a sense that his quiet interlude was about to end. It was summer, and the blossoms were developing into fruits. The nut trees were full with young almonds, walnuts and hazelnuts. In a month they would be ready for harvesting. Roses twisted and climbed with profusions of little flowers, while birds swooped past urgently to feed their young. There was a soothing atmosphere all about him: nature felt the year had been good. For him, memories of fighting with the company were fading, and he was aware of a calmness that had gradually spread over him like a blanket.

The Abbot was walking contemplatively from the church; when he saw Berenger, he made towards him.

'I trust you are well?' he said.

Berenger nodded. 'I feel rested.'

'I am glad.' The Abbot looked up at the sky. 'It is a beautiful morning. I understand from the Brother Infirmarer that the boy you were accustomed to send to fetch more wine has been found to have much time on his hands.'

'I harkened to your words. It seemed to me that my dead wife would prefer that I drank less.'

'And has she visited you since then?'

Berenger smiled fleetingly. 'Not since, no. My sleep has been happier.'

'I am glad.'

Berenger bent his head. 'My Lord Abbot, I would ask you a boon. I have a feeling that I came here because I was guided. I have lived in the world of war for too long. Perhaps I was meant to come here and learn the life of a monk.'

'You wish to join the Order?'

'My body craves it more than anything.'

'Yet you only recently lost a woman you loved, and came here seeking vengeance against her killer. If you wanted to come and live here, all thoughts of romance and revenge must be cleaned from your soul.'

'I think I am ready for that.'

'I shall have to consider. This is not an easy decision. I must pray for guidance.'

Fulk was standing leaning against a tree, whittling at a stick with his knife. Loys was sitting near him; Saul was lying on his back with a broad grin on his face.

'Well, Frip? How is the wound today?' Saul asked.

Loys was still very pale after his fever, but the colour was returning to his cheeks. He said, 'You look better all round, Frip. First time I've seen you looking so hearty.'

'Since my injury, you mean?'

Loys reddened and Saul chuckled.

'I think he means,' Saul said, 'that you look healthier than at any time since Loys met you. Your drinking is more restrained, and you have more watered wine than strong Bordeaux.'

Berenger looked away towards the hills in the distance. 'I do feel well. Ridiculously well. The rest has been good.'

It had. Although he would never tell these men, he felt relaxed and fitter. Two days without wine had made Marguerite's shade leave him. He felt almost as though she had forgiven him. It meant he had less and less of an urge to drink.

'I saw you talking to the Abbot this morning,' Saul said. 'Is he demanding we leave?'

Berenger hunkered down, squatting on his haunches, and picked up a handful of soil, watching it spill from his palm. It looked clean and wholesome. 'Boys, I've been thinking. There are worse lives than these.'

'What do you say?' Fulk said, stopping with his knife half-way through the wood.

'I was just thinking that life here is not bad. It would make sense to take some time to try to do some good.'

'The Abbot's wine has turned your wits. You're addled, man!' Saul said.

'No. I've found peace at last. I will remain here, if he will allow me.'

Loys gasped. He turned to Saul, looked up at Fulk, then back at Berenger. 'You're serious?'

'Never more so. I never intended to be a mercenary. It was just something to do to take revenge on France.'

'So you will foreswear your past and become a monk?' Saul said. He rolled onto his elbow. 'That means no women, Frip.'

'I know.' Berenger saw the door to the Abbot's house open and the familiar features of the Abbot appeared. He stood still a moment, and then beckoned Berenger. There was a short man with him, who moved with a curious gait, like a man who had almost forgotten how to walk. Berenger stood as they approached.

The man with the Abbot was considerably shorter, and very elderly. He had the emaciated body of a man who willingly went without food, and at his throat there were two dangling dewlaps of skin that put Berenger in mind of a cockerel. About him Berenger could detect a sour smell. It seemed to come from his body, an odour more of illness than that of mere lack of bathing.

'My friend, this is Father Jean. He works in the little convent of Sainte Marie some twenty miles away.'

The man shook his head. 'I did.'

'Yes, of course.'

Berenger looked from one to the other. 'I don't understand.'

'A company of routiers attacked it yesterday and destroyed it entirely. The women have all been assaulted, and the buildings looted. There is little enough remaining,' the little man said. His eyes filled with tears and he looked up at Berenger with hopeless despair. 'They even raped poor Mother Superior. She was seventy-two. Seventy-two, and treated with such contempt. They laughed at her as she died with a knife in her belly. The poor woman, martyred for no reason!'

Berenger shook his head, staring from one to the other. His gaze fixed on the Abbot questioningly.

'I am worried that they may come here next, my son,' he said.

'Then you must leave. Pack all that you can, and depart immediately.'

'Give up God's house to thieves and outlaws?'

'If you stay, you risk death, my Lord Abbot.'

'I do not know. If I stay, I may be able to protect the church. Our books, our precious icons, our ...' he waved a hand helplessly towards the buildings that held the abbey's relics and other valuables. 'I said to you only a little while ago, that entering this holy cloister means turning the other cheek, but do I have the right to tell my brothers that they must lay down their lives too?

Yet surely God's House must be defended so that it will continue to reflect His glory. Should we leave, these murderers would no doubt burn the place.'

Berenger felt the keen pressure of anticipation, dreading the answer even as he asked, 'What do you want us to do?'

The first task was to assess the men who remained in the abbey. There were some sixty, all told. Berenger eyed them without comment. Then: 'This is all?'

'We are a religious house, not a castle,' the Abbot responded with asperity.

Berenger walked past the Abbot and stared at a short, bald man. 'How old are you?'

Gums devoid of teeth were displayed as his mouth opened. 'Me? Seven-and-sixty last summer.'

'And you reckon men such as this can hold a sword?' Berenger demanded of the Abbot.

'I can hold one as well as a brat of twenty,' the old man said grimly. 'I've been the blacksmith here for nigh-on thirty years. You show me a child who can use a twelve-pound hammer all day and I'll show you a lad who can equal me.'

Berenger lifted an eyebrow. He was not convinced. The problem was, the majority of the lay-brothers here were incapable of holding a weapon. They were less afflicted with issues of the morality of hurting their fellow men, and more with an inability to hold a weapon and point it in the right direction.

'Very well,' he said. He had collected some lengths of lath, and now he passed these to each of the men. He took one himself and stood near a strong fellow with no neck and legs as thick as his own waist. 'Attack me!'

The man smiled nervously, wetted his lips, and then drew his arm back to strike Berenger. Before his stick had fallen, Berenger had hit him thrice, and then whirled and smacked him across the back with two more blows.

'Abbot,' he said later, when he and the Abbot were sitting at a table with a cup of wine each. 'The trouble is, these men are incapable of fighting. You have raised them to be incompetent in such matters.'

'My son, I appreciate that. You will have to help teach them.'

'My Lord Abbot, with the best will and intentions, I cannot. They will remain incompetent in battle. If I were to set them to defend your monastery, they would all die in the first charge.'

'Then what should I do?'

'If you wish for my advice, I would say you should evacuate this place, take all your people and all your valuables, and escape. You cannot hope to hold it against men such as the routiers which Will leads. You and they must perish.'

'God will not desert us.'

'Abbot, I've fought in many battles, and in each and every one of them, the Lord God has been adjured from both sides to help them. Only one side has ever won, and if nothing else, I have learned that He has better sense than to serve the interests of men who decide to battle for their own interests.'

'This is a different matter. We have a monastery dedicated to His service. It must succeed. He will guard us.'

Berenger stared about him. If they were to leave now, it was possible they would be found on the road, and if that were to happen, they would be slaughtered. 'Well, if you're sure. First, send someone to find help. Second, we have to build defences. Ideally we will have to create areas that appeal to the mercenaries, and into which we may funnel them, so that we can kill them more easily. Third, we must teach your men how easy it is to kill another man, and try to shape them into a force. How long do we have?'

215

'They could be here at any moment. If Father Jean could reach us, they could be hard on his heels.'

'Not so. They will drink themselves stupid first. So, that means we have at least a few days. We must find help from somewhere and . . .'

The cries from the gatehouse made him turn and then begin to run, drawing his sword as he went, convinced that Will and his men had already arrived.

As he reached the gate, he saw it open wide, and there, in the open passage, tottering in slowly, was Denisot. He saw Berenger and held out a hand before falling to his knees in exhaustion, Ethor at his side trying to help him up.

'Thank God,' Denisot said in a broken voice.

CHAPTER TWENTY

'It was terrible,' Denisot explained when they were sitting at a table and the Abbot had placed a large jug of wine before them. 'I could not describe it all.'

'What happened?' the Abbot asked.

They were sitting in his chamber at his great table. Denisot and Ethor were side by side at their bench, while Abbot Andry was seated at the head. Berenger had the other side with Fulk, whom Berenger had grown to trust even more in recent weeks.

'It was the mercenaries. They must have come to the town at about noon. We should have been there. Ethor and I had been down on the road south and east, where some soldiers had murdered a family and burned their house. It is growing all too common now, I fear,' he added sadly.

'What then?' the Abbot asked.

'We conducted an inquiry around the burned house, and then set off homewards. It was late, and in the end we stopped and rested many times. The cart with the bodies was so heavy, we could not push it all afternoon. You do understand that? So it was in the late afternoon when we saw smoke rising ahead and realised the town was on fire.'

'We hurried,' Ethor said. He had lost his ruddy complexion now, and was almost grey-faced. 'As soon as we came to the place, we saw bodies littering the streets. Men, women, boys, girls. They didn't even leave the dogs or cats in peace. Everything they could kill was left there dead. Everything.'

When he stopped and put his face in his hands, it was strangely unsettling. Berenger felt as though his heart was welling with sympathy. He didn't know this man, but to see such a large fellow brought so low by the sights he had seen was oddly affecting, especially since he could imagine those sights so clearly. For a moment he was struck with a desire to put an arm about this fellow, but he restrained himself. He had himself caused so many deaths after attacks, it would be the height of hypocrisy to offer sympathy to this man now.

Yet he felt Ethor's pain like a blow. Berenger thought back to the cities and towns which he had helped despoil. There were so many, it was hard to recall their number, let alone how many citizens had been slaughtered and robbed within the town walls. He felt a quickening shame at the thought that he had helped create such misery.

Denisot continued, 'When we went to my own house, there was nothing there. My maid, Suzette, was dead. She had been raped in front of the house, and left to die after someone stabbed her in the breast. My wife . . . well, I don't know where my wife is,' Denisot admitted.

His face told of his anguish.

When he saw Suzette sprawled where the men had held her down, her face blue in death, tiny explosions of blood in her eyes, Denisot had crouched at her side and wept, mourning for the pretty little maid who had been so vivacious and attractive. He

218

had remained there, crying for his pretty Suzette, before lurching up and rushing into his house, searching with ever increasing desperation. Gaillarde was not there, nor in the garden, nor yet out in the little shed in the field where his cow lay dead. She was his wife, his responsibility, his ward, his love. He should have guarded her, he should have *been* there!

The horror was reserved not only for his own house.

There were many other scenes in his mind that he could not mention. The sight of Pathau in his wine shop, tied to his counter top, his breast torn apart by the blows of some great edged weapon, and the children of his neighbours lying in the streets, their throats cut. There was a great accumulation of men and women in the square, the two sexes separated. While the men were poleaxed, the women were forced to suffer all the indignities of women through the ages before also being killed. Bodies everywhere; buildings burned to the ground, their contents rifled and stolen.

He shook his head. 'All was destroyed.'

Berenger shook his head with dull incomprehension. 'This was not the idea. We were only to take Uzerche and hold it. We wanted some peace from the wars, and we were to take the town and demand tolls from all those who passed along the roads. That was all.'

'Where a man takes the power to himself to take over a town, he will often find it easier to kill than to relinquish his power,' the Abbot said.

'Where a man takes over a company, he may yet find that there are some who will fight rather than submit,' Berenger said. 'Denisot, of all the men of the village, some must have escaped. We need all the able fellows we can find here to protect the monastery. They will come. Will is fully aware that monasteries hold gold and silver in great quantities. We need the means to defend this place. Can you find them?'

'I could try,' Denisot said. 'But there are not many. The mercenaries managed to kill almost all the men. We saw all my neighbours dead in the street.'

'The only alternative is to find others from about here,' Berenger said. He looked at the Abbot. 'Can we call up all the strong fellows from your demesne? We need everyone who can handle a sword or an axe.'

'We have some few, but not enough who have experience in such warfare.'

'I'll find them somehow,' Berenger said, half to himself.

Saturday 13 August

'They come! They come!'

The terrified shriek, along with the tolling of the church's great bell, had Berenger leaping from his palliasse, pulling his chemise over his bare chest, then slipping into a pair of thick hosen and tying their laces. He stepped into his boots and laced them too, before grabbing his sword sheath and hurrying out to the main gate.

There were sixteen men there, a ragtag of scruffy men clad in cheap mail and some armour. They were travel-stained, and there were oil and rust marks on their surcoats and tunics. From the weapons gripped in their fists, he could see that they were experienced fighters, and he was about to increase his speed, when he faltered and stumbled to a halt, his face falling.

He knew two of those faces even from many tens of yards away. If not the face, he could not mistake the immense belly on the glowering fellow in front. He had to stop and gape, and then, seeing another man's face turn towards him, Berenger gave a roar and pelted towards the men.

'*Grandarse*, you old *git*! Never have I been so happy to see a man in all my life!'

'Aye, well, you young tarse fiddler, get your great mitts off me, man! What, do I look like a bloody cock-quaen to ye?'

But for all his coarse welcome, there was no doubting the sincerity in Grandarse's welcome. As Berenger threw out his arms, Grandarse gave a twisted grin, then grabbed Berenger and enfolded him in a bear hug.

Berenger pulled away and then, his face still wreathed in smiles, welcomed the others. 'John of Essex, as I live and breathe! It's good to see you! And you have a vintaine with you? How many are archers? Are there any of the old vintaine with you?'

Grandarse shook his head. 'This is the new batch. The old ones, some of them, are here. They hope for honour, glory, and as much wine as they can drink! Clip and Dogbreath are here, but I sent them back with the men we captured on the ride here. That's how we heard of you, Frip. Eh, but it was a hard ride. A man could die of thirst after a ride like that!'

'If you will help defend this place, you will have as much wine as you can drink,' Berenger said, leading them towards the frater.

Grandarse eyed him keenly. 'What do you do in this place?'

'I was injured, and the good Abbot allowed me to recover here,' Berenger said, but he would not say more before the new-comers had been fed and given ale and wine. Then, while they ate, Grandarse told him of the party of routiers they had found some miles to the south of Uzerche, and how that gave him and his men the direction they could take to follow Berenger. When they were finished, Berenger spoke of his own story: how he had remained in Calais until the pestilence, the deaths of his wife and family, and how he had joined a company of mercenaries who set

221

off to fight wherever they would be paid, and if they weren't, to pillage across France.

'You? Ye turned mercenary?' Grandarse said with some disbelief, but then a broad grin passed over his face. 'Aye, well, I never doubted you'd see sense in the end.'

Gaillarde stumbled on, one shoe already gone, the soft leather torn away. Her light shoes weren't made for long marches, and she could feel how the sole of her foot was tender already. When she put it down on the dry earth, it felt like she was stepping onto brambles. Each step was agony, but the agony was dissipated by its constant repetition. It felt as though her mere existence was itself grown to be a torment. Nothing else existed but the action of placing one foot before the other.

A prod in her buttock urged her on to greater speed, and she acquiesced without complaint. She had seen what happened to others who had argued, who had complained, or who had wept bitter tears. All were dead. The last was a woman of two-and-twenty, who had limped and wept after seeing her husband beaten to death while trying to protect and conceal their child. When he was dead and his body rolled over, the mercenaries saw the child. Three of them played campball with the baby, kicking it from one side of the square to the other while the woman screamed and screamed in horror until her voice was gone. Two of the guards raped her then, and afterwards more, but she never spoke a word. Her eyes were already dead by then. Gaillarde could see her clearly. She breathed, and her body functioned, but her heart was dead within her. It was a terrible sight.

So Gaillarde trudged on, heedless of the direction, not caring where they were going, but determined not to die.

Not yet.

*

It was only a little later, once Berenger had persuaded the doubtful porter and Abbot that these men were safe enough to be permitted into the monastery, that he could stand leaning at the walls, sipping at a cup of wine while Grandarse and Hawkwood drank with gusto.

'Aye, but that's good wine!' Grandarse said, smacking his lips and smiling beatifically at the sight before him.

He had already split his men into two groups. Half were to return to the English army with their spoils, while Grandarse and Hawkwood had decided to take their ease for a few days. The men were unloading the horses and ponies now. There were several large bags on three packhorses that rattled very interestingly, and Hawkwood caught Berenger's eye when two men lifted weighty strongboxes from a donkey.

'We've had a successful rampage,' he said with a smile. 'We are scouting for the King. In fact, we serve under your old master, Frip. Sir John de Sully is with the army.'

'What army?'

'Christ's bones, man, have you been sleeping all year?' Grandarse said. He belched and wiped his mouth with a delicate thumb and forefinger. 'Last year the King was determined to see the French brought to battle. They've been pulling at his beard for too long now, and he wanted to end things once and for all, not that he had any joy in it. The French refused battle at every opportunity. Even when he stood to and demanded satisfaction, King John held himself and his armies away. This year, Lancaster took the battle to Normandy, thinking to force the French to fight, but they didn't. So now we're down here to force the French to fight once and for all. The King wants his French crown, the men want his money and his treasure, and the women want his silks and furs. There's something here for everyone, aye,' he said, and held his empty mazer to be refilled.

'We have been able to stock our stores in the last couple of days,' Hawkwood said. He was quiet a moment, and then added, 'It is good to see you again, Frip. I heard about your wife. I was sorry about that. We all liked her.'

'We all know of people who lost wives, brothers, friends. It was hard, but many had it worse,' Berenger said. He knew he was lying even as he spoke.

'Perhaps,' Hawkwood said. Neither believed it.

'Have you been to a convent a little to the south?' Berenger asked.

'Not a nunnery, if that's what you mean. Is there a rich one nearby, then? We wouldn't mind going and seeing a parcel of naughty nuns if there are some down here.'

Berenger looked around him at the convent and felt an acid bitterness in his stomach. He knew what the outcome would be, were a vintaine to go to a nunnery. He had seen such scenes before. Yet Grandarse would not lie about the places he had been to, nor the atrocities committed, so it had not been he and John with their men who had so devastated that place. Someone else had been there: no doubt it was Will and his men.

'Aye, we've visited a few other places, mind, and persuaded the inhabitants to support us,' Grandarse said, sucking down another long draught of wine. 'On the way here we found a parcel of men. I had them taken back to Sir John. We could do with the extra hands.'

'What sort of men were they?'

Grandarse cocked a shrewd eye. 'You know well enough, Frip. One of them told us you had been at some town with a strange name, and that your friends had decided to do without your leadership. That right?'

'Yes. They tried to ambush me once they had told me I was free. I will meet their leader again and make him pay for his deceit,' Berenger said.

'Aye, well, that will be good. And soon we'll be heading north with the rest of the army.'

'Sir John will be going too?'

'Aye. He was at Bordeaux with the Prince, but they moved to La Réole early in the month. They'll be marching now, I'd guess. They were waiting for reinforcements, but they must have arrived by now. They should be arriving around here any time now.'

'What then?'

'Then? Then we'll prepare for another grand chevauchée! There'll be rich pickings when we ride north. You should join us.'

'I would like to. But I would have this abbey left safe,' Berenger said.

'Aye, well, if you want to get your revenge on this man Will, you won't do it while bolted up inside an abbey, unless he comes to attack you here. And if he does that, you'll be wishing you had a better force to defend the place.'

'They'll have to fight past me. The good Abbot and his monks have been kind to me. I won't see them slaughtered.'

'As they should be to an English archer,' Grandarse said. He cast an eye about the place. 'Little enough, you say?'

'Grandarse, I would not want to fall out with you over a small abbey. This is too small to tempt even you.'

'If you're sure,' Grandarse said.

CHAPTER TWENTY-ONE

Sunday 14 August

'Frip, come with us. We need to exercise the beasts,' Grandarse said soon after they rose. 'Besides, we should ride and check the area. We don't want your old company suddenly springing up and surprising us.'

Berenger was nothing loath. He had been inside the monastery since arriving, and he had a keen desire to see outside the grounds again. With Grandarse and two archers, he set off, trotting briskly along the road that led west. It had been decided that, in their absence, Hawkwood would take charge of the men left behind at the abbey.

'Guard them well,' Grandarse said. 'Fripper's friends are away to the south and west. We will ride south and then scout. I expect it will take two days. Keep a close guard on the roads.'

'We will,' Hawkwood said. 'They'll be as safe with me as my own wife.'

Berenger gave him a long stare. 'Your wife? Would she be safe with you?'

'Well, I wouldn't see her harmed by anyone else.'

Berenger shook his head as he walked away and mounted the horse held by a groom. 'You are an unrepentant bastard, aren't you?'

'Me?' Hawkwood said with mock innocence.

Berenger chuckled as he rode out through the gatehouse.

Once, he turned and stared back at the buildings rising from among the trees, but then he shook off the feeling of slight anxiety and set himself to enjoying the ride.

The sun flared and died as clouds passed overhead, but Berenger was enjoying the feeling of the wind in his face and hair, and the comfort of being with an old friend. They had ridden a mile, and he could feel his mount starting to ease up. It was a palfrey with a spirit to match Berenger's today, and Berenger glanced about him with a sudden feeling that he was as young as a lad not yet twenty. He felt impudent and it was a feeling that thrilled him and made him feel mischievous all at once.

Suddenly he clapped spurs to his beast's flanks and felt the palfrey surge forward like a greyhound seeing a hare. *'Hah! Hah!'* he shouted, lashing the brute's buttocks and bending low.

He heard Grandarse bellowing behind him, and snatched a glance over his shoulder. From that he saw the centener impotently flailing with his reins to try to persuade his mount to hurry, but all to no avail. Berenger grinned and urged his palfrey on.

Flies hit his face like tiny pellets, and he swallowed one, hawking and spitting several times to expel it. It felt as though the creature was stuck in his throat. A corner in the road and a low branch almost unseated him, but he managed to duck lower, laughing and shouting with pure pleasure, and missed it.

227

He had been riding for another mile when he came to a small hamlet in a clearing. A pair of carts and three resting horses spoke of an inn nearby, and he reined in. The beast was content to take a rest, and they soon slowed to an easy trot and then a walk as Berenger took in the sight of the little inn. It was a simple thatched house with two tables and a pair of benches. Nearby there was a ring set into the wall, and Berenger slid from the saddle and hitched the palfrey to it before taking his seat at the bench, looking at the other travellers.

They seemed intimidated by him, and he realised that all three were considerably younger. None had a scar on their faces like his. He touched the old wound unthinkingly. He had won that in the north of England, defending Durham from Scottish invaders, and he had nearly died from it. The wound had healed, but the handiwork of the old tooth-butcher who had doubled as a surgeon on that campaign had left much to be desired. He had not thought of it in a long while. When he was running his little inn at Calais, people knew him and, besides, most of them were old soldiers like him. His face was no surprise to them.

'In Christ's name, Fripper!'

'You made it, then, Grandarse,' Berenger said.

'No thanks to you, you old git.'

Berenger grinned and the men ordered wine. Berenger asked for a pitcher of water from the well. Grandarse watched as he added it to his cup of wine. 'You need to be careful of the water,' he said.

'I find it is good for me,' Berenger said. 'I have drunk enough wine in my time already.'

'Aye, well, I think it's impossible for a man to have had a surfeit of wine, no matter what,' Grandarse said, and tipped his cup into his mouth.

'It is good to see you again, old friend.'

'I am glad to find you,' Grandarse said. 'We have need of all the fighters we can get.'

'Not me, though.'

'Come, Frip, you can't mean it when you say that you'll avoid a fight?'

'I mean to take the tonsure and spend the rest of my days here contemplating all the things I did before. I may even pray for you, Grandarse.'

'Don't waste your breath,' Grandarse said with a chuckle. 'You two, fuck off and leave us to talk.'

Berenger waited until the two archers had picked up their drinks and walked away to the next table. 'What is the route?'

'Far as I understand it, the idea is to go north from here and seek out the French if we can. We want to force him to fight us. But it won't be easy. He seems to enjoy offering battle and then waiting until we get bored or run out of food and drink and have to move off. He did that last year, and I think he avoided battle with my Lord Lancaster earlier this year in a shameful manner. But hopefully we will tweak his tail so badly that he will want to fight us, no matter what his reservations.'

'His father was less than accommodating.'

'His father was brighter. I've heard much about King John. He is not a calculating, rational man. He responds, and often badly. It makes him enemies more easily than friends. We can use that. And I can use you.'

'I don't want to fight any more. My intention is to join a little monastery. I was badly injured again only three weeks ago, and it's taken this long for me to heal. If it wasn't for the help I had from the monks, I'd be dead by now. I owe them.'

'You owe your King, Fripper.'

Berenger's voice hardened. 'I think I've repaid any debts of service long ago. I have the wounds and scars to prove it.'

'Stay with us, Frip. It would be good to have you in my retinue again. You were always one of the first to the front. You want me to beg you? You wouldn't believe the incompetents and tarse-fiddlers I've got in the vintaine!' He shuddered. 'I need a man like you who can knock them into shape.'

'I can't,' Berenger said. He felt something then: a slight shiver of anticipation in his blood at the thought of holding a sword and burying it in another man's breast. 'No! If I fight again, I think I will become a monster. I cannot do it. I had retired to Calais, you remember, and had given up all thoughts of fighting.'

'Aye. I recall. It was a good little tavern you had there. But when I was last there, your tavern was closed. They said you were gone.'

'My wife and our boys died there. They are buried in a plague-pit along with the others who died. That made me mad. I hated everything to do with France and the French. I've been running with a band of routiers for the last years and . . . I've had enough of death and killing, Grandarse. I cannot go back to that. If I do, I think I will lose my soul. I already have a lot to atone for. The monastery gives me an opportunity to make some restitution for all I've done. If I go there and spend the rest of my life in prayer, I will achieve something good from my life.'

'You could come back as a vintener, if you want. I'd even put you in with my best men.'

'Even for that, I think no. It's not plunder I want. It's my soul. I have to find it again, and I think I have seen how to.'

'Aye well, then, Frip, I'm sorry about that, but I won't hold it against you. I'll take the men and leave in a couple of days. We'll return to Sir John and the others. Make sure you keep away from the line of march of the English. If you hear them coming this way, forget the abbey. Just ride. Before I go, is there anything you need?'

Berenger gave a dry grin. 'I'd be glad of a bow and a sheaf of arrows.'

'I suppose I can afford one stave and a sheaf. Make sure you use them wisely, though,' Grandarse said. He smiled. 'I just hope you can find some peace, Fripper, if that's what you want. Me, I have to keep fighting. It's the only way I know I'm still alive. I sometimes think that, were I to stop fighting, I would die of boredom.'

'There's no risk of that,' Berenger said.

Archibald felt the wagon lurch and heard the crack as the massive weight of the cannon rolled over on the bed. He glanced behind him at 'The Wolf' as it moved, and muttered a curse to himself. 'Ed! You didn't bind the gonne!'

Ed was up on the bed of the wagon in an instant, glowering to himself as he lashed the massive barrel again. Archibald watched his efforts with a nod of approval as Ed gave the rope a last turn, tugged it tight, patted the gonne gently as if it was a rounsey that needed soothing, and then sprang down and trotted to his cart, where he knelt on the boards and took the reins Béatrice passed to him.

Archibald blamed himself. He called to the boy in front who prodded the oxen with a goad, the traces creaking with the strain as the huge beasts lumbered into action.

They had already covered some miles, and now the Prince's host was beginning the action that would set the stage for the chevauchée to come.

Archibald had a simple view of the world. He knew that wars would happen whether he willed it or not. Men would kill each other to enrich themselves, and every time someone went to kill a neighbour, whether he be a peasant or a Lord, that act would bring with it the seeds of another killing, this time in revenge.

231

Life, it sometimes seemed to him, was an unending circle of murders and mayhem.

It had all culminated for him in the battle at Crécy ten years before, when the French army was not merely defeated, but was crushed like a beetle in a mailed fist. The pride of France, her glory, her chivalry, were all slaughtered in a blood-soaked patch of grass in Flanders. So many nobles died, it was hard to count their arms.

Archibald had been there. His gonnes had done their bit to add to the horror. His stone balls had scythed through the cavalry and footmen like the Devil's own playthings. After the smoke had cleared, the gouts of flame subsided, he could see rents torn in the French lines where only blood and bones remained. All the men were destroyed.

That was the purpose of his gonnes. To deal death on a massive scale. It was ironic, for a man who had spent his youth in a monastery, but he was content. His toys were there to bring about the end of wars. He firmly believed in that: his serpentine powder could bring about a peace sooner than any number of swords or lances. By destroying the armies of his King's enemies, he could force the parties to stop their feuding. And since the swords and lances were wielded by bold knights and men-at-arms against the innocent peasants, bringing the terror of war to an end sooner was appealing. His gonnes would be able to save lives by causing such catastrophic losses to the French that the war would end sooner with their submission. There was no pleasure in killing, but if it led to a swifter resolution, he was content.

Later, as the sun rose higher in the sky, he saw the shape of the Prince and his household knights ahead. The men who were the Prince's best, most loyal servants were all there, on a little knoll, peering back at the army. Prince Edward often took up a position like this, from where he could survey the long columns of men. Except now his host was changing its deployment. The men were being ordered into new groupings. Rather than a long snake that travelled over the ground trampling a narrow channel, the host was forming a new front. Knights and squires took their servants and archers and extended east and west, short gaps appearing between each, then filling with more men. It took the rest of the morning and into the afternoon for the column to form up into one long line of steel and death.

Archibald climbed down from his board and rubbed the back of one of his oxen while it contentedly chewed the cud. 'Aye,' he said. 'It's a good day for a war.'

Ed was lying back on the grass, while Béatrice stood at the cart's side. She nodded towards the front of the army where the Prince and his entourage stood still. 'Do you think this will be the last?'

Archibald scratched at his balls and yawned. 'No. There will always be a need for another one. Doesn't matter how much we take from the French, they'll always demand it back, and then we'll fight for it again, ceaselessly. It's the way of the rich, woman.'

'It is foolish.'

'So it is. So are men!' he chuckled. 'But men like to fight.'

'I don't think I want to live in France any more.' Her eyes had lost the vicious delight that they had once held at the sight of dead Frenchmen. Her rage had dissipated over the last ten years. She looked at him as Archibald yawned again. 'Rest, Master. You are tired.'

'Aye, I am at that.'

She watched him amble to the wagon and lie down beside his great gonne, tugging a sheet of canvas over him to keep the wind off. He put his arms behind his head and closed his eyes, a picture of comfort and ease.

He could throw off the pressure of his work in a moment.

Béatrice had often felt jealousy rising in her breast, watching him as he relaxed. For her there could be no rest. She had lost her parents, her brother, her family and her friends when her father had been accused of treason and executed. At first she had learned rage and hatred, but gradually her fury had turned to deep sadness. France, poor France, was a tidbit being fought over by two fierce raches or mastiffs. France herself was the victim. Béatrice often felt that with the two rulers snarling and growling at each other, soon there would be little enough of France for either to swallow.

There came a brazen blast of horns. She looked back towards the Prince and his men. Suddenly she saw what was happening. 'Master Gynour, Archibald! Look!'

Archibald sat up, grumbling, and followed the direction of her pointing finger. The Prince's standard-bearer was carefully unwrapping the leather covering to the flag. The flag's staff was shaken to help it unfurl, and then the bearer waved it back and forth so that the vivid colours blazed in the sunlight.

'Aye, well, that's it, then. He's shown his flag like a good warrior should,' Archibald said. He rose and clambered back onto the board, taking up the whip once more. 'He's unfurled the banner of war. Let the killing begin.'

Thomas de Ladit watched the flag in the wind and felt a momentary sadness.

He was not French. His loyalty was owed solely to his master, the King of Navarre, yet he had travelled extensively the length and breadth of France and he was loath to see it destroyed. The rich vineyards, cornfields, and woods and forests that lay in the path of this army would be laid waste, he knew. It was a hideous thought, but there was also the hope that perhaps this fight could see his master released. Navarre's freedom could be one aspect of the English demands. It was possible, and then he could hopefully return to Pamplona with his King and never come back. That would make the devastation worthwhile.

For now, the English had been generous. Perhaps the stern knight with the astute mind had not told the Prince commanding this army about their conversation. Thomas had been indiscreet, certainly, mentioning that Navarre never negotiated in good faith with them, but what else would the English expect? His claim to the throne of France was at least as good as Edward's.

But now there were rumours of the French massing a great army to destroy the English, and Thomas was to be employed as a special adviser to the English. It meant he was here, not in a gaol, which was a great improvement on what he had expected, but it did mean that he was arrayed with an army that stood to assault the French King.

The good-quality food and drink may not compensate for his punishment, if he was captured by the French. Of that he felt sure.

There was a shout from the archers practising at the butts and Hawkwood grunted.

It was fine for Grandarse to hurtle off across the country for a relaxing ride with Fripper, but there was still work to be done down here. Hard work: teaching lay-brothers and some feeble old men which end of a sword they should hold. Not that it was much use. The old fools were so decrepit, they could none of them move a sword quickly enough to block or parry, and even if they could, the idea of then striking a killing blow was alien to most of them. There were some few young fellows who were only recently brought into the monastery and who might make a good showing, but for the most part they were a mixture of the old, infirm and incompetent.

He heard another shout and closed his eyes. The thought of going and witnessing the carnage being done to the grass was too depressing. In preference he returned to watch the men practising with swords and spears. There were some there who were half-capable under the expert tuition of Fulk and Saul, but they still lacked the necessary muscle and determination in his opinion.

Hawkwood swore under his breath. 'All right! I'm coming!'

It wasn't enough that he must try to bring the men at the sword school into some kind of order, but he had to join in with training the archers too. Since Grandarse had sent eight men back, and now he and Frip had taken two men with them, Hawkwood was left with a scant four men to teach the abbey workers how to fight. The others did their best, but the fact of being an archer did not make a man competent to teach others in how to use a bow. It was hard enough, Hawkwood knew, even for a vintener.

He reached the butts in time to see the man at the farther edge of the field pointing urgently.

'Shit!'

The man suddenly jerked and fell, thrown back by the hail of arrows that lanced into his breast. A boy near him began to run back, screaming and waving his arms, but he was soon cut down by the first of the men who appeared, all mounted on sturdy little ponies. Some stopped and dismounted in the formations that he knew so well, leisurely nocking arrows and sending them forward.

'Back!' Hawkwood shouted, waving frantically. 'Back to the walls! Quick!'

Shouting became screaming, and he turned with a scowl to

see horsemen jumping the wall at the back of the abbey, riding on and cutting down three of his trainee archers.

'To arms! To arms!' he bellowed, grabbing at his sword and running towards the threat.

CHAPTER TWENTY-TWO

Grandarse had insisted on sharing another jug of wine before he would leave.

They were at a small village, where a jovial, if wary, inn-keeper had presented them with a good-quality wine. Their ride had taken them south and east in a great loop, but they had dis-covered no sign of a force of men approaching the convent.

By mid-morning they were back on their horses and riding southwards, further away from the abbey, to make a wide sweep and scout for Will and his men. Berenger rode with his eyes watching the horizon before them. From his experience, the first sign of Will would be the rising columns of smoke from build-ings that had been torched.

'So you will turn your face against all the pleasures of life, eh?' Grandarse said.

'Eh? Oh, I can forego the pleasures you think of,' Berenger said. 'But surely you cannot enjoy most now? You've drunk so much wine, cider and ale that your nose is the size and colour of a ripe plum! Surely there can be little joy in drinking even more. You've eaten and drunk your way across the world, haven't you? With your belly that big, you can't see your prick when you're trying to poke a wench, and if you could, how many women will dare lie under you? You'd flatten almost any woman.'

'It's not being flattened they need fear,' Grandarse said complacently.

Berenger laughed. 'It's been good to see you again, old friend.'

'Aye, well, I daresay we can return down this road one day to see how you are, although I would prefer to see you still in Calais. That was a suitable berth for a retired warrior: and a convenient post for a man like me when I had to come to this land.'

'That decides me! I couldn't stay in business if you were to visit too often,' Berenger said with forced amusement. He still could not think of that little house without remembering his wife and the boys.

They rested that night at a barn some miles south and east of the abbey.

'Will ye not miss the life?' Grandarse demanded while they sat about a meagre fire, staring at the flames. Their two companions were silent. Whenever one tried to speak, Grandarse glared until they closed their mouths.

Berenger looked up at the roof with missing thatch, over to the broken door, the thick hay that would be his bed for the night, and thought of a clean sheet on a large palliasse and his woman at his side, warm and eager, and shook his head. 'No. I miss other things.'

'Ach, there's no satisfying some people,' Grandarse said.

Later, when Grandarse was already snoring fit to rock Notre Dame to the foundations, Berenger lay back staring at the stars through a gap in the roof. *Would he miss the life?* he wondered. A life of hardship and brutality.

No, he was sure in his own mind that leaving the battles to others would be for the best.

Monday 15 August

Berenger and Grandarse had ridden eastwards, looking for any signs of a large party of men, but there was nothing apparent. Only once, when they found a ford over a small river, there was a great deal of mess at the entrance and exit.

'What do you think?' Grandarse asked. He halted with the two archers some distance from the stream so that they would not spoil the tracks.

Berenger squatted at the river's edge. 'Some men passed here, but there is little way to tell how many. They were all riding in each other's tracks, and here the ground is wet enough that each subsequent hoof overlapped and concealed the ones before.' He rose and stared towards the north with a frown. 'If it was Will, he will have missed the abbey if he kept on in that direction. Perhaps he rode past.'

'Aye, well, let's hope so,' Grandarse said.

They were nearly at the abbey now. They had bickered and disputed all the way from their overnight rest place, and now they passed around a hill.

'Aye, well, it's good that you would be prepared and happy to tolerate an old git coming to ...' Grandarse was suddenly still. As they turned the last bend in the road, all four men saw the devastation.

'No! In God's name, *no!*' Berenger said, and then whipped and spurred his beast to a gallop.

He reined in at the gatehouse. The gates were left wide, and the porter's body lay a little way inside, his head on the ground nearby. Berenger let his horse amble on. The bodies of lay-brothers and the religious lay scattered all about. He had his mount pause, and he stood up in the stirrups to stare about him, looking for John Hawkwood and the others, for the Abbot, for Denisot, but he could see no sign of them.

'So, the fuckers got here, eh, Frip?' Grandarse said as he came through the gates. 'Eh, but the buggers could have had us too, if we hadn't made it off to scout about. Damn my arse, this is shit!' He looked about him with the wariness of long experience. 'Where are they, then, Frip? Eh? Where'd the bastards go?'

Berenger was already on the ground. He had seen a familiar figure near the Abbot's chambers and he ran as fast as he could to the body on the ground. There was clearly no urgency.

The Abbot's head had been crushed by a mace. The side of his skull was broken and blood, brains and splinters of bone were thrown all over his shoulder.

'I'm so sorry,' Berenger said, kneeling at his side. The Abbot's left eyeball was on the ground, like a spat cherry pip, and the good eye stared at Berenger. It seemed to hold a lifetime of accusation in that unblinking stare and Berenger felt as though his heart was going to break.

He bent his head and began to weep.

The abbey grounds had been trampled to a muddy mess. Grandarse bellowed to the two archers to go and search the undercrofts for supplies, anything that might have been left behind, before joining Berenger to study the wreckage.

The orchard where Berenger had walked with the Abbot had been cut down and many trees burned, but the devastation inside was much worse. In the cloisters all the writing tables had been broken to pieces. Inks and valuable books were spilled and scattered. Leaves from the books drifted in the wind, their gold lettering and bright-blue pigments standing out hopefully when the sun caught them.

Berenger walked about the place with anger in his heart, filled with hatred for what the men had done here. Grandarse kept a yard or two away, and held his tongue. He could sense Berenger's increasing rage.

There was no reason to kill monks. Will and his men had killed them purely because they *could*. They had as little compunction as a fox finding itself inside a hen house. While the creatures fluttered, the fox would slaughter. This was the same. A man with a sword in his hand feels stronger than others purely because he wields the power of life and death. But it was an illusory power. Men could kill, but none could create without a woman. Not for the first time Berenger wondered why men were the dominant sex. God should have created woman first and given her authority, because then fewer people would die in pointless savagery like this.

He entered the church to pray, but stood in the doorway and stared. It felt as though God had left this place.

The altar had been broken, and all the ornaments of their faith had been taken, before all the woodwork had been broken and a small fire started with the pieces. Luckily they had clearly found the Abbot's wine stores and lost interest in the church after that, for else the ceilings must have been burned away. As it was, the timbers were blackened, the white-painted backgrounds and paintings scorched and ruined.

He genuflected, and was about to leave when a glitter caught his eye. He stooped to the fire and found in among the ashes a small crucifix of iron on a rosary of dark wooden beads. It was the one he had seen the Infirmarer wearing. Small and perfectly formed, it was a lovely work of art, and the figure of Christ was gilded, he saw. Someone must have found it on the Infirmarer and stolen it thinking it was gold, only to throw it away when he discovered it was merely gilded iron. He picked it up and walked outside, rubbing the soot and dirt from it as he went.

Outside, Grandarse stood gazing about him with an appraising stare. He had fetched his horse and now gripped the reins as he eyed Berenger. 'Your lot, you think?'

'I expect so.'

'Do they normally collect slaves?'

'No, why?'

'As far as I can see there's no sign of Hawkwood or the others.'

Berenger slipped the rosary and crucifix over his neck as he looked around. Grandarse was right. There were many lay-brothers, but there was not one body of the men who had come with Hawkwood. 'Where have they gone?'

'I'd guess they either disappeared quickly when they saw the odds, or ...'

Grandarse stopped suddenly, his face registering his suspicion. Berenger coldly finished his words for him.

'Or they joined with the mercenaries.'

Gaillarde was grateful at least that she hadn't been offered to other men.

She walked with the stiff gait of the exhausted, her wrists chafed and bloody where the thongs binding her had rubbed. In the last days she had walked farther than in the last year. Her feet were worn. Both shoes were gone now, and if it were not for the help that one of the marching wives had given her, she must have fallen by the wayside. If that were to happen, Gaillarde knew what they were likely to do to her. She would be stabbed and hurled into a ditch.

'Try this, dame.'

She was an unprepossessing slut, this, with raven hair that hung bedraggled half over her face, but she was kind enough. She smeared thick pork fat over two pieces of rag and tied them over Gaillarde's feet, and then wrapped long strips over and about her feet and up her ankles, before pushing a pair of thick-soled sandals towards her. 'Put these on as well. The fat will help your feet heal, with luck.'

Gaillarde had hardly the energy to thank her. This was all a nightmare. As they rose in the morning, she hobbled about like a crone, her legs and back complaining against the exercise. She was only glad that so far only one man had raped her. She wouldn't think about that, though. It was too horrible for words. The bruising, the pain, the vicious speed, his almost embarrassed departure, leaving her without dignity or honour, her legs still spread as she wept. She had never felt so demeaned, so irrelevant. She was nothing more than an object. A chattel to be used and discarded when no longer desired. A *thing*. Even in the worst months of her marriage, when Denisot's and her love had turned sour, he had treated her with respect, if not affection. Good God, but she missed her husband! She would never raise her voice to him again, if she could return to him!

The man had returned to her on the second evening. That time he had brought her food. Some bread, a little cheese, some grapes. He watched her as she greedily stuffed it into her mouth, and he laughed when she could not swallow, the bread too dry in her parched throat. Luckily another woman passed her a leather bottle of water, and she drank it desperately, choking, brackish water spurting from her nose as the lump gradually shifted, feeling like a sharp stone that ripped at every inch of her gullet.

When it was finally gone, she choked but held back her tears, imagining how Denisot would have responded to her. He would have surely shown her some compassion. Alas for her, that he was not here now to protect her!

They had reached the grounds of a large religious institution the day before. At least that meant that she was allowed to sleep in the dry for once. She was given a space on the floor in a hall once she and the other women had pulled the dead out of the room, while the men from the company watched. There were many of them, the dead. All were monks or lay-brothers, and yet the mercenaries had stabbed and slashed at them even when they were already dead. There was no honour in these deaths. It was merely butchery for profit, for as soon as the last monk had been stabbed, the men of the company fell into an orgy of drinking, laughing and arguing about the spoils.

Later that night he had come to her again, but this time he didn't rape her. While she cowered and cringed from him, he shook his head and lay beside her. 'I don't want your body, woman. Just the chance to sleep.'

She had watched him through the dark hours. His nose and beard were shadows in the darkness. She could hear his whispering breath as he snored, ever so slightly. It was that which made her realise he was a little younger than she. When he caught her, she had thought he was older, with his thick, dark beard and glowering demeanour, but now, thinking about his roughness on their first night, and his laughter at her discomfort on the second, she began to realise that he was only young, and being immature, did not know how to behave. That was good, she thought. It gave her a slight feeling of superiority. Perhaps he would respond to her if she were careful in how she behaved around him. It may be possible to inspire his trust, perhaps even win his affection.

Gaillarde was not one to put off till tomorrow what she could achieve today. She had put out a hand to him and touched his beard, just lightly. In response, his eyes snapped open and he stared at her. She smiled, putting into it all the love and sympathy for another that she could.

His fist struck her high on the cheek and she fell away, lights whirling and spinning in the ceiling above her.

She no longer had any illusions about her value to this man. He was a brute. An animal. And when he was done with her, she would be lucky only to be killed. More than likely, she would be passed to another mercenary, or even a group of men.

With that thought she continued. But the rebellious part of her that was still independent swore that she would never let a gang rape her. She would take one of their knives first and kill any who came near until they were forced to kill her. She would not suffer the last indignity.

'So, where are they, then?' Grandarse wondered aloud.

Berenger shook his head and stared around them. 'If I had to guess, they wouldn't head south. They must have heard of the Prince and his army. Will wouldn't want to be caught by the Prince. He'd fear being forced to serve. There's less profit for a commander who is subordinate to a great captain. He'd want to move on ahead of the army and grab what he can. Yes, I'd expect them to ride north, before the vanguard of the army. They were going to remain in Uzerche, if I'd had my way – that was my intention, to charge tolls for the use of their bridge and some of the local roads – but the fact that they have moved off I think must mean that they are determined to make profit before the Prince can plunder all in his path.'

'A good enough plan,' Grandarse said grudgingly. 'What of Hawkwood and the others? Are they with this Will?'

'I don't know. There were so many horses and feet passing up this road, it's impossible to say who was with them. The company – it was surely my old one.' He licked dry lips. 'Shit!'

Grandarse was watching him. 'What's happened to you, Frip? You don't look like the man I left ten years ago.'

'I'm not the same man, Grandarse. I've changed, just as we all have,' Berenger said. There was a crawling, itching feeling under his skin, and he found himself stroking the crucifix. It seemed to take away the feeling of guilt that threatened. He had been the leader of this company. If enough of the men had demanded it, he would have been responsible for the carnage in the abbey grounds.

'Very good,' Grandarse said. 'Well, we can't hope to catch this lot now. Not with only four of us.'

'No,' Berenger agreed. It would be suicidal to attack over a hundred men. And yet ... 'It may pay us to follow their trail, though. We can see how they are camped, how professionally they behave. Perhaps catch a sentry and learn more. It may be possible to free their victims in the dark, or ...'

Grandarse glared at him and then gave a guffaw. He stopped, turned his head as if listening attentively. 'Hear that?'

'What?'

Grandarse lifted a leg and let out a blast that would have deafened a drunk gynour in the midst of a battle, laughing again. 'You are a moon-struck bastard, I'll give you that. Well, if there are two scouts who can take a man from the middle of a sleeping army, it's surely thee and me! That's the great thing about being light on your feet and quiet as a virgin crossing a roomful of randy priests! Ach, there never was a vintener like you, Frip, and there won't be again! This'll be fun. So long as these two puppies don't give us away,' he added, eyeing the archers with distaste.

Remounting his rounsey, Berenger smiled, but inwardly he felt sick. The itching in his hands was noticeably worse, and he had a conviction that if he didn't get a pot of wine soon, he would become weak and ill.

But he wouldn't just give up. If there was a possibility that Hawkwood and the others were still alive, he would do all he could to help them.

CHAPTER TWENTY-THREE

Tuesday 16 August

The four rode as fast as Grandarse's overburdened beast would allow, slowing as they approached clearings, searching the little hills and trees for any sign of sparkling armour or arrow-tips, and only edging out cautiously when they were as sure as they could be that it was safe to do so.

'By my ballocks, Frip. This is turning into a longer hunt than Arthur's for the Holy Grail,' Grandarse said at the end of the first day.

They were sitting in a small stand of trees. The horses were haltered to a rope lashed between two trees, and they were resting their backs against their saddles, the two archers a little distance away from Grandarse and Berenger as they talked quietly, wrapped in their blankets and chewing at dry husks of bread that crackled and crunched between their teeth like snail shells. Berenger had lit a small fire, and now he fed it with dried twigs he had picked from some conifers. The lower branches were dead and gave off little smoke.

'It's a longer ride than I had anticipated,' Berenger admitted. He sucked at a piece of bread stuck between his teeth meditatively. 'I had hoped to be with them by now.'

'We may have to give up if we don't find them soon. The army will be preparing, and I don't have time to be hunting for Hawkwood, damn his cods. I have four other vintaines of archers to command,' Grandarse said apologetically.

'I understand,' Fripper said. He spoke dully, his eyes fixed on the fire. It was a lunatic chase. The old centener was quite correct. They had no chance of finding the company; they didn't even know when the company had attacked the abbey, nor how long they had been travelling north.

From the look of the tracks the company had been hurrying, but there were plenty of people on foot. He had seen their boot prints. Not that this was any surprise. A King's Messenger would travel the same distance in a day, whether he was on a horse or on foot. A horse would cover shorter distances more quickly, but then would need to rest before continuing. A man on foot could keep on all day.

The fire flared. Berenger looked away, his sight blinded, and then had a thought.

During the day, seeing a mass of men through trees was next to impossible, but it was just possible that he might be able to see the light from campfires in the distance. If he saw it, he would know that the company was not many miles distant.

He stood and strode quickly to the edge of their little stand of trees.

'What is it, Frip?'

'Just an idea. If there are a hundred men, they'll have at least ten good-sized fires, won't they? Unless they've found a village or hamlet to take for the night, and have all their fires indoors, they'll make some light.'

He peered through the trees. There was nothing. The sky was clear of clouds, and there was no glow, while the landscape all the way through to where he thought the horizon lay was black. If there were a thousand men encamped out there, he had the feeling he would see nothing. The trees were so dense that even a bright fire would be concealed.

'No,' he said. 'There's ...'

And that was when he saw it. There must be a tiny chink between the tree trunks there, so that when he looked he could just catch a glimpse of light. He thought it was like a star among the trees, and when he moved his head fractionally, the pin-prick disappeared again. It was only in this one place, with his head just so, that the tiny flickering spark was visible.

'What is it, Frip?'

'I've found them.'

They decided to rest for the most part of the night. The sun was still only an imaginary lightening on the far horizon when Berenger kicked dust over the remains of their fire, and they saddled and remounted. It must have been the last hour before dawn, Berenger reckoned. He was sluggish with cold, exhaustion, and most of all the lack of wine. They rode along an earthen track among the trees where the soil deadened the sound of their hoofs, and then into a broad, open area. Here they found a small stream into which their mounts enthusiastically dipped their heads, and Berenger dropped from his horse to fill their water skins. It was cold as cruelty, but refreshing nonetheless, and Berenger felt some of the urgent desire for wine begin to fall away from him again.

He remounted, and they continued. The fires of the company would be dead by now. Although Berenger had always tried to enforce a rule that fires should be covered and sentinels set about any encampment, the men had often moaned and complained when they thought they were in safe territory. Now, he hoped, their laxness would prove useful. He set his rounsey's head in the direction where he thought he had seen the spark, and he and Grandarse made good time, walking briskly, keeping their eyes open for any rabbit holes or other dangers.

It was because he had his eyes fixed so firmly on the ground at his mount's hoofs that he didn't see the ambush until they were already caught.

'Hello, Frip,' a voice called. It was guttural and vaguely familiar, but Berenger was in no mood to analyse it. He whipped his sword out and turned to face the danger, knowing that he was already too late. Any men who had set up an ambush and waited this long would have their plan fixed firmly. He anticipated a stunning blow to his skull, or the sudden impact of a crossbow bolt, or a clothyard arrow to his breast.

He had not expected to see Fulk and Loys approaching, both grinning in delight.

'So, what happened?' Berenger said.

'We were setting up more defences, but we were too late. The first of them came over the wall at full tilt,' Loys said. 'We had some men standing guard at the gatehouse, but their main attack came from the far side of the abbey, over the orchard and past the Abbot's house. You know, where the butts were set up? We had little enough time to form a defence, and even then it was touch and go. The men with Hawkwood fought a good rearguard, but what can twenty do against more than a hundred, especially when the hundred are battle-hardened? Hawkwood managed to get to the stables, and some of his men rode off, while we and a few others did what we could. We killed a few.'

'Remember that vicious little shit Sebastian?' said Fulk.

'From Will's vintaine? Short man, squint, dark hair. He got to the Abbot before anyone could stop him. Denisot saw him stab Abbot Andry, and Denisot ran to him and punched him so hard, he almost flipped in a somersault.'

'It was lucky Fulk was there,' Loys added. 'He got to Sebastian and killed him before the bastard could gut Denisot. He's a tough little shit, that bailiff.'

'I couldn't let the bayle get himself killed for trying to help an abbot,' Fulk said.

'How did you all escape?'

Loys answered: 'We went out the way they came in. It was impossible to get back through the main gate, so we ran for the woods, and watched as they trashed the place. They captured four or five of the lay-brothers, tortured them to learn where the abbey's valuables were, then killed them. By then they were all on foot. John Hawkwood had been waiting for his moment, and he came back at the charge and knocked them away. He held Will and his men back while we took to our heels, and when we were safe, he trotted off after us. Will tried to have his men give chase, but they were having nothing to do with it. Instead, they took to looting everything. They grabbed everything they could, Frip. The gold, the wax, the wine, the lot. Just drank themselves stupid, robbed the place, then packed up and went.'

'They will have been slowed by all the goods they stole.'

'They are close by. Denisot and Hawkwood's men are keeping an eye on them.'

'How many are there?'

'About ninety to a hundred. Not more, I don't think. They have had some attrition.'

'We don't have enough, then.'

Grandarse rumbled, 'If we surprise them, we might be able to . . .'

'These are my men, Grandarse. I know them too well,' Berenger said. 'If we attack them, we may win a slight advantage for a while, but these are war-hardened men. They won't collapse in terror because of a sudden attack. They'll re-form and attack back. There are good archers in among them, and the rest are strong fighters with sword or axe.'

'Aye, but a quick assault with some of these lads, and we'll be through them like a stick through shit! We captured sixteen or so of them last week. That was how we learned where you were, remember.'

'For what purpose? Can we capture them? No. Can we recover all the stolen wealth? No. Can we even free any of their prisoners? Unlikely. More likely is that they will get to hold us off, then attack again and kill every one of us. Like I said, these are professionals, every bit as competent as Walter Manny or Thomas Dagworth's men. They know how to encircle and change their fortunes. I trained them.'

Fulk was nodding. 'He's right,' he said in his deep voice. 'I would not attack them with so few.'

'Ach, if you say so,' Grandarse said. 'But it would be a glorious opportunity.'

'An opportunity to die,' Berenger said flatly. 'But we will need more men if we are to succeed in rescuing their prisoners. Now, take me to Denisot.'

In the bushes, Denisot listened to the sounds of the night, while at his side Ethor lay on his belly. Usually at this time of year Denisot would expect to hear the odd owl, perhaps a wandering cat, the sleepy barking of a neighbour's dog. Here, near the camp, all he could hear was whimpers and weeping from women and others in the camp. He strained his ears, trying to hear her voice. Gaillarde must be there, she *had* to be! She hadn't been left in

BLOOD OF THE INNOCENTS

the town, he was sure. They wouldn't have taken her to another house to rape and murder her. She would have been left in her own house. But someone had taken her with them. They had killed little Suzette and taken Gaillarde.

He looked up when the quiet hiss came from the trees behind them and nudged Ethor. The two crawled backwards from their protective bush, and made their way painstakingly over the grass to the trees. Not until they were five yards in among the trees did they feel safe enough to rise and stretch aching muscles.

'That's the camp?' Berenger asked quietly.

'Yes. You have brought men?' Denisot asked. His voice was harsh with anger. 'They have the women in there from our village. They have my wife . . .'

'No. I'm sorry, but there are only a couple of men with me. Where is Hawkwood?'

'Him? Over there,' Denisot said, pointing to a second stand of thick undergrowth. 'But you should have asked for help, for men to come and rescue our people! I thought you had brought companions to help us save the women! Still, we can do it! We can go now, surprise them. Perhaps we can save some of them.'

It was Ethor who shook his head. 'No, Denisot. You saw the men on guard duty just as I did. They are all alert, not resting. There is no chance of surprise.'

Denisot shook his head. 'Of course there is! We can knock down the sentries, then . . .'

'You *hope* we may be able to break into the camp and rescue the prisoners, but you know that idea is doomed. The women are all held separately with the men, in ones and twos in rooms in an old convent. The men are inside, too, all gathered together. To get to them, we would have to race through all the sleeping routiers. Then we would have to release the women from any shackles or bonds holding them before trying to escape. In that time the entire camp would be awake, and it's unlikely we could liberate any of the women before we were slaughtered. I don't think a single woman could be rescued like that. More likely, the mercenaries would slay them as soon as the alarm was given.'

'We have to leave,' Berenger said. 'We can go to our knight, Sir John, and bring him back. These fellows may listen to him and surrender their captives for a fee.'

'Fee?'

'A ransom. They will be happy enough to release the women for some money.'

'What money?' Denisot asked. His voice was louder than he intended and when Ethor put a hand on his shoulder, he nodded. 'Yes, I know,' he said more quietly. 'We have no money, Master Fripper. All we had, they have stolen. What would you have us do, go and rob someone else to pay these thieves? Kill someone to pay these killers?'

Berenger looked towards the camp. 'Perhaps there is another way, but there is nothing we can do without more men. We have to go to the English camp.'

'You go, then. I will stay here and watch for my wife,' Denisot said.

'You don't even know that she's there,' Berenger said. 'She could have been slain and left in any one of a number of places between your town and here.'

'These men do not bury their victims or hide them! They kill and leave the bodies where they lie! My wife is there. I am sure of it!'

'If you remain here, you will be likely caught and killed yourself,' Ethor said. 'Denisot, go back with these men. I will stay and follow them.'

'To what purpose?' Berenger asked.

'If they move from their path, I can show you where they have gone.'

Berenger shook his head. 'My friend, if you think that the English army cannot see a swathe of destruction such as these men are leaving, you are blind. And if you were to come to the English camp and call out, you would be killed as a spy. If you were captured when the army came to you, you would be slain. None of you can remain. Denisot, staying here will mean your death. If you come with us there is a possibility that you can save her. If you don't, there is none.'

Denisot turned and stared back towards the mercenaries' camp.

'I failed her before. She still blames me because I could do nothing to save our children. I could see it in her eyes: she held me responsible for their deaths. If I go now, I will be—'

'Helping to rescue her,' Grandarse said. He belched and hoicked up his belt. 'Aye, well, we'll be rescuing no one if we don't get our arses back to the English camp soon. Best hurry.'

'I will stay. I may be able to help her,' Denisot said. He stared hard at Fripper. 'I saved your life once. You owe me this. You should stay with me.'

'I could not help you against so many,' Berenger said. 'You stay, but keep safe, and we shall bring back more men so that we can rescue your wife.'

'You will come back? This you swear?'

'Yes. I will return with men.'

Denisot nodded as though to himself while Berenger stood, waiting. Ethor shrugged and muttered, *'Eh, bien.'*

'You are with me?' Denisot said.

Ethor nodded and the two stood staring at each other. At last, with a heavy heart, Berenger muttered his farewell. 'God watch you.'

Denisot said, 'Godspeed.' He looked at Ethor, and the two men turned and made their way quietly back to the edge of the trees. Berenger watched them disappear into the gloom.

He felt as though he was betraying Denisot and his wife; he felt as though he was leaving them both to their deaths.

CHAPTER TWENTY-FOUR

Wednesday 17 August

The English camp was in turmoil when Berenger and the others arrived. Sentries forced them to stop on their way in, and even when they had passed inside the camp, they had the feeling that they were being watched suspiciously as they sought the pavilion of Sir John de Sully.

'Eh, this is a bugger! I feel like a spy, even though I'm as innocent as the day I was born,' Grandarse said.

'If that's true, you must have been a remarkable babe,' Berenger said.

'I was that. I was noted for my intelligence and skills.'

'At eating and thieving?' Hawkwood said with a grin.

'Aye. And clipping saucy bastards from far-off parts round the head, too, ye ignorant git!'

Berenger smiled, but only fleetingly. He felt curiously ill at ease here in the midst of the English army. It was so familiar, so much a part of his past: all the noises, the smells, the scenes, were engraved on his mind from a dozen campaigns: the ringing and clattering of hammers from the smiths and armourers, the coarse bellowing and swearing from vinteners trying to urge on recalcitrant recruits new to marching and fighting, the smell of baking clay as new-made bread ovens dried, the all-pervasive odours of ten thousand men urinating, sweating and defecating in the warm air. It was all so poignantly familiar, and yet it was foreign too. It had been so long since Berenger had felt a part of a campaign like this; to return to it now made him wary and nervous, like a pup waiting for a kick.

'Come, Fripper,' Grandarse said.

Sir John's pavilion was easy to find. Grandarse and Berenger walked to it and announced themselves to the steward at the door.

'My friends, I am glad to see you!' Sir John exclaimed when he saw them. 'Fripper, it does my heart good to see you well. I had heard you were dead!'

It took little time to tell him what had happened to them since Grandarse and Hawkwood had left in search of Berenger. Sir John's face grew serious as he heard of the sacking of the abbey. 'These men are not serving the Prince or our King. They are making war on their own account. If we find them, they can expect little sympathy from me or any of my men here,' he said.

'There is no justification,' Berenger said. 'They murdered the Abbot of St Jacques, just as they murdered many others about Uzerche.' He didn't want to mention Alazaïs. Not yet. He had a natural reluctance to talk about her murder. There was always the risk that Sir John might think he had a personal feud with Will over the woman. 'If I find them, I will kill their commander,' he said.

'Quite so.' Sir John turned away.

Berenger looked at him as Sir John filled his mazer from a

jug, waving a hand towards Berenger and Grandarse so that his steward would serve them too. Berenger took the cup and sniffed the heady odour of strong wine. He set it down untouched.

He could remember the battles in which he had served this knight: many battles, most of them victories, and some few disasters. But in his mind still all he could see were the faces of Alazaïs and her two boys as Sir John spoke once more.

'Now, to cheerier matters. Grandarse, I assume you will happily command Fripper again as a vintener?'

'Aye. Gladly.'

'Then I think that the men he has brought with him shall be a benefit to all of us. Please take him to the fellows he will command and introduce him.'

'There is another matter, Sir John,' Berenger said.

'Yes?'

'I must take my men to find the company who were guilty of these crimes.'

Sir John peered at him over his cup. 'I do not think that the Prince would be happy to learn that I had agreed to deplete my forces just as our campaign begins.'

'It is essential, Sir John. My friend's wife is held captive with the company.'

'Then it may be better if he doesn't win her back, don't you think?' Sir John said. 'If she has been raped and assaulted for the last week or so, I doubt whether she will be the same woman.'

'He must win her back,' Berenger said. 'It is a matter of honour.'

'Well, I can admire his determination, but to lose a vintaine would be difficult. We do not have the manpower to fritter away our forces.'

'It would have to be more than one vintaine,' Grandarse said. 'They have a force of over a hundred.'

'So you'd want five or six vintaines? I don't think . . .'

'Then I must go back alone. I owe this man my life. I will not leave him when he needs my aid.'

'Berenger, you are part of the Prince's army now.'

'I have no contract, I've accepted no money, and I have not even taken provisions from you. I am a free agent.'

Sir John rubbed his chin and contemplated the man. Berenger looked pale-faced and fretful, which was unexpected. In the past he had always been determined and firm, but he had a core of obedience that had remained unshaken. Now he looked like a man who was willing to risk all in order to help this man he called a friend. 'How far are they?'

'Perhaps forty miles yesternight. Now? Maybe another twenty. They have many on foot still, and those must slow the march of the entire column.'

Sir John considered. Berenger was a useful leader, but to send him and a force of men after this company may well cost more than a few of their own troops. The English could ill afford to lose more men. They were short enough as it was.

'Grandarse?'

'Aye, well, I think Fripper is keen, Sir John,' the centener said.

'It was one thing to allow two vintaines to make a reconnaissance, but different to have a centaine riding off in force,' Sir John said.

His squire leaned forward and whispered in the knight's ear.

'Yes? That is possible, certainly,' Sir John said, frowning in concentration.

'What?' Berenger asked.

'Since we left Périgueux we have had two forces of cavalry watching our line of march. They must be riding on to warn our enemies where we are. Perhaps you could find them and capture some of their men? Any of them brought back here would be worth a great deal in terms of information. And if you kill them all, that will leave the Compte de Poitiers blind until he finds a new force to track us. What do you think?'

Berenger nodded and glanced at Grandarse. 'We should be able to do that. How strong are these French forces?'

'Perhaps seventy men-at-arms. You will need to take a strong force.' The knight gazed at him impassively. 'Perhaps a centaine.'

Berenger grinned. 'Thank you, Sir John.'

'Bring my men back safely, Fripper. And if there are any good fellows in this man Will's company, we could use them, too.'

Gaillarde was ready to collapse in a heap when they reached the latest camp, but first she must gather up sticks and twigs and make a fire while the men rested, the dark-haired man watching her from narrowed eyes.

His name, she had learned, was Bernard. He at least had little in the way of an accent. She could understand him. That was not the case with many of the other men in the company. More were like the fair-haired fellow called Owen, who had a dreadful cut in his cheek, and spoke in some guttural tongue she could barely understand. Perhaps it was the recent wound that was giving him his speech impediment, but she doubted it. His eye was horrible, too: it had a bruise that had turned the eyeball to a violent scarlet.

Even with those, she found Bernard was the more terrifying of the company. He was quiet, watchful, intense, like a hunter stalking a hart. Always at his side was another, nervous and terribly shy. This was Arnaud, a younger fellow who was so nervous, he barely dared to look at her. Whenever his eyes lit on her, he instantly reddened and looked away; Bernard was one of those men who was always looking at her as if he could see every line of her beneath her shift and tunic. His eyes were everywhere, all over her body. It made her feel as if slugs were crawling over her. He was terrible; he made her feel sick.

The younger fellow reminded her of a cousin who had got into trouble in Limoges when he went as apprentice to a saddler and got into the wrong company. Poor Guillaume! When there was a dispute between the apprentices and others, he joined a gang that ran about the town, hurling stones and getting into fights with sticks and clubs. At the end of their brief reign of terror, the apprentices were punished severely, and Guillaume was fortunate not to have been caught. From that evening onwards, he was a quieter, more peaceful man. He had settled and raised a small family, making all forms of leather purses, pouches and scabbards for local folk, vowing never to travel to the city again.

'Mistress?' It was the fair boy.

Gaillarde turned to him, giving an involuntary whimper as the skin on her cheek was pulled taut over her bruise. It was painful at all times, but when she moved her head without wariness, it was worst of all. 'Yes?'

'You want some pottage?'

Bernard stood and stepped between them. Gaillarde drew away as he leered at her, then turned his back and pushed the other back again. 'Leave her, Arnaud. She doesn't need anything from you.'

'She likes me, and I want to feed her. You give her nothing.'

'She is mine, Arnaud. Not yours. Leave her alone or you'll answer to me.'

His voice was low, quiet, but there was no mistaking the menace in his tone. Arnaud looked past him at Gaillarde, and in his eyes she saw his soul as though it was stripped naked. He was no mercenary, not in truth. These thieves and murderers must have captured him and brought him here against his will. They seemed to keep a close eye on him at all times, so far as she could see. Bernard in particular seemed to think he might run away at any moment, and perhaps find friends to rescue her too, she thought.

Gaillarde had to fight to hold back a sob. The back of her throat felt tight and strained, and her breast was like a clenched fist. All the muscles were taut. She let her head hang.

'He likes you,' Bernard sneered. He took her arm and pulled her along to his bed. 'He thinks he can take you like he's taken others.'

'He wouldn't!' she burst out. 'He's not like you!'

He pushed her suddenly. A heel caught a stone, and she fell back on her rump with a short squeal of pain as a sharp piece of rock bit into her buttock.

'You listen to me well, woman. You are mine while you're in this company, and you'd best remember that. I'll have you keep your eyes downcast when you look at other men, else your life will grow painful.'

'Why? So you can keep me in good condition for whenever you want to rape me?' she snapped.

He slapped her face suddenly. It was not hard, but it caught the bruise where he had hit her before, and the sudden pain flared like a torch, scorching her face. 'Don't talk to me like that,' he said, leaning close. 'If I want to fuck you, I will, you whore. You have no one here will save you. Don't forget that for a moment. I'm the only man here who's keen to keep you alive.'

'Why? Tell me that!'

'Because ... because I would see you safe.'

He wanted to keep her for himself, no doubt, but he had no affection for her. That was proved by his abuse.

'You should be careful! I am wife to the bayle of my town!'

'So you're the wife to the bayle? That is good to know. I know much you don't realise, woman. I know a bayle's wife is worth money. So I'll keep you alive and I'll sell you back to him when I get the chance. But if you make my life hard, I may just think that it's not worth the fight. I may decide to leave you to the others to be gang-raped and killed. If you want that, you go on making sheep's eyes at Arnaud back there. Otherwise, if you want to live and see your husband again, you'd best learn to be nice to the one man here who's protecting you.'

She turned her face away while he glared down at her, and then he was gone. She dared not move for a few moments, thinking that he might still be there, but he had stalked off, and was seeing to his pony. Carefully, fearfully, she turned her head a little further and saw Arnaud. He was standing a short distance away, and as his glance caught hers, he slowly dropped an eyelid in an elaborate wink. She felt relief course through her veins. It was as intoxicating as a draught of strong wine.

At least she had one friend here.

Berenger and Grandarse took their leave of the knight, walking back into the sunlight. Saul was sitting on the grass with his back against a trestle; Fulk and Loys looked up hopefully from a bench they had commandeered for their own use, and rose to follow Grandarse when he beckoned them.

He led them between carts and wagons, past men gambling on barrel-tops with dice, and out past the butchers slaughtering captured cattle. The noise here was deafening. There were hawkers bellowing their wares, women offering themselves, armourers clattering and hammering in an irregular timpani, smiths beating out horses' shoes, while others were spinning the grinding stones, sharpening blades ready for the coming battles, sending sparks flying in all directions.

'This is a vast army!' Loys said breathlessly. Working men stretched away in all directions.

Grandarse looked about him dispassionately. 'Not so large as we had ten year ago, eh, Frip?'

'No. Then we had twelve or thirteen thousand, I think.'

'Half as much again as this, then,' Grandarse said. 'Still, at least there are some folk here who're useful.'

He led them around a series of smaller, lighter wagons, and at the other side Berenger's face broke into a grin. 'Master Gynour!' he bellowed, and hurried to meet Archibald.

Archibald smiled and grasped his arm, but even as he did so, he thought how unwell Berenger looked. 'You are well, Master Fripper?'

'Never better,' Berenger declared.

Not so, by my troth, Archibald thought. He could see the bloodshot eyes, the pallor of the skin, and he could tell that Berenger was thinner than he had been when they had last met. 'Come, have a little cider with me.'

'You have cider still?' Berenger chuckled. He knew only an overwhelming pleasure to see this old friend again. 'You always preferred cider to ale, didn't you?'

'Sometimes, yes. Today I am very thirsty. Do you have water?'

He poured the drink, and saw how Berenger's hand shook slightly as he took the cup. That explained much.

'So how is your collection of toys?' Berenger said when they were sitting.

'My gonnes? I have command of a small company now. We have four great gonnes and some ribauldequins.'

'What are they?'

'Small barrels set on a frame like a handcart. I have two that Ed and I serve, each with three barrels. We can set them off one after another, so that they cut down more men. They are the way

267

of the future, Frip! The great guns are good for knocking down walls, but these little ribauldequins, if we had one for every ten archers, would revolutionise warfare.'

His eyes took on a dreamy look. Berenger smiled to himself. He knew how Archibald's mind worked. In his mind, he was seeing massed ranks of these handcarts, all belching smoke and flame like an army of dragons, and before them, swathes of French knights and men-at-arms falling like sheaves of corn before the scythe.

'So Ed is still with you.'

Archibald's attention came back to Berenger, reluctantly, from his dream. 'Him? Oh, yes. And Béatrice, too.'

Grandarse left Berenger and the others to return to Sir John. He was standing near a fire, and his shrewd glance fixed on Grandarse when the centener appeared. Grandarse thought it was like being spitted on an ash spear three yards long.

'Grandarse, will Fripper be well?'

'He'll be fine, Sir John. Just give 'im a few days and he'll be the same Fripper you knew before.'

'You've seen as many men like that as I have,' Sir John said. He stared down at the ground by his feet. 'It is sad to see a man who was once so hearty and eager changed. Don't deny it, Grandarse. His spirit is broken, isn't it? I saw how he set his cup of wine down, as did you, I dare say. He has fought in one battle too many.'

'He'll be fine. Give him a chance. It'll only take the first action to bring back the old Fripper,' Grandarse said as reassuringly as he could.

Sir John cast a glance at him and was rewarded with the shifty look of a thief with the purse still in his hands. 'Really?'

'I'm sure of it, on my ballocks,' Grandarse said. 'He'll be fine. He was the best vintener I ever had, and he will be again.'

'I hope you're right,' Sir John said. 'Because if there is any doubt about his skills, his judgement or his abilities, you will leave him. We have a long ride ahead of us, and I will not endanger our task because of one feeble-minded fool who depends too much on wine for his courage.'

'You question his courage?'

'I question everything about him, Grandarse. Keep him with you, then, and ensure that he is safe. I want no man who is not safe and firm in the line.'

CHAPTER TWENTY-FIVE

It was his eyes that she noticed first of all.

Béatrice had known Berenger for almost a year when she last saw him. He had remained in Calais, while she went with Archibald, originally to London, and then, a year ago, to Bordeaux. When she'd left Berenger with his new wife, he had been happy. If ever a man could be said to be contented, that man was Berenger. He had at last found a wife, and his future looked happy. Looking into his eyes, Béatrice could see only happiness as he gazed over at his woman.

Now his eyes were empty. There was life glittering deep in their depths, but this was not the man she had known ten years before.

'It is good to see you again, Master Fripper,' she said. It was a formal greeting, but somehow suitable. Neither of them was young, and neither was unmarked by the passing of the years. She had been orphaned during the crisis in the year before the battle at Crécy. Her father was accused of treachery and executed, and it was only the English under Berenger that had saved her. She owed him and his group her life.

'I hope you are well,' he said.

'I have a good master in Archibald.'

'You never married?' he asked, and glanced at her sidelong. She was as attractive as he remembered.

'Me? No. I never found the right man,' she said, staring at her hands. 'You were married, I thought?'

'The pestilence.'

She nodded, her head on one side. 'I am so sorry. You were happy?'

'For a little, yes. She bore me a son, too. But the boy died. They all died,' he said. 'What of you?'

'I am content,' she said firmly. 'It has been enough for me to be maid to Archibald and Ed.'

She could not explain it to him. How could he understand? She was a woman without lands, money, or even family. Her life was ruined in France, and in England she would always be looked at askance. Men in England were the same as men anywhere: they thought that a hand on a woman's rump or breast was a compliment, just as an offer of money for a quick knee-trembler in an alley would be accepted with alacrity. The more wine a man had drunk, the more convinced he became that his tarse was the only one in the world that could interest a woman. Especially, she had come to realise, a French woman. She was exotic, compared with the standard fare at the docks or in the stews south of the Thames. They all thought that she was delectable and assumed her to be ever-available. At least living with Archibald and Ed, many of the less welcome overtures could be evaded.

Especially since most men still viewed Archibald's talents as being only a short walk from devilry.

'You never thought to wed either of them?'

She blinked. *Archibald?* she wanted to say. A fat, old man

271

with a beard so thick that she was almost convinced mice and rats lived in it? A man who could never wash away the blackness from his skin because the powder burns had tattooed him? Or Ed, a boy who was still younger than her. 'It would be like marrying my father or brother,' she said.

There came a bellow from Archibald, and she turned to see her master carrying a heavy barrel and putting it on to a wagon.

'I am coming!' she called.

'I will see you on the march,' Berenger said.

She nodded and began to hurry to Archibald, but after only a few paces she turned and watched Berenger as he walked, his head bowed, back towards Grandarse.

'They would never match the man I wanted,' she breathed sadly, and then pushed the thought from her mind. Time enough later for mourning, when she was in her blankets and could indulge her misery to the fullest extent.

Berenger had never noticed her feelings for him. He couldn't reciprocate her affection in the past, and although she was shocked to find that her heart was still devoted to him, it was clear that he had no feelings for her.

That evening Berenger sat about the fire and observed his new vintaine as the men chatted.

There was an atmosphere of half-suppressed excitement among the men. When Berenger was presented, he sensed the immediate suspicion and distrust. It wasn't like the old days, when he'd had Jack Fletcher and Matt and Geoff and the others; then he could read the temper of the men in an instant. Now he was aware of wariness from all the men under his command. God, but he needed a pot of wine!

The only two whom he had known from previous campaigns were Clip and Dogbreath, and they were both locked in their own worlds so tightly it would be a miracle for him or any other man to get any sense from them.

These others, though, were hard to read.

Robin of London was a pale-faced man of perhaps thirty years, with the build of a smith. He had a naturally slender frame, but his muscles were taut and wiry under a thin skin that spoke of long weeks with little to eat. Every muscle stood out clearly when he moved an arm, and although there was no great bulk to him, when asked he could lift great weights. He was reluctant to talk about his past life, but because of his paleness, Berenger assumed that he was one of those who had been gathered from a gaol and offered a pardon if he would fight for his King. He certainly had the mistrustful look of a prisoner, shooting little glances all about him as though expecting an attack at any moment. Sitting on his rump now with a bowl held to his mouth, he had his hands gripping the bowl in a way that concealed the contents. It looked much like other men Berenger had seen in gaols. Yet Clip had told him that this Robin had commanded the vintaine for the last weeks, and had done so well.

There were also the two Guyennois: Père et Fils, as the others called them. The older, Pierre, was a rugged-looking man whose hands showed none of the calluses or scars of a working man, and he shivered. He was better accustomed to the warmth of a hall's fire than living out of doors. His son, Felix, had deep-set eyes that looked away when someone peered in his direction. He bore clear signs of guilt, and Berenger wondered what he had done. It seemed clear enough that the two had left their home because of some crime committed by the boy, but what it might be, Berenger had no idea. Nor did he particularly want to know. He was happy to think that the past of any members of his vintaine were their own business, so long as they obeyed him when he needed them to.

He had enough shame and guilt to bear as it was. He didn't need to take on another man's. A sudden desire for wine came over him. Rather than dwelling on his own inadequacies, he glanced at the others. He would have to get to know them all as quickly as possible. He must know their strengths and weaknesses before they were thrown into a fight.

One, a taller, fair-haired man with a narrow face and swift, birdlike movements called Baz, was picking at a bone with his teeth. He glanced at Berenger with disinterest, as though he didn't think the vintener would be around for very long and wasn't worthy of his attention. Beside him, slurping pottage from a bowl, was Gilles, a chubby fellow of not yet twenty, who had the look of a stable-boy or similar. He was plainly here on a great adventure, and was desperately keen to fit in with the other, more experienced and older men. Imbert, behind him, was tall and watchful. He listened a great deal, but tended to keep his own council. Berenger thought he could be a source of dissent in the group, because men like that tended to hoard secrets. Occasionally they might share their perceptions with others, and that could lead to disputes.

There were two fellows from Bristol, Gilles and Nick, who had known each other for years. In their middle to late twenties, Gilles was under middle height, slim and had a quick sense of humour. Nick was shorter. He had a smile constantly fixed to his face. He wasn't a deep thinker, from what Berenger had seen, but he would be an asset in terms of building camaraderie in the unit. There were few men like him, who could generally find something humorous in any situation.

For all that, he was happy that he had Loys, Fulk and Saul in his vintaine. All were known to him, and their abilities were respected. His only reservations lay with Fulk, who was not by nature an archer, but he had the strength to draw a bow and loose it. In a general mêlée, that would be adequate. Accuracy against a mass of horses and men was less essential. Speed mattered more.

Yes, Berenger felt that there were enough characters to meld a coherent fighting unit from all these men. His main doubt was his own ability to lead them and fight. He was not so young as when he had led the vintaine to Crécy and Calais ten years ago.

Looking down, he realised that all this while he had been fingering the crucifix.

He was not the same man at all.

Thursday 18 August

'They want to send us away? We only just got here!' Saul said despairingly.

'Sir John wants to see how we work,' Grandarse said. 'Every horse, every ox, every man has to be used to their burdens. He wants to know ye're accustomed to our packs. The beasts too. Aye, and as we ride on, every bishop in their churches will mutter curses towards us, and the townspeople will stare and wonder, quaking at the thought of Englishmen marching towards them. The alarm is spreading throughout France. Their King must hear that we are here, he must tremble to hear of our approach; he must fear us so much that he gathers his army and comes to meet us.'

'So he will come all the faster to meet us? That doesn't sound sensible,' Robin said. He snorted and leaned back on one arm. 'You are saying that all the French will be prepared for us? The towns and villages where we hoped to find plunder will be deserted and emptied, and instead we will find soldiers and archers to contest our path?'

Fulk looked across at him. 'You thought there would be none? The longer we sit here and practise what we must, the better a force we become. In the last day I have learned how to hit a target with a bow. You have learned how to fight with a sword and axe. We grow more strong as we learn.'

'For my part I would just hurry on,' Felix said.

Berenger looked across at Grandarse. He stood like a rich merchant viewing a new market. Before him, the men looked less convinced. Pierre looked grey-faced and fretful at the thought of fighting.

'Do not wish for excitement,' Berenger said. He prodded the fire with a stick, urging the flames to cook his oatcake more swiftly. 'Excitement is the last thing a soldier should crave.'

Grandarse gave a loud belch. 'Aye, Frip's got the right of it there! Peace, rest, ale and women, yes, but not excitement. Excitement isn't all it's said to be. Give me boredom and a wench, and I can fill my time.'

Pierre and his son were staring into the flames as the men waited for their cakes to cook through. Berenger had always insisted that his men should have something in their bellies before he asked them to ride or fight, and Grandarse knew better than to try to persuade him to change that habit.

'What is our actual task?' Berenger asked Grandarse as the other men began to chatter about women they had slept with and the best taverns in London or Bordeaux.

'If anyone asks, we are scouting ahead. If we happen to run into someone called Will, and liberate a woman he is holding, that's up to us. Especially if the thieving scrote happens to have a lot of plunder with him that we could usefully look after!'

'So it is approved for us to ride on ahead?' Fulk asked.

'Aye, lad. But we have to be careful. There is likely a large French army coming down to meet us, man. If we're found pulling our tarses out there, we'll get more excitement than we'd want!'

Gaillarde could see the men gathering in a huddle. She was cold, and while her feet were less painful than they had been, she was yet aware that they were not healing as she would have liked, with the constant marching.

They were close to another village, but this time Will and his men turned west and moved off the main track. Soon she saw why. Smoke was rising through the trees, and there was a series of buildings deep in the valley.

Suddenly the atmosphere changed. It was like being out when a storm was brewing. There was a feeling that the men, their animals, their prisoners, all were charged. To touch another would lead to painful sparks. But there was nothing there in the space between people, it was in the people themselves. It was a thrilling of excitement and tension in the men as they prepared themselves for another raid on an unsuspecting community.

She would have rushed forward to warn them, if she had the strength. But she didn't. She was empty of all feeling. She was aware of compassion, but there was no power in her to bring it to bear for the benefit of another. Instead, when Bernard pointed her towards a gap in the trees and told her to wait there with the other women and prisoners, she meekly complied. Two men were set to guard them all, and they stood with their knuckles white as they gripped their polearms, watching their captives, but all the while listening to the other sounds.

Gaillarde set her back to a tree and slowly allowed her legs to give way until she was resting on the ground. She was exhausted. The thought of moving on any further was hideous. She had no more energy. She could not cope with another mile.

There was a scream. Then another.

The two guards laughed, and one slapped his thigh to hear the panic. They could hear bellows and whoops, like huntsmen after a hart, and then a long shriek that died away shivering like an ululation at an unimaginable distance. On the wind they heard more screams, muffled now. Some of the women with Gaillarde wept at the sounds. They knew what was happening further on in the woods. For her part, Gaillarde was too weary to feel sympathy, compassion or anything else. She was only aware of a heaviness of spirit that left her feeling empty.

There came a shout, then a series of cries that seemed to be getting closer, with a crashing of twigs and little branches. Gaillarde looked up in time to see a nun hurtling through the undergrowth. She had a wimple trailing, leaving her hair enclosed within a coif, while the skirts of her robe were held up in her hands to allow her to run as best she could, but her clothing was snagging on twigs and brambles, and her shins were bloody from scratches and cuts. Her eyes were wide with terror and she was running as though the hounds of Hell were on her scent.

She did not see the clearing and the women until the last moment. Suddenly she burst through the surrounding undergrowth and found herself in their midst, staring about her wildly. One of the guards tried to reach for her, but she darted to one side with a squeak like a hunted rabbit; but that put her in reach of the second guard. He swung his polearm and the pole hit her at the back of the head. Her skull was thrown forward with the strength of the blow, and she fell to her knees.

When he grabbed her arm, pulling her to him, two more men arrived. These were the ones who had chased her from the convent beyond the woods.

'Leave her alone! She was ours!'

The guard watching laughed. 'Go find another!'

'She was ours, though.'

'You make good beaters. You drove the game to us, and for that we're grateful! Get on! You're getting all the fun already!' the guard standing said, still watching his colleague. The two men stood muttering as though to dispute the two guards' right to take their prize, but then they heard more screams. Cursing, they turned and hurried back the way they had come.

Gaillarde put her hands to the ground and found herself touching a great wooden branch that had fallen from the tree above. Without thinking, she grasped it and stood.

She was almost in a dream, or so it felt. There was nothing in her mind: no emotion, no concern, no fear. She stepped quietly to the nearer guard, who was watching his companion trying to kiss the captive nun. Perhaps he heard her steps, or saw a shadow. Whatever the reason, he began to turn to face her just as she swung her branch.

The wood crashed into his face, mashing lips and teeth into a bloody froth. He grunted and thrust out with his polearm, but she was already swinging back, and his pole was out of the way when the branch crashed into the side of his head. His temple was crushed like an egg shell, with a sound like a wet cabbage hit with a bar. The man fell without a word, without a cry.

She hefted her branch. The other guard saw her approach, but he seemed incapable of comprehending his danger. Her branch fell on him and he fell back, letting the nun free. Gaillarde struck him again, once, twice, thrice, and his eyes rolled up into his head as he fell, blood blackening his hair like tar.

Gaillarde pulled the nun away. The young woman was still only partially aware as Gaillarde led her away, in a daze herself.

Picking up the stick had been an automatic reaction. As soon as her fingers met the branch, they enfolded it as though acting on their own volition without any need for her to instruct them.

Standing and swinging it at the guards was the inevitable consequence of her picking it up. There was nothing that required thought or planning. Each stage of her attack flowed on as a natural consequence of the stage before. And now two men lay dead.

The nun stared about her with petrified eyes, her hands clutching at her robes as though fearing a fresh attack at any moment. But, for now at least, she was safe. Gaillarde patted the nun's head, hugged her, kissed her gently, and pushed her away, up the road in the direction that the mercenaries had come, back to safety.

Then Gaillarde returned to the other women. They looked up at her dully. None made a comment. They were all too weary and emotionally drained. None had the strength to rise or run; none of them cared.

She should have run. She knew that. But she couldn't. She was so very tired.

She sat back at her tree and closed her eyes.

CHAPTER TWENTY-SIX

Berenger and Grandarse had left before the second hour of the day, their men clattering along behind them.

Now, with some seventy-five men, supplies for two days and a bag of oats tied to the saddle, Berenger was leading the way deep into the French countryside and for the first time in days he wasn't upset. His hands weren't shaking, his head felt good. The thought of a cup of wine now, even this early in the day, was enough to make his heart beat a little faster, but it was not an all-encompassing passion.

Just now, though, there was more to his life than mere drink. He was more keen on the idea of finding Will.

In short, he felt elated.

'So why are we being sent out, Frip?' Clip asked in his customary whine. 'Why's it us?'

'We're going to find the men who destroyed the convent, the other men from the routiers you discovered, Clip. I have a friend who is following them. They took his wife, and it is our task to find them and rescue her and the other prisoners they took.'

Imbert scowled at that. 'I thought Sir John told us to go and find the French scouts who were . . .'

'Don't listen to conversations that weren't meant for you,' Grandarse snapped. 'We will look for them, too. We have more than one mission, man.'

'The scouts should be easy to find, Grandarse,' Berenger said. 'They will be searching for any stragglers themselves. If we continue on the road to St Jacques, we may well find them.'

'If I was their commander, I'd sit on my arse towards the middle of our army, and I'd have my riders sent out to the flanks of the English army to see how broad a swathe of devastation we were determined to make.'

'They won't need to,' Robin said. 'They'll see the smoke.'

'Yes, you may be right. But they'll know we've seen them, so they'll expect a welcoming party trying to catch them. They may be feeling secure just now, mind. They may think the English won't care to catch them.'

'So we shall have to be greyhounds.'

'What does that mean?' Gilles asked. He was sitting on a short pony that suited his diminutive size. At his side his friend, the taller Nick, snorted derisively. 'Have you never set a hound loose at a hare?'

'I've seen it done.'

Berenger said, 'The hound will always be swifter, over any distance. But oftentimes it will miss its quarry because the hare is smaller and can turn faster. As the hare jinks and twists, the hound overshoots, if it is unused to the quarry. A young greyhound will be a great deal faster than the hare, but it will miss every time, because it is untrained and unused to the hunt. But get an older, slower hound, and he may well take the hare because he runs behind the younger, faster hound, and can antici-pate the hare when the youngster misses.'

'What has that got to do with us?' Nick asked after absorbing this for a few minutes.

'You'll be the young greyhound, while we're the older, cleverer ones, aren't we, Frip?' Clip said, adding self-consciously, 'When you've been on as many campaigns as us, you'll see.'

Grandarse hawked and spat, pulling up his belt again. 'They are few and fleet. We are the greyhounds, more likely to catch them over time if we get into a chase, but it won't be easy. So we will use guile and try to catch them that way.'

'I hope we are the greyhound,' Berenger said. 'I hope we are not the hare. But the scouts for the French know their land, and they could easily trap us like conies in a net if we are careless, so be vigilant.'

Imbert gave a snigger. 'You think some French monkeys will catch us? We're English!'

'English we may be, but if you enter a fight, it is safer to consider the enemy to be more powerful than you. Assume they are more powerful and more clever, more devious, more dangerous than you.'

'Pshaw!' Nick exclaimed. 'Why? We know that Englishmen always win in a fight even when we're outnumbered.'

'Is that what you've been told?' Berenger said. 'That is good. But Englishmen who believe that often die because their arrogance makes them forget that their enemy is intelligent too. Think on this: if we all die this morning, but Prince Edward goes on to win a great victory, all will say that the English are invincible. They will remember the Prince's name over the centuries as a great warrior, they will remember the names of all the knights who fight at his side. But us? We who die here today? We will be forgotten in a week. No one will want to remember the little force that was wiped out to a man by a cleverer French captain. So keep your eyes open and be as vigilant as a cat hunting a mouse. For that is the only way you will survive.'

The rest of that day was a blur. Gaillarde was unsure whether she had truly killed those two guards, but the bodies were there as proof.

When the two men were discovered, Will came to view them and soon came to the conclusion that someone had heard the attack on the convent and thought to come and save the nun before she could be injured or killed. That was the thought of the mercenaries, anyway. Gaillarde took little interest in the proceedings. She was so weary.

The convent had been a small commune of thirty nuns and some associated workers. The nuns had been captured, all bar the last, and raped before being put to the sword. Soon after the women were taken to the place, past the bodies and into the cloister where other men were grabbing all the silver and valuables. Books were thrown to the floor and trampled, until a routier collected them for the fire later. There were barrels of wine in an undercroft, and the men became very merry as they drank their way through as much of it as they could.

But not Bernard. He had come through a little while after the nun had disappeared. He glared at the women waiting there in the clearing, and Gaillarde thought he was staring particularly at her. She refused to meet his eyes, but remained with her gaze fixed on a tree at the other side of the clearing, until he strode to her and squatted before her.

'Where did she go?' he asked.

She focused on his shoulder. That way she could almost ignore his fierce eyes. He slapped her hard on the cheek, and her face was turned.

'Where, bitch?'

She heard his knife scrape as it was pulled free of its rough scabbard, and involuntarily her eyes flitted right even as he touched the point to her throat. It wasn't her fault, she couldn't help herself. Her eyes moved without her meaning to. Later she would tell herself that it wasn't her fault, that he would have found her without Gaillarde's help, that her own eyes hadn't betrayed the nun, but all the while she knew the truth. It was her fault.

He made an incomprehensible snarling sound, rose, and was away, running in pursuit of the nun.

Not long afterwards they all heard the horrible scream of a woman in terror.

Ethor and Denisot had followed after the men for two days, and after the constant marching had been exhausted when they reached another village and found more bodies. It was somehow even worse than discovering their own village. These were innocents. They had no money to steal, no gold, no valuables, only their lives. The company had treated them like animals, slaughtering them all.

Denisot found himself weeping as he passed in among the bodies. He was looking for Gaillarde, but there was no sign of her. He just hoped and prayed that she was still alive and had not been slain on the march. But even through his tears, he felt his anger increasing. It was a rage that demanded satisfaction. He would find the men responsible for this violation of his land and make them pay, he swore.

He was hungry. Starving. It was more than a day since he had last eaten anything, but the urgent need to follow the company and try to rescue his wife overruled all else. He peered into a couple of the houses that were not too badly burned, but at a brief glance there was nothing inside that they could eat. He was reluctant to enter any of the buildings. It would have made him feel like a despoiler himself, as though he was joining in the plunder of the village.

'Denisot, we have to find some water,' Ethor said.

'Yes.'

There was a well, and when they drew the bucket, both drank their fill. It was cool and refreshing, and both felt better for it. Ethor had a wineskin, which they filled, and then they set off again in pursuit of the men who had killed all the folk in the village.

They had been walking for the whole day and Denisot was blundering along, already half-asleep. A yard or two behind him, Ethor was little better. After covering so much ground, both of them were plodding mechanically, barely aware of their surroundings. Denisot was remembering an Easter feast day with his children and wife back in those happy days when Gaillarde still loved him and he her. It had been a lovely, bright but cold day, and the children had been happy, running about as they made their way to the church to celebrate the feast day, when Denisot heard the squeak of leather and jingle of harnesses and instantly thought to himself that this was wrong: there had been no noise of horses on the day he was remembering.

And then his eyes opened and he saw the company in front of him. They had waited and waylaid him, he thought as he saw the leader canter towards him, drawing his sword.

'*No!*'

Denisot heard Ethor's roar and a moment later he was thrown to the ground as Ethor rammed him aside. There was a shock as he was flung to the ground, then a jarring as his neck was ricked back, and he tried to clamber to his feet, but a hideous blow slammed into his head and he fell forward, his brow striking a rock as he went. He felt his neck explode into white-hot agony as something made it bend too far sideways, and suddenly there was nothing but anguish, and he was riding high over the ground on waves of pain that rolled and crashed like surf over his head, and he drowned in it and mercifully knew no more.

Friday 19 August

Grandarse and Berenger agreed on a camp not far from St Jacques, and the next morning it took them little time to reach the place where they had kept watch over the routiers that night.

Now it was a desolate spot, with the mess of the ruined village. At one side of the square a series of men's bodies had been piled; the rest of the place was deserted. There was no living thing that they could find, only the reek of burning and the sight of broken spars and beams sticking into the air like the broken ribs of a gigantic animal.

Berenger saw Gilles and Nick blench at the sight and smells. Behind them, Felix was already puking while his father stood with a white face, shocked, his hand patting his son's back like a man calming a horse. A short distance away Baz stood gazing on as if in a trance.

'Look on, men. This is what war is like,' Berenger said. He indicated the bodies. 'You must get used to this. You will see many more men and women like this. Gutted, beheaded, tortured, raped: this is *dampnum*, a war of terror. The French King cannot protect them. All he can do is mouth pointless platitudes.'

'Who did this?' Pierre asked, his voice quiet.

'It was the men who tried to kill Fripper,' Grandarse said. 'That's why we're aiming to catch them. So, back on your horses, and let's get moving!'

The party remounted, for once without the usual complaints. Berenger took a good look at the men and was reassured to see that even Clip and Dogbreath were grim-faced as they rode past the pile of dead men. They had both seen enough horrors in their time as soldiers, but there was always something particularly hideous for a new recruit about the sight of a fresh pile of corpses. Especially when they were not even soldiers.

'These were English, Frip?' Robin said. He had joined Berenger unnoticed while Berenger was looking at the other members of the vintaine.

'Yes. Most of them. They are the same as any other company. Some are Guyennois, some Navarrese, some Saxons – men from everywhere. There is nothing that distinguishes one killer from another, in my experience. A man who is prepared to slay another can be from any background.'

'I hope we find them soon.'

'Aye. And then we can copy them and kill all of them, just as they killed the men in the village,' Nick said dully.

They found a clearing at the edge of a river, and as the sun was fading, Grandarse gave the order to dismount and make camp. It was a relief for all the men. Even those who were more experienced were relieved to be able to climb from their saddles and rest sore thighs. Even releasing the grip on the reins was consoling. Berenger felt as though his hands were formed into claws. After so many days of resting in the Abbey, the ride had been an unaccustomed effort for him. The others were little better.

Berenger walked about the camp as the men set about seeing to their beasts, collecting firewood, pulling tinder from beneath their shirts where it had been stored to keep dry, striking steel with flint, mixing oats to make cakes. Soon there was the soothing odour of wood-smoke mingled with boiling peas and beans in pots. Clip disappeared for a while, and when he returned he carried a pair of chickens.

'Where did you find them?' Grandarse asked.

'There was a peasant's cottage up there,' Clip said, jerking his thumb over his shoulder as he plucked the bird on his lap. 'No one in, but these two were scrabbling about, so I caught them.'

'How does he do it?' Grandarse demanded of the world in general.

'It's a skill,' Berenger said, grinning. It was good to see that Clip had not lost his talent. He had been known as the most skilled forager in the vintaine when he had been fighting with Berenger during the last campaigns.

The men were so tired after their long ride that they mostly collapsed where they sat, rolling themselves in their blankets and sleeping where they were.

Berenger refused to sit. He knew that to sit would mean to sleep and he dare not sleep yet. He must set sentries and watch for danger first. The sight of the people in the village earlier should have warned all the men of the dangers of this area. He walked to the perimeter of the camp, and stood staring out as the night drew in. As the veil was pulled over the countryside, he felt a strong sense of loss. He was relieved to find that he had no desire for wine. Once, by this time of day, he would have had to have become drunk before he could sleep. And then, as his eyes closed, he would see those faces again ... not tonight, though, he promised himself. Tonight he would be free from them.

'You all right, Frip?'

'Sorry, John,' he said, startled from his reverie. Hawkwood had joined him and now stood gazing out over the short area of plain before them. A half-mile away there was a stand of trees, but here they had a clear view of the land before them.

'We need to post guards,' Hawkwood said after a moment. 'I'll stand the first watch if you like.'

'I am fine here. I'll wake you when I get tired,' Berenger said firmly. He had chosen to take his post here and he was not ready to be commanded to leave it.

'If you're sure. Wake me when you feel tired.'

Berenger heard him tramping back to his men and settling. Meanwhile Berenger stepped forward, a little away from the fire-lights. They were too distracting to his eyes.

There was a knack to watching in the dark. A man could not stare straight at an area and see it clearly. Only by gazing close to an area could he see sudden movement. Berenger watched the horizon, carefully concentrating on points just above the land-scape, looking for a shape that could be slipping over the ground. It was times like this that he found his imagination would work its magic. He would see wolves, snakes the size of men, demons and dragons, all advancing towards him with the ponderous slowness of a starting mill-wheel in those moments when the water first lands in the topmost bucket.

The dark was his friend. He had grown to like the night. Most people were terrified of it, thinking they would be attacked by *sanguisuga*, the vampires who flew on the wind to suck the blood of the innocent, or that ghouls or ghosts would appear and snatch a man's soul. Berenger had no fear of such things. He knew his soul was gone: it had been taken when his wife died. Since then, he had only rarely thought that he could win it back. Perhaps if he helped Denisot to find *his* wife, Berenger would find some peace. He had thought that he would find comfort with the Abbot, but Will had taken that, just as he had taken the vision of happiness that Alazaïs had offered.

He would find Will and make him suffer for his crimes.

CHAPTER TWENTY-SEVEN

Saturday 20 August

The next morning was grey, overcast and full of a fine mist that seeped into the men's clothes and left them wet and grumpy.

Berenger rode a little behind Grandarse as they left their camp. He had insisted that they should all set off with an oatcake as usual, and forced them to relight the embers of their fires so that they could cook them, but there was little joy in it. The men went through the motions, mixing, shaping, then cooking on hot stones near the fires, but there was none of the easy bickering that spoke of happy soldiers. Instead there was a sullen silence that matched the weather perfectly. Even Grandarse seemed to sense the general atmosphere and sat grimly eating his cake and sipping some watered wine. Imbert and Baz sat close together and glowered about them.

It was a relief to mount and ride away, as if they could leave their feelings of misery behind.

'What's that?' Hawkwood asked.

Berenger peered towards the trees where Hawkwood's finger pointed, but he could make out nothing at that distance. His eyesight, never terribly good, was much worse since his forty-third birthday. 'What is it?'

'A man, I think,' Hawkwood said. There was a crisp incisiveness in his tone now. 'Clip, take two men and see about that man. See him? Catch him and bring him back here.'

'Why me?' Clip said.

'Just do as you're told!' Berenger snapped, and soon Clip was cantering along the grass with Pierre and Felix lumbering behind him.

'Hold on!' Hawkwood said, rising in his stirrups and peering towards the man. 'Isn't that Denisot?'

'What happened to you?' Berenger asked.

'The company,' Denisot said. 'They killed Ethor.'

He looked like a man who was already dead, Berenger thought to himself. He had a lump on the side of his head the size of a goose's egg, and his brow had been opened, which meant his face was slathered in blood. Black streaks had run down his face and coagulated. Now they had cracked like the ice on top of a pool in winter when the boys have smashed it. Denisot's face was full of misery and confusion. He looked like a man who had not eaten or slept for days. He sat on the ground while Hawkwood, Grandarse and Berenger stood about him, the rest of the men remaining on their mounts, Clip and Dogbreath warily surveying the road ahead.

'What happened to you?' Berenger said.

Denisot shook his head as though in weary confusion. 'We were walking, walking . . . they came out of nowhere, a company of a hundred men or so, and they rode at us. Ethor pushed me to safety, but they hacked at him till his head was broken open.

They hit me,' he said, gingerly touching his head, 'but they didn't kill me. I don't know why.'

Looking at him, Berenger felt he knew why. The man's face was so bloody they must have thought he was dead.

'I came to and ... I found Ethor was dead, lying on top of me. I had to push him off. It was difficult ...'

'When did you last have something to eat?' Grandarse said. 'You look as though you're starved, man.'

'I don't know. I have to find the men, though. Gaillarde is still with them.'

'You're walking back the wrong way, Denisot,' Berenger said. He glanced up at Grandarse as he spoke. The centener pulled a face. Both had the same thought: Denisot was so badly hit about the head that he had become confused about the direction the men were travelling.

'You must have something to eat. Give him some food,' Grandarse called. 'Frip, Hawk, we'll rest here a little to let him gather his wits. We need a fresh mount for him, too. Poor devil hasn't the energy to lift one foot in front of the other.'

'Put him on the cart with the arrows. He can rest on that,' Berenger said.

'Aye. Clip? Give him food and be quick. If you have wine in that skin, so much the better.'

Once Denisot was rested, Berenger and the vintaines rode on steadily until they came to the place where Ethor lay. Denisot had been right about the man. His head was cloven almost in two, with a great blow that must have instantly killed him. Berenger stood over the man and said a prayer for his soul. He set four men to dig a hole for him while the rest of the men rode on at a gentle trot to where smoke rose.

The smoke enveloped a small wood. There, snuffing the air,

Berenger knew what he would find. There was the clean smell of wood-smoke, but mingled with it he could detect burned fat and the unmistakable odour of roasted human flesh.

'Denisot, you stay here,' he said.

'Why?' Denisot asked, and then blanched. 'No! If it is her, I have to come too.'

Berenger pulled a face. 'If you're sure. Let's get it over with.'

They rode at a walk into the woods, their path taking them through the trees and past a clearing on their left. Berenger sent Saul and Hawkwood to investigate and make sure that there was no risk of ambush from there. Clip and Dogbreath he sent over to the opposite side. He could hear Clip's whining complaint as he went: 'Why's it always me, eh? Sending me off into the trees like this, like I was the man he could most easily lose, eh? It ain't right.'

'Shut up!' Dogbreath snarled.

'Oh, aye, that's the way of it. You mark my words, man, we'll all get killed on this ride. Ye'll be killed same as me.'

'Ye'll be killed all right if you keep on,' Robin said. 'I'll fucking kill you myself!'

Berenger listened with only half an ear as the complaining faded away into the distance. There was a curious silence. From here, all he could hear for a while was the heavy breathing of the mounts, the occasional jingle of harness and thud of a hoof on the road as the beasts moved and stamped, but even those sounds seemed dull and flat here among the trees.

Saul and Hawkwood returned. 'It's clear there, Frip,' Hawkwood said. 'But there's been a lot of people held in there, from what I could see.'

'Prisoners?'

Hawkwood nodded. 'I'd say so. Looks like a lot of people

sat down. If I was a routier here, I'd have the prisoners kept back while I rode down to wreak mayhem on my target.'

Berenger nodded. It was how he read the ground, too. They waited for the still-complaining Clip and Dogbreath, and then made their way down the track to the source of the smoke.

There was little enough left. Only two walls of the main convent remained. The others had collapsed as the appalling heat of the fire had cracked the limestone walls. The rocks had shattered, and now all that remained was a foul midden of burned spars with a tall chimney in their midst. Scattered among the ruins were the bodies of the nuns and lay-sisters who had kept this little convent alive. Berenger gave them a brief glance. There were no men lying in between them, so he assumed that the attacking force had surprised the women living here when they rode into their midst.

'Christ Jesus!' Berenger heard Denisot say. Berenger threw him a look of urgent surprise, wondering if he had seen something nearby to shock or alarm him, but then realised that the man was staring down at the bodies.

Berenger looked again and this time his eyes were opened. He didn't see a collection of dead nuns. In their place, he saw a woman of some sixty years with her legs wide, her habit thrown over her belly, and a gaping wound in her stomach; he saw a younger woman with an expression of horror and hatred twisting her figures, her throat slashed so deeply he could see the cartilage of her severed windpipe; he saw a nun who could have been his own Marguerite, eyes full of sorrow and even, perhaps, forgiveness. He saw women, some little more than children, lying crumpled like discarded toys in a midden. They were a collection of innocents and the most religious, destroyed because of the savagery and greed that lay at the heart of men in war, and he felt shamed to the core of his soul that he had not the wit nor the imagination to see that at first glance as had Denisot.

Denisot was not sad, he saw. The bayle stood and gazed about him with determination, as though he was memorising every aspect of this fresh atrocity, that he might be the more resolute when he visited revenge on those responsible.

Berenger had a thickening sensation in his throat. It was the choking that came with the realisation that he had mislaid his humanity since leaving Calais. What sort of man was he?

'She is not here,' Denisot said. He was stumbling through the place like a man in a nightmare.

Berenger shook his head. 'They will have a better use for her,' he said.

Just then there came a call from further up the road. It was Clip.

Berenger ran to the call, his heart pounding, but Denisot was in front of him when they came upon the scene. He gave a gasp of horror, and sank to his knees.

She was fixed to two trees. Her wrists had been tied with tight thongs, stretching her body between the two trunks in foul imitation of a crucifixion, her head hung down, her hair covering her face and breasts. Berenger glanced at Denisot; the man had hidden his face, and his body was racked with silent sobs. Berenger's heart went to the man. He could imagine his own despair, were this his wife.

'She was a nun, see, Frip,' Clip said.

Denisot looked up. The woman's robes had been cut and ripped away, and now lay as shreds of black material lying all about her.

'Berenger!' Denisot managed.

'This woman was only young,' Berenger said, and turned

away as Denisot wiped away his tears with a face hardened and grim once more.

The wound that had killed her was the thrust of a knife to her left ribcage. From the look of the blood, it had penetrated her heart.

'Why would someone do this?' Berenger said.

'Dear God,' Denisot said. He was giving thanks for the fact that this was not his wife. Now he looked, it was ridiculous to think it was Gaillarde: the woman was thinner, without the thickening at her waist where she had borne children. He had caught a glimpse of her magnificent hair and made the assumption – and now he felt guilty at the relief that washed over him upon realising it was not his wife. 'Another child – my God!'

'What is this?' Berenger asked.

'I told you when we first met that I was looking for a man who had killed children and young women. He rapes them, and crucifies them like this before leaving them to die.'

'Who would do such a thing?' Berenger wondered aloud. It was incomprehensible to him. But some men viewed women and children as little better than animals. Perhaps this was one of those men who considered that a nun was only a female who could be taken. Possibly that was why he had stripped her naked first, so that he wasn't reminded that she was a nun, whereas the other men in his party were less fastidious. They would rape a woman, nun or not, clothed or not.

It was a strange thought, that this man could be more fastidious than his companions, Berenger considered. He did not like the fact that he could look on the body so dispassionately.

'It must be one of the men in the English company. One of your men,' Denisot said. He could not help himself. With a sneer and open contempt, he waved his hand at the victim's slumped body. 'This is the sort of man you were leading, Master Fripper.'

Hawkwood glanced about them. They were near the main road at the top of the track to the convent, and the sun was filtering through the trees like lances of light and dust. He sucked at his teeth.

'Rape I can understand. Men who have been in a battle and need a woman, that is at least understandable, just as I can understand killing. Many men will do that when the blood is still hot and lust is all they know ... but to kill like this? To tie up this woman and make her suffer, then stab her? It makes little sense.'

'What does it matter?' said Clip, picking his nose. 'Enough others suffered and died here. What's one girl more or less? At least he gave her a quick death in the end.'

'A quick death in the end – yes, that's what I don't understand. Why would he do that? A man who enjoyed torturing a child, who watched her suffer – why would he suddenly end her pain like that?'

Berenger said, 'Cut her down and carry her back to her sisters.'

'Who, me?'

'Yes, Clip: you! Get on with it.'

While Clip climbed from his horse, grumbling to himself, Denisot glanced at Berenger. 'This is the same as the bodies I saw near my village. It is as I said: the man who did this must be with the company you once led.'

Berenger looked at him with a frown. He would have argued as an instinctive reaction, but then he nodded. He could not dismiss the proof of his own eyes. 'I cannot imagine which of my men could have done such a thing. In my company, there was none, I am sure, who had the brutality to attack nuns in this way.'

'We have men who have raped and killed often enough,' Hawkwood commented. He saw Berenger's expression and held up his hands. 'Frip, I'm not arguing, I'm just saying that there are men in our company now who have done so. Grandarse himself used to enjoy taking women when we sacked a town. God's cods, so did I, in my time. Younger men who are less disciplined can do this sort of thing. Older men who've had violence more ingrained in them, too. It's not unique or particularly rare for men to behave in this way.'

'Yes,' Berenger said. Clip had cut the body down, and was now struggling to heave it over his horse. The nun's figure was stiff and as easy to manoeuvre as a sack of grain. 'In God's name, someone help him! Yes, John, there are men who could do this sort of thing once in a while, but this man is committing his crime more regularly. He is killing wherever he has the opportunity. He enjoys watching his victims die, I think.'

'I heard from a shepherd who saw him,' Denisot said. 'The shepherd saw a company of men go and rape a woman, but then, once they had left, one returned and crucified her. Perhaps this is what the man likes, to see his victims as they die? He would be a very cruel soul to do that.'

'Or a madman,' Berenger noted.

Berenger stared at the nun again. She was surely only some fifteen years old, a slim little figure with her hair moving in the wind from beneath the coif that had tried to enclose it, fine and golden. A novice, then.

Then another thought struck him: if he'd had but a little more time in Calais before God sent the pestilence to deprive him of wife and children, he could have had a little girl like this. She would not be so old yet, but . . . He pushed the sadness down. He would not succumb.

Clip was muttering and complaining, struggling with the

unwieldy body, trying to shove it up over his saddle, while his horse skittered sideways, eyes rolling.

'Denisot, remount. We have to find the men who did this.'

Berenger was surprised to find that the rest of the vinteners would not ride away and leave the nuns in this condition. Grandarse ordered some to make fires while directing others to help.

Soon two vintaines were collecting up the bodies and bringing them to the cemetery, where the rest of the men were set to digging. Even Imbert for once needed no urging. He slaved like the others. Denisot walked among the women's bodies muttering the *Pater Noster*. His eyes were wide and half-vacant, like a man who has been moon-struck. This was a man who had travelled past horror and was halfway to lunacy, Berenger thought. And then he wondered if he had looked the same, when he was at Uzerche and a dozen towns before that.

John Hawkwood watched. 'Are you sure about this, Frip?' he asked. 'We ought to be carrying on.'

It was Denisot who answered. 'We have to. We cannot leave nuns to the mercy of wild animals.'

'I agree,' Berenger said.

'Well, if you are sure,' Hawkwood said. 'I don't know . . .'

He was about to comment further, and Berenger saw in his face the same expression he had seen on Will's face at Uzerche. The thought that Hawkwood could be like Will was enough to make him suddenly angry, as though it was a proof of incipient disloyalty.

'I am sure,' he said, and turned away.

CHAPTER TWENTY-EIGHT

Sunday 21 August

The force under Grandarse had ridden hard that morning. Without delays they made good time, while the men they pursued were in no such hurry. They sacked and despoiled all in their path: churches, farms, villages, all fell to them.

It was in the late morning that they came to the little village. Smoke still rose from the ruins of the chapel in the midst of a reek of burned buildings and slaughtered cattle. In among the dead animals Berenger could see the hands and faces of numerous villagers. He sat on his rounsey and surveyed the scene, trying to control the dull throbbing at the back of his head as he took it all in. War was foul enough, but at least the King fought in order to impose his rightful claim on the land and the people. This, though, was mere outlawry. Men who demanded gold, food, lives, just because they could.

'These people ain't been dead long,' Clip called. He was rootling about in the midst of the corpses with the optimistic air of a man who might find something of value. 'Maybe a day or two.'

Behind him, Gilles, the chubby youngster, peered with interest, his neck craning past Clip to see the body behind. On seeing a woman who had died a grim death, he turned a shade of green and pulled away again. Berenger soon heard his retching. 'Longer than the nuns, though,' he added, lifting a leg and seeing how the rigor mortis had stiffened the body.

Berenger muttered, 'Clip, just hurry up.'

'Aye, Frip. But don't you think it a waste to leave all these here?' Clip said hopefully, waving a hand at the carcasses of cattle. 'Just a leg or two would suit us for the evening.'

He was correct, Fripper knew. The company had several carts carrying essentials, and he ordered one to wait while a butcher recovered some steaks. Meanwhile the rest of the men picked up bodies and set them into neat piles.

Clip, as usual, was at his complaining best as he picked up a young woman by the arms. Gilles stared, but stood away, and Clip's voice grew louder, rising to a derisory whine. 'Come, you thick fucker, give me a hand! Pick up her legs. Sooner she's up, the sooner we can go and dump her. Shit! Come on, will you? You want me to clump you about the head? Are you asleep?'

Berenger snapped, 'Just get on with it, will you?' but even as he did, Hawkwood span and stared into the distance.

Père et Fils were riding back at speed from where they had been scouting. Both were excited, and Felix panted as he said, 'They're up ahead! We saw them!'

Archibald gave the metal a last rub with his oiled cloth, then pulled the coverings over the gonne again.

'It'll survive,' Ed called.

'This damned weather is foul,' Archibald grumbled. He disliked the drizzle that fell constantly in this land. Today was dry, but he was sure that the gonnes could sense the weather to come. And whether or not his massive tubes could be affected, he was absolutely certain that his barrels of powder would be. 'It'll get into all the powder, and when we need it, we won't manage more than a damp hiss if the weather keeps up like this.'

'It will be fine. The barrels are all well coopered and sealed,' Ed said.

'When we stop tonight I'll have the lids off every third barrel. We'll test the powders and see how they are.'

'Very well, Master Gynour,' Ed said.

Béatrice was silent. She sat on the wagon's edge and stared ahead without speaking.

'What, no comment?' Ed said half-humorously.

'There is nothing to comment about,' she said.

Archibald raised his eyebrows and glanced at Ed. She was not usually so reticent, but since the day Berenger had returned, she had been like this. Whereas before she would have argued and insisted on her own point of view, her own way of working with the powders, which were often irrational but sometimes more effective than Archibald's own, now she was listless and uninterested.

Ed and Archibald exchanged a look. Archibald wasn't sure how much Ed understood about the woman, but for his part he was quite certain that it was the disappearance of Fripper that had led to her introspection. He was sad. She had adored Fripper when they first met all those years ago. She had confessed that to Archibald once, six or seven years ago, when she was miserable and deep in her cups, but the two had never discussed the matter again. He knew that she would be humiliated to think that he could remember the conversation. She was too proud to think of sharing her feelings with another. And since she would not discuss them, she withdrew into herself like a snail hiding from the sun.

She had been so much better these last few years, too. It was sad to see how she had changed. Archibald checked the ropes holding the gonnes down, and climbed back onto the wagon, a foot on the axle, second foot on the wheel's rim, and up. Béatrice did not look at him as he rested his buttocks on the wall of the cart's bed and took the reins from her. 'All well?'

'Why should I not be?' she asked.

Archibald shrugged. The army was starting to move again, and he snapped the reins. The bullocks began to move as the boy with the prod jabbed at their rumps, and Archibald rolled with the wagon as it lumbered over the ruts and bumps in the road.

The army was spread over a vast front. Someone had told Archibald that the devastation wreaked by this little army covered a front of some thirty miles, and he could believe it. Here he was surrounded by perhaps a centaine of men who had been instructed to ensure that he was safe and that the gonnes and serpentine powder were not put at risk. The French would dearly love to be able to capture both, or at worst send the powder and its manufacturer to meet his maker. Black powder was becoming a vital element in battle, terrifying horses and disrupting charges before the knights could muster. Yes, archers had their uses still, but Archibald knew full well that his powders were the way of the future. It was powder that would reduce a castle to ruins in the future, powder that would horrify and shock whole armies into submission on the battlefield, powder that would drive the English to victory over the French. Nothing could match the effect of a number of gonnes belching flame and smoke to their own thunderous timpani.

As yet there was no French army to dispute the right of the English to trample this land into the mire. There were still occasional scouts visible, watching, but no force. Archibald was beginning to wonder whether they would ever show. In the past, the French had been most agile to avoid any encounters. There had been little fights, yes, up and down the country when captains like Dagworth and Manny had forced local French soldiers to come to blows, but they were sporadic little events, not pitched battles. The only time that the French had succumbed to the rage that English depredations had caused, they had been so heavily defeated it was hard to believe they would dare risk another drubbing.

'Ten years ago,' he mused.

'Hmm?' Béatrice turned to him.

'I was thinking: ten years since Crécy. That was the last real battle fought by the French. They have deliberately avoided all English armies since.'

'They cannot continue to do so.'

'No. They'll have to contest our rights at some point,' Archibald said. The wagon rolled heavily down a larger rut, its massive weight crushing rocks in the soft mud of the roadway. 'Else they will find they've lost the kingdom without a fight.'

But he did wonder when they would begin. There were rumours of the French King having laid siege to some town in the north, taking over lands that had once been owned by the King of Navarre, but Archibald was doubtful. The French King was considered a vacuous fool, easily cowed. He had not the heart and stomach of an English peasant!

It was as he was smiling to himself, reflecting that there was little that could stop an English army, when the first horn blasts came from the English vanguard.

'What in God's name?' he muttered, and then Archibald

305

grabbed for his long-bladed knife, staring out to the east of their cavalcade.

There, in the murk of the dust kicked up by hundreds of hoofs and booted feet, he could vaguely make out a party of horsemen.

'Shit!'

Berenger and the men rode along a broad, flat plain with a ridge of trees on their right. Further ahead trees rose on both sides, as if they were entering a funnel. A long range of hills, blue with distance, stood clear on their left.

He rode along deep in his own thoughts. Grandarse tried to speak to him, but Berenger only shook his head. The morning's discovery at the village had been sobering. Many of his troop were still unused to the sight of death, and he was not sure that he was acclimatised to it himself.

The landscape here was empty. No smoke rose from fresh victims. In the far distance there was a hamlet, but it looked undamaged. The only sign that his company had passed by lay in the broad path of flattened grasses and ruts where carts and wagons had trampled the ground.

'Frip? What's that?' Saul was peering ahead and pointing. 'Is it smoke?'

Grandarse held up his hand and the call was sent back to the others to halt. Berenger glanced at Hawkwood. He had the better eyes. The younger man stood in his stirrups, but even with his eyesight he could discern little. 'It could be mist. Perhaps there is a river down there?'

Robin of London was peering with a frown wrinkling his brow. He had good eyes, Berenger knew. 'What do you see, Robin?'

The tall man turned his head a little, favouring his right eye.

Then he reached down to the bow that was at his back. 'To me that looks like dust kicked up by a large force of men. I think it's your company, Fripper.'

'Dust?' It had been raining much of the previous day, and yet already the sun had dried the mud enough for hoofs to stir it.

Berenger looked at Grandarse, who nodded and then wheeled his mount around.

The centener bellowed, '*Company!* Ahead are the men who have caused all this damage. They are riding on to their next victims. One of their prisoners is Denisot's wife. He wants his wife back, and I want the head of the man responsible for looting and stealing all this way. So we will break their campaign now! Archers! *Archers, dismount and string your bows!* We'll ride with lances to the front, archers at the rear!'

Berenger cast an eye over the men nearest him as the archers swung their legs over the rumps of their beasts and began to drag bowstaves into their familiar curves, sliding the string up to the notches where they held. It was impossible to string a bow on horseback. In his own vintaine, Loys and Fulk sat on their horses gazing ahead, fingering their swords, while Saul sat behind them on his short pony drawing his bow and releasing it, getting a feel for the string under his fingers. Clip too had strung his bow, and now slouched grumpily in the saddle, scratching his cods. Berenger knew he would be bold enough in any battle.

Clip glanced at Dogbreath. 'Makes no sense.'

'What?' asked Berenger.

'Those bodies back at the last place were cold and solid,' Clip said. 'If these had just been there, I'd expect the whole lot to be warm still. I'd have said they were dead for days.'

'No matter,' Berenger said. 'These are our men.'

The archers were all remounting now, and Grandarse pointed towards the dust cloud.

'When we are in bowshot, lads, dismount on my command and loose as fast as you can. Don't delay, but send your flights as quickly as possible and stop when you see us reaching them. I don't want a clothyard in my back just when I engage the buggers!'

Berenger called to his men. 'Imbert, Felix, Pierre, Gilles, you will ride with me. Fulk, Saul, Loys, you know your work: stay at my side. The rest of the vintaine, you follow us. We will ride them down swiftly, with luck. Denisot, you stay at my side. Is that clear?'

Hawkwood and the other vinteners were making their own dispositions while he spoke, and as Berenger finished, there was a lull. Hawkwood nodded to him, and Grandarse clasped Berenger's forearm, then did the same to each of the other vinteners in one last sign of comradeship.

His best archers he left with the other bowmen. 'Robin, Clip, Dogbreath, I leave you here with the archers. Keep them together, make sure they don't hit us, and when your arrows are spent, take your knives and join us. Fulk, Saul, Loys, when we have broken into their party, you will hopefully be able to separate the prisoners from them. When we have engaged them, form a guard between the fighting and their prisoners. Denisot, are you content?'

'I am.'

'Good.'

Then, as Grandarse raised his clenched fist and began to trot onwards, Berenger stood up in his stirrups and drew his sword. 'Let's catch those bastards and kill all who will not surrender immediately! Come!'

They rode forward at a steady canter, the men with lances at the fore. Berenger felt the first stirrings of excitement, and he was shocked to find that he was anticipating the shock of their collision with glee. He glanced to left and right and saw that Fulk and Saul were riding steadily. Neither looked concerned at the imminent clash. Imbert looked more nervous, while Denisot looked grimly determined.

Ahead the mistiness was growing. Gradually Berenger became aware of a large mass at its centre: a wagon. At either side he could see men tramping on over the dry ground. The trees on either side were closer now, standing over the road and leading the riders into the narrowing gap. It would, Berenger thought, make it harder for the company to disperse and hide in the woods. So much the better.

A pang of doubt struck him, but he quelled it, swinging his sword over his head like a berserker of old.

Berenger decided he would reduce the distance by a half before commanding the archers to take position, and then he would charge the company with his men.

Onward another fifty paces, he thought, and then he could allow the archers to fall away. That would be enough. Then ...

Something was wrong. The way that the dust rose: it wasn't heavy enough for a party as large as Will's. The doubts returned to him, redoubled. This was *wrong*.

'Company!' he shouted, and he was about to raise his sword to the sky when a sudden movement to the right, in the trees, warned him. He hauled back on the reins, then pulled away to the left bellowing, *'To me! Ambush! To me!'* even as the first of the arrows and bolts began to hiss past and into the men. He heard the hideous *thwack* as a quarrel slammed into a man, heard the fellow's hiccup of shock, then another wet sound as a bolt flew into a man's head and toppled him from his horse, already dead. Six others fell, either they or their horses injured, before Berenger could withdraw the rest of his group.

The archers had already dismounted, and were sending flights in among the trees on either side, covering their retreat, and as Berenger and the men reached a safe distance, Robin bellowed at them to cease and save their arrows.

Fulk was at his side. 'They got the idea of an ambush before us.'

'I should have realised. They know me too well,' Berenger said heavily.

'Aye. We should both have realised,' Fulk said.

Grandarse sat on his horse puffing and blowing, interspersed with regular snatches of curses.

'I can't believe that! Fuckin' treacherous, lying ... fucking bastard fuckin' mercenary ...'

Berenger was staring ahead. 'What are they doing?' he said to Robin, who was standing a short distance away with the archers.

'Looks like they're regrouping. There are a lot of them.'

'How many?' Berenger asked, cursing his lousy eyesight.

'I'd think about a hundred, hundred and twenty. Not more than that.'

One of Hawkwood's men was panting and sobbing with pain, a bolt protruding from his left shoulder. He snarled through his gritted teeth. 'Let me get to them, Hawk. I'll take three of them with me!'

'You won't have to,' Hawkwood said, squinting. 'They're coming.'

Berenger turned his horse and pointed to the archers. 'Clip, Dogbreath, you take the left flank. Robin, you take the right.'

Grandarse spat into the dirt. 'Yes. Hawkwood, we'll dismount and receive them here.'

Berenger nodded and shouted, 'Archers! Wait until I give the order! Clear?'

There was no ground for defence, no time to dig pits to make the horses stumble. All they could do was stand and wait as the men-at-arms in the dust ahead of them casually climbed onto their mounts and formed a cavalry squadron. As Berenger watched, he could see them forming a long line, the horses jerking their heads and pawing at the ground, as excited as their riders, thrilling to the shouts and orders. Then, as Robin and Clip and the other archers stood nocking their missiles to their strings, Berenger glanced ahead and saw that the dust was rising higher. The sun had dried all the puddles and mud into solid lumps that were shattered and pounded into a fine powder that would clog a man's throat in moments.

'They are coming! Prepare!' Berenger called, glancing left and right. Eleven men had lances clutched in their fists held low, butted against the ground to take the force of any charge. Behind them a second rank of men held their lances overhand. It was not enough, but it would have to do. More had taken their place in among the archers, ready to step forward when the enemy approached closer.

'Where are the prisoners, Frip?' Hawkwood murmured.

'They must have them held in the woods,' Berenger said. He threw a look over towards Denisot, who stood with a long-bladed knife in his hand, pale and resolute as he watched his wife's kidnappers advancing. At his side, Fulk was gripping his great axe, his fingers clenching and unclenching as he stared at the enemy.

The line of horses began to pick up their speed, from trot to slow canter, all in perfect unison. Berenger frowned to see a knight in the middle of the line, and then he saw three more men in modern armour, scattered among the line. *Will must have stolen a knight's steel,* he thought, and then he saw the banners proudly declaring their owners' pedigrees, and gripped his sword more firmly. The line began to gallop.

These were not his old company!

'These are French scouts!' he shouted.

They were better trained than Berenger's old company, but while the men in armour hurtled on, other riders were slower to urge their beasts to follow, and the line had begun to fracture. Men riding faster began to fill the gaps where slower men had fallen behind. Now the front men were only two hundred yards away; a hundred and fifty; a hundred; ninety . . .

'*Archers! Draw!*' Grandarse yelled.

Eighty . . .

'*Archers: aim! Archers: loose!*'

The whistle and hum of fletchings catching the air, strings vibrating, and then a thin mist seemed to plunge into the riders.

'*Archers: nock! Aim! Archers! Loose at will!*'

That familiar sound again, as though a flock of geese had swept past, and already the men racing towards them were falling. Berenger saw a destrier dive forward, head down, and the rider was hurled over, only to be crushed when the hindquarters of his mount flipped over and landed on him; another was thrown when his beast reared, trying to bite at the arrow protruding from his breast; a third and a fourth were hit in the face or chest and were flung back from their horses. More men fell, tumbling and rolling in the dirt like a child's rag dolls, as insignificant and as lifeless.

'*Loose!*' Grandarse roared one last time, and this time the arrows were aimed almost flat at their targets. Five men disappeared, but the horses came on.

'*Spears!*'

The men with the archers lowered the points of their weapons, aiming the leaf-shaped blades at the approaching horses.

'*Aim for their chests, boys!*' Grandarse shouted, and the tips went lower still.

'Fuck, Frip: these aren't English, are they?' Saul said.

'No, we've done what Sir John wanted; we've found the French.'

Still the men came on, their horses maddened with the noise and the thrill of the charge. Great destriers, fast rounseys and palfreys, all galloping wild-eyed and crazed. The men on their backs were whooping and cheering, crying to Saint-Denis and France as they came on, and then their lances came down and they crouched in their saddles.

'Here we go, lads!' Berenger called. *'For God, for the Prince, and for Saint George!'*

CHAPTER TWENTY-NINE

Béatrice and Archibald stared about them as the noise approached. There was a din of shouting and horns blowing, and Ed ran to them, a sword in his hand. 'Get down!' he called. 'They'll ride straight to you when they see the wagon.'

'Why?' she said.

'Because they'll think you have valuables in it, you fool!' he snapped. 'Get down from there, you too, Archibald!'

Archibald wasn't listening to him. The horn blasts had ceased, and he could dimly perceive that the men who had approached were talking with the vanguard. A knight trotted forward and was also chatting. Then the column began to move again, and as Archibald watched, the men who had appeared were moving through the column.

'Who are these men?' Béatrice asked.

'I've no idea. Nobody I know,' Archibald said. He saw the leader, a tall, well-built man with sandy hair. Behind him rode a motley assortment. 'They look like the worst mingling of archers, men-at-arms and mixed scoundrels as ever graced an outlaw band.'

'You don't see Berenger?' she said.

'No. Not him and not Grandarse neither,' Archibald said. He saw her slump a little as though she had held herself taut against the possibility of seeing Berenger again. 'He'll be close by, maid,' he added kindly.

The leader of the men passed close by their wagon. 'God save you,' Ed called.

'He will, I am sure,' Will said, and rode on. He glanced at Béatrice and smiled at her.

She thought he had a kind face.

A spear-point grazed Berenger's cheek, and he angrily clubbed it away with his forearm even as the man wielding it was thrust through with an English polearm. A thunderous concussion made the ground tremble as a horse was brought down but dust and grit were thrown into the air, blinding Berenger and making him blink and wipe at his eyes.

More men and beasts were falling. They tried to force their way through the English lines, but the out-thrust spears were enough to deter the horses, and the riders were forced to lunge with their weapons at the English from too far away. Their tips would not reach Berenger or his archers. Gradually, those men at the front were whittled down as arrows were sent to them from only yards away. Those with mail or plate armour were not safe at such close quarters. One man Berenger saw remained on his horse even though he had two arrows piercing his armour. He tried to lift his sword to fight on, but already his chin was resting on his breastplate, and soon his sword arm fell to his side and he slumped, toppling from the saddle.

Berenger blew a blast on his horn. 'Forward!'

The archers and lance-men began to move, stamping down with their left feet, shoving with their lances, stamp and stab, stamp and stab, stamp and stab. A man on a maddened horse tried to wheel to face the danger, but his mount would not obey, and he was run through with a spear as he tried to spur and rally the beast.

Berenger roared, 'Hold! Hold! Enough!' but none of the men would listen to him. To his horror, his own men began to rush forward.

The enemy were terrified, having seen their comrades pushed from their horses and hacked to death, but the English were too blood-crazed to hear anything in the heat of the moment. Berenger saw Denisot run to a man on the ground, stabbing him repeatedly in the throat with his knife, not noticing that he had already broken his blade. Fulk was whirling and spinning, his massive axe dealing death on all sides as he darted in between their enemies. The French fell back before him, terrified by his weapon and his seeming invincibility.

There was a man who turned, Berenger saw, and fled. A second saw him, and also left the fight; then a knot of three others copied them. He saw Loys, that foolish grin still fixed to his face, run to a man-at-arms on the ground, lifting his sword to strike, but before he could, Berenger saw the man attack, and his blade came through Loys' back, slick and oily with Loys' blood. Loys fell to his knees, and then hacked down with his own weapon, and Berenger saw his opponent's face erupt with a thick mist of bloody spray, before Loys fell on top of him. He saw Gilles dart forward, stumble, and stare down at the man who had swept his arm from his body. Gilles stopped, staring about him as if bemused and, as his eyes caught Berenger's, his enemy's weapon swept back and took his head from his shoulders.

Berenger roared, 'No!' and sprang forward, but Hawkwood was already there and Gilles was avenged.

There was one knight still on his feet, slashing and stabbing about him. As Berenger watched, an archer fell, writhing, with a great wound in his belly.

'Enough!' Berenger shouted. He snatched a bow and arrow from a man nearby and nocked and drew in one easy, fluid motion. 'Sir knight, drop your weapon and yield, or by God's bowels I'll send this into you and leave you to die here! Drop your sword!'

Sir John was riding with his esquire when the men arrived, surrounded by a strong force of men-at-arms and suspicious-looking archers.

'Sir John, this man has asked to speak to you.'

'Really? Who are you, then?'

'I am called Will, Sir John, and I am commander of this company.'

'I have heard of you, Will. Was it not you who sought to kill Berenger Fripper?'

'Kill him?' Will looked at his companions in appeal. 'No! He threatened to kill me, Sir John, but for my part I had no wish to see him hurt. He was a good man, although in recent months his skills were blunted.'

Sir John eyed him closely. 'How so?'

'He suffered from that malady that men who run their own taverns will often develop: an over-fondness for the ales and wines he sold. It was manageable mostly, but then he decided to indulge his desires and it grew to overwhelm him, I am afraid. I am sorry if this is hard news, Sir John, but Fripper became a keen drinker. The men could no longer trust him. And then he developed an affection for a woman and would hear nothing to moderate his passion.'

'Which woman was this?'

'Alazaïs, a lovely lady of Uzerche. She was beautiful. It is no surprise that men would desire her – but Fripper became infatuated. He grew convinced that his adoration was reciprocated, and that she wanted to run away with him. When she told him she wanted nothing to do with him, he grew enraged. I have never seen such a display, even among drunkards! He threw a tantrum fit for a child, and even tried to threaten some of the men. After that we had no choice but to overthrow him.'

'You mutinied?'

'No, I would not say so. Rather, we held an election and I won the vote of the majority of the men. Berenger, I fear, was unreliable. A company depends on the leader, and if the company loses confidence in him, they lose their confidence to fight. We had to remove him.'

'And what then?'

Will would not meet his eye. 'We let him go.'

'You tried to kill him?'

'No. We agreed that he would leave. That was all.'

Sir John threw a glance at Richard, who shook his head. The squire did not believe the story, but Sir John remembered Berenger's bloodshot appearance, the slight shake of his hands and the tremor of his voice when he was talking. Fripper had definitely every appearance of a man steeped in wine.

'There is more. Tell me.'

'Truly, there is nothing more that matters, Sir John. He left with some companions. A great, hulking mountain man with the choleric temper of a lunatic bitten by a rabid hound; a man with the appearance of a child and the same innocence; another who was taken in by Fripper's tantrums. There will always be men who have such simple minds that they will believe what they are told, and drunks are good at spinning a story that will entrap the innocent.'

'There is more. You are keeping back a part of the tale.'

Will shook his head, but threw a look at the black-haired man at his side.

'If you won't tell them, I will,' Bernard said. 'It was this, Sir knight. The man Fripper was mad. When he fled the town, he tried to force the woman to join him, and when she refused, he put her to the sword. Not only her, but her children too, and a physician who was there at the time. He killed them all for jealousy and lust. Nothing more. That is Fripper's temperament now: those whom he feels thwart him are given short shrift. A woman who refuses his advances will be slaughtered and her children besides.'

'I see.'

'We ask nothing. If you prefer, we can ride away,' Will said. 'But do, please, consider that I've done nothing to deserve your enmity. However, we are fighters, and as soon as we heard that the army was here, we wanted to come and join the battle, if battle there is to be.'

'That is good. We shall be marching before too long.'

Richard Bakere watched as the party of mercenaries were taken away to join with Sir John's force.

'What is it, Richard?'

'Sir John?'

'I recognise that look. You disapprove.'

'I simply wonder about that man and his story. We know Berenger Fripper well. That man's story does not tally with the Fripper I know.'

'Fripper's lost all in the last ten years. Wife, sons, tavern – who would not change?'

Bakere was silent. In the end Sir John turned to him and demanded that he speak his mind.

'In that case, Sir John, I think Berenger Fripper deserves

more credit than you give him. I would trust him with my life, and that means I suspect that man Will of lying. And if he lied about Fripper, what else did he try to deceive you about?'

Archibald and Ed went through their routine checking of the barrels and gonnes while Béatrice went about her duties, fetching water, buying a little meat from a vintaine which had discovered some cattle, chopping up leaves she had found in a hedge, mingling them with some grains of barley she had found at the bottom of a food chest, and adding a sprig or two of rosemary from a bush she found in the garden of a house they had passed that day.

She fetched herself a cup of wine, and sat while the pottage seethed and simmered.

It was good that Berenger was not here. She had missed him so much, and perhaps she had dreamed of him more than was healthy, but now that he was no longer in sight, she was content. She had seen for herself that he was happy enough. But he had given her no sign that he held any feelings for her. Why should he? He had marched with her before, to Paris and back to Calais, and afterwards married another. She was foolish to think that after all this time he would feel differently towards her. She had enjoyed seeing him again, but she recognised with a languid melancholy that he would never be hers.

Béatrice grunted to herself as she finished her cup of wine and stood listlessly. There was work to be done. She had used most of the water to make the pottage, and now she walked to fetch more.

The stream was a short distance, but to reach it she must make endless detours around other groups of men. Most, when they noticed her at all, were quick to look away. No one wanted to be too close to a woman like her. She saw some making the sign of the cross to ward off her evil eye.

It was enough to make her curl her lips in contempt for the poor fools. They understood nothing about making the black powder and assumed that there must be some kind of magic woven in among the grains in order to make the explosions. They didn't realise that it was only a simple mixture. Making powder for the gonnes was like making a loaf of bread. It meant using the best ingredients and mixing them in the right proportion. The only difficulty was, making sure that the cake of powder was safe from sparks and flames. Still, the powder burns and scars on her arms and face meant that all too often the soldiery would look at her with horror, as though these were proofs of her association with the Devil.

Béatrice didn't care. It meant that on the whole she was left safe from the men of the army. It was more than most women could expect.

Near the river she stopped. A woman was there already. She was older, from the look of her: her gown was matronly in style and cut, like a mother in her thirties, although her face was lined and creased with care and woe. She looked like so many French women whom Béatrice had seen in this sorry country: worn down with fear, haggard with grief, hunger and exhaustion.

'What are you doing?' Béatrice called.

The woman was surrounded by four men, all from other companies. One was taller than the rest and stood laughing uproariously, while his three shorter companions held their arms out like men trying to catch a sheep or piglet. They were laughing too, as men will when they see that their prey is almost in their grasp. And there was little doubt what they intended for this woman when they had her.

It was all too reminiscent of Béatrice's experiences ten years ago, when other soldiers tried to catch her to rape her. She was armed only with her wooden bucket and a small knife, but the two were adequate. She only hoped that the men were most of them drunk. That would make her attack all the more easy.

The nearer man must have heard her feet or sensed his danger, because he began to turn even as the bucket was hurtling towards his head. It struck his nose and cheek with a crack that could have been heard in Paris, Béatrice thought, and then she was swinging it towards the second man. He must have been partly drunk, for he turned only just in time to see the pail rising. He dodged backwards and it missed him by a quarter-inch, but his hurried evasion meant that he fell back heavily onto his arse, and while he was there, Béatrice continued onwards, letting the bucket clump against his forehead. The heavy rim left a thick welt on his brow and he remained where he lay.

As she turned, she found the tall man in front of her. He wasn't smiling now, but stood with his sword outstretched and pointing at her breast. 'Who are you, bitch?'

Béatrice walked around him until she was at the side of the woman. 'I am named Béatrice. If you want to find me, you will find me with the men of the Prince's artillery.'

'I've heard of you – you are the witch with the serpentine powder, then? You think yourself so fearsome that I will quail at your approach? I am not so easily scared, wench. But you are more wholesome than this old drab. Perhaps I ought to take you in her place, since you have been so keen to injure my men to protect her. The best protection for her would be to be supplanted. You will be an adequate replacement.'

Béatrice nodded as though in agreement. She weighed the bucket in her hand. The tall man was not alone. His last companion was still nearby, although he said little. Béatrice could easily raise more support by screaming for help, but there was no telling what manner of support that would bring. It was as likely to bring more men who would decide to rape her for their personal gratification. They might not realise she worked with serpentine.

So Béatrice did not scream or call for help. She stood her ground, watching while the man stepped forward, his short riding sword held with the ease of experience. He advanced until the blade touched her breast-bone, and he smiled then.

She took a step backwards. From the corner of her eye she could just see the last of the men. He was sidling around to move behind her, and she feigned surprise to see him. All at once she was some inches from the sword-point, and she lifted her bucket, shoving it over the blade and pushing down and forward, trapping it. The sudden attack surprised the tall man. His sword was dragged to the ground, and Béatrice stepped on the cross. He could not lift it from that angle, and even as he released his grip on the hilts, he felt the prick of her small knife under his chin.

'Be very careful, master,' she hissed, 'for I am nervous. I would not wish to slit your throat from fear. What is your name?'

'I am called Quilter.'

'Good, Master Quilter. Now, tell your man to step back. I will not hesitate to kill you. Believe me.'

'I believe you!' he said, then, 'Back away! I don't want to be gralloched just because you misread her determination!'

'That is good, master. Now, you will step away too.'

'What of my sword?'

'You may find it later. Step away.'

'I will remember your face.'

'Do so. It is familiar to many. So is the face of my master, who is the Prince's favourite gynour. If you have a desire to pick a quarrel, feel free to do so. I have enough men to protect me.'

*

323

Arnaud tramped along the path with a nervous smile on his face. Bernard looked so grumpy always, glaring about him with his habitual frown, while his latest acquisition trailed behind him.

She was desperately unhappy. Arnaud could see that. And while she no doubt deserved her current afflictions, he did feel sorry for her. He would have liked to take her away from Bernard, to soothe her and comfort her and reassure her. Not that Bernard would allow him. Bernard didn't like him associating with women, which was ironic really.

This army camp was scary. All these English soldiers in every direction. It was the sort of place Arnaud and Bernard would usually avoid, since the horror of almost being caught up in the arrests and killings at Rouen when the King of Navarre was captured. A horrible day.

They were passing by a great pavilion as he thought this, and he stared down at the rugs that covered the floor inside. Rich, glorious colours all but blinded the eye, and he was taken by an urge to roll on the sumptuous carpets.

It was when he looked up that he saw Thomas de Ladit again.

CHAPTER THIRTY

Tuesday 23 August

Berenger and the others rode into Saint-Amand-Montrond with their captives and made their way to Sir John de Sully's pavilion.

The knight rose when he saw Grandarse and Berenger approach. 'In God's name, I am glad to see you back,' he said, clasping Grandarse's hand and smiling broadly. 'I had feared that you were dead or captured. It does me good to see you both safe.'

'Aye, well, we failed to catch the men we wanted, but we did bring you some French scouts to question,' Grandarse said. 'They say that the French King is building an army to meet us.'

'So much the better!' Sir John said. 'Yes, so much the better. The sooner we can meet him in battle and force a decision, the better.'

Berenger nodded. 'The French are gathering at Orléans. King John plans to collect all the nobles and knights he can. He has brought his armies from the north and is mustering all the local peasants to fight too.'

'Peasants are no match for English soldiers,' Sir John said.

'An ant is no match for a bee, but given enough ants, they'll overwhelm the bee,' Grandarse said.

'That sounds like philosophy, Grandarse. You're learning.'

'It's not philosophy, only sense. If they have five or six times our number, we will be at risk. From what our man says, the King of France is determined to destroy us and put paid to any future English invasions.'

'It is hardly surprising,' Sir John said. 'From all we have heard, he was disgusted with his father's failure to halt English attacks, and yet now he is as incapable of preventing them as his father was. We should keep up the pressure on him and force him to submit.'

His eyes moved to Berenger as he spoke, and Berenger was sure that the knight was uncomfortable.

Grandarse grunted his reluctant agreement, and the three men lapsed into silence for a moment. Then Berenger said, 'The company we sought killed another man. We didn't find the women they had captured, but they left a trail of destruction.'

'Which is what the army is expected to achieve,' Sir John said. 'It is a war of *dampnum*, after all, Frip. You know that. You've been involved in our wars before.'

'Yes, but this is violence against the local population for their own profit, not to further the Prince's ambitions.'

'Perhaps the two aspirations meet. It is possible that the Prince's ambitions could be advanced by these actions.'

'A band of routiers murdering and stealing wherever they want?'

'You yourself were their leader once.'

'Yes, but . . .'

'They will surely add to the Prince's desire of seeing the populace driven to despair. His men will add to the burden of misery that afflicts this land, so that when the Prince promises to bring all into his peace if they obey his laws and recognise his authority over all, they will take his invitation with open arms.'

'You mean you support the man?' Berenger said.

'He has brought his company into the Prince's army. He has been accepted.'

Berenger felt as though his stomach had fallen to the floor. He opened his mouth to speak, but no words came.

'He has given his oath to the Prince, to serve for this campaign, Frip. You need to forget him.'

'The man took my—'

'Your *what*? Your position as leader of his company? The company you say should be hunted down and destroyed because of its crimes, even though you were the commander originally, when the company began its depredations? Or because the woman you lusted for chose him? Yes, I have heard the story.'

'That's not true! She left the town to be with me!'

'That is not what I heard, Frip, and his tale was convincing. As things stand, he is a captain in the Prince's army. You must leave him alone, no matter what. Grandarse, Berenger will stay under your command. You will keep an eye on him at all times. I will not have fighting in my ranks. I hope that is understood. Meanwhile, if anything untoward happens to Will, I will hold Fripper responsible. However, I will try to ensure that your men are always some distance away from him and his company. I hope that is understood.'

'Aye, Sir John. But I don't like it,' Grandarse said.

'You don't have to like my orders, so long as you obey them,' Sir John said.

Béatrice had told Archibald about the woman and the attack as soon as she returned to their camp. She had learned Gaillarde's name as the two backed away from Quilter and his men, and Béatrice had stood in the trees with her knife, watching in case they were followed, but when she turned, Gaillarde was nowhere to be seen. She had fled.

'You shouldn't get involved in things like that, woman,' Archibald had scolded. 'You might have been injured.'

'You know my history. I would not allow that to happen to anyone else,' she said firmly.

He had glowered at the ground then. When she was young, he had seemed so confident and self-assured, but as she grew to know him she realised that this was mostly for show. His confidence lay in his appreciation of how others would react when they heard he was a gynour and knew the magic of the black powders. When people got to know him, he was a warm, genial companion, but he was still shy around women, he was so determined never to give offence. If Béatrice wanted something, or needed to silence him, she knew her best approach was to square up to him. He would invariably back down if confronted.

'I don't want to upset you,' she said in a more conciliatory manner. 'But I could not leave that woman to her tormenters.'

'I understand.'

He didn't, of course. He had never experienced the sheer, white-hot, mind-numbing terror that overran a woman's mind when faced with a group of men who were determined to take her body. There was nothing that a man could suffer that could possibly compete with that.

The rest of the evening had passed quietly, but now Béatrice was walking about the camp, trying to find Gaillarde again.

There was something about the woman's face that had touched her. Her panic was not only due to the four men about her, she was sure. There was more to it than that. Was she an unwilling marching wife? Men had tried to force Béatrice to be one such in her time, and the experience had scarred her. The hatred with which she looked on the men who tried to force her to them in gangs was rivalled only by her hatred of the men who had killed her father. But that was a long time ago.

So now, when she went to find water, when she went to fetch bread and meats, when she was sent on errands, she would always search for that face in among the other women of the army. She was resolved to seek her out.

But in an army of thousands, spread over thirty to forty miles, there was no telling where the woman might be.

Denisot waited with Clip, Robin and Pierre and Felix, guarding the French prisoners outside the knight's pavilion while Grandarse and Berenger were inside.

When Sir John was finished, Denisot and the others relinquished their responsibilities, passing the men to Sir John's guards and following Fripper.

'You can't do anything, Frip,' Grandarse was saying.

'It is true, then? I heard his words aright?' Denisot said.

'You shouldn't have listened,' Grandarse grumbled.

'You cannot help but hear a conversation inside a tent,' Berenger said.

Denisot ignored them both. 'The man Will is to be permitted to remain in the camp here? What of the people he has murdered? What of my wife?'

'You heard what Sir John said,' Grandarse said. 'So you heard him say we have to respect Will as a commander here. He is captain of his company, and that is all there is to it.'

Denisot turned and began to stalk away.

'Hoi! Denisot, where are you going?' Grandarse shouted.

'He's going to find Will and kill him,' Berenger grated. 'And I'm going to help him.'

Grandarse grabbed his arm. 'No, you don't, Frip! I won't have you throwing your life away for no reason.'

'No *reason*? Will had my woman murdered before my eyes, Grandarse. He killed her and her two children, just to make me angry before he had me killed. Well, he failed to kill me, so now he'll have to cope with the result.'

'Frip, don't do this. I swear, I don't want to see you injured or killed. Sir John made his views clear, didn't he? If I have to, I'll have you tied down, man.'

'Then hurry up, because I'm going now,' Berenger said, snatching his arm away and hurrying after Denisot.

Grandarse rolled his eyes. 'Hawkwood, get your lardy Essex arse over here!'

When Béatrice had to fetch water again that evening, she was careful to keep an eye open for Gaillarde, but she saw no sign of her.

She moved carefully between the trees and the men at their encampments, most of them averting their gaze as she appeared. The men of the army were nervous in the presence of Archibald and other gynours, but when it came to her, many were openly scared.

It was good that she was left alone. There were few who, like Quilter and his companion, were unafraid of her.

She filled her bucket from the nearest well, and set off back to Archibald and Ed, but on the way she saw a group of men. Something about their voices piqued her interest, and she went to see what they were doing.

As she came closer, she recognised a few of the men, and they moved apart as though in fear of her, more than one crossing himself as she moved in among them and could stare down at the bodies of Quilter and the man with the sword.

Berenger caught Denisot as he was passing the armourers. 'Wait!'

'What, do you want to stop me too?'

'I want to be with you when you find them. Don't forget, I have reason to want to kill Will too.'

'Then you can. After I have.'

'I don't think that's likely.'

'You think I'll fail?'

'Have you looked at your dagger since the fight?'

'Yes. When I cleaned it of the blood. I killed two men that day, you know.'

'And you still carry the broken blade with you.'

'Why do you think I came here, to the armourers?'

Berenger nodded. 'I had thought you were seeking Will out at once.'

'Do you think me a fool? How would I find one man in an army of thousands? You think that I could find one man in a morning?'

Hawkwood and Grandarse caught up with them both as they were fingering different knives and testing them against their thumbs.

'Eh, Frip, but you gave us a fright back there, man. I thought you were off to find Will immediately.'

'I know my place,' Berenger said. He did indeed. However, he would not allow Sir John's demands to affect his determination to have his revenge on Will as soon as he could. Will had tried to kill him and had killed Alazaïs. He would die for her murder.

'What of you, Denisot?'

Denisot felt the edge of a foot-long knife and nodded to himself. 'I seek my wife. Nothing else. I want to see Gaillarde or, at the least, learn what has happened to her.'

'Well, man, there's no harm in that. Perhaps we'll find her at the next town, eh?' Grandarse said.

Denisot nodded while testing the weight and balance of the

knife. He nodded to the armourer. 'How much for this one? My friend here can pay.'

Grandarse glanced at him, then at the knife, before looking over at Berenger. 'So there's no nonsense about killing this man, eh?'

Berenger met his eyes firmly. 'Of course not. We have been given our orders, haven't we?'

Thursday 25 August

The rain was falling steadily and Berenger pulled off his hat with a curse, the sodden fabric floppy as he wiped his brow. He wrung out the felt, leaving the brim and crown disfigured, and tugged it back on again. It was little good in this weather.

'Not much to see,' Robin said.

Berenger grunted. They had been slogging north for the whole day now, leaving the main army behind as dawn broke, detailed to ride out with the Captal de Buch, a fiery, indomitable commander, and a favourite of the Prince of Wales, together with a large force of his Guyennois. Berenger felt as though he had been cut adrift. The rest of Grandarse's centaine remained behind with Sir John, but he had heard that he had been recommended along with his vintaine because he had such a close working knowledge of this part of France after bringing in the French scouts.

'A man cannot see through this rain,' he agreed. 'If only this weather would improve!'

They had set off in bright sunlight yesterday, riding past Chateauroux and continuing up to the flat valley here. Their duty was to search the land for any signs of French soldiery, and then not to engage them, but take news of their size and direction back to the Prince's party. Yesterday their journey had been easy, but overnight the rain had set in and now all were soaked. Hungry, weary and unrested, they slogged on through the mud, dreaming of hot fires, hot food, and steaming drinks of wine or ale sweetened with honey. Berenger could almost taste the sickly sweetness on his tongue.

'What's that?'

Berenger held up his hand and peered questioningly at Robin. There were few men whom he would trust in almost any conditions, but he was quickly learning that Robin's hearing and eyesight were as good as any man's, and a great deal better than Berenger's own.

'Well?'

'I thought I saw something there,' Robin said, pointing. Berenger stared through the mists, but he could make out nothing against the backdrop of grey misery. Just vaguely he thought he could see a path through the trees as a paler grey. 'Just a squall blown by the wind,' he hazarded.

'Perhaps,' Robin said. He continued to stare.

Berenger sighed. 'Did it look like men?'

'Possibly.'

'Well, I don't want to ride into a damned ambush again,' Berenger said. 'If they want to tempt us that way, we should continue and then work around behind them – if there are men there.'

'Very well.'

Berenger sunk his chin on his breast and glowered at the rain on the road ahead. He could see the little detonations where the drops were pocking the mud and puddles like pebbles thrown into a stream. When they hit his back, they felt like slingshot. The rain here was heavier than any he had known before, a torrent that tumbled from the sky like a wall of water. It seemed almost impossible, as though the entire ocean was being poured over them, and then, all in an instant, it was gone. Where he had been all but shivering from the chill, suddenly the clouds were peeling back from the sky, the sun burst out with blinding ferocity, and Berenger could see the steam rising from the dark coats of the horses, from the thick cloaks of the men and from the road.

It matched his mood. He was ferociously bitter about the way Sir John had turned him from the centaine, passing him on to this Gascon raiding party as though he was an embarrassment to be disposed of. He was here, while the rest of Grandarse's men were enjoying a gentler ride some miles south of him now. He ought to have been with them. If possible, he and Denisot should have been seeking out Will, and when they found him, executing him. The man had to atone for Alazaïs and her children as well as for Gaillarde. Yes, he would pay for his murder of the woman and for his attempt to kill Berenger.

The urgent desire for revenge was like a drug. Berenger had felt as though he had returned from alcoholic oblivion to his youth when he discovered the Prince's army and was reunited with Grandarse and the others. Now he was doubly outcast, it seemed, as reviled and despised as an outlaw, and all because he wanted to punish the man who had tried to kill him. There was no justice. Well, it would be put right when he returned to the army. He would find Denisot, who would with luck have learned where Will was – Denisot had not been sent with Berenger, but had been left behind, told to help Grandarse. When Berenger returned, he would find Denisot and the two would look for Will. And kill him.

'That! Did you hear that?' Robin demanded. He was turned in his saddle, facing back the way he had pointed before. 'I heard a clatter, like a sword being dropped. There are men out there, Frip.'

'I heard nothing,' Berenger snapped.

'Then wait here, *Vintener*, while I ride to discover what it was I heard,' Robin responded sharply. 'If I am right and there is a force there in the trees waiting to attack us, we could all suffer for your bitter mood.'

Berenger bit back his curt rejoinder. Instead he held up his hand to halt the vintaine, then shouted, 'Clip, Dogbreath, Felix, Pierre, Nick, Baz, ride with me!' To Robin, he said more quietly, 'You're right. Wait here. Fulk, you too, and Saul. Have the better archers prepare, just in case, and make sure of your targets before you loose. I don't want one of your arrows in my back.'

'Yes, Frip.'

Berenger took his horse back down the line until he was back at the place where Robin had first seen something. 'See anything in there, Clip?'

'I can see trees. What else do you expect me to see?'

'We'll ride in along that path, Clip. Keep your eyes and ears open, all of you. This could be another ambush,' Berenger called, and spurred his mount onwards. He had no desire to ride at a slow pace to allow a crossbowman time to draw a line on him. Instead he rode in at a sharp canter, close to the line of the trees on the left, studying the trees at the other side of the track, searching for a paler smudge in among the ferns and bushes that thickly filled the darkness. There was nothing, only large oak and elm boughs and occasional chestnuts. He saw only verdant growth, heavy, hanging branches, and . . . a face. And another.

'*Ware!* Ambush!'

CHAPTER THIRTY-ONE

Berenger roared and clapped spurs to the beast's flanks, bending low as the first bolt flew over him, and already he was flying along. There was a man before him, then two more, all with crossbows, all aiming, but before they could loose their weapons, he was on them, jumping over the middle of the three, the horse's hoofs striking his assailant on his helmet and knocking it away with a ringing clatter. Berenger landed, his horse wrenching from side to side, and Berenger had to tear the reins round to attract its attention, then he was hurtling back, his sword out and flashing at the archer on his right. The man went down with a shriek, but the last man had slipped back into the forest again, out of sight.

Pierre and Felix were sitting on their mounts with mouths agape, while Clip and Dogbreath were darting hither and thither from one man to another lying on the ground. When Berenger approached, he saw that Clip was weighing a man's purse in his hands and pulling a face. 'Hardly enough for a loaf of bread. I tell you, these were all peasants.'

'How can you tell?' Felix said.

'Even you can see they made their attempt too soon, can't you? We weren't all in their trap, and the men who tried to kill us had no skill.'

Berenger explained, 'They loosed their bows with their eyes shut, desperate to send their bolts at us and then run, so they all missed, and when we got closer, they were so panicked they ran along between the trees. If they were sensible, they'd have jumped in among the trees. We couldn't ride there to hunt them down, and they could have spanned their bows again and taken us one by one. As it is, these peasants died for nothing. They harmed none of us, and gave us every opportunity to kill them. Fools!'

He was bitter. All thoughts of eagerly accepting death, such as he had known at Uzerche, were gone now. Berenger could not die and leave his men to be misused in the way that these peasants had been. Their lives had been flung away as though they were worthy of little more than death. They were mere stalks of wheat to be scythed down. It was wasteful, sheer foolishness.

Then he began to wonder whether there was some reason after all. 'Clip, did you find their commander?'

'No. Only these lummoxes,' he said, kicking the nearest body.

'Why would they throw men like this at us? They must realise that we would trample them into the dirt.'

'It's too few to cause us a real headache,' Clip said.

'But enough to hold us up a short while,' Berenger said.

'Why bother?' Felix asked.

'Clip, Dogbreath, remount, fast!' Berenger said.

'Just let me . . .' Clip began.

'No! String your bow and get on your horse now! This must have been a distraction while they attack our vanguard. Why else would they throw so few without effective leadership at us here? Quick! Back to the Captal!'

*

337

It was the early evening when Béatrice happened to see her.

There was a line of women who were marching wives to the men, some women who had been captured and forced to submit, but mostly girls who had seen in the English army an opportunity for money and food. Many were peasant children orphaned by the wars, although some had been attracted to a specific man and chose to march with him and his comrades. Some remained with the one man, although others were happy to offer their affections to many in return for money, food or drink. Some were raucous, flamboyant characters, while others trudged reluctantly, heads hung low.

It was when they stopped that Béatrice walked about the women's part of the camp and saw her again.

Gaillarde was foraging, and there was a fair-haired man with her. Both were hunting about for sticks and tinder, preparing to make a fire for their evening meal, and Béatrice felt a flood of warm relief wash through her.

'Gaillarde!'

The woman's head snapped around, and Béatrice saw the fair-haired man look from Gaillarde to her, and then over to a little fire. He looked suddenly terrified.

Béatrice stepped forward to Gaillarde, but even as she did so, she saw Gaillarde shaking her head vigorously and stepping away. 'Go! Go away! Quickly, before he . . .'

'What is it, Gaillarde?'

But Gaillarde and the scared man were drawing away. And then Béatrice saw the black-haired man at the fire. His eyes were fixed on her and she suddenly realised why the other two were so scared.

He had the face of a Devil.

Berenger galloped from the woods with his pony puffing and blowing like an aged nag, his men straggling behind him as they urged their own beasts to greater efforts.

'Robin, that was a diversion!' he bellowed as he came closer. 'The main attack must be ahead! Ride now, warn the Captal de Buch!'

Robin needed no second encouragement, but clapped his heels to his pony and took off after the leader of their army, Berenger clattering along behind.

The force under the Captal de Buch was over a thousand strong, and it marched slowly, the men carrying heavy loads as well as their weaponry. There was no certainty of obtaining food while they were on the march. Berenger rode along behind Robin, wiping away the spatters of mud that Robin's horse threw in its wake, until they were past the main column and had reached the vanguard.

'Robin!' Berenger shouted. 'There! The Captal!'

Robin heard his call and followed his pointing finger, riding to the group of fifteen knights and squires who were plodding on in the muddy road.

That was when the trap was sprung.

A flash of powder and a thick cloud of smoke on the left showed that there was a gonne of some sort, and Berenger felt as though his bowels were going to dissolve. A large stone ball was flung from the midst of the smoke and over the heads of the startled Captal and his commanders, and then there was a loud hissing, and Berenger saw a plume of greasy grey smoke rising from the trees. A scream came from that direction, but he ignored it, riding to the Captal, shouting, 'Ambush! Ambush!'

His warning was too late, he saw, and he groaned. A sudden flurry of heavy bolts and arrows flew from the front and a little behind, and while the men were recovering from that, a second flight struck them. Horses shocked and terrified by the gonne's shot were stung by these darts, which, while they were not driven by bows as powerful as the English longbows, were enough to penetrate the *cuir bouilli* of the mounts. Maddened by the stinging barbs, several horses reared and plunged, throwing their riders and hurtling off. Berenger saw a movement from in front, and then the main attack was launched: thirty or more horsemen screaming and yelling, lances couched, riding straight at the Captal and his men.

But the Captal was no novice to fighting. He gave a command and his men-at-arms spread out, donning bascinets, pulling down visors, and advancing. On a second command, the first men trotted forward, then cantered, and suddenly they were galloping. A third command and the Captal himself and the remaining men were hurtling in the wake of the first row, and then the squires and sergeants were following with remounts. Meanwhile two centeners had already cursed and bullied the archers from their mounts, and had them string their bows and send the first of many flights of arrows into the trees where the French archers and gonnes were.

Berenger watched with his heart pounding as the Captal and his men crashed into the French. There was a rattling sound like a thousand pewter plates being thrown together on a stone floor, and then the English were through the French, leaving a number of inert bodies. The Captal's horse seemed crazed, rearing and kicking, then trying to bite another beast with a Frenchman on its back. There was a man on the ground looking dazed, sitting and holding his head. The Captal's mount came down heavily with both forehoofs and Berenger didn't see him again.

Meanwhile the little plain was filled with the ringing of steel as the warriors drew their swords to finish the battle. In only a short time the French cavalry had been put to flight.

Exchanging a glance, Berenger and Robin rode for the place where the blackened undergrowth spoke of the gonne. Berenger avoided the powder-burned bushes, but rode to the side where the undergrowth looked thick, and as his horse entered, he saw three men fumbling with a barrel of powder. He rode at them, panicking as he saw the powder spilling all over the ground, and when his horse stood in the middle of it, but their serpentine was damp or ineffective, because nothing happened. He lunged at the nearer of the men, and saw a spear-point thrusting at his belly, knocking it away with only a moment to spare, and then he was kicking his beast on again and hacking at a man, who held up a broken barrel for defence, but Berenger's blade caught all his fingers and chopped them off as easily as a knife cutting through chive stems. When the man screamed and threw the barrel at Berenger's head, Robin was behind him, slashing at his bare pate.

They moved through the undergrowth with caution, but soon they were through the woods and at the far side they could see the remnants of the infantry running away over the surrounding fields. Soon, from either side, they saw English riders in pursuit.

'You want to join them?' Robin said.

'No. I've killed enough today,' Berenger said. He looked down at his sword. There was a notch on the blade that had not been there earlier. He pulled a face and wiped the steel on his sleeve, then thrust it away into his scabbard before leading the way back to the column.

The Captal de Buch was waiting when they both rode back to the column. The Captal pulled his bascinet from his head and nodded to Berenger and Robin. 'How did you know that was going to happen?' he asked.

Berenger explained about the diversionary attack and how he had immediately thought that there could only be one reason for it.

'You did well, Vintener.' His stern, square features suddenly broke into a grin. 'Although you were almost too late, hey? Next time, more quick. But I thank you.'

He rode on, leaving Robin and Berenger. They took their horses back along the column towards their own men.

'At least he will remember your name, Frip,' Robin said.

'Perhaps,' Berenger said. He grinned without humour. 'So does a King's Justice when he gives a death sentence!'

Thomas de Ladit wanted to return to the safety of Navarre. He was the King's man, after all, and while poor Charles languished in prison, waiting for the King of France to forget his anger, it was Thomas's duty, so he thought, to go and keep the administration of Charles's lands in good order. It was categorically not his responsibility to remain here in France, at his own risk, to help the English, allies of King Charles though they may be.

He left the Prince of Wales's pavilion. They were inside, staring at maps and trying to make sense of the landscape about them, and he was, frankly, fed up. He didn't know this part of the land, and if they were so keen to have better information about the terrain, they should ride out themselves and view it. For his part, he craved only a real bed and a chance to sleep for a week. Being on campaign with an army like this was little better than hard labour. Constantly marching, riding, stopping and having a scrappy meal of pottage and bread, and then sleeping on a tree-root or stone as best he could, before lurching up and being forced to repeat it.

This was no life for a man used to the comforts of life in King Charles's court.

He stood and stared out at the men all around. Thousands of them, sprawling out in every direction. Armourers and farriers belting out their own irregular timpany; cooks bellowing for salt as they sweated over their fires, kicking at their servants; soldiers sweeping their whetstones over swords or daggers already razor-sharp; dogs bickering and snarling at each other – the noise was deafening.

Strolling away from the worst of the hubbub, he found himself in among Gascons, and then more English. The voices, the dialects and languages buffeted his ears like a stormy sea striking a harbour. There was no regularity.

'Thomas!'

Suddenly he was grabbed from behind, and he found himself staring into the face of Bernard.

'What are you doing here?' he cried.

Friday 26 August

They passed an uncomfortable night, with the rain still falling in a desultory fashion as though it was itself as bored with dampening the men as they were of being soaked. Berenger sat with his cloak over him, his hat dribbling water like an old man trying to drink with a broken jaw, squatting before a fire, his back to a tree. Before him in the flames of the campfire he saw his wife, smiling, and then looking at him with sadness in her eyes; and then her face smoothed out and rounded, and he was looking into the face of Alazaïs, the widow of Uzerche, and she was beseeching him to avenge her murder and the murder of her boys. Their faces, too, he saw in the flames, and then in the embers as the rain slowly drowned the fire.

He must have slept.

Berenger came awake startled, all in a sudden, with the shock that makes a man draw a deep breath, like the first inhalation of a newly born child. He couldn't tell what had woken him, but all about him the sun was beginning to brighten the sky. Berenger rose stiffly, feeling the tendons and joints moving roughly, like old bolts sliding in unoiled channels. He was old. Too old for this kind of life any more. He didn't know how Grandarse managed, nor Sir John. They both of them were older than he, but neither, he thought, woke with this dullness behind the eyes. It was debilitating to always have this sensation of thick, clogged weariness on waking.

But a man had work to do, no matter how he felt. Berenger rose and shook out his cloak, wrung out his hat again, and studied it with dispassionate appraisal. It was oddly bent and twisted from too many occasions of being cleaned and dried. It was comfortable, but surely, when they took a fresh town he would have to find a hatter who could provide him with a newer garment that would offer greater protection from the elements. He hoped so.

He saw to his own gear, then woke the men. The only man missing was Robin, who reappeared later, when the men were almost all on their feet. He had gone to defecate, he said when asked. Berenger didn't care. He had spent his time reigniting the fire and forming his own oatcake, setting it to cook with his sign – a 'B' – cut into the upper surface so no one could claim it as their own. When it was hot and toasted on the outside from the too-vigorous flames, he packed his gear and was soon ready with his horse saddled and bridled. When Robin appeared, throwing his blanket over his pony, then setting the saddle and tightening the girth, Berenger peered at him.

'Imbert. Is he the one?'

Robin hesitated without meeting his gaze. 'What do you mean?'

'I know you don't sleep with the rest of the men. You wander off and return in the morning. But if you're trying to avoid Imbert, that won't work. He'll figure out one day, and then he'll be able to hurt you away from all the rest of the vintaine.'

'So I should stay here and wait for him to come to me in the night? I should allow him to kill me at his leisure?'

'No. But if you are here, it will be easier for you to get the help of others to subdue him. He is not popular with the other men. You are.'

'What does that matter? He's strong and powerful. He is accepted by all the leaders here.'

'The Prince and the Captal de Buch are more appreciative of their archers than a meathead like Imbert. But if he tries to attack you, I will see him flogged. Unless you have a better idea?'

'No. A good flogging will suit him fine,' Robin said. He finished tightening the girth, and then paused, looking up at Berenger. 'Thanks, Fripper.'

'I'll tell him. Just make sure your dispute doesn't make for bad feelings in the vintaine.'

They crossed the river early that morning.

Berenger had a feeling that this would be a day he would remember when he spoke to Imbert and had to threaten the man of the consequences if there was more trouble between him and Robin. Later, staring down at the remains of the bridge over the River Cher, he knew he would have good cause.

Uprights were leaning drunkenly, and even as the army watched, the last hammer blows broke the final supports. As Berenger stared, he saw the last sections of the bridge move slowly from the verticals and begin to fall into the waters, individual planks pulling away from the rest of the structure, then the heavy beams that took the full weight of the bridge, all traffic tumbling after them, and the whole of the main roadway floating away like a vast barge. At last, the noise of hammering and then cries and the sound of wood rending and tearing came to them on the air.

'That looks like the furthest extent of our ride,' Robin said.

Berenger glanced at him. 'You think so? If there's a town up there, and there's a river here, that means someone used to cross the river before the bridge was built. So, somewhere down there is a ford. All we have to do is find it.'

'A ford?' Robin said. 'Over that river? It's huge!'

'Not as big as the Seine when we crossed that ten years ago,' Berenger said. As he spoke, the command to proceed came, and before long Berenger was being called to the front.

'Sir?'

The Captal looked as though he was ready to beat to death the first man who answered back or who seemed to thwart him. 'I want to know . . . How can we cross that river? We must get to Vierzon on the other side.'

'You want me to seek out a ford near that town?' Berenger said for him.

The Captal eyed him bleakly. 'I have heard you know how.'

'It's what I did when I served the King in the chevauchée that ended at Crécy. The enemy had torn down all the bridges, and we had to find fords then, too. If there is one, I will find it with my vintaine.'

'Do this for me and I will see you rewarded, you *and* your vintaine.'

'They will be happy to hear it,' Berenger said.

'Good. Godspeed, Vintener.'

That was at least an hour of the morning since, and Berenger and the others had spent all the intervening time wandering along the river banks east and west from the bridge's broken structure. So far they had seen nothing that could help. Usually a ford was indicated by the low, sloping banks where wagons and carts could be driven down to the water prior to being drawn through the river, but here there was nothing to indicate that a ford had ever existed.

Berenger had seen such places before, where townspeople destroyed the old ford so that all wheeled traffic had to use the new bridge and pay the tolls for the privilege. But then usually a man could see the line of a road which had once led to the ford, or the line of shallower water. Here he could see nothing. Only the deep, dark river waters.

There was a line in the water, though. A darker shape, as though the shadow of the bridge had indelibly marked the river-bed here, staining it a deeper shade than all the rest of the river. He dropped from his horse and walked to the waters. Here, where the bridge had stood, the water was a cold green that looked impossibly deep. Berenger looked upriver and saw that the water was paler. The same was true downriver, and he wondered why the water should be deeper just here. That was when he realised that the darker colour was the weed. It was darker because the weeds were nearer the surface.

'Archers! Here!' he bellowed, and instructed them to prepare to loose their arrows at any force approaching on the opposite bank, before lifting his sword in its scabbard over his head and stepping into the water.

It was chill. He felt it reaching into his boots, icy fingers stroking his thighs and licking at his cods. That made him draw in his breath, but he continued. The water was up to his belly now, and then his breast, but he kept on walking, the breath coming harder now as the pressure of the water squeezed the air from his lungs, but already he was past the middle of the river, and he could see the farther side closer and closer, and he felt a ridiculous grin fixing itself to his face. He was almost there, and then he was rising, and his legs were feeling as though the air out here was colder than the water, and his boots were squelching and farting as he climbed up the sandy bank and peered cautiously around him. There was no one about. The people of the

347

town were either so convinced that an army would find the river impassable, or else they knew nothing would stop the English and had remained behind their town's walls.

Berenger turned back and waved both his arms. He could see the Captal de Buch on a knoll a short distance away, pointing with a sword, and saw the command being issued, and soon the whole Guyennois force was approaching the ford. While engineers cut logs from the destroyed bridge to construct ramps for the wagons, archers rode quickly across the river to form a bridgehead to protect the men crossing. Berenger sat on a log watching them with a strange feeling that he should not have found this ford.

He was growing despondent. If he had not found this ford, the army would have stayed on the other bank and perhaps fewer Frenchmen would die. It would have been better if he had done that. The world would have been better.

In truth, the world would be better without him.

CHAPTER THIRTY-TWO

Robin brought his pony to him and passed him the reins. 'You were right. There was a ford.'

'There's always a ford if you know where to look,' Berenger said.

'Why do you stare at the men?'

'I was remembering the last time I was stuck looking for a ford. That was a few days before Crécy, and the French had harried us all the way up north, with our escape blocked by the Somme. We had no choice but to continue then, following the river, hoping that we would find a path across, because else we were dead.'

'You were trapped?'

'The sea on one side and ahead of us, marshes and salt flats, the river to the right and the army of the French behind us. No sensible place to have a battle, no defensive position and no escape. We kept on moving because they could have surrounded us if we stopped, but there was no food to be had, so all they need do was wait and starve us out. But then we captured a man we thought was a scout, and it turned out he was a fisherman, and had been born English. I think he was also born a smuggler, because he knew a path over the Somme at low tide.'

'And that saved you?'

Berenger nodded.

'And this reminded you of that?'

'Yes. Then it saved us. I begin to feel that when we reach a river and cross it, that itself helps us. If the rivers of France are all set to protect us and aid us when we need their help, surely that means the land is for us too, and that means God is on our side. With Him to look to our interests, how can we fail?'

Robin looked at him. 'You believe that?'

Berenger watched as Clip, Dogbreath and the rest of the vintaine clattered up the ramp. Fulk was behind them, Père et Fils a little ahead of Clip, who was berating the river, the weather, the town ahead and all the army. Did he believe it? Sometimes, perhaps. More to the point, he knew what to say to enthuse his men.

'You can't see the injustice?' Clip said. 'We're sent here to find some Frenchies, and what do the others do? Grandarse has them cosy and warm with the Prince and the rest, all of them in nice, warm billets, dry and comfy, while we slog our guts out in the rain and the winds. And now we have to ford rivers like this fucker here.'

Pierre turned to him. 'But you were telling us that you wished to be at the front of the army, for that was where the best pickings and winnings were to be won?'

'Yes, the front of the army, not here in a sodding scouting party.'

Robin chuckled. 'You call this a scouting party?'

'Well, isn't it?'

Fulk rumbled, 'It is a large scouting force, then?'

'It's away from the main army, is what I'm saying. Dogbreath understands, don't you?'

Dogbreath gave a nervous smile and managed to look like a fretful hound unsure of a command.

Pierre frowned. 'So you think we are hard done by because we are at the front of the army?'

'I think we're hard done by because we're the poor fuckwits who always end up in the middle of any nasty battle that's going.'

Fulk laughed aloud. 'You want the glory and profit without the danger?'

'Some profit would be good,' Clip said. 'It's all right for you now. You think you'll live forever, but the sad fact is, we're all going to get killed. Just you wait. We'll be thrown into the next big fight and get our arses cut from us. There'll be no safe resort for us once the Captal decides he wants something. The commanders, they're all the same. Throw away our lives without blinking, the lot of 'em. So, say your prayers carefully, make sure you have the priests shrive you when you get a chance, and live like a saint.'

'Like you, eh, Clip?' Fripper said. He and Robin had fallen in alongside their vintaine.

'I like to think . . .'

Fulk laughed again, earning him a black glare from Clip.

'I was going to say, before that fat mountain man belched, that I have lived a good, virtuous life.'

'What would you think would be an evil life?' Robin wondered aloud.

While the vintaine resorted to bickering, Berenger allowed his mind to wander. He recalled the abbey and the kindly Abbot who was so keen to help see him healed, but who was determined to expel him once he was fit once more. He would like to see the Abbot once more, to talk to him and . . . and what? Ask

351

his forgiveness for the last few years of debauchery and violence? Or ask him for his blessing for a religious life?

'What?' he asked. He had been startled from his reverie by the appearance of a herald, who cast a contemptuous eye over the men in the vintaine.

'I said, the Captal de Buch, your leader, asks if you are ready for your reward?'

Berenger found the Captal de Buch standing in the shade of a large beech tree, staring at the town with a broad grin on his face. 'Ah, Fripper. You did well finding the ford. You have my gratitude.'

'I was asked to come that I could claim my reward?'

The Gascon gave a wolfish grin. 'Ah, but yes. We shall shower your reward over you shortly. The town there. I have heard that it is a valuable place, filled with riches. All we need do is storm it and take what we want. You will be with the first parties. To you will go much of the glory when we seize it. And all the riches you find, you may keep, you and your men.'

Berenger stared at him, then at the town. 'You mean we shall ride in there and take what we want, no matter what the towns-folk say?'

'The town is yours. However, I would not send you in alone, my friend. No, you will have the whole army at your side and back.'

Berenger had a vision of Clip's face as he listened to his orders. Clip was mouthing, 'We'll all die, I'm tellin' you,' as the Captal finished. There may have been other words in his mouth as he glared at Berenger, but then the Captal said, 'Is that clear?' and the mental image mercifully disappeared.

'Yes, sir.'

*

Clip stared, his mouth open. 'What?'

'You heard. Come on, Clip.'

'I'm not goin'. I'm not! That's fucking unfair! We were the first down here as scouts, we were among the first over the river. You were the first, Frip, weren't you? And now some Gascon ape says he wants us to go into the town and get our arses fried as if it's a reward for good behaviour? Are you mad? Tell him to piss off and get another vintaine that's ready to die. I'm not. I'm not going!'

Fulk glowered at the ground. 'He is not being wrong. This time, I think Clip has the fair idea of the justice.'

Berenger glanced at all the men and puffed out his cheeks. 'What of the rest of you? Père? Fils? Saul? Robin?'

The father and son glanced at each other. There was hope in the boy's eyes. Meanwhile Nick and Baz stood. 'We're with you, Frip.'

Fulk was still sitting. He took up a twig in his fingers and snapped it. 'This is not right. Some other vintaine should be found. Clip is right.'

'You want me to go to the Captal and tell him that you all refuse to obey his orders? I can do that, of course. But you know the consequences. You'll likely be hanged as an example of what happens to the disobedient. You want that?'

'Worse,' Robin said, 'when we come out of there with all the merchants' furs and gold hanging off us, we'll come and tell you all about it.' He settled his sword on his hip as he stared towards the town. 'I'm with you, Frip.'

'Right,' Berenger said as he glanced at the men who remained squatting or sitting. 'Godspeed to you all. I don't disagree with you, but we are soldiers. We have to do as we're told; else, how could any commander achieve any victory? The Captal has to be able to rely on his men. If he cannot, he may as well give up his staff of office now.'

He turned and began to make his way up to the road that led to the main gate of the town.

It was not a great city, but a goodly sized town nonetheless. Robin joined him, and the two marched along the dirt road.

'Did I lay it on too thick?' Berenger asked quietly.

'No. But you needed a good shovel to set out the soil and flatten it.'

Berenger glanced at him. Behind him, he heard Clip's whine.

'I'm buggered, I am. This is a fucking stupid army. Why am I here, eh? I ought to be at home with a roaring fire and a pot of ale, not trudging through the mud to go to a town where some evil harpy's likely to cut my throat as soon as I look at her.'

'She'll cut her own throat at the thought of you touching her,' Robin called.

Berenger licked his lips nervously. To left and right he could see parties of men moving forward. None seemed to want to overtake him, but instead they moved at his speed. But there was no sign of the defenders. 'What is going on?' he asked.

Robin smiled at him. 'I think the good Captal was honestly trying to reward us, Frip.'

'What?'

'Do you see any men on the walls? Do you see any smoke from a fire? There is nothing, is there?'

He was right. The town was deserted.

Saturday 27 August

The next day Berenger sat stiffly on his horse and watched the end of the little farmstead.

They were fifteen miles from Vierzon, and from where he was, he could see perfectly clearly the cloud of black, filthy smoke that was rising from the remains of the town as the men of the Prince of Wales's army moved in to destroy it. There was to be nothing left.

'Riders, Frip,' Robin said.

Berenger nodded to Clip. He stood with Nick and Baz, and now gave them their instructions. Soon they had their torches alight, and they moved in and about the buildings. It took little time for the dry rafters and inner thatch to take the flames to themselves, and once the timbers were crackling and spitting, there was nothing to do to save them.

This had been their task since they had arrived at Vierzon, to destroy everything for miles around. The Gascons under the Captal de Buch had taken to their new task with enthusiasm, putting to the sword any living creature they found, and burning, burning from farm to village to field. Nothing was to be left standing, and the Gascons were most competent at their work. But it was soul-destroying. Berenger had seen little farms that must have been home to three generations of peasants being consumed. He had watched as working mills were destroyed, as stores of food and drink were broken, ravaged, and then thrown onto the reeking pyres. The folk of this land would be utterly ruined, losing home and belongings, losing their livelihood, their possessions and all the foods they had expended so much effort to grow.

Berenger could understand the need to deter men from going to the French King, but this was surely not the way to achieve the Prince's ambition. The Prince wanted to have the people learn to despise their King, and to deny him a rich source of tax income, but by attacking all the people, destroying their towns and farms and homes, burning their crops and their stocks, he was only giving them cause to fly from the English. It made no sense. None of them would want to come under the Prince's protection, surely. The people would be like those at Uzerche who stared sullenly at Berenger and the company, reluctantly accepting the truth of their position, but not doing so with any enthusiasm. They did not see a group of strong men who deserved their honour and respect, but only a company of thieves and mercenaries. It was not surprising. What else were the men in this Gascon force, other than plunderers and opportunists, just as were the men in Will's company. Would a townsman decide to surrender to Will in order to win the protection of the routiers? It was unlikely.

'Frip?'

Berenger turned to see that the riders were much nearer. He recognised one of the men at the front as an Englishman who had been in the Captal de Buch's army. He was a short man, but very broad-shouldered, with eyes that seemed always on the verge of a smile. Today he had nothing in his eyes but shock.

'Fripper, is that you?' he asked as the riders came to a halt.

There were two vintaines with him, thirty-four men in total.

Racking his brain, Berenger finally remembered his name. 'Bill. How is the trail that way?'

'Evil, I swear. I haven't seen such deaths in many a year. Some men must have come across refugees up yonder, and they slaughtered them all. Men, women, children, all lying in one pile.'

Berenger nodded. 'It is a dreadful sight.'

'Usually it is sad. Today it was dreadful,' Bill said.

Bill accepted the offer of some of their food with alacrity. He and his men had been riding all day, he said, and they were thirsty after their exertions. The weather had been spitting with rain, and the dust had been kept down, but even without it the men had endured a hard journey.

'We were off before dawn to scout about for the French, and to see whether we could find a crossing over the Loire.'

'Did you have any luck?' Clip asked excitedly. He had convinced himself that there would be easier pickings north of the great river, and was keen to make his way to Orléans or Chartres and take whatever he could in plunder.

'Nothing yet, but there are other scouts searching towards Meung and Blois. Audley and Chandos have taken sizeable forces with them to see if they can find a passage. If so, all will be good. We shall have a clear path to the north.'

Berenger nodded. Most of the men were aware that the Prince intended to head north and west, hoping to link up with the army of the Duke of Lancaster. With the two armies of the Duke and the Prince, the English would be a match for any French force.

Clip was disappointed by the news. 'You didn't find any crossing?'

'No. But we did find other things,' Bill said. He took a long swallow of wine and glanced at Berenger. He had lost all joviality now. In his eyes there was only a restless wonder. 'I tell you, Fripper, there are some men who'd deserve a long, slow death for their actions here.'

'What do you mean?' Berenger asked.

'I found a young maid up there today,' Bill said. His voice dropped, and he wouldn't meet Berenger's eye as he spoke. 'A maid of perhaps thirteen, fourteen summers? She had been raped, but when they killed her, they did so by lashing her to a beam, and then cut her throat.'

'Where was this?' Berenger asked sharply.

'To the north of here, perhaps two leagues.'

'Were there any English near?'

'Not that I saw at the time, but they have been that way. I expect it was one of Chandos's companies. They seem to have passed that way. Why?'

'I have seen another body like that. I have heard of many more,' Berenger said. He cast an eye about his men thoughtfully.

'Whoever this man is, he should be cut away from the rest of the army,' Bill said. 'It is one thing to obey orders to kill as a punishment, but another to kill with cruelty for sport.'

Clip shrugged. 'What is the difference? If we're told to kill everyone in a town, what does it matter whether a girl is stabbed once, or killed another way? She'll be just as dead.'

'If you cannot tell the difference, you are lost,' Berenger said sharply. 'You remember Béatrice, don't you? If she were to be killed, better that she should suffer as little as necessary, rather than she should be forced to submit to rape and then be killed in as slow a manner as possible.'

'What says she died that slowly?' Clip asked. 'Being tied to a board to be raped, and then had her throat cut. Doesn't sound too bad. Many are slowly strangled. I'd think that would be worse.'

Berenger was going to answer, but he had no words. 'Tell the men to prepare to ride,' he said. He was thinking: the other deaths all happened when Will and his men were about. Now another body was discovered.

Bill was soon back on his own mount. 'I tell you, Fripper. There was something about that child's murder that made me think. I'll need a quart of wine to sleep well this night.'

Berenger nodded and patted Bill's horse's neck. 'I know. I recall only too clearly the woman I saw treated in the same manner.'

'And I keep thinking, it could be anyone in our army,' Bill said. 'When I sit and eat with another man, I will always wonder whether that was the man who killed that child. Whether it was his hands who tied her and made her suffer, then cut her throat, and those same hands are now breaking the bread for me. How can a man sit while thinking that?'

'The man who did that before was in my company. I was ejected from the company, but the man who killed girls and children that way was still there. Have you seen any sign of the company under Will's command?'

Bill frowned quickly. 'Will? I saw him only two days ago. He is with Audley searching for a crossing point.'

Berenger tried not to sound too eager. So, this latest victim was found only a matter of a day or so since Will's party had ridden this way. Which of the men could be guilty of this, he wondered. None of his old party struck him as so crazed that they would treat a child like this.

He said, 'Two days ago where?'

Robin was at Berenger's side as Bill and his men took their leave of the vintaine, and he glanced at Berenger's face as the little group rode off.

'What?' Berenger asked.

'Frip, I trust you, but you have too much interest in this man Will and your old company.'

'I have little interest in them.'

'So we shall not ride off after them?'

'Of course not. We'll ride to check any possible crossing points over the river. That is all.'

'And if we run into this man Will's company, what then?'

'If we run into a group that attacks us or tries to ambush us, we will respond as Englishmen,' Berenger said levelly. He looked at Robin. 'And if I find a murderer in my path, I will execute him as I would any wolf's-head.'

'Are you seeking this man for revenge because he stole your company from you?'

'No! I seek him for other reasons.'

'It's true that he stole your woman, then?'

Berenger's mouth gaped. 'Who told you that?'

'It is common enough news about the army. You were enraged when he took your woman and—'

'*Ballocks!* He wanted my woman, but when she chose to leave her house, her town, her life in order to be with me, that prick had us waylaid on the road! It was only the presence of Fulk and Saul that saved me from dying just as she and her two sons did! If you doubt me, ask Fulk! He was there too. He can tell you the truth!'

Robin nodded slowly. 'I will ask Fulk and Saul, but even if they tell me you are speaking the truth, Frip, what does that mean about hunting down Will? Will it help the Prince or our army to chase him, even if he is the killer of a number of French girls or women?'

'You don't mind a man doing such things? You condone his actions?'

Robin's eyes went hard and flat. 'I condone nothing, Frip. But I won't see this vintaine thrown into a fight against this man just because you have a beetle up your arse and dislike the man enough to risk your life and all ours in order to get revenge.'

'You would allow him to—'

'I allow *nothing*! You do not listen to me, Frip. Listen carefully now: I will not see the men of this vintaine killed needlessly to satisfy some whim of yours for revenge, however well-meaning it may be; and I will not see the men thrown into a pointless chase when it goes against all our orders. So if you mean to test your men's mettle and seek your own oblivion at the same time, I will not help you.'

CHAPTER THIRTY-THREE

Sunday 28 August

They were up before the dawn.

Berenger felt light-headed, almost as though he had the start of a hangover at the back of his head when he climbed to his feet. The heavy dew overnight had sprinkled his blanket with moisture until it looked like frost. There was more in his beard, and when he rubbed his face, his hand came away wet.

They had ridden hard last afternoon, reaching this place just after dark, all the men weary, the ponies and rounseys exhausted, almost too tired to eat as they were rubbed down and set to crop the thick grasses. The men themselves muttered and complained about the location, the lack of decent firewood, the smell of the place – everything. But it was a quiet grumbling, not the whining of true bitterness. After some cold food, all had settled quickly.

He had an old felted cap, and he pulled this on now against the cool morning air. It was wet, but it kept the wind from his thinning hair, and he was grateful for it as he moved among his men, kicking a foot here or there and calling all to arms.

'Oh, aye, we can't expect a late morning on the day we're to move north,' Clip grumbled.

'What, do you want the French King to get to Tours before we can sack the place?' This was from Nick. His dark eyes had worn a perpetually nervous expression since the death of Gilles. The two had already been comrades when he first met them, Berenger recalled. Now he looked like a peasant who remembered he should have locked away the chickens, and it was too late. The fox had already got in among them.

'When you've marched over as much of France as I have, and seen as many friends killed as I have, then you can take the piss, Nick. Till then, just hope that you'll survive like I have.'

Nick's face took on an alarmed horror as he absorbed the vision that was Clip. 'Dear God in Heaven, you mean that is the *best* we can hope for?'

'Go swyve a . . .'

Berenger was content. While the men were bickering and complaining about the food, the weather, their horses, the quality of their leadership, and making humorous comments about Clip, he knew that they were happy. It was when they became quiet and pliant that he knew there was a problem.

It struck him suddenly that this was the kind of thinking he would have known during the Crécy campaign. In those days he had been a professional soldier, he thought, and that made him realise just how far he had sunk in the intervening years. It had taken a decade for him to be broken. Once he had been a respected fighter. Now, he had gone through hard times, losing his wife and children, and had discovered a new life viewed from the bottom of a jug of wine.

But now he was himself again. He truly felt that.

*

Berenger and his men rode solidly that morning, and they were rewarded early in the afternoon by the sight of Sir James Audley's column.

'We're English!' he bellowed to the scouts sent to challenge him. They soon accepted him and allowed him to approach the main force.

There was a fierce excitement in Berenger's breast at the sight of the force ahead of him. At last he felt as though he was close to Will and would be able to exact revenge. He could feel the flames of his rage licking up from his stomach to heat his chest and heart until his lungs themselves seemed clogged with it, and he thought that if he were to have any more anger in him his soul must be consumed.

He hunted all along the column as they rode past, looking for a face, a familiar slouch, a hat or cloak that reminded him of any of the men from his old company, but as he went he saw nothing. There was no one. He cast a glance back at Fulk and Saul. Fulk sat shaking his head as he jogged along on his pony, clearly disapproving of the venture, but Berenger would not allow any man to get in his way today.

He was determined to find Will.

As Berenger rode off to overhaul the English, there came a blast on a horn and then bellowed commands.

'They want to talk to you, Frip,' Fulk rumbled. 'I think they want to know why we are in so much hurry to get in front.'

'Shut up, Fulk,' Berenger said. He looked about him. 'Robin, Fulk, you will ride on. I'll catch you up later.'

He turned his pony and trotted back to the main column.

Audley welcomed him. 'I know you, don't I?'

'Berenger Fripper, sir. I'm vintener in Sir John de Sully's force.'

363

'I see. Where are you riding?'

'I've been instructed to see if I can find a bridge over the river. I was attached to the Captal de Buch's column, but I seem to have overtaken him, so I thought I should ride on here and see what I could learn about the enemy. There are tales of French cavalry ahead.'

'I hope not,' Chandos said. 'We are riding to see if we can cross the river soon. With luck we'll find a bridge or two that can still be used.'

'I hope so, sir. If I find one I shall send men back to tell you and give you directions.'

'That is good. Carry on, then, Fripper.'

'Sir.'

He rode away, feeling a thrill of excitement deep in his bowels. It felt to him that God was determined to remove all impediments to his successful capture of Will.

But even God can have a change of heart.

They rode through a narrow defile and on up a valley, before finally breasting a hill; there they were presented with a series of fields, the crops ripening nicely. It was a scene of rich plenty. 'I could live in a place like this,' a man said, and Berenger thought, *yes*. This was a land worth winning. A land worth fighting for, a land worth dying for. Perhaps he would be able to come here and live with a monastery. A kindly abbot may allow him to live as a lay-brother, working to erase the stains he had earned on his soul.

They came to a lip, and before them they could see a wide plain leading to the river.

It was a strange place. Dykes criss-crossed it, the water in them gleaming silver in the sunshine; stands of coppiced willow dotted it, and alder, and reeds formed great green swathes. The reek of marshes came to them on the wind.

'I hope there is a bridge,' Fulk said.

'Aye, shite, I can't swim, Frip, you know that,' Clip whined.

Berenger followed their eyes. The rains of the last days had filled the river so that where a meandering watercourse had once lazily idled, now a torrent raged.

He stared with encroaching despair to see the mad waters. It was thick, wide and brown with silt and sand, and it had broken over its banks and flooded large parts of the plain before him. At first he stared keenly, trying to strain his eyes to see the company of men which Will had taken from him, but as he peered at the view, he could see nothing. There was no sign of a group of men riding over that sodden landscape, no glint of steel in the sunshine, no rising dust from four hundred hoofs. Nothing.

He slumped back in his saddle struck dumb with the enormity of his disappointment. All the way here he had been convinced that he would encounter Will and that somehow, before the end of the day, Will would be dead. To be confronted with this emptiness was shattering.

'Is that him?' Fulk asked.

Berenger shot him a look, and then gazed in the same direction. There, over at the farthest extent of the plain, far over to the west, there was a thin line. Of course there was no dust, he told himself. The whole area was drenched in water from the rain and now the river, but that looked like a winding line of men making their way through an unfamiliar and rather dangerous landscape.

'Yes! It must be them!' he cried and spurred his horse.

The road took them down a slope and then on towards the Loire. It was not steep, but after all the rains, the road was slippery and treacherous, with shifting gravels making their beasts slide and slither uncomfortably. Soon they reached the bottom, and were thundering through the puddles and mud towards the little line of men in the distance.

Berenger cursed his eyesight. He was sure that Will was riding on at speed, but it was impossible to tell with his eyes. Normally it would be possible to gauge distances by the height and thickness of the plume of dirt and dust that were thrown up by the hoofs, and without that he felt oddly naked, as though he was being watched by hundreds of unseen eyes. There were few trees nearby, but as they rode, Berenger was aware of rows of small bushes and thick scrubland that could hide a hundred crossbowmen. It was daunting to ride along, expecting at any time to hear a screamed command and see ranks of archers rise with crossbows ready, hear that hideous thrumming of strings, and see the bolts flying at them. At close quarters like this there was little a man could do to protect himself from crossbows, apart from pray for safety and hope that the first wave of missiles missed him. If the first missed, there was always the hope that a man could ride in and hack at the archers before they could latch their strings to their belt hooks to span them a second time.

But blessedly there was no array of archers here and Berenger rode on with his unease dissipating. Not entirely leaving him, but at least losing some of its intensity. Soon he would be in front of Will, and then . . .

'Frip, I don't like this,' Robin said.

'What is there to like? We'll ride to them and . . .'

'They don't look English. That looks to me more like a party of men-at-arms than English bowmen. They are all armoured, and I can see no bows. Can you?'

Berenger was not prepared to discuss the imperfections of his eyesight. 'Are you sure?'

'Shit!'

Clear on the air there came the sound of orders, a blast on a horn, and the whole line of men before them halted and began to turn to face them.

Berenger looked up at Robin. 'You are sure?'

'Of course I'm sure!'

Fulk peered ahead. 'They all bear lances.'

Clip said. 'Aye, well, we're all going to get killed this day.'

'Shut up, Clip,' Berenger snapped. Now he could see them more clearly. They were turning in the narrow way. 'Vintaine! Let's get out of here! Retreat!'

CHAPTER THIRTY-FOUR

Berenger knew that the lightly armoured archers had only one chance of escape, and that was to make it to the hillside once more before the French could catch them. Once they were rising up that slope, the French beasts would tire much more swiftly, and with luck the English could reach the top and make some distance before the men-at-arms could do anything. If they were enormously fortunate, he realised, the English columns might also have closed the distance between them. Perhaps the hunters could become the hunted.

They were lashing their beasts now, hurtling up the slope as quickly as they could, the ponies lagging on their shorter legs, the rounseys taking longer strides, but suffering with the loose stones, scrambling up the roadway as fast as they could, the panic of their riders communicating itself to them. Berenger glanced over his shoulder to see that the French were gaining on them already. There was a lip at the top, and he found he was urging his pony on with jerks and wrenches of the reins, as though his own efforts could help the beast on, but even as he rode, he could feel his mount flagging. There was a rattling like hail on a wooden panel as its hoofs caught on stones and pebbles, unable to lift its legs as high as before.

'Frip!' he heard from Robin, but he gritted his teeth and drew his pony to the right of the lane to give his men space to escape. His pony tried two more great lunges with his hindquarters, but that was all he could manage, and Berenger could feel the energy seeping from him as the pony tried to gulp in air after his massive effort.

'Ride on! Go on!' he shouted at his men as they stared at him. Clip had a look almost of despair, and then Dogbreath reached him.

'Aye, fuck this. I've never liked horses,' Dogbreath declared, and dropped from his saddle.

'What are you doing here?' Berenger roared. 'In the name of God, mount up and ride back, you fool!'

'Swyve a donkey, Vintener! I'm stayin',' Dogbreath said, smiling his horrible leer as he grabbed his sword.

'Oh, *shit*!' Berenger said. 'Follow me!'

He sprang from the road onto the loose scrub and slippery pebbles that lined the edges of the hillside here. Running, he hoped to evade capture again. When he glanced over his shoulder, he saw that Dogbreath had grabbed his bow and a handful of arrows from his quiver, and now was chasing after Fripper.

There was a shout from the roadway, and he saw three horsemen turn towards them. The rest carried on up the hill, labouring under the weight of men and steel, and Berenger wondered that none of them had died with all that cargo on their backs.

'How many were there, Dogbreath?' he asked, panting as his foot slid on the loose scree.

'At least a hundred, I'd think.'

Berenger glanced behind him. One of the horses was making

ill weather of the hillside, and had slid down six feet. For a fully laden warhorse this hillside was no fun. Berenger continued, trying to keep his footing on the treacherous slope, but suddenly he heard a yelp and saw Dogbreath go tumbling down the slope on his backside, before fetching up in the midst of some ragged bushes, where he remained, cursing volubly and with imagination on the subject of France generally and French men-at-arms in particular.

There was a shout, and Berenger turned to see the nearer pursuer pointing to Dogbreath. The man who was already lower on the slope urged his beast straight for him.

'Dogbreath! String your bow!' Berenger bellowed. 'Quick! There's a man after you!'

In answer Dogbreath held up the two broken halves of his bowstave. He gave a sheepish grin. Berenger saw the man-at-arms couch his lance and ride for him. Dogbreath stood still.

'*Dogbreath!* Are you going to die by a Frenchman's lance! Move your arse!'

Dogbreath said nothing, but his shoulders sagged and Berenger knew real horror as he realised the Englishman would do nothing to protect himself. He had given up his battle.

Then Dogbreath reached down and picked up a heavy stone. As the lance came closer, he hurled it with all his might at the horse's head. It struck with a sound like a hammer striking rock, and the beast jerked sideways. The lance went wide as the rider tried to keep his balance, and then the horse whinnied in panic as his hindquarters started to slide, and the brute tried to turn to face up the hill once more, but the weight of the man-at-arms made him overbalance. The horse and rider seemed to hold themselves at an impossible angle for a moment, and then, with a crashing and clattering like a dozen sacks of heavy plate, the horse reared up, and fell back, crushing his rider, and the two went rolling and tumbling down the slope.

Berenger was of a mood to clap and cheer, but before he could think of anything like that, he saw the last two riders coming at him. He had little time, but he picked up a stone in each hand too, and began to hurl them. One struck the leading horse on the shoulder, but that only sent the creature into a deeper anger, and he saw the rider was urging the beast on at him. He flung the second, and as he did so he saw Dogbreath running back towards the road. It was no surprise, the man could do nothing useful here. He had arrows, but no bow. He would only be a target if he were to remain.

Berenger grabbed another rock. Perhaps he could be lucky. First he had another thought, and began to scramble for his life, up the slope. It grew steeper, and then must grow more shallow, he thought. He could only see the nearer lip of rock, and then all was sky, and he hurried as fast as he might up the loose pebbles, slipping and falling flat on his face, tasting the mud and grit in his mouth, and then spitting it out as he grabbed for clumps of grass to help himself up the rest of the way.

He heard panting and snorting, and turned to see the first horse was a matter of yards away now. There was a large, irregular stone near him, and he grabbed it, hurling it, but it went wide, and he knew that he was almost done. He turned and started to clamber higher, and then he heard the familiar *tock* sound. There was another, and he turned as the horse began to neigh and jerk about, trying to reach the arrow that was embedded in his flank through the saddle. Even as Berenger watched, he saw another arrow strike the rider, this one high on his shoulder. Another hit him in the back, low, and glanced away, but one was already stuck in his back, and now another hit the horse in the shoulder and, maddened with pain, the beast tried to bite at it. His hoofs seemed to lose their grip all at the same time, and suddenly he was sliding down the slope. His rider was already slumped, head forward, and as the horse went, the man slowly spilled from his saddle.

The last man-at-arms was now alarmed and he tried to escape by turning his mount to the slope, but Dogbreath had the distance now, and sent five arrows swiftly at him. Dogbreath had many faults, but inaccuracy was not one of them. Each of the arrows found its mark on the man's flanks, under his arms where the armour was weakest, or in the shoulder and neck of his horse. A sixth hit the horse just behind the ear, and the brute collapsed like a pole-axed bullock, all legs folding simultaneously.

Berenger looked about him and felt the shivering begin in his cods, and rise through his stomach to the top of his skull, so that his teeth chattered. He wanted to speak, but there was no strength in his lungs to say a word.

'You all right, Frip?' said Dogbreath. He was already running to Berenger, apparently concerned that his vintener might be injured, but as Berenger fell back to sit on his backside, he could not help himself. He began to laugh.

Béatrice met Gaillarde again when she was filling her water bowl from a small stream, and the woman snapped round to face her, fear in every line and bruise, at the sound of Béatrice's call. 'Oh, it's you!'

'You look fearful. Are you not here willingly?'

Gaillarde sank onto the ground and sobbed. Gradually she told her story, about her husband, about the men who had taken her village by storm and killed everyone, and the one black-haired man who had caught her and forced her to become his marching wife. Although he had made no overt advances to her, he was always nearby, watching her.

'Where is he now?'

'He rode off with his leader, the man called Will. I don't know when they'll be back.'

'But you can leave them, woman! You are free, if they do not watch over you.'

'And what then? I am with the marching wives, but if I run, someone else will catch me. I cannot leave here. If I run, they will come and find me. And then I will have the same hardship and punishment. And where can I go? My husband is gone, probably dead, and my home is burned and ruined. I have nothing: no family, no home, no hope!'

'Get up, Frip! Get up!'

Gradually the urgency of Dogbreath's words got through to Berenger. He took a deep breath and nodded. With Dogbreath's help, he made his way to the top of the hill, both of them falling many times, until they lifted themselves over the lip of the ground and could see the plain before them.

Only a half-hour or so earlier they had ridden past this area. Berenger could remember the tranquillity of the fields, the sound of birdsong. All was destroyed now. As he watched, the remnants of the French formed a long line, perhaps fifty strong, turned, and charged the English column. He could see that Audley and Chandos were already in the fray, battling with a number of other English knights against a smaller force of French. His own men were nowhere to be seen, and he wondered what had happened to Robin, but when he mentioned them to Dogbreath, the wizened little man curled his lip and pointed. 'Rob's goin' all right. He's over on the left flank there with the rest of the archers. Looks like Clip's there too. Couldn't kill him if you tried.'

Even as he spoke, there was a cry, and the French charged, their mounts thundering over the damp ground. Berenger could feel the pounding of their hoofs through the ground under him.

Suddenly a force of knights flashed out from the English lines and rode around to take them in a vast circle. As Berenger stood up, he could see the manoeuvre and the way that the English charge had disrupted that of the French, making them fear that if their own continued, the English must entrap their whole force. What had started as a little skirmish for the French was turning into a disaster. As Berenger and Dogbreath made their way back towards their ponies, the battle was already mostly over. French men-at-arms lay on the ground, dead, while a number hurtled away, bloodied and desperate.

'Not so bad,' Dogbreath muttered.

'No,' Berenger agreed, but as he spoke, in his mind was the question: where did Will go?

Thomas de Ladit was marching again, his feet tender and blistered after so many days of slogging onwards, but his mind was not on his feet or the soreness of his legs. He was still thinking of the brief discussion with Bernard three days before.

It had been such a shock to see him, and they had little time to talk. The only thing Bernard was interested in was making sure that Thomas would make no mention of the women killed in Normandy. Those peculiar rumours of a killer who was keen to savage women, to rape and crucify them. The stories had grown to terrify the entire community, as Thomas had seen. No one dared leave young girls alone lest they be captured and slain.

But why was Bernard so keen to see those stories suppressed?

He trudged on, and when he glanced to his side, looking at all the soldiers marching, hearing the jingle of their mail habergeons, the squeak of their leather scabbards, belts and sometimes the *cuir bouilli*, he studied their faces. There was such a variation in appearance between these men. Some were the sort who would grab and rape any women they captured. Others had a less brutal look about them. They appeared more like any man to be found in a market town at midday. Which sort was Bernard, he wondered. Amiable or brutish?

Imagining Bernard's grim face, it was easy to think him capable of the most heinous crimes, he thought, and then his face was struck with a dawning realisation.

There was a lot of questioning later. Berenger was given a large cup of wine, and he drank it quickly, gasping as it passed down, warming him all the way to his feet. It was tempting to demand another, but he forced himself to do without. He didn't want to break his run of mornings without hangovers.

'You were lucky, Vintener,' Chandos said. 'Your men reached us quickly, and we were able to kill many of the French.'

'It was a sharp battle, Fripper,' Robin said. He held a jug, but Berenger shook his head and asked for water. 'We breasted the hill, and there before us was the whole column. We shouted our warning, but our speed was enough to give the alarm. They soon had the whole battle fixed. It was magnificent!'

'The men are trained,' Chandos said. 'I hear you killed three yourself?'

'No. Dogbreath did. He killed the first with a stone, knocking him from his horse, and then reached my bow and killed two more.'

'Good! The French can never win while England has her archers, eh?' Chandos said, slapping his thigh. He had a cut under his eye and his left arm was hanging as though he had injured it, but he would not speak of his wounds. 'So, we still have no passage over the river, far as you could see, eh, Vintener?'

'From all that we saw there is no bridge. We were not able to get close enough to search for a ford before the French came at us,' Berenger said.

'Well, we caught eighteen of them. They can be questioned to see if there is anything,' Audley said. He was the slimmer of the two men, and had a way of keeping his head lowered so that he peered at the world from his beetling brows. It made Berenger wonder whether he had injured his neck. A man who wore a heavy bascinet daily and regularly took a heavy axe or hammer blow on the crown would often be injured and lose some of the muscles at the back of his neck.

'What do you think?' Chandos said to Berenger. 'Is there likely to be another bridge to the west?'

Berenger tilted his head doubtfully. 'When we were here before Crécy, the French were adept at destroying all the bridges in our path when they wanted to keep us away. It worked for them then. I doubt not that they will do the same again to keep us to the south of the Loire. The river is greatly swollen compared with its usual course, I think. If I were to guess, I would expect the bridges all to be down. If you want to pass north, you will have to build a bridge, but the river is very wide ... and while she is overflowing her banks ...' He shrugged expressively.

'So you don't think it possible?'

'I served the King during the whole of the Crécy campaign, and in all that march we never managed to overcome an obstacle the size of this one,' Berenger said. 'I think it unlikely that we can do so now.'

Audley nodded to himself, then glanced at Chandos. 'Are we in agreement?'

'Yes,' Chandos said. 'Fripper, you have new instructions: we require that you ride back to the Prince and tell him all we have discussed here. We think you must be right. We will have some more scouts sent east and west to check the river and we will question our captives, but the likelihood is that there is no crossing point here.'

'So you wish me to suggest an alternative?'

'For now, we must assume that the passage north is blocked.'

Monday 29 August

Berenger and his men rode into the Prince's army at Vierzon in the middle of the morning, and Berenger felt only sadness to see the destruction.

In the two days since leaving the town, the place had suffered. Although there had been some fires started when Berenger and his men were there originally, in the days since almost the whole town had been consumed.

'Fripper, I hope I see you well?' Sir John de Sully was in an expansive mood in his pavilion outside the town. He had seen his tent pitched far enough from the town to ensure that the smell of burning would not reach him. 'We have been busy. I trust you have too?'

Berenger had been given a written note from Chandos, and he passed this over now. Sir John glanced at it long enough to ensure that the seal was still complete, before passing it to his clerk. 'This is for the Prince. See to it that it is delivered swiftly.'

The clerk nodded and took it as gingerly as a man passing a barrel of Archibald's powder with a lighted fuse clearly visible. He slipped away as soon as he had it.

'Now, Fripper. Tell me what it's like up there,' Sir John said, sitting.

Berenger told him all he had seen: the swollen river, the flooded plains, the mud, the overflowing dykes and irrigation channels.

The knight listened, his face growing longer as Berenger completed his tale of floods and mud, and then, when Berenger spoke of the attack from eighty French men-at-arms, Sir John scowled. 'I have been fighting for the King and the Prince for more years than I care to remember. I must not live many more summers. I'm five-and-seventy years already, in God's name! Will I never see this war ended? Surely the French must come to realise that their nobles and King cannot protect them? Yet their men-at-arms will still come and contest the land. It is maddening, and so wasteful. The courage of so many, all being killed for such a foolish argument, for so ridiculous and petulant a King! Do they not see that God Himself fights on the side of England?'

'I think they see the depredations of the English fighters and resent us more than they dislike the failures of their nobles,' Berenger said.

'Our English fighters do their duty, no more. We fight to bring to the attention of the peasants the fact that they must all be far better off in the safety of the King's Peace,' Sir John said dismissively. 'And now, Fripper, go and find yourself some food. You and your men must be tired after your action.'

Berenger was glad to find Archibald not far from Sir John's pavilion.

'What of the others? Where is Grandarse?' Berenger asked.

'He has been sent, moaning and grumbling, to scout out to the west for the day,' Archibald said. 'There are rumours of a French force. He was not happy!'

The two were sitting before a small fire built at a safe distance from the wagons containing Archibald's serpentine powder and gonnes. Berenger could not help but glance in their direction every so often. He almost expected to see a demon clambering all over them. While he tried to squash his superstition about the powder, there was still something malignant and terrifying about it and the way that it would explode like a thunder-crack, deafening all and slaughtering men and beasts yards away with its massive stone balls.

Béatrice walked to them. She looked at Berenger, but when he glanced up, she looked away quickly so that he was uncertain that she had been looking in his direction in the first place.

'How are you?' he asked as she moved past him.

'I am well. I hope you are also?'

He shrugged. 'If my arse never has to sit on a pony again, I'll be happy enough.'

She chuckled. Archibald said nothing, but was pleased to see that there appeared to be no shaking in Berenger's hands when he took a cup of wine. His eyes were clear, and his smile looked less forced, too.

'What will you be doing now? Have you been told?' Archibald asked.

'I have some unfinished business with people here,' Berenger said. He looked about him. Berenger wanted to find Denisot again and talk. And then he still wanted to find Will. That was becoming his most fervent desire of all.

'Who?' Béatrice asked, and then, as he told her the story of Will, his own Alazaïs, and Denisot, her mouth fell open. 'His wife was named Gaillarde, you say?'

'Yes.' He caught sight of her face. 'Why?'

CHAPTER THIRTY-FIVE

Tuesday 30 August

Next day, Berenger rode beside Grandarse towards the little town of Romorantin.

He had not told Denisot about the woman yet. If Denisot was to try to liberate her from her captors, there was no telling how the matter would end. Better for Berenger to see if he could learn more about her first. Perhaps Will's men would let her go for a small ransom.

'Why's it always us, Frip?' Clip was whining. 'They always send us out first, don't they? Why's it always us have to go do the hard work?'

'They took one look at you, Clip, and saw an easily disposable archer,' Robin said.

'Me? They wouldn't want to get rid of me in a hurry!'

'I suppose you would make a useful target for a real archer,' Imbert sneered.

'Me? You'd never dare loose an arrow at me!'

'You want to try me?'

'Enough! Shut up, Imbert, you lunatic little turd,' Grandarse bellowed, and held his hand up. 'That's it, then, Frip.'

Ahead of them a little walled town had appeared from between the trees. The land here was so flat that a small copse could conceal a city, but now they were presented with Romorantin, a small town with an inner citadel that towered over the walls. The walls themselves were pale, a cream colour, with some darker stones intermingled with the rest, and Berenger found himself studying it with interest. There were some areas that looked shaded, as though the sun was behind a cloud just there, but with his eyesight he could not tell if that was an illusion or not.

Sir John had been riding behind them a short distance, and now he caught up with Grandarse and the others. 'Well, there's the next objective,' he said.

'Is it worth the effort?' Grandarse said doubtfully. He looked over the worn walls. 'It doesn't look like it has a lot worth plundering.'

'No. It may well not, but it does have Amaury de Craon and some hundreds of men inside, according to some scouts we captured. We cannot afford to leave them here as we pass. They might take it into their heads to fall on our rear. We have to try to take them.'

Grandarse shrugged. 'Well, it shouldn't take too long. It's tiny, isn't it?'

Friday 2 September

'Remind me never to listen to you when you predict whether a job will be easy or not,' Berenger said.

'I wasn't to know, was I?' Grandarse said.

The two were sheltered in an abandoned merchant's shop and house, the vintaines dotted about the street in similar accommodation, sipping from cups liberated from a potter's further up the town.

It had taken only a matter of hours for the English to breach the walls and take the town by storm. The walls were in no condition to keep out a determined army, and Berenger had watched as men-at-arms had clambered up the scaling ladders, while archers loosed flight after flight to force the defenders to keep their heads down and stay away from the walls. The English took the outer walls while the defenders were still trying to gather and organise themselves. They soon left the walls and the town to the English and moved to the castle itself. The outer bailey was taken after some hard fighting, and the defenders had to move into the keep.

And now, two days later, they were still there.

'It didn't look like they were going to offer much fight, did it?' Grandarse said defensively.

Berenger looked up as the sound of hammering and shouting came across the street. 'Doesn't look like they're going to give up soon, does it?'

He could see the walls of the castle from here. The citadel loomed over the town now, since so many of the buildings nearer had been destroyed. Those which the English had not pulled down had been smashed by the rocks hurled with such abandon from the walls of the castle by the defenders. Now the English were collecting all the spare beams and planks from the shattered remains of the houses and were building mobile towers from which to assault the castle walls. They had plenty of time, after all. The castle was showing no signs of surrendering to the English.

Berenger bit off a hunk of bread and eyed the walls. Smoke drifted in front of them and he wiped at his eyes as they began to smart again. There was little attractive about a battle of this sort. There was a bare foot sticking out from a pile of rubble at the other side of the street, and he wondered who the owner was. If he were to dig down, would he find a man or woman? Someone of great age, or a mere stripling? War was a leveller. All people were brought to the same height. Some were fortunate and would be buried in their own graves, but all too many wouldn't find their way, and would be left to rot, eaten by wild creatures and maggots.

He stared at that foot. It looked so forlorn, lying there in the dirt and mess. He tried to imagine the owner, a faceless, sexless being wandering the streets here, but all too soon the creature became a woman, and then it took on the appearance of Alazaïs.

Berenger had to look away. He could not meet her accusing gaze. He should have found Will by now.

Will had not appeared for two days after the attack at the river. He had trotted back and rejoined the army hours before the town came into view, but Berenger had not heard until that night, when Archibald told him, and by then Will and all his vintaine had been sent to another place in the line of march.

He would find the man, but it was taking time. He had thought Will would be easy to find here while they all laid siege to Romorantin, but so far there had been no sign of him. It seemed clear to him that someone was trying to keep him away from Will. Perhaps Sir John had decided to avoid any embarrassment by ensuring Berenger would never find his enemy. If that was his intention, he may have sent Will on more scouting duties.

If he had, it would at least have the merit of being a sensible action. They had to try to find where the French were. From all that they had gleaned from towns and French scouts for the last days, King John had demanded that all men of fighting age should join him at Orléans, ready to fight the English. He would have to come down and find them soon.

When he did, Berenger hoped that they would have left this place far behind them. He did not want to be caught in this crumbling, devastated town with the might of the French army waiting outside. The idea of being held in here was not appealing.

'Come! Archers and men-at-arms!' a man bellowed from further up the street.

Berenger cocked an eyebrow at Grandarse, who shrugged, stood, and hoicked up his belt. 'They probably need new latrines for the senior commanders, Frip. You'd best take your men over there. I'll gather the rest of my centaine.'

'*Vintaine!*' Berenger called. 'To me!' When he had counted them, he led them to the man who had called them, a burly, ginger-bearded sergeant Berenger had met before called Art.

There was already a jostling, tense group standing about the fellow. He wore a rusted mail shirt and ripped tabard, but his voice was clear and precise. He stood on a lump of broken wall, and called as though speaking to friends in a tavern. 'Englishmen, we have a task for you that will be to your liking, I think. We must take this tower. Your Prince is determined that we shall not waste any more English lives unnecessarily, and storming ladders are pointless. We need you to come with us. We have siege engines set about the castle now, and we shall attack from all sides. By evening we shall have the castle.'

'I like his use of the word "we",' Robin murmured.

'So, vinteners, follow me and bring your men,' Art commanded, and stepped from his platform. He led them up to the siege tower. It stood a full two yards above the castle's walls, and was set on a number of tree trunks. It would roll forward, and the men could pull the last roller from the rear of the tower, drop it in front of the tower, and then repeat the process to push the great cumbrous device right up to the walls.

Berenger gazed at it and gradually his eyes rose up the sheer sides of it, to the fighting top many feet over his head. It was a massive construction, deeper than it was broad at the base, although it looked as though the uppermost platform would be square. The sides were smothered in untreated, fresh ox hides. It would be difficult for any burning arrows to make them catch fire.

'Come on! *Push!*' the sergeant roared, and Grandarse puffed out his cheeks, took two deep breaths, and set his shoulder to the beam at the back.

'Come on, you lazy tarse-fiddlers!' he roared, and Berenger and the others bent to it. Berenger reluctantly took hold of a rope, pulling from in front, and while the rest of the men fell in and took hold of his rope or the one next to it, Berenger glanced up at the walls. It would not be long before the men on the ropes would present an irresistible group of targets to the men with bows and bolts up on the walkways.

'*HEAVE!*'

Berenger leaned forward, all his body's weight against the rope, the strain along the taut cable lying from his shoulder along his back. In front of him was Imbert, who was several inches taller, and the rope was lifted higher than was comfortable for Berenger, so he turned and pulled instead, his heels slipping on the dirt of the street's surface, his teeth clenched and his lips tightly pursed. There was a sudden gradual movement, then a lurch, then a rumble that the men could feel from the ground and the rope, almost as though it was a thrumming in the air itself.

There was shouting and cursing, and a sudden scream as a man's muscles tore, and then Berenger had to take a step, and he saw the men carrying the first of the massive logs, more than he could be bothered to count, as they ran before the tower and dropped it in its path, then ran back to fetch another.

Berenger felt his stomach muscles tightening and clenching with every effort, and the tower slid forward another few inches as the men pulling and those pushing sweated and swore, their muscles as hard as the cord he gripped so firmly.

When they had manhandled the tower from that street and into the open area before the castle's keep, the archers in the castle had a free rein.

There was a shriek and Berenger saw a man fall with the fletchings of an arrow protruding from his left shoulder. The whole of the rest of the missile was buried in his body, and he rolled about, kicking and jerking, his mouth opening and shutting like a trout thrown on the river bank, and Berenger could not be sure whether he was speaking or screaming because his world was full of the sound of creaking timbers and cords, the rumble of tons of wood rolling over logs, the roars and bellows of men urging their companions on, and then he became aware of the steady 'tock, tock, tock' of arrows plinking into stones nearby. They bounced up and rattled, but every so often there was another, wet sound of a man's body being struck, and then the shouting grew louder as sergeants and others urged the tower on.

Berenger turned and now he saw a hellish sight. Men were on the ground, flailing at their injuries as arrows and crossbow bolts flew at them almost vertically. More and more men were toppling.

'This is mad,' he muttered, and then, when he saw a man pinned to the ground by an arrow through his calf and foot, he came to a conclusion.

'Drop the ropes, men! Back! Behind the tower! Push, leave the ropes!'

Nothing loath, the men scuttled back to the safety of the area behind the tower, and Berenger hurried to Grandarse. 'We need archers to keep their men from the walls, Grandarse. Let me have two vintaines and enough arrows and no more of our men need be killed.'

Grandarse was staring at the carnage before the tower. A man was trying to crawl back to the tower, with a bolt in his lower back and another in his leg. As he watched, another bolt hit him between the shoulder blades and he slumped.

'Fetch your bows, Frip,' he said, and gripped Berenger's shoulder. 'Kill those fuckers!'

Berenger soon had his men back. They stood, studying the walls contemplatively.

'Remember, aim a little high,' Berenger shouted so that they could all hear him over the noise of the battle. 'You will need to use your arrows fast at first, and then sparingly. Don't waste your missiles!'

There was a bellow, and the tower began to creak and grind forward again, making a graunching noise as logs rolled over and crushed rocks and timbers under its ponderous weight, and then there came a high, shrill cry of horror like a rabbit caught in a snare, and Berenger saw that a man had fallen, and the first log was rolling up his leg. His ankle was already gone. It was only a smear of blood when the log rolled on, and luckily two men darted forward, an axe swung, and the screaming man was dragged away. Bolts from the walls missed the three only narrowly.

That was enough to make Berenger set his jaw.

'Archers! *Nock!*'

He had his own bow at the ready, and now he raised it high over his head.

'Archers! *Draw!*'

He drew the string, bringing his arms down, the bow bending as he felt his back muscles tightening, until his hand was beneath his ear.

'Archers! *Aim!*'

He felt the intolerable pain begin in his shoulders as he squinted along the arrow, letting the tip touch a figure at the castellations, then lifting the point so it was over the man's head.

'*Loose!*'

The relief as the arrows flew was better than release with a woman: a great surge went through him as though it was passing through his very soul, and his left hand jerked as the string snapped straight, and he saw his missile leap into the air like a live thing, climbing quickly until it reached the top of its flight and dropped swiftly to his target. He saw it miss and strike the wall before the man, but then a second arrow smacked into the man's head and he was thrown down.

'Archers! Loose at will!' he bellowed, and pulled another arrow ready. It was nocked and aiming almost before he had finished speaking, and when he loosed it, he saw his target fall.

Beside him the men were roaring and stamping their feet as the tower was shoved further, the logs snatched up from behind and carried quickly to the front, then the same crackling and rumbling as the tower was pushed and cajoled forward.

Berenger sent six more aimed arrows into flight, but then he saw the men being detailed to climb up the tower. Some of the first were archers, and he urged his men to hurry and keep the men down from the walls. Soon there were more arrows being sent towards the keep from the top of the tower, and a cheering from inside the tower spoke of the morale and confidence of the men inside. They were being urged to great feats of courage, and Berenger thought to himself, 'Rather you in there than me,' and he looked across at Grandarse, and saw that he was thinking the same. There was no need to speak. Both had been at the forefront of a battle often enough in the past. They knew the dangers.

There was a fresh rattling as the chains were slipped, and now the great drawbridge of the tower fell and crashed onto the stones of the battlements. A scream went up from the walls, and then Berenger was sure he could see a figure with a crossbow. He lifted his bow, but the man had loosed already and the first of the Englishmen fell tumbling from the drawbridge before his feet had touched the walls, pierced through with a bolt.

It was then that the French sowed the seeds of their own destruction. A fire had been prepared, and now pots of boiling pitch were hurled at the drawbridge, each shattering and showering the wooden frame with the sticky, foul contents. And men tossed three burning torches into it as the attackers were running across the bridge.

The bridge flashed like a barrel of black powder. A great roiling, orange and red flame leaped to the sky, and from its midst Berenger saw burning figures rush forward, or topple and fall, still alight, all the way to the base of the tower where their screams were mercifully cut off. But the French had miscalculated. The tower was so tall that the bridge dropped down to the wall. When the containers were hurled onto the drawbridge, it was so warm that it ran like water, and dripped back inside the castle's walls. Some of the English ran onwards, and fell, burning, inside the walls, and as they did so, the pitch that had fallen inside was soon ablaze. There was little the French could do to put out the flames while the poor demented devils rolled and wriggled, screaming in agony as their flesh burned away. Water would not kill the flames. Soon it was clear that the keep itself was on fire.

The planks of the tower were well alight already, and there was nothing to be done to save it. The men inside were ordered to leave, and the archers from the top soon evacuated their posts, just in time as the rest of the tower began to burn, filling the square with the reek of burning hair and flesh from the ox hides spread over it.

Berenger had seen enough. He called to his men and they returned to their room, sitting and waiting for the next command to go to fight, all of them seeing again crushed men, and men burning like torches.

The keep surrendered the next day.

CHAPTER THIRTY-SIX

Tuesday 6 September

They were marching again when the rain suddenly fell in sheets.

It was a grey day, a miserable day, in which the men slogged on, the infantrymen with mud up above their knees, while the horsemen and archers hunched their shoulders and sought what cover they could by pulling waxed hoods on, if they had them, or just endured the grim weather with the patience of those used to living outdoors.

Berenger could hear the men's rising irritation.

'When're we going to stop swimming and get to a place with a roof?' Clip demanded.

'They said that the end of the world was coming, and there'd be floods,' Felix said. 'This could be the start of it.'

'Best look to building an ark quickly, then,' Imbert said. 'We wouldn't want to think your boots could get wet.'

'No problem with my boots,' Felix said with a surly glance at the bigger man.

Imbert sniggered to himself.

'He means if it's the end of the world, your feet will get wet if you're not in a ship,' Dogbreath said.

'I don't think it's very funny to joke about things like that,' Pierre said flatly.

Imbert sniggered again. The other men drew away from him. Even Baz, who was closer to Imbert than the others, threw him a disgusted look. There were times when his difference in attitude would bring all the vintaine together in their mutual dislike of him.

Denisot ignored Imbert. He rode along with a bitter expression twisting his features as they covered the miles. Berenger had still not told him of the woman held by Will and his men, and he had failed to learn anything more about her, even though Béatrice had sought her. Gaillarde could have been spirited away. Certainly Béatrice had enjoyed no success in finding her.

'Ach, I'm buggered with this shite!' Grandarse said. He pulled off his hat and rubbed his hand through his lank hair. 'I tell you, for a penny piece I could tell the army to go and take a ...'

'Yes, Grandarse?' Sir John enquired. He had ridden up behind the men without being noticed, and now he sat eyeing his centener with amusement.

'I could tell the army to take a more gentle road and wait till better weather, Sir John. How good it is to see you,' Grandarse said with hardly a change in inflexion.

'I am glad to hear it,' Sir John said.

'Sir, where is the next town?' Berenger asked, keen for a change of conversation.

'We are heading for Tours.' Sir John stared ahead in silence for a moment. 'We have received some good news, some bad, which necessitates our hurrying westwards. First, the Duke of Lancaster is in France and is heading to us to swell our numbers. We are aiming to find him in the next week, I believe.'

Grandarse nodded. 'Aye, that is good. But you said there was bad too?'

'Yes. The King's original idea was to sail to Picardy and from there to join up with Lancaster to attack King John from the west. We were supposed to march north and meet them, hopefully assaulting the French in the rear or flank, and thus win a glorious victory.'

'And now?'

'The French have hired Aragonese galleys. Our King cannot risk the Channel while they threaten the crossing, so we are on our own. Tours lies in our path and blocks our passage west to meet the Duke of Lancaster. We cannot cross the river because all the bridges have been broken, and now we hear that the man who calls himself King of France is on his way to meet us too. Which means we have need of some haste.'

'I see,' Berenger said. He could hear the silence behind him, which meant that all his archers were listening to their conversation with interest. It was hard not to spin in his saddle and confront them. Yet it mattered little. It was better usually that the men understood the reality of their position. Besides, if they didn't hear him talking, they would gossip among themselves and come to a nonsensical conclusion.

'Grandarse, I want you to send some men to the south and keep a close lookout for French forces,' Sir John said after a few moments of reflection. 'We must be on our guard at all times. It will do no harm to have more men watching the flanks. Is that clear?'

'Yes, Sir John. Frip, you can go and take the first watch.' Berenger nodded.

Sir John glanced at him. 'Be careful, Fripper. You and your men. We are entering a dangerous stage in this campaign.'

'Much like the chevauchée before Crécy, sir.'

393

Sir John chuckled. 'Yes. Before we managed to cross the Somme we were all in fear of our lives, were we not? And yet from the jaws of that disaster we managed to snatch a sudden victory that is still spoken of today.'

'We were very lucky.'

'We have God on our side, Fripper. Never forget that: He is with us.'

Berenger would remember his confidence later.

They were riding along on the flank, keeping up with the Prince's column, when they saw the little huddle of people. Before long there was a desultory assault.

It was an embarrassment. An irritation. From the perspective of an army, it was less than the bite of a horsefly on a stallion's rump. For Berenger it was little short of a crime.

A local bayle had ordered the peasants from their fields to come and deter the English army by force of their arms. The arms they had were some antiquated bills fixed to ash handles, a couple of swords that had seen more service in the local wood-piles than hewing limbs from men, and some bows that were better suited to stunning rabbits than killing men with or without mail.

Berenger would have let them leave without punishing them, but when the arrows began to fall more thickly, Imbert lashed at his mount and hurtled off after the peasants. Pierre and Felix followed suit, plainly thinking that they were duty bound to follow any man who sought to attack the enemy, and in moments Berenger saw that he had no choice. The first rule of any army was that the men should not run after the enemy until com-manded to do so, and that would be only when the commander had been assured that this was not some feint intended to draw the men apart. And now, because of the rashness of Imbert, more than half his force was already riding like men-at-arms in their first charge.

'Saul, Fulk, keep with me; Robin, Clip, Dogbreath, I trust you with your bows. When we're in bowshot, watch for any signs of danger. If there is an ambush, don't wait for the order: loose at will. Is that clear? I'll have Imbert's balls for this!' And then he was off, haring after the rest of his vintaine as fast as his little pony could go. It was not fast, and he was not quick enough to catch up with Imbert or the others. He bellowed at the top of his voice to them to halt, but he knew it was in vain. In his own ears he could hear little but the irregular thunder of his pony's hoofs, the snap and crack of his cloak as the wind tugged at it, the rattle of chains, the creaking of leather, the stertorous breathing of his mount; the sensation of his hair being tugged back, the hissing and rushing in his ears, was as good as a pint of wine after a filling meal. It made him feel complete – whole.

Then the scene was ruined as he saw the flare of red. He saw Imbert's sword high in the air, and the youth's throat opened wide like a second mouth, and the bayle who stood, the bow shaking in his hand as he saw the red death in Imbert's eyes and tried to draw, but the arrow was released too soon and missed its mark as Imbert ran him down, kicking him in the face, springing from his mount and hacking at the man as he lay screaming, trying to cover himself with his arms, but his arms were no defence against two feet of English steel, and the man was defenceless and left to die as Imbert ran to the next, a pair of young boys who stood sobbing in their terror, as petrified with horror as rabbits seeing the fox approach.

'Stop! *Enough!*' Berenger roared as he approached, but he was too late. He heard them crying out: it sounded like one was calling for his *soeur*, his sister, perhaps to save him. Most boys would call for their mother, not a sister, but maybe these lads were orphaned and their sister had looked after them. What in Hell's name did it matter now?

Berenger saw that Felix and Pierre were copying Imbert's example, Felix slashing about him with the abandon of a man in a horrible dream, while Pierre looked as sad as only a reluctant executioner can.

Berenger looked about him. There was no ambush. Here, strewn about the grasses and the mud, were only a collection of peasants pulled from their fields that morning, with no training, and given a rudimentary collection of weapons. They had not managed to injure even a single man of the vintaine. The two boys killed by Imbert looked as though they were too young even to hold a sword. They were shorter than the adults by a full head. They could only be some ten or eleven summers old. Only a little older than Alazaïs's boys, he thought, and that brought a tear to his eye.

'French bastards!' Imbert shouted. He was kicking at the corpse of the bayle still; the red mist had clearly come down over him.

Berenger turned and beckoned to Robin and the others before riding to Imbert. He pointed to Nick and Pierre. 'Hold him,' he snapped. 'If he tries to kick someone again, I'll break his fucking leg. And *you*!' he added to Imbert, 'will wait and do every painful duty for the vintaine in the next week to remind you that you wait for my orders before you risk your life and theirs in a reckless charge like that! Next time, I will leave you to ride on to your own doom without our support!'

He waited for the rest of his vintaine, and as he did, he cast his eye over the landscape quickly, wary of another French party arriving. There were men over to the south, but they appeared to be watching, not considering approaching and disputing the right of the English to be there. Then he saw a mounted force approaching from the ruins of a village in front of the army.

'Riders!' he shouted. 'Archers! Dismount and nock an arrow!'

There was a rattle of hoofs from behind him, and he heard Clip's muted 'Fuck!' at the sight of the youngsters, but then the men were all leaving their saddles and stringing their bows, snatching arrows up and nocking in preparation. Clip had seven arrows already stabbed into the ground in front of him as he stood with his bow at the ready. 'You want me to drop one o' them, Frip?'

Robin scoffed at that. 'Can you see them yet, old man? I thought your eyesight wouldn't pick them up yet.'

'My eyesight's good enough to hit an arsehole at thirty paces, and you're nearer than that!'

'A glowing endorsement. You can hit a man at thirty paces. Impressive,' Robin said.

'I'll ...'

'Shut up, both of you!' Berenger snapped. He was peering at the riders with narrowed eyes. 'Can anyone see whether they're ours or French?'

Fulk suddenly leaned forward and stared. '*Scheisse!* It's Will, Frip. I can see him riding in front.'

Denisot heard and he strained to see the horsemen more clearly.

'Keep him back!' Berenger ordered, and then squared his shoulders as Will and his party came nearer. Berenger felt the anticipation like acid in his belly. His bow was not in his hand. That was fortunate, because if it had been, he might have drawn and loosed before Will had approached any nearer.

'Fripper, God has been kind to you!' Will called. He held up his hand and the company slowed to a halt, before Will himself allowed his horse to walk forward. It looked expensive, and Berenger felt a sudden shame to be mounted on such a lowly beast as his pony. 'You look as though you are better than when you left me. Your liking for strong wines then was the most obvious driving force in your life, but now you look almost like a man who is happy without. Or do you have a large wineskin about you now?'

'What are you doing here, Will?'

'Such a cold voice? I am surprised. And I thought we were—'

Fulk and Saul moved to stand at Berenger's side as he cut Will off. 'You are a fool, Will. You think to embarrass me before my men, but they know me well enough already.'

'These? Fulk and Saul, I know. Where is Loys? Oh, but I heard, he died, didn't he?'

'Not from the wounds your ambush gave him,' Berenger snapped.

'Oh, I know that. I know much about you and your men.'

'What does that mean?'

'Have you never thought about that? How we never met on the march until today?' He smiled then. 'You cannot continue a feud in the army, Fripper. You will get yourself into trouble.'

'You will have trouble enough. I will have revenge on you for having Alazaïs murdered with her children.'

'Who?' Will smiled. 'The little French widow? Oh, she was nothing. But she did like me. As for having her murdered, it's a little rich to blame me. If you had left her behind she would still be living now. Her death is another of your responsibilities, Frip, I fear.'

'What of *my* wife, then?' Denisot blurted, trying to wrest his pony from the two men holding him back. 'What of her, and the others in my little village?'

'Who is that, Fripper? A keen little ferret you picked up

along the way? You always liked your little rescues, didn't you?'

'Get off your horse, and we'll see who's—' Denisot blurted, wrestling to free himself.

'Much though I'd like to, I have to get back. I am a scout, you see, and our vintaine is due some rest once we have reported. Not all of us can enjoy such exciting sport as killing children, after all,' he added, looking down at the youngsters lying dead.

Berenger almost threw himself at him. Will was so arrogant, so smooth, so confident. 'Command has served you well,' he said. 'You come across as assured, but I know the weakness at your core.'

Will laughed long and loud. Still smiling, he leaned down until his elbow was on the crupper. 'You dare say to me that *I* have a weakness at my core? When your hands shake even now with desire for a pot of wine?'

He was still laughing as he rode past.

Wednesday 7 September

There was a thin mist over all the land when Berenger woke the next morning. It was cooling and attractive, but it did not soothe his blood. He had a choleric disposition that morning. The memory of Will's laugh and his smile was enough to make Berenger clench his fists and tense his belly. There could be nothing better than to wipe that smile from his face forever.

He rolled up his blanket and went to the fire's embers from the night before. There was no heat in it, and he would have to start again from scratch. As a task to distract him, building a fire would be effective, so he gathered some drier twigs and pulled out his own tinder in its draw-string leather purse. His flint was in there too, and he took it and began the laborious job of striking a spark, succeeding after many attempts, and carefully blowing on the tiny spark, enwrapping it in some charcloth, blowing more firmly until the tinder and the charcloth were showing a small flame, and then setting it down with some more tinder and wood shavings.

When he had a good fire built, he rose. He saw Robin watching him. 'Well?'

'You appeared to be doing well enough without my help.' Robin rose from his bed and stretched. 'Is it to be another wet day today?'

Berenger pulled a face. 'It seems better to me. The air is clearer. With luck it'll be warm.'

'You're still angry, then?'

'It's that obvious?'

'Leave him, Frip. Wait until we have a battle and you can drop him without anyone seeing.'

Fripper gave a dry grin. 'Is that how it's done now?'

'Hasn't it always been?'

'That bastard. He's won. I can't do anything to him.'

'Why not?'

Berenger shook his head. 'He even knew about Loys. How could that be, unless he has a friend here in the vintaine?'

'You suspect me now?'

Berenger glanced at the two huddled bodies at the far side of the clearing: Saul and Fulk. Had one of them been spying on him?

Robin laughed. 'Them? And how did they broadcast your news? By letter, sealed and delivered to Will? Think, Frip. More likely it was a cook or baker who heard of your plight and Loys' death, and Will heard tell. You think Fulk or Saul would betray you after all the time they've been with you?'

'I don't know. I'm going to go and ride about the camp.'

'Alone?'

'Yes.'

'I don't think that is a good idea.'

'You think someone could attack me?'

Robin said nothing, but his expression told the tale. He believed Berenger was going to seek Will.

'You wait here,' Berenger said.

He saddled and bridled his pony and trotted off into the early morning. The last vestiges of darkness still lingered, and he didn't feel comfortable about riding at speed, but he was desperate to get away from all the men for a little while, if he could. He set his mount's face to the west and cantered along easily enough. The wind in his face, the feel of the pony beneath him, the sight of a fresh morning, all served to calm his angry spirit. Some of his choler left him, leaving him feeling bitter, but less angry. Instead he began to become aware of a melancholy settling on him like a cloak, dulling his awareness, but not so much that he was unaware of the horse riding after him.

'So you cannot even obey a simple order, like stay where you are?'

Robin gave a short laugh. 'If I had been that obedient, I would not be here now.'

'Why? What brought you here, Robin?'

'You suspect me of spying on you?'

'You didn't answer the question.'

Robin gave a wry smile. 'So you do suspect me now? In the first place I am here because Grandarse caught me in Bordeaux. He found me in the streets when I was hungry and thirsty, and he bought me food and drink. But when I found myself here, I thought, "Why not?" After all, everyone in England has heard about the amounts of money made by the soldiers who joined the

King and the Prince in previous chevauchées. And I had little to look forward to at home.'

'Why?'

'I am here because I was forced to abjure. I killed a man at home, and although I managed to make it to the church and claim sanctuary, the coroner gave me the usual punishment. Exile for life. I gave up all my possessions, everything was forfeit, and made my way here.'

Berenger watched him as Robin stared out over the flat landscape, a land of fields and trees. 'You look like a man who has found a place to live.'

'I love it,' Robin said. 'But I wish I could see it in happier times.'

'Yes,' Berenger said.

The two rode on. There was a natural path that took them between stands of trees and on towards a distant smoke. Both paused, Robin gazing about them diligently, while Berenger stared down at the ground, deep in thought.

He said, 'Perhaps there is someone who is keeping an eye on me and the vintaine. It could be someone from Sir John's entourage. It could be Sir John's clerk, or the squire. There is his sergeant, too, and his . . .'

'There are men enough in the army to spy on you, I agree,' Robin said. 'But not too many would have . . . What is that?'

Berenger stopped his horse and turned in his saddle to peer at Robin. 'What?'

Robin said nothing, but urged his horse into a slow walk along a pathway cut in the bracken that led to a small copse.

'Oh, Christ's bones!'

She was young, but still, a woman not a child. Her arms were spread between two trees, bound with thongs, and her body had slumped back, her chin pointing up at the sky. She had been killed slowly, from the look of her. Blood was all over her pale breasts and between her legs.

'Sweet Mother of God,' Robin whispered.

Berenger dropped from his pony and walked to her. The blood had congealed beneath her, so she had not died very recently, he guessed, but when he touched her throat, he discovered that she was still warmer than the air about them. It looked as though her killer had raped her with a spear or knife, from the blood at her thighs.

'Poor child!' Robin said.

Berenger nodded and took his hand away, contemplating her. He had taken women in his time as a soldier; he had seen many women slain after the sack of a town; and yet this death struck him as more sad than all the others. She was not beautiful, she was not rich. She was a mere peasant woman, scarcely old enough to be wedded, and she had been brought here and tortured for no reason except possibly her killer's twisted lust.

'He's getting worse,' Berenger said. 'At first it was just killing. Now he's torturing his victims. And he's killing more and more. Look at this woman! I've seen rapes, I've seen women killed. I've seen them forced to witness their husbands and children being slain before them, but that was soldiers killing when their blood was up, or when they were drunk. This is a sober man who chooses to kill because he enjoys it. And every time, it is just after Will's company has passed by.'

'There are many in our army who enjoy killing and raping,' Robin said.

'There are some. But most kill because they have to, because if they do not, their opponent will kill them. In the company, when I still ruled it, women were raped. I tried to stop it, but even then the men were more likely to rape a woman and let her go. It was rare that she would be slain, and if she was, it would be because she tried to defend herself and hurt her assailant. It was an immediate, drunken reaction, not because the assailant needed to see her die for his satisfaction!'

'I doubt many of the peasants about here would recognise such a fine distinction.'

Berenger pulled out his knife. 'Perhaps they wouldn't. But I do, and that's what matters to me just now.'

CHAPTER THIRTY-SEVEN

Berenger could feel the eyes of the men on him as he rode into the camp.

Imbert frowned, then grinned. 'You had good taste, then. A nice young cony!'

If Berenger had looked at him just then, he would have killed the man. As it was, he rode on, and did not halt until he found a priest only a short distance from Sir John's pavilion.

'Here, Father,' he called. 'I have a maid for you.'

'Eh?' the priest was a fellow in his middle thirties, with a fair paunch and jowls that wobbled as he spoke. 'What has happened to her?'

'Someone from our army captured her, raped her, crucified her, and then killed her slowly.'

'You sound very sure.'

'I have seen this work before. I know what he does.'

The priest looked at him closely. 'Come in here, and bring her with you.'

Inside the priest's tent, Berenger laid her gently on a bench before the altar. 'She shouldn't have died like this.'

'You said you knew of the man who did this?'

'Yes. And if I can, I will stop him.' Berenger studied the priest. He had the look of a lad who had been born to privilege, and who had enjoyed a soft life in the Church, but there was also something else in his eyes: a hardness; a resolution. 'I am sorry, I don't know your name.'

'You can call me Father Paul.'

'Thank you, Father. What else can I do about it?'

'If the man is here, I can have him punished for his crimes. The Prince wants bold men who will fight men for him, not weaklings, cowards, and those driven by the Devil to assault women. Tell me all you can.'

So Berenger spoke of the man, Denisot, and the girl he had found, and then all the other bodies that had been discovered in the last weeks. 'He killed this maid only last night. He will do so again. Be assured of that.'

Thursday 8 September

Berenger was with the vintaine on the far left flank for much of the day after depositing the girl's body with the priest. They slept where they halted that night on top of a little knoll, all the men exhausted after their efforts riding up before the rest of the main columns, checking the houses and barns that lay dotted about the countryside.

Twice the day before they had run into optimistic groups of peasants wielding scythes and billhooks and had to fight them. They had no difficulty in routing them. Berenger's men were growing more experienced by the day, and Robin was already showing his worth as a subordinate, taking Berenger's orders and reining in the men when their natural enthusiasm for chasing and hunting down the fellows who bolted took over. Even Imbert appeared to have taken Berenger at his word and now remained with the others. Several times the peasants bolted towards woods and copses where Imbert was keen to follow them, and only Robin's stern commands stopped him. Imbert was beginning to realise that without the rest of the vintaine, his life would be in jeopardy if he was to get into a fight.

Today, however, Berenger and the rest were sitting near their horses and waiting for something to happen.

They had ridden up here to this hillock overlooking the town of Tours last night, and now they sat and watched as English soldiers will.

'Aye, not worth the fight, I tell you,' Clip said in his whine.

'Look at it, man! There must be ten thousand people living in that place! It's huge!' Saul protested.

'Big is fine, but it doesn't mean they have money, does it?' Clip said.

'Look at the place!' Imbert said greedily. He licked his lips. 'Of course they have money!'

Clip shook his head. 'Ye haven't the brains you were born with! Look, two little enclosed areas, there and there, both with a wall, and then another wall to surround the two others and the suburbs between. And how do they look? They look like they're falling down already. Do ye think they'd let their walls get in that condition, if the merchants and burgesses inside had money?'

Robin peered at the walls. 'If they didn't expect to be attacked, they might well allow the walls to become dilapidated, and that third construction looks as though it is unfinished.'

'Man, they've heard of us in this area for months now. I'm telling you, if they had any money, they'd have spent it on the walls.'

'What do we care?' Pierre said. He and his son were sitting close together as was their wont. 'We will be thrown at it, anyway. We must hope that there is something inside that makes the sacrifice of so many men worthwhile.'

'There's nothing there worth the taking,' Clip said. 'We'll get thrown at the walls anyway, and we'll all get killed, and that for nothing.'

'Shut up, Clip,' Robin said in his automatic response to Clip's whine of their impending deaths.

'Aye, well, you can tell me to shut up, but it'll happen.'

'Why?' Imbert said. 'If there's no money, why would the Prince ask us to take the place? You're talking shite.'

'Am I?' Clip said, leering horribly.

'It is the bridge,' Denisot said wearily. 'The Prince wants that bridge.'

Clip nodded. 'Do you know nothing, Imbert? See, there's a nice stone bridge over the river, isn't there? And the only thing stopping us crossing it is that shit-hole of a town. Doesn't matter whether the men living there are the richest in the land or the poorest. Our Prince will want to cross and meet with the Duke of Lancaster on the other side. He won't do that while the town blocks his path, will he? So he'll throw us at it. It's always us, after all. We'll all get killed.'

When the summons to see Sir John de Sully came, Berenger was still chuckling to himself at the sight of Saul and Robin wrestling with Clip, who shrieked and complained continually until Imbert threatened to fill his mouth with horse dung.

'What is it about Will and his men?' Sir John demanded as soon as Berenger approached.

'Sir?'

'I've just had Father Paul talking to me. He tells me that you have been going on at him about Will again. I don't want to hear any more about it, Frip!'

'I believe he's responsible for the murders of these children and women.'

'Perhaps he is! If not him, it's someone in his company. So what? This was *your* company once, Frip. You've allowed your anger that he took your men from you to colour all your actions since.'

'That's not fair, Sir John! I only—'

'You only what? You only thought it was reasonable for women to be raped and murdered by your men while you were their leader? You thought it was all right while the men were acting under your command? Tell me, Frip, because I do not understand!'

'These are children, Sir John,' Berenger snapped. 'You haven't seen them. Raped, crucified and murdered, like so many—'

'Like so many victims of this army, Frip. We are here bent on destruction, Vintener, to bring the full horrors of war to everyone in the community here! It is our task to bring about the collapse of the people so that they no longer want to support the man who calls himself their King, but come over to the legitimate Peace of King Edward! It is the aim and desire of the Prince that this army of his shall wage war so ruthlessly and unmercifully that the people will submit to him without loosing an arrow, and you say that a few children dead is a reason to call into question the commander of a successful company?'

'If you want to bring the people into the King's Peace, it is better to show them that there is at least a semblance of justice and law under his rule,' Berenger said.

Sir John stared at him for a long moment. At last he said, with forced control, 'If that is how you feel, Berenger Fripper, perhaps it would be best for you to leave the Prince's army now. I will not delay you. Robin seems a competent leader, and I am sure he could take over your responsibilities without difficulty. If you wish to leave the Prince's service, and mine, you can go freely, in honour of the good service you gave him ten years ago.'

'No, I don't want to leave.'

'Then I will have your word that you will leave this matter alone. I want nothing more to do with dead children and crucifixion. Do you hear me?'

'Yes, Sir John.'

'Do you not think we have enough to worry about as it is?' he added.

'Sir?'

Sir John had turned and was standing at his table reading messages passed to him by his clerk. When he spoke, it was without the rancour of the last minutes. He was engrossed. 'Eh? Oh, it's the same as ten years ago, Frip. The French are snapping at our heels now. They'll want to bring us to action as soon as they can. Never mind. I'll have Will and his men at the rear of our column and we'll see how we get on. I'll want your men to the fore again. But for now, we have to concentrate on this town. We'll attack in the morning.'

'*My* men?'

Sir John appeared to focus on him. He frowned. 'Yes. You can join them. You will be led by Bartholomew Burghersh. I will inform him.'

'Gaillarde!' Denisot shouted.

He was hunting down a drink of something to make him feel less waterlogged and more human, when he saw the figure moving between fires and huddles of men. 'Gaillarde!'

There could be no doubting who it was! It was his wife! She

had turned half-towards him and he recognised her profile as the firelight caught her. He ran towards her, and then a large man stood in his path, and he slowed, baffled, as he took in the face.

'It's all right, Bernard, don't hurt him!' Gaillarde called. The man before Denisot, a large, dark-bearded man with a scowling face, moved aside. As he stepped from Denisot's way, Denisot saw that Gaillarde was watching the man as though fearfully.

'Gaillarde! Come, I'll take you back with me and we can ...'

'I don't know who you are, but she's staying here with me. She's married to me.'

Denisot was so stunned that for a moment he could only gape. Then he shook his head. 'She is my wife, and has been many years past.'

'She is mine now.' Bernard pushed past Denisot and took his place in front of Gaillarde.

'You have not the right!'

'She has chosen. Now fuck off!'

'Gaillarde! Come with me.'

'You heard him, Denisot. I am his wife now. I am safer here.'

'*Safer?*' he cried, but Gaillarde turned away, and Denisot, head downcast, watched as she crouched at the nearer fire next to a younger man who was laughing at his expense.

'It was humiliating,' Denisot said to Berenger later. 'I didn't know what to do or say.'

'You came away. That was the right thing. It means you're still alive. Don't pick a fight with those men,' Berenger said.

Imbert grinned wolfishly. 'Let's go and get her tonight. We could creep in among them and take her. If any of them try to keep her, we ...'

'Would kill them and then be hanged for mutiny or fighting among our own,' Berenger said flatly. 'No. Denisot, did it never occur to you that the woman might have been willing to go with them? She might have considered you likely to be dead, after all.'

'Well, we had a bad few years after the children died,' Denisot admitted. He was close to tears. He simply could not believe that his wife, his loyal, if unhappy, companion had chosen to desert him. After all those years of loneliness, he had thought that they were about to enter a new period of happiness.

But she had chosen another man. Denisot, after such a long journey to rescue her, had been rejected by her. He walked away from the vintaine, seeking solitude to nurse his hurt and incomprehension.

CHAPTER THIRTY-EIGHT

Friday 9 September

'Into line, you maggots!' Grandarse roared, and the men shuffled and jostled into the semblance of a straight row. 'And get those strings strung!'

Berenger stood in the drizzle and felt the water running over his brow and down his neck. His waxed cowl and hat were no help when the weather was like this. The rain had fallen steadily for the last two hours, all while the men had been standing to, waiting for the assault, and now, at last, it seemed that they were going to be moving.

He watched the rest of his vintaine. The words of Sir John had cut, as the knight had intended. Berenger had never yet run away from a battle or left either his men or his King when he was needed, but that was clearly what Sir John had expected. Or he had threatened him with expulsion and exile from the army in order to shock him into his senses.

Berenger didn't know whether he was mad or not. Only a matter of weeks ago, he would have been unconcerned about women and girls who had been killed unless, as he had seen at Uzerche, the death of the victim might have an impact on him or his men by rousing rebellion among the population. Pointless murder was just that: pointless. In an army like this, there was logic in creating fear and horror. But it was one thing to inspire dread, and quite another to harbour a man who, for his own perverted reasons, wanted to torture and kill in that cruel manner. A man like that must be weak. He wanted his gratification at the expense of those so much more weak in comparison to him, so that he must pick on young girls.

Berenger heard a horn blow, then another, and the mass of men on his right began to tramp along the plain towards the French walls. One and a half thousand men armed with shields and spears began their walk towards battle and death.

There was a shout, then cries went up from their enemies and Grandarse gave a hoarse bellow, '*Archers!*' that was repeated along the line of bowmen as each vintener took up the call.

'Archers! *Nock!*'

Berenger heard the familiar commands up and down the line. They were acted upon almost without thought now.

'Archers! *Draw!*'

The noise of creaking as all the men lifted their great bows overhead and then drew them, both arms lowering, the yew tensing and crackling in their hands, the strings taut as wires, the men grunting as they held the weapons on target, shoulders burning already with the immense effort.

'Make sure you allow for the distance, you shitheads! Don't hit our fucking men! Now: *loose!*'

A flurry of fletchings catching the air, the whistle as the shafts sprang away from their bows, and the men were ordered to nock again, and a second and third flight were gone before Berenger could take three breaths.

He nocked a fresh missile and prepared himself.

The men were moving more urgently now. He could see their leaders at the front, urging on their companies by their own example, waving their swords or holding spears aloft, and then starting to trot onwards. Suddenly the entire line of English was moving more swiftly, breaking into a faster pace as it reached the flatter lands before the town.

But then the line faltered. A series of volleys were launched at them from crossbows at the walls, and even with his eyesight Berenger saw the front row collapse like reeds under the scythe. The next ranks were already there, but they too stuttered, and there were splashes as men fell.

'Bastards must have dug pits or something,' Robin said.

The men were floundering now, some with their arms waving as if to aid them walking. Berenger could just make out the French darting from their walls, loosing their bolts, others with slings releasing their stones, while occasional gouts of flame spoke of small gonnes at the walls.

'Archers! *Archers!* Give them support, in Christ's name!' Grandarse bellowed, and the men sprang to their duties again, sending shafts sleeting towards the walls. No time for worrying about picking a target at this range: it was a case of putting as many arrows into the sky as possible, hoping that even if they missed the enemy, the fact of their arrival would drive many French defenders to seek the safety of an overhanging roof of some sort.

The English were making heavy weather. They struggled on, but it was clear that they would not breach the walls. Men fell and were trampled, and over the noise of the trumpets and shouts, the screaming of the wounded was growing louder. Still the English moved on, depleted now, but determined.

Berenger held up his hand. 'Stop sending arrows now,' he said. 'They're too close to the French.'

The English had made it to the line of the outer wall, but there they were held. There were too many defenders, and for every Englishman that reached the weaker points, there were three Frenchmen with rocks to be hurled, or crossbows, or even spears to stab the man in the face or at the throat.

That was when the rain began to fall in earnest. Berenger was blinded immediately as the rain pelted down. His hat was nothing more than an encumbrance, and he pulled it off, tucking it into the front of his jack, but there was little point. The rain was so torrential that all he could see before him was a grey mist, with unrecognisable shapes that may or may not have been men, ebbing and flowing like wraiths in the wind. The very thought made him swallow uncomfortably. Perhaps the ghosts of past French warriors were here to repel the English invaders?

'Archers! Hold fast!' Grandarse called, and this time Berenger could hear the weariness in his tone. Even Grandarse had endured enough marching and rain in the last few weeks.

They did not even penetrate the main wall.

Later, as they marched back to their waterlogged camp, Berenger was struck by the atmosphere among the men. There was a sullenness about them all. The men were not despairing, but they were not far from it, and that was a cause for concern.

Berenger was sitting in the limited shelter provided by a cloak tied between a couple of trees and two thongs that took the lower corners to pegs in the ground when Archibald found him that evening.

'Space for a small one?' Archibald asked.

Berenger grunted and shifted to one side. There was barely enough room for him, and he took up less than Archibald, but there was a feeling of comradeship between the two from their past service.

'I heard you were helping with the assault?' Archibald said.

Berenger had tried to light a fire, but the wood was so damp that his tinder could not light even the thin sticks of pine he managed to rescue from the lower branches of the trees.

'Yes. We were there to give what aid we could. Not that it was much use in this rain. The bowstrings got damp, and then the arrows would not travel as we needed. There was a risk of falling short and skewering our own men,' he said.

'If only I had some gonnes set up nearer. I could have blasted a hole through their walls, had I a large enough toy!'

Berenger smiled. Ever since he had known him, Archibald had been convinced that his devices would be able to batter a city to gravel in a day. Yet when he had been given his chance at Calais, his shots had bounced from the city, chipping fragments, but leaving the main city walls whole. To take a city an army needed tunnellers and bold men who could clamber scaling ladders more than gonnes. But he didn't say so.

'They did their best,' he said instead.

'A ridiculous way to waste men! A storming party of one and a half thousand men running forward, only to be confused by a line of ditches, by thick mud caused by the rain over so many days, and finally, by the fierce defence of the townspeople. Most of them, so I've been told, were women and children. They picked up rocks and beat the brains out of our fellows,' Archibald said.

Berenger smiled thinly. 'Small children? Lifting rocks large enough to break a man's head? I doubt that. The truth is, there were only a few weak places where we could attack, and the French had the sense to concentrate their men-at-arms at those spots. War is not a precise art, but nor is it terribly difficult. They fought well. That is all.'

'And now we will be forced to hurry away.'

'Why? What have you heard?'

'Nothing. But the French cannot be far away, and we have a depleted army since our foolish assault today. It would have been better to go around the town and straight over the bridge.'

'If we could, yes. But if you leave a town behind you, you leave an attacking force that will cut you off, if you are not careful. We could not leave Tours standing.'

'Well, we shall now.'

Berenger shook his head. 'No, we'll take the place tomorrow.'

Sunday 11 September

Berenger's faith in the Prince's ability to capture the town was misplaced, as he was soon to learn.

All that Saturday the English had struggled to continue the fight. Men stumbled and fell and staggered onwards under a withering barrage of rocks, arrows, bolts and even stakes and posts. Berenger and his men kept up what support they could, while the rain poured down and the mud grew viscous, thick and stodgy, and the stench of blood and intestines and shit rose to their nostrils. Berenger stood and stared down, barely able to see a single individual with his dreadful eyesight, but instead seeing the battle, from his distance, as if it were not a phalanx of men, but a great beast that consumed them, gorging itself on their bodies, while they fought and struggled and killed and died, trying to keep the beast at bay. But they could not: it was stronger than them.

'Why?' Robin asked as the day passed from morning to afternoon. 'What's the point of more slaughter?'

'That town is in the way,' Berenger explained. 'Archibald told me that the Duke is over there somewhere. We have to cross the river to get to him. And we're safe enough here on this side of the river for now. The French army is to the north, and they won't be able to cross over the river any more easily than we could.'

'If you're sure,' Robin said, unconvinced.

His lack of faith was shown to be justified shortly afterwards when the command came to pull off the attacking force, strike camp and march south.

The French army had crossed at Blois and now the full might of the French was heading towards them.

The rest of Sunday was one long slog southwards.

Berenger's pony was weary and fractious, and Berenger's mood was not improved as the beast tried to bite him and kick other people. He managed to force the little brute to his will in the end, and then the vintaine was pushed ahead once more to scout the land before the English and warn of any enemy forces that appeared.

They came to one river and crossed that without too much mishap, although a cart with stores on it was washed away when the horse drawing it fell on a slippery rock, breaking its leg. A butcher's axe put paid to that. Then the army continued marching in a thin, chill rain that penetrated all clothing, all flesh, through to a man's very soul. Berenger felt as though the rain was filling his body, until he reached a stage when he thought his belly would begin to swell and gurgle with the extra liquid. It was uncomfortable to be so cold, and all the men could feel their softened flesh chafing against leather straps, rough linen and saddles. Few that night would be without sores and blisters, he knew.

Some miles further on, they reached another river. Berenger and his men crossed warily, but there was no danger with this little course. It was shallow and broad here at their ford, and the men passed over and on to higher ground with a sense of relief as, at last, the clouds parted and the sun broke through. In only a few minutes the men had steam rising from their bodies where the sun struck them, and Berenger could feel the heat like a warming salve smothered all over his back.

Even the men felt the sudden uplift in their spirits. Berenger could hear their voices rising, and there was an occasional foul remark about another man's ancestry and sexual inclinations that caused much ribald humour. He was tempted at first to remind them that they were in enemy territory, and try to curtail their laughter, but even as he opened his mouth to remonstrate with them, he saw Clip and Dogbreath's eyes moving over the treeline ahead. He saw Saul issue a disgusting comment about Dogbreath while he stared fixedly at a building in the distance, and Berenger kept his counsel. There was no need to tell this vintaine anything. Their long march had moulded them into an effective team, and they knew the dangers as well as he.

It was only a short way to the next town. This was, so Berenger heard from a peasant they caught, the town of Montbazon, a smaller community than Tours, but still significant enough. There, since darkness would fall before long, Berenger decided they would halt. He sent Pierre and Felix back to the main army to guide them, and then he had Clip and Dogbreath ride on with Robin to check the land about while the rest of the vintaine waited. When the Prince arrived, they took the town.

CHAPTER THIRTY-NINE

Monday 12 September

Sir John de Sully waited in the hall for the Prince.

For once the sun had risen in a clear sky, and the whole land was full of the odour of fresh loam and good soil. It reminded him of his manor at Iddesleigh in Devon. For a moment he felt himself transported to a morning some years before, walking with his wife, Isabel, in the pastures before the hill near his manor, breathing in the clean, pure air, holding her slim body close, staring out at the black hills of Dartmoor in the distance.

No. That was long ago, and very far away. Today he had a sterner task.

There was a call from outside this chamber in the castle. Sir John walked to a window and leaned in so that he could gaze out through the narrow slit. Outside he could see the river and the crossing. The army had taken the town the previous evening, and at last the men had been able to sleep in the dry, under shelter that was more substantial. All looked better rested.

But now he could see the cavalcade they were all expecting. He withdrew from the embrasure and gestured to one of the heralds. The man nodded and went to the Prince.

There came from outside the noise of the horses, the clattering of hoofs on cobbles, the rattle of cartwheels, the commands of a body of men, and then the orders and sound of many booted feet.

Before long, the Prince joined the men in the hall, walking to a seat and standing by it. When the doors opened, the newcomers were faced with a row of knights and noblemen on either side with, in the very middle, the slim, tall figure of the Prince.

Sir John eyed the two Cardinals with distaste. He had heard of the fat man who walked in with a sneer of distaste curling his lips. This was Niccolo Capocci, a man who was supposed to come from princely Roman blood. From all Sir John had heard, he was a determined man, who was never backward in giving his own thoughts and voicing his opinions of other men. He was not an easy man to like, and seemed a curious choice for a negotiation that the Pope must have known would be difficult.

If Capocci was a strange choice, the second was a slap to the English cheek. Sir John knew this man, as did all the noblemen in England: Élie Talleyrand de Périgord. A haughty, arrogant fellow who had been made a bishop at only twenty, he thought himself superior to all men except, possibly, the Pope himself. Only thirteen years ago the English Parliament had complained to the Pope about the number of foreign religious prelates who were arriving on England's shores and taking English livings. This Talleyrand was the man they used as a prime example of the abuses. He had an army of clerks and servants whose sole duty, from the point of view of the English, was to ensure that his already fabulous wealth was protected and increased at every opportunity. He was detested in England.

Sending him to negotiate with the Prince looked like a deliberate insult. With negotiators such as these, Sir John felt sure that the likelihood of a peaceful outcome was remote indeed.

The Cardinal de Périgord, Talleyrand, entered the hall with the haughty demeanour of a man who was ready to impose his will on a pack of truculent and delinquent hounds. His manner was that of a man sorely tested by the fractious behaviour of his charges, although he was determined not to lose his temper. He must always demonstrate his love, and while he must be stern, he must also be forgiving.

Behind him came his entourage of clerks, servants and magnates. They stood nearer the door as the Cardinals made their way along the hall, along the corridor of English noblemen. The clerks stood with their heads downcast as if in prayer, hands clasped over their bellies, while the fighting men stood warily, hands on their swords.

To Sir John, Talleyrand looked more like a politician from the highest echelons of the Church bent on bringing a rebellious upstart to book, and it put his back up immediately. From the way that Bartholomew Burghersh made to move forward, only to have a restraining hand placed on his arm by Sir James Audley, he was not alone.

Not a word was spoken, but the Cardinal must have noticed the heightened tension. The fact that he had been reported to the Pope as being 'the greatest enemy' of King Edward in the papal curia would have come to his attention. Not that there was any indication of distrust or unfriendliness in the smile with which the Prince greeted him.

After the preliminary welcomes and smiles all around, then prayers for the success of the mission of the Church to prevent bloodshed between the rulers of two such important nations, the Prince drew the Cardinals to a bench, at which wine and meats had been set out. He took his place at the head, and while panters and bottlers moved about the table, the guests washing their hands in the lavers' bowls and drying them on the towels, the Prince kept up a witty and respectful chatter, speaking of matters within the curia, discussing affairs in Portugal and Galicia with a charm and sophistication that few rulers in Christendom could match.

Sir John had to smile. These Cardinals would have already met with King John of France, a man known to be a bully, obstinate and sulky when thwarted, who admittedly was a fine figure of a man with the build of a knight and courage to match, but without the intellect and wisdom that a ruler like King Edward possessed. Sir John thought the Prince was in every way his superior. The Prince had the benefit of strong advisers whom he trusted. From all Sir John had heard, King John trusted all too few people. He was always suspicious, never trusting except with a small number of adherents whose own abilities were all too questionable.

The Prince was asking for the reason for the Cardinals' arrival. 'I am always glad to welcome my friends from the Church, but you must be aware that we are close to a battle. I may not tarry long, however much pleasure I take in the company of two such eminent Cardinals.'

'Holy Mother Church is shaken to the core by the idea that there could be another battle here in France,' Talleyrand began.

'In France?' the Prince said mildly.

'This is France!'

'This is a part of the English territory. We consider France to be a part of our territory.'

'We understand your demands,' Capocci said, 'but you must understand that we wish to negotiate and bring this war to an end. You are depopulating a vast tract of land. What will happen to the noblemen when they wish to see their fields ploughed and planted? Who will see to the cattle and the sheep? You are harming the men of your own rank.'

'Perhaps they will come to realise who is their rightful King all the sooner, then,' the Prince said smoothly.

'You have signed and agreed treaties to prevent further death and destruction,' Talleyrand said, holding up a finger to indicate to Capocci that he should maintain his silence for a little. 'We would have you hold to—'

'Which?' the Prince interrupted.

'The treaties are agreed on both sides in order to ensure that peace can be maintained.'

'But which treaties do you mean?'

'Any treaty freely entered into should act as a—'

'You forget that the Treaty of Guines was gladly entered into by my father, the King of England, but it was torn up and ignored by John, who likes to call himself King of France.'

'It was an unhappy affair, but you must keep to your agreement.'

'What?' There was an edge of sharp hostility in the Prince's voice, Sir John noticed. 'You say that we, the English, must adhere to all the conditions of a treaty agreed by both sides and ratified by the Holy Father, but when the French throw it away, we must ignore their actions and still hold to the basic agreements? I tell you plainly, Cardinal, I do not think my father would agree to that.'

'A new truce will give us time to negotiate a fresh treaty, and that is vital. The Holy Father wishes it. He demands it. A truce based on the same lines as the last.'

'On the same lines as the treaty which the French ignored?'

'It was good enough for you last time,' Capocci said. He reached for a tidbit of meat, sucking his fingers loudly.

The Prince threw him a look, and quickly fitted a smile to blanket the open contempt in his eyes. 'The French swore to return Aquitaine in full sovereignty. In addition the Limousin and Poitou were to be ceded, and all other lands south of Normandy, while England would retain Calais. In return my father promised to renounce his legitimate claim to the crown of France. We gave you peace then, and England ceased waging war on land and at sea, but France did not uphold the treaty. It was used solely as a breathing space to rearm and plan more destruction.'

'It gave you more land than you could ever have hoped to win in battle,' Talleyrand said with a voice as sharp as a dagger's point.

'No. It gave us land without having to go to the extreme of fresh battles and slaughtering still more Frenchmen.'

'Give us peace and we can give you the same assurances as at Guines.'

The Prince laughed. 'Cardinal, your humour is profound! We can win the same assurances as those which were ignored or tossed aside with as much consideration as a gnawed bone, you say? And that is intended to reassure us that this time the man calling himself King of France will honour his agreements?'

'You question the honour and integrity of a King?' Capocci said.

'*Be careful* how you speak to me, Cardinal,' the Prince said. 'I am a Prince and the son of a King. I know my father deals with all fairly and honourably. But I also know that Aquitaine remains disputed, that Poitou is not in my father's Peace, and the Limousin appears to remain under French control.'

'You must negotiate with us. We will have a peace agreed!' Capocci said.

'I am here at the command of my father,' the Prince said, and leaned back in his seat. 'I have my instructions.'

That was when Sir John first understood that the Prince was playing with them. He had no desire for peace.

He wanted his battle.

The atmosphere in the room was tense as the Prince stared unblinking at the Cardinal. Then he relaxed and leaned back. 'So, Cardinal Talleyrand: what is it you want to propose?'

'A truce. I require you to remove your soldiers from all lands ruled by King John and withdraw to Guyenne. As soon as you are there, we shall ensure that negotiations continue at speed to bring about a lasting peace.'

'And we shall gain how?'

'You will lose no more men. Look at your army! Bedraggled, weary, many of them without soles to their boots! Come, it is time to stop this foolishness!'

'So there is no advantage to us. Once again you would have England abase herself, give up all that we have won, and give our adversaries time to rearm and prepare themselves to attack us. No. I will not do that.'

The Cardinals exchanged a look. Talleyrand shook his head sadly. 'But consider, Prince, how this must affect others. Think of the poor nobles and barons who live here and—'

'And depend on the poor peasants for their support. Yes, you said.'

'You would see them impoverished?' Talleyrand said, looking about him at the barons and knights in the chamber with them.

'We would have them join us in the King's Peace.'

'Think of the lives that must be lost! Think of the

honourable, good, kind men of France, the knights, squires and men-at-arms who will die. Think of your own men, for the army gathered by King John is mighty, far more mighty than yours.'

'We are glad to hear it, good Father in God. A victory against an equally matched foe is hardly worth the effort,' the Prince said.

'Sire, you make a jest of the matter?' Talleyrand's voice had a hint of steel in it. 'Take pity on the men about us here, for you may well join them. Are you so convinced that you are in the right with this whole sorry affair? If you pull back even now from the brink of war, God and the Holy Trinity would look favourably upon you. The rewards in Heaven could be great.'

'In Heaven? I have long enough to wait before that, with God's mercy. We know what you say is true, Cardinal, yet you also know what I state is true. The quarrel is just. It's not an idle whim that led my knights to take on armour and travel here. When Valois was crowned, the nearest heir was my father, King Edward. It was to him that all should have pledged allegiance. But no, Philippe Valois stole the crown and now his son reigns.'

'You would hinder peace. It is pride that speaks here!' Capocci said.

The Prince shook his head and Sir John could see that he conquered his anger with difficulty. When he spoke, his voice was amiable and gentle, but only so gentle as the finest lamb's wool in the scabbard that protects the steel blade. The blade was yet there.

'No, Cardinal. It is not pride, and neither do I wish to hinder peace. However, I cannot broker peace without instruction from my father. I have my orders. Still, if you can win my father's approval for peace, that will be well. I will agree with alacrity if it will save a number of men's lives and all the damage and loss that must ensue.'

428

'So you will agree to a truce?' Talleyrand said hopefully.

'No. First you must persuade my father to change his instructions to me. I will happily avoid war if that is his wish. However, I am here on his command. He did not give me permission to seek peace while I was here. I cannot in all honour break my oath to him to obey his orders. So, gain his approval and I will gladly change my plans to suit his wishes. But be aware of this: I am so convinced of the justice of my cause here, that I have no doubt that God, our Lord and Master, will grant me victory when I meet the French King in battle. I will not delay that battle, nor will I seek to avoid it. So, if you wish to speak with my father, be swift, else you learn that all has already passed before your return.'

'If you demand this, the battle will have been fought!' Capocci spat.

'Then I suggest you hurry to speak to him. Because as you know, not only am I without instructions, but there is an army under this supposed King John which is even now riding to meet me. I will not negotiate while he approaches to trap me.'

Sir John smiled to himself as the Cardinals rose and made their farewells. The Prince stood too, gracious as ever, as the two swept along the hall to their men, and gradually the chamber emptied.

'He had tears in his eyes,' Sir John heard the man on his right say.

'Talleyrand was keen to bring this all to a conclusion,' Sir John said. 'Perhaps he truly feels sorry for those who will die.'

'It's more likely his family has land about here and he will see his income reduce,' his neighbour said cynically.

'My Lords!' a herald called over the sudden hubbub. 'Your Prince would speak with you on a matter of great urgency!'

*

The weather had improved. That at least was some relief, Berenger thought as he jogged along.

None of the vintaine had the slightest idea what had happened at the town, and it was a relief to see Sir John riding up late in the afternoon.

Clip was quick to put on his most wheedling tone. 'Sir John? What's happening? We were comfortable there.'

'Aye, well, sometimes even you have to suffer a little hardship, Clip. We are marching to the next town.'

'Why, though?'

Sir John looked across at Clip, then up at Berenger, and along the line of the vintaine, as though assuring himself of the quality of the men, and satisfying himself that they would not falter.

'We have a trained army, Clip. We have the best men in a fight in all Christendom. Not because our knights wear harder armour, or because we are stronger than the Frenchmen, but because we are trained and prepared. When the French muster their men, they gather up all the local farmers. Well, they're hardy enough, and they have the muscles to swing an axe or a sword, but they don't have the experience of actually sticking a blade into another man's guts, or taking an axe to his head. You do. That makes you better in a battle. You're less likely to freeze and show fear.'

'Aye, well, I don't know fear,' Clip said complacently.

'That is because you have few original thoughts in your head!' Sir John said. The men laughed. 'But when we go to battle, we have the combined force of archers like you laying down a blanket of death over any field. We saw well enough at Crécy how that would allow us to dominate any territory. Well is it said that for a French army to have a superiority of four to one would make a battle unfair. We would still have the advantage of them!'

'Aye!' Clip said, and Dogbreath gave a snarling cheer.

'The French know this,' Sir John said, and his eyes were roving over the land ahead now. 'They know it well. And the fact is, that they have a good strategy. If they can hold us against a river or the sea, and then attack at a time and place of their choosing, their numbers may weigh against us. So they manoeuvre to try to get beyond us and cut off our retreat, while we must hurry to prevent them, and find a defensive site where we can place the archers and men-at-arms to best advantage. And that is the game we play now: we race south, while the French try to catch us and overtake us. If they succeed, we shall have to look to our swords and our courage. If we succeed, we shall win the day again, as we did at Crécy.'

Robin exchanged a look with Saul and said, 'So you think they will want to fight this time?'

'I have no doubt of it. The French are led by an impetuous, impulsive ruler. He has heard all through his childhood of the battles that his father avoided. His father was an intelligent man, although a poor leader of men. But he was sensible. Clip and Fripper here can tell you about the siege of Calais, when the French suddenly appeared and almost swept us from our camp. They could have made our lives difficult, but we were lucky enough to have good commanders, and our camp was at the base of Sangatte, where there are only a few paths that can be safely trodden in between the marshes. There was no means by which the French could attack us there without being slaughtered in a few narrow pathways. Their commanders took the only sensible route: they retreated, to the disgust and contempt of the besieged in Calais. It was the only course they could take, but it resulted in obloquy. Shame was heaped on the heads of all those present who recommended retreat, and that kind of shame leaves a burning scar in the mind of a man like King John. He feels that most

431

keenly and constantly strives to show that he is a better man than his father. It is his firmest ambition to beat the English in battle. He will do anything to catch us in some manner so that we may not escape, in a place where we must be destroyed.'

Berenger saw Felix and Pierre give each other an anxious look. 'But, Sir John,' he said, 'although they have a rough plan, we have the commanders to foil it, do we not?'

'Oh, aye, Fripper. We have the better commanders by far,' Sir John said, his eyes creasing in a smile. 'We have Sir James Audley, the Captal de Buch, and the Prince himself. With men such as these, and with the archers and our men-at-arms, we shall not only prevail. We shall win another victory of the kind not seen since Crécy! We shall kill their nobles by the score until the ground is drenched in blood! Their knights will die in their armour, just as before.'

'But first we have to find a good location for the battle,' Robin said.

'Not only that,' Sir John said. 'We must also seek the locations where the French wish to fight and avoid them, and we must discover as soon as we may exactly where the French are. Those are our most urgent tasks. And for that reason I would ask that you ride to the south and east, Fripper. Take your vintaine and Hawkwood's, but you will be in command. As soon as you make contact with the enemy, ride back and do not engage.'

CHAPTER FORTY

Tuesday 13 September

Twenty miles. It was only twenty miles.

Berenger took the men at a leisurely pace to the south and east as he had been ordered, and soon they were in a large forest, with trees that rose on all sides. It was silent, and the wind seemed to miss them, but gusted over their heads. The clouds were bucketing past high overhead, and the sun flared and burned them for minutes at a time before fading as a fresh cloud smothered her. The path they followed was narrow, a mere peasant's path through the woods, and there was thick undergrowth on either side at the line of trees; after some time the road began to climb gently into the hills. Berenger kept looking at the trees and recalling the ambush intended to distract the men that had nearly gone so badly for him and the vintaine. Where was that? On the march to one of the towns they had captured. He couldn't remember which now. The assaults and towns all merged into one. An unending series of attacks and killings.

'Keep your eyes open,' he called quietly to Robin, who rode along behind him.

He heard the message pass back along his column of men, and he knew that to his left, Hawkwood was doing the same. Hawk was out of his line of sight on another track through the trees, and Berenger's ears strained all the while to hear any sounds of a fight: shouts, ringing of steel on steel, the whinnying of a horse in agony – but there was nothing. Only an occasional burst of birdsong, the hiss of leaves catching a breeze, the irregular clatter of men and horses at a fast trot. The road climbed a little more steeply, and the land to the left fell away, the tops of the trees falling lower and lower until Berenger could look over them all.

'Ah don't like this. We'll all get killed, you know.'

'Shut up, Clip,' Berenger said automatically. He didn't need that sort of comment now. He was struck again by the conviction that no matter who else died in battle, it would never be Clip. The man carried his own defensive aura of impregnable certainty with him. There was nothing could penetrate his confidence, not even a bolt from a Genoese crossbow, and . . .

There was a sound up ahead, and Berenger held up his hand. The column halted; apart from the blowing of the ponies and the occasional pawing of hoofs at the dusty ground, Berenger could hear nothing.

'What is it, Frip?' Robin said. He had ridden to Berenger's side and now sat on his own mount, listening intently.

Berenger shook his head, his eyes narrowed, and then he dropped from his saddle and took his bow. He strung it and took five arrows from his riding quiver, signalling to Robin to remain where he was, then Berenger trotted up the track, his shoes making little noise in the dusty roadway. There was a slight rise and then the road curved to the right, and Berenger crouched lower as he approached. Stopping a moment, he listened, and then he caught the noise again.

It was not a discernible sound, but a low grumble that almost seemed to come up from his feet. He knew at once what it was, but he edged forward carefully nonetheless, dropping to his hands and knees as he approached the edge of the road and could stare down at the plain.

'Shit!'

Wednesday 14 September

The response to the vintaine's news was instant. Berenger met with Hawkwood's men on their way back to La Haye, and when Berenger had reported to Sir John, Hawkwood was able to corroborate the main facts: the French were hurrying south in an attempt to overhaul the English and block their path. If they succeeded, it would hold the English forces and the French could call on other levies to come and help crush the Prince's army.

At dawn on the Wednesday Berenger and the vintaine were already on their horses, riding warily south and west and looking for any further sign of the French. They searched from the high ground, with Berenger grumpily sitting on his horse while Hawkwood and Robin, with their better eyesight, searched diligently for any flashes of armour, rising dust from a column of troops marching, or any other indications of movement. There was nothing they could see, and the English army soon reached Châtellerault. The town had the sense to surrender without a fight. It meant many would lose much, but at least most would remain alive.

Berenger stood at the town's walls and stared at the land all

about while the men about him dug pits and erected wooden barricades to break any assault in the lands before the town's gate.
The clatter of picks and hammers was everywhere.

The hills rose, rippling like giant waves, curling each on
another, but in the town itself there were few vantage points to
see the countryside around. It left him feeling enclosed: trapped.
He longed to find a horse and escape this place.

'Not happy, Fripper?'

'Archibald! I didn't hear you.'

'No, well, I rarely hear much myself now,' the old gynour
commented. He poked a finger into his ear and wiggled it
experimentally.

Berenger gave a grin. 'I expect so,' he said.

'You should come and see us,' Archibald said. 'We have a
quiet little shed where the powders can be kept safe and dry, and
Béatrice is proving to be a marvellous cook. She can work won-
ders with a couple of pigeons or conies.'

'I have many duties.'

Archibald eyed him with a look of grim distaste. He looked
like a father peering at a wayward son. 'Oh, is that so, Master
Fripper? What is it that scares you? In the past it was an irrational dislike of my powders that kept you away. Now it's your tarse,
isn't it? Or is it that you fear your prickle would do nothing?'

Berenger felt the flash of anger like a torch in his breast. He
took a step forward, and he scarcely realised that his hand was
on his dagger until Archibald's voice came to him.

'Old friend, I didn't mean to make you quite that angry. It
wasn't my intention. My apologies.'

Berenger looked down to see that his dagger was more than
half-drawn. Archibald's hand was on his, and as the gynour saw
his glance, he gently removed his hand.

'I . . . I'm sorry, Master Gynour,' Berenger said. He thrust the dagger back into its sheath and suddenly felt enormously weary. A shudder convulsed his frame. 'Come, let me buy you a cup or two of wine, my friend.'

'What is it, Fripper?' Archibald asked as they walked.

'I am too old. When my wife died, when my children died, that was terrible. But then another woman was murdered for her growing affection for me – or perhaps because of her fear for her life if I had left – and her death brought me back to my senses. I saw the look in Béatrice's eyes when we met again. She wants my love, but every woman I touch comes to harm, and I will not be responsible for another woman's hurt and injury. I cannot.'

'What will you do?'

'I will find a monastery and install myself there as a corrodian. I will tell the novices all about my great history and make them excited and scared to hear that such an ancient old bastard could have had so exciting a life. And then I will die, shriven and content, and await the judgement in peace.'

'You will go and rest? You? I never thought to see the day I would hear you say that!'

'I have killed enough men already. I've been responsible for the deaths of too many, Archibald. That knowledge takes its toll of a man.'

'You should see her, Fripper. She will have no man but you.'

'What of Ed? The Donkey was a good fellow, as I recall.'

'Well, he is a strong worker. So is an ox. It doesn't make the ox any more attractive to a woman.'

Fripper grinned at that. 'Perhaps not.'

'Come and see her, Frip. She would like that.'

Berenger turned back to the hills and felt again that tight, anxious feeling of being imprisoned. 'I will.'

*

The barn which Archibald had taken was near the southern part of the town. It was enormous, and it had been easy for him to manipulate the wagons into the space. Now, when Berenger walked in, there were fifteen men sitting at a fire outside the main wall. Archibald stalked inside quickly and cast his eyes about the room with a quick suspicion before turning to Berenger with a shrug of apology.

'It's my task to ensure that the powder is always safe,' he explained. 'It is so choleric that a man wearing the wrong type of boot can set it off. If he has studs, if he strikes a spark from a cobble, if a fellow grinds the powder too long and too hard, or any number of other problems will lead to its explosion.'

'It is still dangerous, then?' Berenger said, looking at the small barrels stored so close.

'It is safe, my friend. Never forget, these are the very powders that will save our lives. It is these that will drive our missiles towards the enemy and ravage them, rending the limbs from their bodies.'

'You speak most eloquently.'

'And you speak like a fearful soldier,' Archibald chuckled. 'Come!'

He had a chamber created at the farther end of the barn. A doorway led to a small yard, and here Berenger met Béatrice once more. Archibald walked out, loudly calling to Ed, and in an instant Berenger was alone with her, silently cursing Archibald under his breath.

'Maid, I hope I see you well?' he ventured.

She nodded. Béatrice was wearing a simple tunic and chemise, and she stirred a pot of meaty broth that gave off a delicious odour.

He sat on the ground. 'I am glad.'

'I am content. You have ridden far while scouting, I hear tell?'

'Aye. We have found the enemy's army.'

'Good. You said your wife died of the pestilence,' she said.

'She – and our boys,' Berenger said. He felt the grief as a pin-prick to his heart, but he resolutely pushed it down. It was too long ago.

'I am sorry.'

'It was a long time ago. There's no need to be.'

Berenger looked up at her and as he did so, she was looking at him. All at once he felt the pain in his breast again, that poignant sensation of loss and grief and hope and despair all thrown together and carefully mingled like Archibald's serpentine. 'Béatrice, I . . .'

He got no further. There was a scuffling of feet outside, and then the steady trot of a company of men on horseback, and even as he looked up, he saw the gynour and Ed return. Then, through the open gateway he saw the men riding. In the front was Will, then a line of other men from his company. 'What is it?' he snapped.

'Ed's gone mad, that's all!'

'No, I swear it was him, Master. It was the man from Bordeaux!'

'What man from Bordeaux?' Berenger asked.

'The man I saw crucify and murder a young child,' Ed said. 'He was there, that big, black-haired bastard. I want to see him pay for that!'

Thursday 15 September

'So, Fripper, you wanted to speak with me?' Sir John said. He was breaking his fast with a slab of cheese and a pot of wine. He had a small round loaf of peasant bread on his plate, and was chewing hard. 'I don't know how the peasants here keep their teeth,' he grumbled. 'There is more stone in this than flour. Even the peas seem hard as gravel. Come, Fripper, what is it?'

'We have discovered who the murderer was.'

Sir John leaned back in his chair and stared at him. 'You are still pursuing this feud when I told you to desist? I think I said to you that I would not stand in your path, were you to leave the army, but that you were to be silent on the subject.'

'And I have been. But last evening the Donkey saw a man whom he recognised from his time in Bordeaux. He saw this fellow kill a young maid in the city, and when he saw the man again yesterday, he could not hold his rage. The man crucified his victim in Bordeaux and then sat down to watch her suffer before stabbing her.'

'As I said to you before, this matter is closed.'

'Sir John, the Donkey is enraged to find the man. He will not rest until he sees this man punished.'

'And let me guess, it is Will, is it not? Your personal feelings are getting the better of you, Fripper, and will undo you.'

'No, Sir John. It's not him. It's one who was not long in the company when I left. A black-haired man with the look of a Breton or Cornishman. You know the sort of fellow: black hair, blue eyes, strong build, not too tall. This was the man who has murdered children and young women all the way from Bordeaux to Uzerche and now with the Prince's army. He is evil, Sir John.'

'In which case half the army is evil, and—'

Berenger lost his temper finally. He brought his fist down onto the knight's trestle table, making the cheese leap up and wine slosh over the cup's rim. 'In God's name! Will you not listen to any man who talks sense to you? Should I demand that Paul the priest come here to advise you? Should I bring in the Donkey that you may interrogate him? It took us an hour of the evening to calm him when he saw the man, and if you do nothing to slay this murderer, you will find that you will lose me and the Donkey and others because we *will* see him pay for his manifest crimes!'

'For the sweet love of Jesus, man, do you not realise what is happening out there?' Sir John bellowed in his turn. He swept his arm out, encompassing the town and environs. 'A matter of miles away to the south, the French have set up camp in Chauvigny. That was why Will came back to us here, to warn us that we run the risk of being blocked. If the French have scouts watching us, and you can be very certain that they do, they will be able to tear into our columns in force while we are on the march once we leave here. But you would have me accuse and arrest a man who is a most competent fighter and archer, because you feel sadness for a few women raped and slain? Are you *mad*? We need every strong warrior we can field just now. We need to protect this town, and if the French do not come, we will need every soul ready to fight as we march away. If I were to worry about this one fellow, the rest of the army will suffer!'

'Sir John, if you do nothing, the men will take matters into their own hands,' Berenger said.

'Are you threatening me?'

'If the men see a man getting away with this, they will lose respect for discipline. It is different when they capture a town and are set loose on the women there. This is a man who takes pleasure from crucifying and slaying children. They do not want to be about him. He will be slain, whether you like it or no. And when that happens, you will have a matter of military discipline to resolve. Instead of only that man, you will have one, maybe two more to execute, and the army will be three men fewer when we have to face the French.'

'You drive a hard bargain.'

'It is no bargain. This is a deal with the Devil.'

CHAPTER FORTY-ONE

Berenger took half the vintaine with him when he strode to seek out Will and his men.

Will's men were resting in a tavern that they had broken into, liberating casks of wine and some beer, and as Berenger stood in the doorway, he saw the men, many of them sprawled across tables and on benches. There was a soft, warm odour of a byre: bad breath, farts and the sourness of urine and spilled wine.

'Where is Will?' Berenger asked. The Donkey and Robin walked in with him to stand at his side, while Clip and Dogbreath sidled in as though looking for a purse to cut.

'What do you want with me? Oh! Good God, it's Fripper! Remember him, boys? He was the commander you used to have before me!'

Will was bleary-eyed after a night's carousing, and his smile was twisted as though he was yet half-drunk. He had a green pottery drinking horn in one hand and he lifted it now in ironic salute. 'This is the man you had to get rid of. Remember?'

Berenger had a clear vision of how he had appeared when he was still in command of the company. Will was drunk, yes, but so had Berenger been almost every day when he was leading the men. Now it was he who was sober, and Will who was embittered, miserable, sullen and steeped in wine and beer. 'I have no quarrel with you, Will.'

'Oh, but you do, I think.'

'You're drunk.'

'You dare say that to me?'

Berenger looked into Will's eyes and saw the desperation. Will had aspired to command, but now he had the position, he hated the solitude. He was no original thinker, and planning what to do with his company had taxed him. Suddenly Berenger realised why it was Will had joined the English army. It was because Will craved orders from above. Here he felt secure again.

Will continued, 'You want your men back, don't you? Not this rabble of pipsqueaks, but a real fighting company of mercenaries that will help you win treasure and glory.'

'No. I never wanted either,' Berenger said, but his eyes were roving over the floor. 'Donkey, is that him?'

There was a man with a thick beard and black hair at the rear of the room, lying with a large woman and a younger, slim lad beside him. He glared back at Berenger with suspicion. Seeing Donkey and Berenger approach, he suddenly sprang to his feet and watched them with growing anger.

'Is it, Donkey?' Berenger said again.

Donkey nodded. 'Let me take him, Frip.'

Will drank his wine and let the horn fall to the floor. It smashed. 'What is this?'

'You've been harbouring a murderer,' Berenger said, moving through the bodies on the floor and benches. 'That man has killed women and girls all the way from Bordeaux.'

'Don't talk nonsense!' Will said. He moved forward to try to grab Fripper's cotte, but he stumbled and missed.

The younger fellow was standing now, and he gazed from Berenger to the black-haired man with fear. His hand was on his knife.

'Don't pull your dagger against me, boy,' Berenger said. 'You'll be putting yourself between a King's Officer and a felon, and that won't work well for you.'

'You can't take Bernard!' the younger man said.

'Shut up, Arnaud,' Bernard spat.

'But, Bernard, what would I do? You're my brother!'

'Leave me, Arnaud,' Bernard said. He reached down to the woman, who squeaked in alarm. 'Come with me, Gaillarde,' he said more gently, but she pulled away from him in terror.

'Then die here, you bitch!' he snarled, kicking at her, and then he was off. There was a door at the rear of the chamber, and he darted through it like a ferret into a warren.

'Get him!' Berenger shouted, and was after him as fast as he could go.

The room behind was a store room, filled with crates and bales and barrels. Berenger had only moved two paces when his shin caught the corner of a chest and he almost went down, but he was soon hurtling along through the dusty air, through to the door at the rear.

This gave out into a yard filled with firewood and the detritus of a tavern: shards of broken pottery, shit, old bones and rotting vegetables. A hound was lying dead at the far side, killed while guarding his owner's tavern, no doubt, and there was a mess at the farther end of the yard that Berenger thought might be the owner himself, but then he was out and into a small lane. Up ahead he saw the black-haired man, and took off in pursuit, his men behind him. They raced through puddles of rainwater and urine, their boots thundering in the narrow corridor between buildings. There was barely space here for a handcart, let alone a wagon of any sort. A flailing tendril of bramble caught at his brow, the thorns ripping a ragged tear in his flesh that stung, but then he pulled his cap further over his head and hurried on.

They came out into a thoroughfare. On a normal day this would have been filled with people visiting the market, but today it was almost deserted. So many of the inhabitants had fled on hearing of the approach of the English. Now Berenger saw the fleeing figure heading towards the church with its two towers. 'Robin! Don't let him inside!'

His archer squinted at the figure, then took up an arrow, nocked, bent his bow and let fly all in one easy movement. Berenger saw the arrow climb into the sky, swoop like a hawk, and then plummet. It fell into the man's upper thigh, and he was thrown flat on his face, stunned as his forehead struck the cobbles.

Berenger and the others ran after him, and as though suddenly realising his danger, Bernard clambered to his hands and knees, shaking his head. He stood, tottering, and as Berenger reached him, he saw how pale and blanched the man's face had grown.

'It's easy to murder children, but you don't like pain yourself, though, do you?' Berenger snarled through gritted teeth.

Gaillarde had fallen onto some old pots, and now she sat up, nursing her forearm where a shard of pottery from Will's drinking horn had torn a long cut.

'Are you all right?' Arnaud asked, his handsome young features anxious.

'Yes, nothing that won't heal,' she said.

'You must be careful of things like that,' he said. 'You are a woman, and you have so much to atone for.'

'Me?'

'The Fall, the temptation of Adam with the apple. Women are responsible for so much.'

'I don't think we—'

'You are lucky. I will protect you,' he said. But then he held her hand tightly. 'But you must stay with me. I can't protect you if you leave me.'

'I don't need any protection. I can go to my husband.'

'You would leave me here alone?'

She looked into his face and saw his devastation. 'Perhaps I will stay here for a little while.'

After all, she thought, Denisot may not want her back after her rejection of him. He wouldn't realise that Bernard had been threatening her with death, were she to leave him.

Sir John listened to the evidence in the hall of his own building. The owners had been successful merchants of some sort, from the look of the tapestries and wall paintings. Biblical scenes were portrayed on all sides, and Berenger thought it was a most incongruous scene, with Sir John sitting on a throne-like seat with his sword in his lap, while the vintaine stood behind him, apart from Robin and Imbert, who stood on either side of their captive as if to emphasise how much shorter he was than they.

Will and his men were grouped near the door facing Sir John as he began. 'What is your full name?'

'Bernard of Rouen.'

'You have been accused of the rape and murder of a number of girls and women. What do you say?'

'I'm innocent.'

'Very well. This is not an English court of law, but a martial court. I am judge here. Who will speak against him?'

Donkey stepped up first, and stood staring at the knight.

'Come on, Donkey. Give us your name.'

'Ed of Southampton.'

'What do you say?'

'It was when I was in Bordeaux, before I made my way here. I saw a girl hanging from a wall. It was only as I got closer that I saw she was a child, little more. Her hands had been nailed to the wall of a building, and there was blood, you know, between her legs.'

'You guessed she was raped?'

'Yes, Sir John. She was only a child. Perhaps nine years? No more. And in front of her, I saw this man,' he said, pointing. 'He heard me and ran away, but not until he'd stabbed her. She was dead when I reached her.'

'I see. What else?'

'That is all, Sir John.'

He was allowed to return to the ranks of the vintaine, while more men were called. One was Denisot, who stood and told of the bodies he had found.

'Did you see the man who was said to be guilty?'

'No, sir, but the herdsman who saw the men rape the girl outside her parents' house described the man he saw return and kill her. It was the image of this fellow, sir.'

'Wait, Sir John,' Will said. 'Will you not have any dispute of the facts?'

'This is a martial court. There are no pleaders and justices of gaol delivery here,' Sir John said. 'Is there anyone else who has something to add?'

'I do,' said Thomas de Ladit. He had been at the back of the crowd and now he was glad to be able to speak. He recalled the stories of all the girls killed in such despicable ways all those years ago and glared sternly at Bernard. 'I am named Thomas de Ladit, and I am the Chancellor to his Royal Highness, King Charles of Navarre. I know this man.'

'What do you have to say?'

'I knew Bernard and his brother when they were in the entourage of my King, before his illegal capture by King John of France, and they were, I thought, good, loyal men. However, when I was myself caught and brought here to the English army to help with your Prince's war, I met Bernard. He told me I should not talk to anyone about certain deaths about Rouen.'

'What deaths?'

Thomas grimaced. 'Many young women, some children, were tortured and murdered: they were crucified. These deaths shocked all in the area. The peasants were alarmed and anxious, wondering what kind of a Devil could commit such offences.'

'And this Bernard commanded you to hold your tongue on such matters?'

'Yes. On pain of death.'

Sir John looked again at the man standing between Robin and Imbert. 'You, Bernard of Rouen. What do you have to say to all this?'

The man stared back at the knight, then nodded with his lip curled. 'It was me, aye. I did them.'

Sir John shrugged towards Thomas. 'Then let justice take its course. Fripper, you see to it.'

'Sir John.'

There was a great oak out by the main gate to the town. Berenger walked out from Sir John's hall to where a cart was waiting. He held the pony's halter while the priest came out.

He began to intone the *Pater Noster* as the men helped Bernard up onto a cart. The captive's hands were bound to a ring in the cart's body, and the vintaine took up position all about the cart before they began the slow march to the execution site. Behind them, some few of Will's company stood and then straggled along in their wake. Arnaud was there, his face downcast, his hat in his hands like a man before an altar, but Will himself merely spat at the ground as his man was pushed onto the cart, and then made his way back to the tavern with most of his men. Berenger thought that they would be spending the rest of the day with wine and women, rather than helping with the town's defences. That was good. He wanted to see as little of the man who had tried to kill him as possible.

His bitterness was undimmed, but now, having seen Will, he was surprised to find his feelings had altered. Where he had once been enraged to think of the death of Alazaïs and her boys, now he felt mere contempt for the cowardice and deceit of the man who had caused her murder.

Will had once been a proud, competent fighter, an ideal sergeant and second-in-command, but now he was a husk of his former self. The loneliness of authority had sapped his confidence. He had once been the darling of the men, but once he was placed in command, he had learned that the loyalty and affection of the troops was as reliable as marsh gas. From the moment he began to give his commands, he would have found how much more hard it was to lead a group of other vinteners and men, rather than the twenty he was used to commanding. He had learned the sad truth of command. A commander has no real friends, only willing servants. If a commander tried to ingratiate himself with his men, they would no longer respect him. Berenger had learned that early on, and it was a lesson he would not forget.

Their path took them along a broad thoroughfare, and as they reached the gates, Berenger glanced back. Bernard and Arnaud were staring at each other, Bernard with a fixed determination in his cold, dark eyes, Arnaud with a reluctant misery.

'They were brothers, you remember?' Saul said.

'I'd forgotten, but yes. Now I recall.'

It was an added burden, Berenger thought, to know that you were leaving a brother alone in the world. Arnaud looked like a boy who could hardly remember to tie his laces, let alone fight in a battle. He would have to take care of the lad.

They reached the tree. The priest stood beside the cart as Clip sprang up into it and flung a rope at the nearest limb. It struck the limb itself and he cowered with his hands over his head as it fell back on top of him, to the ribald amusement of the men all around. Clip glared at them, looped the rope once more and hurled it with similar lack of success. Robin pushed him from the cart and made a large knot, gathered up the coils, gazed up thoughtfully, and then threw it. The knot ran over the limb, but stayed tangled in the branches. In the end, Dogbreath climbed up the oak and crawled out along the limb, dropping the rope to the cart.

Eager hands untied Robin's knot and fashioned a loose running knot. It was tied off at the base of the tree, and the noose placed over Bernard's neck. He breathed in as the knot was tightened, while two men gripped his wrists to stop him trying to remove it. The priest asked if he had any comment to make, but he shook his head. His eyes were still fixed on his brother.

Berenger waited until the men on the cart nodded to him, before smacking the rump of the pony. The beast moved, startled, and the cart was pulled away. Bernard fell from the back, his hands going to his throat as the desperate fight for life began, his heels jerking spasmodically while his eyes bulged.

His mouth opened to release a guttural, bestial sound, but nothing else came. Gradually, over some minutes, the movements eased and grew more gentle, as if he was only going to sleep, and instead of the creaking and crackling of the rope, all Berenger could hear was the soft sobbing of Arnaud.

CHAPTER FORTY-TWO

Saturday 17 September

'What're we doing here, that's what I want to know!' Clip whined.

They were sitting about the fire in the middle of the packed earth of the floor. Cheery sparks and spitting flames lit their faces and made their cooking biscuit glow orange. The day before all had been working on the defences in the anticipation of the appearance of the French army, but there had been no sign of them. Instead the men had resorted to throwing insults at each other. Last night they had fallen into their beds moaning about their aches and pains after so much heavy digging and working with barricades, fences and trenches.

This morning all had risen quickly with the dawn. All the men were more or less comfortable, although it was not obvious, Berenger thought, to listen to them.

'You have food, drink and a dry bed. What more do you need to know?' Robin asked.

'We ought to be going out about the place, seeing what's happening,' Clip said.

'Oh, you mean robbing any poor travellers you find on the road?'

'Well, if there's someone about the place, we should question them.'

'And if you happen to find a farm, it would be a crying shame not to see if there were any chickens or pigs that needed to be looked after,' Fulk said. 'You are nothing better than a felon, Clip.'

'Aye, but at least I know who I am,' Clip said.

'What does that mean?' Fulk demanded.

'Ach, I've been fighting all my life, and always in the pay of the King. But you, you are a farmer really. You don't know what you're doing here.'

'You think me a farmer?'

Robin was chuckling to himself. 'He thinks anyone who was not born in a city must be a farmer, Fulk.'

'But I am a farmer. Where I live, the farmers are not like you. We are free, since we the slaughtered the French at Morgarten more than forty years ago. All men are equal in my country. We have no Lords, no Barons, no Counts and no King. So I am free to come here and fight.'

Clip was staring at him open-mouthed. 'You're *free*, and you come to fight for our Prince? You must be mad! You could be sitting on a stool in a tavern with a wriggly wench on your lap, and you chose to come here to fight and die?'

'Ah, but I will not die.'

'Ye'll die. We'll all die. This French army they're sending after us, it'll stop us.'

'We are stopped,' Berenger said mildly.

'Ah, because we're held here in a trap, Frip, don't you see?

453

We have no escape,' Clip said with grim cheerfulness. 'We'll all die here.'

'Not you, I've no doubt,' Berenger said. He was serious.

'Why are we all here, Frip?' Baz asked.

'The Prince is searching to find where the French army has gone, and this is a moderately good defensive position. I think he wants to learn whether or not the French truly desire a fight.'

'Why would they have sent their men after us if they didn't want to fight?' Dogbreath said. He was pushing at his oatcake, trying to make it turn on its hot stone without burning his fingers.

'They could want to hold us to one point and try to besiege us. That would be my fear,' Saul said.

'They could, but don't forget that the Duke of Lancaster and his men are supposed to be joining us,' Robin said.

Imbert grunted. 'You think those pricks will show up in time for a battle? They'll discover every bridge broken against them, just as we did near Tours.'

'The French will likely leave one or two standing,' Berenger said mildly.

'Only if they have great cities and defensive positions to keep us from them,' Imbert sneered.

'Perhaps so. If you are correct, then it may explain why the Duke is delayed,' Berenger said. 'But if that is so, it is still a good reason for us to wait here.'

Clip took his oatcake from the hot stones and stood tossing it up and down to cool while he blew on it. 'Well, it doesn't matter. Ye'll all be killed here.'

'Still forecasting death and destruction, eh, Clip?' Grandarse boomed from the doorway.

'Aye. I'm a realist. It's just that none of you realise,' Clip said, undaunted.

'Fripper, to me!' Grandarse said, ignoring his comment.

'What is it?' Berenger asked as he joined his centener at the doorway.

'Change of plans, man. You and your vintaine are to come with me. I'm taking you and all my other vintaines to the roads south to see whether we can find the French. The King needs eyes and ears searching for them.'

'Which road do we take?'

'The whole army's following us. We cross by the bridge here, then down to the Clain. We have to find a ford or some other crossing point. Then we head to the south. If we're lucky, we may catch the French partway over the river, half this side, half the other. If we do, we can slaughter them with ease. If not, well, we'll have to figure out a different route to victory.'

As they rode across the bridge over the Vienne, Berenger could not help but throw a look over his shoulder at the rest of the army. There was something about leaving the army behind that made him feel horribly lonely, even with the rest of Grandarse's men all about him.

'Eh, keep with me and we'll be all right,' Grandarse called to him.

Berenger grinned to himself. He drank deeply from his water bottle and then, as he looked down at the river, he thought he should refill it, but with all the men moving, it would be difficult to stop now. Better to wait until later, and refill it then, he thought. There was bound to be time when they took a break to rest the horses.

'Come on, you daft beggar!' Grandarse called.

It was good to have a leader like Grandarse. He always seemed to understand what was going on in his men's minds. Not one to consort much with the men who worked under him, he kept their respect. In almost every way he was as unlike Will as he could be.

Seeing a waving hat, Berenger peered, and was almost sure that it was Archibald and Béatrice standing on their wagon to give him their farewell. He waved back, hoping it was them, but then steeled himself for battle. He settled himself in the saddle once more.

They had not a long ride, but an important one. Now, at the western bank of the Vienne, they must ride south with haste. They would soon meet with the River Clain, Berenger had been told, which was considerably smaller and, with luck, easy enough to ford. After that, they would make their way south in the hope of catching the French on the march. If they did, they may be able to maul them so viciously that the French would be routed. That, at least, was the hope.

'If we find 'em today, that could be the end of this chevauchée,' Grandarse said ruminatively.

'What then?' Berenger asked.

Grandarse looked across at him. 'For me? Hah! You know, I always thought I'd settle down with a filthy-minded little strumpet. I'd go to the Bishop of Winchester's stews south of the Thames and pick a wench who was looking a little old and tired, and rescue her from her life of harsh, unremitting toil, so long as she knew how to cook and sew and keep my bed warm at night. It's not a bad little dream, eh?'

'No.'

'Ah, I forgot, man. You had that dream once. And you caught the opportunity when it floated past you, too. I admire you for that, Frip. You showed good sense. You ought to again.'

Berenger gave a laugh that was little more than a sigh. 'You think I could settle down? I tried that, Grandarse. It's not for us, old friend.'

'It could be, Frip. You have to carry hope here,' Grandarse said, clenching his fist and striking his breast. 'Without that, man, what is there left?'

'I think I had my opportunity for happiness at Calais.'

'Your woman died. It's sad, but it happened to many others, Frip. Don't hold one death against God. He might yet surprise you and make you happy again.'

'I doubt it.'

Grandarse pulled a face and glared at the road ahead as though it was arguing with him. 'You have the means to be happy, Frip. You shouldn't throw it away.'

'I've thought,' Berenger began, 'that I might join a monastery.'

'*You?* Oh, eh, man, you said that before, but now I know you're just making fun of a daft old git because you can! Ballocks to that! You? A monk?'

And he rode on, guffawing loudly, while Berenger jogged along behind.

Berenger reckoned they had been riding for almost five leagues through a forest when there was a hissed cry from in front.

His head snapped up immediately. He had been riding in a half-doze for the last few miles, but at that sound he was fully alert again. The column of scouts waited hesitantly, and Berenger had a feeling of nervous excitement thrill through his body as a pair of riders appeared. They were from Hawkwood's vintaine, he saw. Hawkwood had ridden on with his fellows to act as vanguard some time ago. These two must have been sent back to warn Grandarse of a danger ahead. Berenger urged his mount forward a little so he could hear the conversation.

'We've missed them, yes. They passed by on the road. We're coming to it shortly. It's a good mile or two ahead. But we've definitely missed them.'

'You're sure it's the whole army?' Grandarse asked.

'The trail is broken for three wagons' width. If it's not an army with heavy supplies, I don't know what it is,' the scout returned.

'Very good. Ride back and warn the Prince. We'll ride on and wait for his orders.'

Grandarse gave the signal and his column moved on again, but this time with a renewed vigour. All the men were aware that the French were very close now, and they rode with the keen attention of men who knew that battle could strike at any moment.

At the head of his vintaine, Berenger paid close attention to the darkness of the trees. With luck, there would be no assault here. If the scouts were right, the army had passed across their line of march and continued on.

It was only a mile and a half to the road, and here the men paused. Berenger had the feeling that crossing that road would be inviting disaster. He could imagine a charge of knights hurtling along the road to slam into the flank of the English army. It was not a welcome thought.

'Grandarse, let me dismount a strong force of archers and take them to the roadway. If there are any French dawdling behind, or if some scouts come along that road, we will need to kill them before they can form a charge.'

'Aye, good idea, Frip. Take your men, Hawkwood's and two other vintaines to the west. I'll have more head to the east. Keep within two bowshots of us here, and if you see anything, send a man back to let us know before you all get cut to pieces, eh?'

Berenger nodded. He called to Hawkwood and two of the other vinteners and explained what they were to do, and then went to his men. 'Archers, dismount,' he called, then, 'String your bows and collect ten arrows each. We're going to ride west along this road just to make sure we don't get any nasty surprises. Keep close, keep careful, and for the love of all the saints, keep quiet. We don't know how far away the French are.'

They remounted and set off. The road here was a rough track, and as they went the dust caused by so much heavy traffic rose thickly. The men coughed and covered their faces as best they could, but Berenger kept his eyes open, blinking wildly.

At each curve in the road, he would slow and peer warily about the trees, trying to discern whether there was any sign of men. This road was over hilly ground, and didn't follow a stream or river, but instead followed the hillsides. It made for a road with little incline, but it was nerve-wracking to endure the ride expecting at any moment to hear the shouts and grumbles of an army on the march, to see horses and men, to experience that horrible, slow realisation of approaching disaster.

They rode on, the dust clogging the throats of men and beasts alike. Berenger's nostrils felt as though sand had been poured into them, and his throat was parched. It was hard to imagine that only a few days ago they had all been complaining about the rain and hoping it would stop. Now he would give much to have a little drizzle to keep the dust down. Without thinking, he reached for his leather bottle of water, but when he shook it, it was empty. He had known he should have refilled it at the river. It was a basic rule of soldiering, to take every opportunity to refill water and grab whatever food there was available.

He was still berating himself as he took the next turn in the road. There, he stopped, and stared.

Before him, almost hidden by the thick clouds of choking dust, he could see the slowly rumbling wagons, the horsemen, the marching peasants, of a great army.

'Frip, I really think we should go back rather than trying to engage that lot,' Robin said quietly.

*

The Prince and his commanders were already at the edge of the road when Berenger and his men returned.

'Sir, the rear of the French army is just up there, about two miles away up beyond a steep bend in the road,' Berenger said, pointing. 'They are turning slightly south, from what I could see. They may be preparing to make camp.'

'How many?' the Captal de Buch asked.

'I couldn't say accurately, sir. The ground could have hidden more, and the line of trees too.'

There were more discussions, but there were several facts clear to all. The French had already passed this way; Grandarse's men had run into the rear of the main force, and to continue along this road would bring them into contact with the French.

'We shall follow them, but rather than take the road, we shall travel through the trees,' the Prince decided after consulting with his commanders.

'Aye,' Grandarse said. 'It'll keep us hidden from the enemy, right enough, but it'll be more of a bugger for all us.'

Berenger knew what he meant. The men had already covered over twenty miles that day, and most of that by narrow tracks in the forest. The ruts, the thick undergrowth, the mud and the irregularity of the paths were taking their toll on the men, the beasts and their wagons.

'To enter another wood and push on through, that will be hard,' Berenger said reflectively later as Grandarse related the news to his vinteners.

'No one ever said that war would be easy,' Grandarse said sternly.

'Except you.'

Berenger was called to Sir John de Sully as the men were preparing. Grandarse was already there, his face grim.

'Frip, we have need of a good centaine at the front of the army. I'm putting Grandarse and you out there. I want you to ride on the right flank and a little ahead of the main column. The men here will be Guyennois, and I know the Captal de Buch formed a good opinion of you when you were up near Vierzon. Do you stay there on the flank and ahead and keep your eyes open for any enemy scouts.'

'Yes, Sir John.'

'There's another reason why you're up there, Frip,' Grandarse told him as they marched back to their men. 'He's put Will and his company on the left flank. He still thinks you have a problem with Will. Is that so?'

Berenger shook his head. 'That's forgotten for now. I'll not endanger the army by picking a fight with him on the eve of a battle.'

They had reached Grandarse's horse, and now he puffed and blew as he tried to launch himself up onto his mount's back. Berenger helped him with a shove that almost pushed him head-first over the other side of the beast. 'Watch what you're doing, man!'

He settled himself, then looked steadily down at Berenger. 'If you were to be trying for a job with a new abbey, just remember this, Frip. God doesn't take kindly to the idea that His monks could have violence in their hearts. If you want to settle down like that, man, you'd best think on those words about gentleness and turning the other cheek.'

'And forego my revenge, you mean? I don't think so. I think God believes in justice too. He would expect me to destroy Will for what he did.'

Berenger walked back to his men with resentment burning like a torch in his breast.

'You all right, Frip?' Robin asked.

'Yes.'

He saw to it that his men had their orders. All bows to be strung and ready, each man to have ten arrows on him, to ride quietly and carefully and keep their eyes open in case of ambush.

To Berenger it was irritating that Sir John could have suspected him of risking the army because of his anger at Will: he had taken on a feud with Will because the man had killed his woman, not because he had taken Berenger's company. But he wasn't worried about that. He did want to avenge Alazaïs, as well as the kindly Abbot, the cynical, prickly Infirmarer and all the others from the monastery, but having seen Will over the matter of Bernard, Berenger was coming to the opinion that the man was already living in Hell. And from the look of his men, and the way that they looked sidelong at him, it was likely that the man would not long retain command in any case. If Berenger was any judge of men, the fellows of his company would soon take matters into their own hands. And from Will's expression when he had gone to arrest Bernard, he knew it.

He could almost feel sorry for Will.

CHAPTER FORTY-THREE

They were moving off through the late afternoon. In among the trees no wind could ruffle the branches, and the men were soon sweating.

Berenger had taken an entry point into the woods some fifty yards away from the main column. As he sat on his mount, waiting, he could see the Captal de Buch and his men-at-arms on their beasts. The Captal was working his reins through his gauntlets, pulling them tight, loosening them, pulling them tight again, while his mount vigorously nodded his head up and down. The tension was getting to all of them, men and beasts. Berenger found himself touching the hilts of his sword, his dagger, the arrows stuffed into his belt, almost as though they each held talismanic qualities. But it was less that, more the fact that he wanted to know they were all there, in place still. He didn't want to throw himself into a fight and discover that his weapons had disappeared.

There was a raised arm from the Captal, and then all the men were plunging into the woods.

All at once it was dark. There were cries and the crack of whips over to their left, but they could see nothing of the rest of the column. Only the sounds, the occasional crackle of a sapling being broken down, the rumble of the wagons' wheels thundering over rocks and roots, the crackle and rustle of brambles and bushes being trampled into the mire.

Berenger and the men continued onwards. So limited was the line of sight, that even Berenger could see the trees at the edge of their vision. Beyond was a blur of tree trunks and thick vegetation. It felt at every pace that the trees were creeping closer and closer, as if they were sentient and determined to squash these intruders.

Usually Berenger would not be prey to such superstitions, but here in the woods it was easy to be struck by atavistic terrors, when any tree could conceal a Genoese archer or French man-at-arms with a hundred bowmen at his command. And still there was no stream.

Berenger had to snap at Imbert and Baz, who were engaged in a loud argument about the quality of French wine compared to good English Bordeaux (Baz hated both) and tell them to be silent.

He was very thirsty. The dust and warm weather were making him sweat in his thick, padded gambeson. The feeling of thickness in his throat was more due to the grit he had inhaled, and he could do with refilling his bottle as soon as possible. There had been no opportunity to refill it on the march, and now he looked about him for a stream running through the woods with increasing urgency but no success.

His men were making more and more noise as they went, but it was the noise of horses: rattles and clinks of chains, the creak of leather, the snapping of twigs and occasional whinnies or blowing of nostrils. At each sound, Berenger cringed, and he felt his back stiffen as if in preparation for a crossbow bolt or slingshot, but there was nothing. After the first mile, he began to relax a little. After the second, he was able to ride without ducking at every loud crack of a breaking branch, and by the third he was comfortable enough.

They had travelled four to five miles when he had a sudden shock. The trees began to thin, and through them he could see the sky at last. They were nearing the edge of the wood.

'Hawkwood, take the left,' Grandarse said. 'Frip, we're at the edge. You need to send someone to the Captal to warn him. Then you come with me. We'll go and protect the right flank from attack that side.'

'Yes, Centener. We should have more men.'

'Will two more vintaines be enough?'

Berenger nodded and soon they had disposed the men. Now Berenger took his men to join the force of some fifty dismounted archers. Taking their bows in hand, their arrows in their belts, he led them to the thick vegetation that grew at the edge of the trees. He crouched, signalling to the others to do the same, and peered ahead, aware all the while of Grandarse's stertorous breathing behind him. There was no sign of man nor beast on the road. He beckoned Robin and had him gaze along the road. Berenger looked at him, and was about to signal to the men to join him, when Robin grabbed his sleeve and shook his head.

'There are at least five hundred of them, sir,' Robin said. 'At the edge of the woods, I could see them. It looks like they're beginning to settle for the night.'

'Where do they come from?'

'I saw many flags, but I don't know what they mean,' Robin admitted. 'I don't know the heraldry of France.'

The Captal de Buch peered at him from those shrewd little eyes for a moment longer, before turning to Berenger. 'You?'

'You can trust Robin. He's never been wrong before.'

'I see. In that case, we shall attack. Gentlemen, we are evenly matched in numbers, but we have the weapons and the hearts of Guyenne. Ready yourselves.'

'Guyenne? More bleeding England,' Berenger heard Grandarse mutter as he hurried back to his own men, who grabbed additional arrows from their cart. As he looked along his own vintaine, Berenger could see the different emotions displayed. Robin was standing almost stock-still, head slightly back, gazing into the distance as he calmed himself, his fingers running along the fletchings of his arrows; Baz was fretfully working at the laces tying his hosen, as though they might fall in a fight and embarrass or entangle him; Imbert was thoughtfully swiping his sharpening stone up and down his sword in a meditative manner, as though he was considering the hordes of men whom he would slay; Clip was swearing to himself in a steady monotone.

'What is it, Clip?' Berenger asked.

'Ach, we're all going to die. What's the point moaning? We're all going to be killed.'

Berenger heard Saul mutter, 'Shut up, Clip,' and grinned.

For himself, he was aware of a fretfulness. There was an anxiety that would not leave him. Perhaps it was the atmosphere here in among the trees, or the thirst that was raging in his throat, but for some reason he felt as though his hearing and his sight were more keen than ever before. He felt as though he was soon to die, and that his body and soul were not ready yet.

'Holy Father,' he began, but then stopped. He had no idea how to frame a question or request of God. It was impossible to know how to start. In truth, the only prayer he knew was the *Pater Noster*, after long familiarisation. He was about to start reciting it, but then lifted the Infirmarer's crucifix to his lips and kissed it. Just then, Grandarse farted and pointed forward with a grin.

'They're over there, lads! Let's go and get stuck into them!'

With a crash and roar from two hundred voices, the Gascons spurred their great mounts forward. Berenger and his men darted across the road and waited while the Captal de Buch and his men-at-arms thundered along the track.

They had come to a farmstead in the trees, and now the men were pounding along the track at a fast canter; as they approached the French, they spurred their destriers to the gallop as the horns blew, and their gay lance-pennons dipped in unison as the men couched them for the first clash.

It was a slaughter. The French had been settling for the evening, preparing their cooking fires and pots, and had never thought that the English could appear behind them. The idea of passing through the forest had not occurred to them, and to suddenly be confronted with a glittering array of lance-points threw the entire camp into confusion. Men scattered wildly, struck with terror, throwing down pots and pans in their mad rush, while only a few tried to rally and grabbed swords or lances for their defence.

'Archers! Ready!' Berenger bellowed, and the archers moved with him to follow the men-at-arms.

There were three wealthy noblemen who had moved to join each other and stood now with a handful of squires and sergeants, all gripping swords and preparing to sell their lives dearly. Behind them Berenger could see men running. Already a number were lying dead, trampled or stabbed and flung aside.

'Nock!' he called. There were others moving up already. It would be useful to have some archers held in reserve to avert a fresh attack.

'Frip, you're joking, aren't you?' Clip said. 'There're good hostages up there! Look, there's no one else coming!'

Berenger was about to argue, but as he looked about, he could see Clip was right. 'Men! Take what you can!'

A bolt hurtled past Berenger's ear, and he was startled into a run, the others with him.

Clip had been right. The other archers and men-at-arms were already congregating around small knots of men, some risking their own lives, throwing themselves onto the richer, better armoured men in the hope of winning a valuable prize, while those with more common sense and foresight fetched stones or ropes, and tripped or stunned their victims to make them safe.

Not all the French were worthwhile catches. The peasants, grooms and others were of little or no importance and thus pointless prisoners. Those who submitted might be fortunate and left alive. All those who challenged the Gascons were put to death as swiftly as possible, with an arrow or two from close range, or simply overwhelmed by numbers and stabbed when down.

Berenger headed for a knot of soldiers about a bearded man in a thick padded coat. He was roaring at his tormentors, a hand-and-a-half sword in his hands, which he whirled about before him and behind as the men advanced. Berenger pushed the men aside, taking off his gambeson as he walked, and then wrapped it swiftly about his left arm. When the man's sword next passed before him, Berenger took hold of his arm, pulled, and held the man's sword against his protected arm as he threw the man bodily over his shoulder and onto the ground. 'Yield!'

'Not to a damned peasant!' the man spat. Berenger nodded understandingly, and then slammed his elbow into the man's face with as much force as he could muster. He felt the man's nose break, and in the momentary peace, he wrenched the sword from his hands and held it at the man's throat. '*Fuck you!*' he said.

He had an argument with two of the men who had been ringing his captive about, but he knelt on the man's back and bound his hands with a cord, ignoring the complaints and commentary about his ancestry. 'Grandarse! You want a share?'

The older man walked to him, kicking and shoving the arguing men aside as he came, and agreed to share in a third of the value of the man. With his agreement, Berenger rose and helped Grandarse lead their prisoner away.

'Well?' Grandarse said.

'He was a knight,' Berenger said. 'With luck he'll bring in some money.'

'Aye, not a bad day's work,' Grandarse said.

He was lying on his side near their fire. The English had taken the booty and prisoners and left the farmstead to the dead, retreating back deep into the forest, and now with a strong party of sentries surrounding their camp, the English were resting after their labours.

'Not bad at all. We killed or captured some two hundred and fifty, and there were two Counts in among the prisoners, as well as another important French courtier. There will be some fortunes made today.'

'All to the good. And hopefully, tomorrow we will be away from here before the Frenchies notice. Ach! I love this life,' Grandarse said with satisfaction, rolling over. 'Just as a man thinks all is going to shite, we catch some French monkeys and get the chance of a decent night's sleep.'

Berenger nodded, but he had one thought uppermost in his mind just now: the whole vintaine needed water. He and others had looted the French camp for whatever they could find, but now he was thirsty again. With luck they would find water on the morrow.

They ate biscuits and some meat they had liberated from the French camp, and a few of the men were already snoring when a boy came through the trees. He was wearing the particoloured hosen and tunic of a King's Messenger, and every so often would call out. 'Centener? Centener?'

'Aye, boy, I'm here,' Grandarse grumbled, rolling over until he was sitting up again. 'What is it, lad?'

'You are to have your men ready before dawn, Centener. The captured French have told us where the French army is to be found, and we expect to fight them tomorrow.'

Grandarse cast a look at Berenger. 'Ballocks! Into the fire again, Frip.'

CHAPTER FORTY-FOUR

Sunday 18 September

They were clear of the woods before sunrise. All the men were aware that this could be the day that they met the French army at last, and the usual noise and ribald comments on each other's cleanliness, appearance and ability to fight were notably lacking. Many of the men were nervous; not scared, after so many long miles of marching, but feeling that anxiety that fills a man's belly and makes his hunger dissipate.

Other vintaines had been sent to scout, leaving Berenger and his men in the main column, a short distance in front of the Prince and his knights.

The vintaine had tried to keep all noise to a minimum, so as to avoid warning the French soldiery, and made their way with caution. Berenger was pleased to see the great abbey nestling in the hills and trees. The tower stood out proudly, and he could hear the Benedictines in their church. It would have stopped their music, had they realised how close by the English were marching, he thought, but then he was taken by another sound, and he dropped from his horse quickly, running to the chuckling river and filling his leather bottle before cupping his hands and drinking his fill. It was against the rules, but just now he didn't care. He was not going to ignore the cardinal rule of a soldier, making sure that he had sufficient water.

He was not alone. Many other English archers and fighters who had likewise suffered a thirsty night were also there, their horses alongside them. It was good, Berenger reflected as he rose, dripping, to be full and have an appetite for meats satisfied, but it was a better feeling by far to have been thirsty, and to be able to drink until replete.

They continued past the abbey and along a curling road shaded by great trees on either side, until they came to a point where the road fell down to the river, and then rose up a hill on the farther side. This road they kept to, in a long, ragged column of men, horses and wagons, and they were riding up the hill when there came the clattering of hoofs and a man bellowing for space. He rode at the gallop straight towards Berenger, and hurtled past them on a horse that looked already blown, as though it had run a hard race.

They would soon learn why.

They marched on, and soon on their left there was a vast, thick hawthorn hedge. There were occasional breaks in the hedge, but for the most part it made a good, all-but-impregnable barrier to horses and men. Berenger nodded to himself. This was a good defensive position, he thought, and then he came to a gap and could look out. The sight made him pause. Up before the English, ranged along a hill in the plain between Poitiers and Savigny-Levescaut, was the entire French army.

'God's teeth, Frip!' Grandarse said when they caught sight of them. 'There must be fifteen thousand of them!'

Berenger could see the dark mass of glittering metal and gleaming flags. Banners moved in the wind, and the colours of the tunics and tabards was startlingly bright in the early morning sun. 'Robin, how many are there?' he asked.

'From here, I wouldn't want to guess, Frip. But I can see at least eighty banners. They must have every nobleman in France up there.'

'Eighty?' Clip said.

'There's a lot of money on that hill,' Dogbreath said.

Saul sighed. 'Do you never think of anything else?'

'Aye,' Clip responded. 'Death. We'll all get killed here, you see if we don't.'

'Shut up, Clip,' Robin, Fripper and Fulk said.

The Prince had no intention of attacking an army placed in so strong a position. Instead he had the men form up on the hilltop where they stood, just a little north of Nouaillé. It was not a bad position. To their left, the land fell away to the little river, the Miosson. Although the hill was not steep, it was severe enough to slow a galloping destrier or wind a battle of men trying to charge up it. To guard this, the Prince placed his first battle with the Earls of Oxford and Warwick in command. On the right he placed the Earl of Salisbury, while he himself took the centre. Berenger and the rest of Grandarse's centaine were sent to the rear as a fighting reserve, along with three other centaines. From there they could be called to any point where they were needed.

It was a fortunate location. There was a slight knoll, and from the top Berenger and his men could see forward over the heads of the English troops before them. This was farming country, and there were many pastures, vineyards and woods. Before the English was a thick hawthorn hedge, no doubt placed there as a barrier to animals trying to escape their pasture, while behind them was the forbidding darkness of the Nouaillé woods. To the left were the marshes of the river, deep and impossible to cross for men and horses in armour.

'This is where we'll fight them, then,' Berenger said. He touched the crucifix.

'Aye, and it'll be a bugger of a battle,' Grandarse said grimly.

The men-at-arms were already dismounted. Spears were catching the sunlight, where the men were preparing to use them, butted on the ground, to deter cavalry, and men were moving about in front of the hedge with picks and shovels, digging one foot square holes to frustrate any charge.

Berenger could not help but think, as he stared across the hill, that this was a good place to be forced to fight. It would serve the English very well.

But before they could fight, they had some visitors.

The wagons clattered and creaked over the rough ground, but the oxen pulled with a will, and Ed led them down to the River Miosson at the ford, then up the pasture and fields to the brow of the hill. On his right was the thick forest of Nouaillé, and he glanced at it with approval. It would be hard for anyone to launch an attack through that.

A herald rode to them and addressed Archibald. 'Master Gynour, this will be our place for the battle. I am asked, could you take your gonnes down there, to the far left flank?'

Archibald followed his pointing finger. Here there was a great barrier of thorns and thick boughs, and as the ground fell away towards the river, which looped nearer, giving the English a shorter line to defend, he could see a small contingent of archers preparing the ground for defence.

'Aye, I can do that.'

'Good. From there you can harry the flank of any men sent to attack us, and protect our line.'

Archibald nodded and turned the wagon to the loop of the river, but it was soon obvious that the land here was not ideal. It was marshy and the ground was treacherous. However, it meant that the archers had their own defence. Archibald took his own position a little further up the hill, where the ground was at least solid. With the archers to his left and the beginning of the English line on his right, he felt sure that his precious gonnes would be safe enough.

He halted his wagon and began to put together the arms of his hoist so that they could remove the trestle on which would rest the largest barrel from the bed of the wagon and set it up, while Ed and Béatrice brought the two carts which held the three-barrelled ribauldequins. With them, Archibald was happy that he could hold off a large force for a while.

It was only when he sprang down from his wagon that he realised his mistake. Here, the ground rose slightly. It meant that there was a lip in the ground some eighty yards away, Until the French were that close, they would effectively be hidden from him. While any surprise to him would be matched by the surprise of the French to meet him, that was little consolation. They would have to charge him, but after he had fired his gonnes, they would be able to overrun his position with ease.

He glanced to his left to where the archers waited. At least he was protected by them, he reflected.

Berenger was standing and peering over the heads of the King and first battle when he saw the approach of the Cardinal of Périgord with a large complement of clerks supporting him. He had been with the French forces, and now passed between the two armies, trotting on their valuable horses until they were in hailing distance.

'My Lords, Sire, I have urgent messages from the King of France!' the Cardinal called as he came nearer.

'Let him pass! Let him through to see the Prince!' was bellowed from the Prince's battle, and Berenger heard the sudden creaking as taut bows were relieved of their pressure safely, the arrows taken from the strings and replaced in their quivers. The Cardinal rode forward. As he came nearer, the Prince and senior advisers left the battle and walked behind it so they were between Berenger's reserve and the main centre.

The Cardinal reached the space a short time after the Prince. About him the Prince had a number of his household knights, and with the Cardinal there were lawyers as well as the clerks, Berenger saw. However, more interesting to him was the appearance of Talleyrand. The Cardinal had tears streaming down his face.

'What's up with him?' Grandarse muttered.

'He's had his ballocks in the French King's vice too long,' was Dogbreath's unsympathetic view.

'Perhaps he really wants to stop a fight?' Baz said. There was an optimistic tone to his voice.

'Who's that?' Robin asked.

Berenger saw him pointing to an ordained priest. 'Him? He was there at the trial of Bernard, you remember? Thomas de Ladit.'

'Why's he there?'

'Because he is keen to prevent a fight too?' Berenger guessed.

Clip snorted. 'Why would he want to stop a fight? It wouldn't earn him another estate or money, would it? No, don't get your hopes up, Bazzer. We'll have our fight. And we'll all . . .'

'Don't say it,' Robin said.

'What?'

'We all knew what you were going to say, Clip. Just don't, that's all.'

'I was going to say we'll all have a fight today or tomorrow.'

'Really?'

'Yes. And we'll all get killed!' Clip added with an evil grin, ducking under Robin's fist and running away, laughing.

'Sire, look at the men all about here! How many must die for this quarrel to be ended?'

'Good Cardinal, if you have any proposals, please speak them quickly. I would prefer to spend the day in battle than in preaching.'

'Sire, you can see that the King of France has a mighty army. He will do battle with you today, and he intends to wipe out your army and kill you, too. He is the most powerful King on Earth, and he has called together all the most notable Lords in his land! Look on his banners! Look on his men! Their armour shines so brightly, it would dazzle the eyes of any attempting to fight him.'

'Good.'

'Sire?'

'My Lord Cardinal, I have been seeking to bring this army to battle for weeks. All too often the French avoid battle when they might have held their honour by daring to challenge us. If they will now seek to prove their mettle against us, that is good.'

'But look at all these men about you! How many noble souls will you see destroyed in your search for victory?'

'I am keen to allow the King of Heaven to show His justice in the matter,' the Prince said. 'He will show today perfectly clearly who is the rightful claimant to the inheritance of this country. I place my faith in Him.'

'But He would prefer that England and France should join forces to throw the unbelievers from the Holy Land. You could go on Crusade with him and save Jerusalem, or . . .'

477

'You think the French would allow us to negotiate and leave here?'

'With my good offices, Sire, yes! You are both noblemen, and if you would work with fairness and honour to negotiate, who knows what might be achieved? After all, you can see the strength of the French positions. They hold the land before you, and you cannot spread out, can you? You are hemmed in by woods and rivers on all sides. Consider: the King of France has an enviable position. If he wishes, he can hold you here and starve you out. You dare not flee now, for as soon as you do, he will fall upon you like a wolf upon lambs, and tear your army to pieces! You must remain here, hoping that he will attack you, but the King is no fool. It will give him a cheap victory if he merely remains where he is and lets you starve into submission.'

The Prince shook his head. 'You think we have a weak position? I tell you plainly, Cardinal, we have supplies to last us days.'

'And what then? After those days are passed? Will you then demand a truce to negotiate? You cannot retreat before such an army. And King John has supplies and fresh troops arriving hourly. Look how his banners catch the wind! There are so many groups from all over France, that it would be difficult to name them all. I must say plainly, Sire, to remain here and fight must expose you to ridicule. Noblemen would look at you and wonder whether this was only a prideful escapade, smacking of presumption on your part.'

'You dare to say to me that—'

'I speak only of how others could interpret your behaviour, Sire,' Talleyrand said. He held out his hands in supplication. 'Please! I beg you, allow a truce, agree to send negotiators to meet with the King's own in the land between the two armies. Come and discuss peace. You will be honoured by all the angels in Heaven if you do so, and your place will be guaranteed. If you refuse even to discuss peace, God will judge against you when you come before Him. But if you agree to talks, God will bless you!'

'I do not fear battle, but I have a responsibility to my men. I will not reject peace,' Prince Edward said. 'Ride back and ask the French to send their negotiators. I will send my own men to meet them between the armies.'

The marching wives were all kept at the rear of the English battles, detailed to bring food to the men through the long day, but their most important duty was to fetch water.

As the heat of the day rose, Gaillarde bore her yoke with two buckets down to the Miosson and filled them repeatedly. She went with the other women, enjoying the walk down the hill before trudging back with full loads of water. The men gratefully filled leather pottles or drank from cupped hands as the women walked past, trying to ensure that both buckets emptied at the same rate. It was hard work to carry one full, one empty.

By the time the sun was overhead, she was already exhausted. She continued up the ranks of the men, and as she reached Berenger's men, she saw her husband.

Denisot caught sight of her at the same moment. He ducked his head and looked away. She was reminded of him when she first met him, when he was a gangling youth, fearful of rejection, terrified that any advances would be thrown back in his face. He had always been anxious and fretful, she recalled, until they had their children. The children made him grow, made him mature. They gave him confidence, and it was largely because of the man he became that he was elected as bayle in their town. Men respected him, and his confidence grew as a result. It made her heart sing with love for him to see him like this once more.

Gaillarde smiled haltingly in the face of his anxiety, unsure how to speak to him. The years since their children's death, the hurt she had given him in the last weeks, the hurt she had given him by allowing him to think she wanted to stay with Bernard. He looked desperate, his eyes full of melancholy, but she took her buckets to him. 'Drink, husband,' she said. 'Please.'

'You should return to your man.'

'Denisot, when I refused you, I had no choice. I was held by that man for weeks. I feared for my life at all times with him. When you appeared, I thought he would kill you – and me as well. You don't know what he was capable of.'

Denisot nodded. 'I saw the girls he killed. He butchered them, just for the pleasure of seeing them die.'

'His brother was kind to me,' she said. 'But if you would have me, I would gladly return to you, husband.'

Denisot felt as though he was being choked. 'You are sure?'

Her buckets were empty again. She reached forward and touched his cheek, bringing him closer, and kissed him. 'I am your wife, Denisot. Even Bernard could not take that away.'

Further along, in the line of trees, Arnaud's face paled. 'But you are mine!' he whispered. 'You promised!'

Berenger felt the Prince's eyes on him even as the Cardinal hurried away, puffing and blowing with the urgency of his mission. He beckoned Berenger to him.

'I know you. Your name is Fripper. I remember you from Crécy and Calais. Many years have passed since those days, eh?'

He looked as though the weight of the lives that depended on him had just fallen onto his shoulders. 'Fripper, a man cannot fight when the Host of God stands against him. If we fight now, without seeking a peace, I will be damned for all time. Any death will be laid at my door.'

Berenger was unsure what to say. He nodded as though in understanding.

The Prince turned and faced him. 'Go with the negotiators, Fripper. Take your vintaine, and stand away with your bows ready. If there is any sign of bad faith, any sign at all, you will protect the English negotiators. You understand me?'

'Yes, Sire,' Berenger said.

Messengers were sent and returned, the primary negotiation being who should take part, and where. As soon as that was agreed, Berenger had his archers formed in a column. As he and the men waited, they could see a similar body of men forming in front of the French army, and when they began to march towards the English, Grandarse hoicked up his belt. 'You be careful, Frip. Keep your bow in your hand and an arrow ready to nock, but in God's name, don't let fly until you are certain there's a need. If you do, you'll take on all the guilt of Judas for starting a battle that wasn't needed. Mind you, if you do, we'll thrash these Frenchies. Never have any doubts about that.'

Berenger nodded.

Clip shook his head. 'Aye, ye know, we'll all . . .'

Berenger grasped his shirt and pulled him to him. 'Clip. If you say it, I'll knock your teeth so far down your throat, you'll be shitting them for a week. Leave it.'

There was no humour in his words. Berenger was aware of the responsibility the Prince had settled on his shoulders. If he misread the signs and precipitated a fight, he would be one of the first to pay for it, but it could also cost the rest of the English army dearly.

Clip nodded, shocked, and when he was released he returned to his place and stood silently.

'*Archers!*' Berenger called. 'March!'

CHAPTER FORTY-FIVE

As Berenger marched on, he glanced about him. The Earls of Warwick and Suffolk, Audley, Chandos and the King's closest adviser, Sir Bartholomew Burghersh, were riding with them, as was the dark-clothed priest, Thomas de Ladit. That man walked, keeping a little apart from the rest of the men as though he felt he was separate from the Prince's army, as he was – there to act as witness to the negotiations on behalf of Navarre.

It was curious to march down the plain towards the French, always aware of the eyes on them. Before him, Berenger could feel the hatred of the French as if it was vitriol flowing through the ground towards him, and behind him he could feel the English army staring at his back, some in hope of peace, others desperate for the battle that would end these wars forever. And one man, the Prince, who watched with the keen desire for a battle, but who must first give peace every opportunity.

The Earls stopped and waited for the French to come closer. Suffolk, the grey-haired veteran of a hundred fights, turned and pointed at the ground. 'Archers! Remain here. Do not approach unless you are called.'

Berenger nodded, and the men spread out on his command. The French had a group of men-at-arms and Genoese crossbow-men with them, who were also detailed to wait some fifteen paces behind the negotiators, and then the Cardinal approached and stood between the two parties.

Berenger could hear the names of the English representa-tives being called out, and then the French side was introduced: the Count of Tancarville, Jean de Talaru, Charny, Boucicaut and even the Archbishop of Sens, along with some other men Berenger had not heard of.

The discussions began coolly, with the French disdain-ful and apparently determined to force through demeaning demands. The English remained calm but obdurate, until the Cardinal began to lose his temper. It was already close to eve-ning when Talleyrand proposed resolutions to the problems. 'This truce is to the advantage of the English. If we have a battle, the majority of the casualties must lie with the English. For peace, clearly the English must give back all the lands they have taken. I suggest that all the possessions they have taken in the last three years should be returned to the French crown. Further, the English should make reparations. Perhaps a quar-ter of a million nobles would suffice to compensate the French King?'

'You want us to pay how much?' Suffolk demanded. Always choleric, his face had become the colour of a ripe plum.

'Perhaps less, then. Let us say two hundred thousand nobles. But in return, the Prince could marry the daughter of the King of France, thus sealing the peace for all time. She could bring Angoulême as her dowry.'

'I would rather fight to keep the lands God has given us in

battle!' Chandos roared. He clenched his fist, adding, 'And take Angoulême as well!'

Thomas de Ladit winced to hear the man's hoarse bellow. This was no way to conduct talks to avoid war.

He was sure that he recognised an esquire on the other side. A slim fellow with mail habergeon and some *cuir bouilli* armour, he was instantly familiar, but Thomas was not sure where he had met, until a memory sparked and he realised that this was Martin de Rouen, the esquire who had been with him when King Charles of Navarre had been captured.

While the Lords bickered and squabbled, he edged his way around them all. He saw no reason not to talk to an old companion. Others in the two parties were mingling. So many were friends with men on the opposing side, and it was only natural that they should speak and discuss mutual friends while their Lords argued.

'Martin? Esquire?' he said.

'Thomas de Ladit!' the other responded, and the two smiled and clasped hands, for a moment without words.

'I had thought you were captured,' the esquire said.

'And I you.'

'I was fortunate. The King decided he had little use for an esquire to demonstrate his anger on, when he had so many others,' the esquire said with some bitterness.

'And what do you do here now?' Thomas asked.

'Oh, I am here to see that Rouen doesn't suffer,' Martin said.

'And have you heard of our Lord?' Thomas wondered. 'I have heard nothing from him since his capture. I have myself been forced to wander about the lands, trying to work my way south. I was captured here by the English, and now serve that Navarre may have a record of what happens here.'

'I am in much the same position,' Martin said. 'I hope that the two armies here can agree a sensible peace. Did you hear of Bernard of Rouen?'

Thomas told the esquire of the murders and the capture of the guilty man, and Martin nodded seriously. 'I am glad to hear it. There were many rumours of the killings. The peasants barely dared to leave their children for a moment or two.'

They continued chatting, but the two groups of negotiators began to separate and draw apart. Martin and Thomas exchanged another hand clasp and wished each other Godspeed.

Later, Thomas would not know what prompted him. For some reason, as the two began to walk towards their joint parties, he asked, 'What of the Dauphin and the King?

The reply was enough to make Thomas want to hurry from the field and speak to the Prince.

The parties separated and returned to their armies to take counsel. Berenger and the archers marched back to the English lines and waited while the advisers told the Prince what had been discussed. To Berenger's surprise, Thomas de Ladit insisted on talking to Sir John, and shortly afterwards he and Sir John hurried to the Prince's pavilion. Thomas and Sir John were soon back, and Berenger was surprised to see a fresh excitement about Sir John. There was little disappointment to be seen in the faces of the negotiators either. The men strode back to the place of truce without a look back. Berenger was not sure how to take that. He had his archers stop at the same point as before, and the English delegation continued to the negotiation.

Soon the French and the Cardinal had arrived. Talleyrand looked pale, Berenger thought. The day's efforts must have cost him dearly.

'What does your Prince say to the Cardinal's proposals?' the Archbishop of Sens asked brusquely.

Suffolk glanced at his companions, and then said quietly, 'He will accept the proposals.'

'He will accept the fair demands of the French King?' Talleyrand said, thunderstruck.

'If they are sworn, yes.'

'When the lands are returned, he will need to return all the prisoners captured in the last three years as well,' the Archbishop said. 'And furthermore, he must swear not to take up arms against France for seven years. We will not negotiate a truce for now, only for him to come with a fresh army as soon as one can be gathered.'

'Very well.'

'And you will swear to be bound to this?' Charny asked.

'Yes. Subject only to one condition.'

'Which is?' Talleyrand said.

'That the treaty must be ratified by King Edward, his father.'

'That is not possible,' the Cardinal said with a smile. 'We would have to wait for weeks to hear back from your King. We cannot accept that.'

'That is the Prince's firm determination. Without his father's approval, the peace would hold no force. He has no right to agree to anything without his father's agreement.'

Charny peered at him. 'You are serious? He will agree to nothing?'

'Perhaps a short truce. No more.'

'There is nothing more to discuss,' the Archbishop snapped. 'This has been an exercise in bad faith!'

'Bad faith?' Suffolk growled.

Berenger's hand moved towards the arrows at his belt. He glanced at Clip, who nodded.

'You never had any intention of honourably negotiating,' the Archbishop spat. 'You wanted to hold us here and delay the battle. To rest your men, and give them the food you have looted from the farms about here!'

'Whereas your men wanted to come and view our meagre forces,' Chandos said.

The two groups separated with a bad grace, Talleyrand piteously pleading with both parties not to report the failure of the talks. Instead he begged that both sides should warn their leaders that he would return later with further ideas.

It was already late, and Berenger was glad to be marching back to the camp. With his eyesight he could see glowing balls of light at the French lines, but although he knew they were campfires, he could see nothing of the men who waited there for the moment when they would be sent into battle.

He found himself close to the priest, Thomas de Ladit. As the light faded, Thomas was walking nearer as though seeking comfort in companionship.

'What do you do here?' Berenger asked him.

'Me? I represent my King, Charles of Navarre, and will seek to advise your Prince as well.'

'What will you seek to advise him?'

'If he asks me, I will say that nothing King John offers can be believed. I have seen his uncontrollable rages. He is ungovernable when in a fury, and now he is determined to crush you and your army. He will not negotiate your freedom lightly.'

The negotiators were soon back, and Berenger and his men were sent to find food for themselves. Later, Berenger saw a lone torch approaching, and the Prince once more met Talleyrand and his little entourage near Berenger and his men.

'Sire, I have spoken to the French King and he does not accept your proposals.'

'He does not?'

Talleyrand looked like a man close to the end of his tether. 'The Bishop of Châlons is there, and I fear he spoke against you. He declared that the English would do all they could to link armies with the Duke of Lancaster, and then begin to assault French towns and cities once more. They believe you will not surrender any towns or people, but will continue until you are stopped, and your army is destroyed. He was able to persuade the others that the best time to fight you would be now, when you are already trapped.'

'So all our promises were ignored?' Suffolk said.

'If you will not agree to terms on your honour, but continue to demand that everything must be approved by your father the King, Châlons will convince others that you do not negotiate in good faith,' Talleyrand declared, and there were tears in his eyes.

'So, it is all done. You can bear witness, along with all my Lords here, along with these good archers, that I have offered much. I accepted your proposals in good faith, and I offered my own assurances. It is he who has rejected the chance of peace, and so I confidently place myself in the protection of God. He must adjudicate, and I ask that you pray for Him to grant the victory to our side because ours has the most justice. Our cause is just, as He will decide, I am sure.'

'Please, do not submit to war! Give me something to negotiate with, and I will see if I can change their minds!'

'Such as what?'

'Well, Sire, the King of France did offer you a truce for this night, if you swear not to use it to leave the field and retreat to Bordeaux. He is determined to give you battle.'

'Is he? Well, you can assure him that I am also keen on a

fight. But I will give him no assurances of remaining here, no. I didn't come here with his permission, and I do not intend to ask it to leave either. I am here, and if the man calling himself King wishes to stop me from leaving, he must use his troops to do it.'

'Sire, could you not give me space to negotiate? A truce in which you will not attack France again? That would at least give them some comfort!'

'For how long?'

'As long as is necessary!'

'I will consider a truce,' the Prince said. 'You may tell the French that I will consider a truce.'

'My Lord, I am glad!' Talleyrand said, and in moments he was gone.

'So, Fripper,' the Prince said when the delegation was gone. 'What do you think?'

'Me, Sire? I think he is keen for a truce.'

'Yes, but why, I wonder? Is it to save lives, or just to hold us here with no means of replenishing our stores of food, so that we can be more easily dealt with when it comes to battle later?'

'I don't pretend to understand the ways of negotiators,' Berenger said. 'It's all over my head, Sire. My task is to serve you, and that I'll do as best I may.'

'Good. Then set guards about the camp and get your head down, Fripper. For in God's name, I believe tomorrow we shall have our battle.'

Monday 19 September

Berenger and the men slept at their positions and were up and ready before dawn. He passed around his small sack and they began to make their oatcakes as the sun started to light the far hill. Campfires were lighted, and the men went to warm themselves occasionally, but for the most part the men stayed where they were. None of them had a satisfying sleep.

Then, as the sun rose, Berenger saw her light spread across the French lines. Their banners and flags moved sluggishly in the gentle dawn breeze, but that did not detract from the awesome sight of thousands of men in armour standing in the cool morning while tendrils of mist moved slowly.

'Shite, Frip! There's more than yesterday,' Grandarse muttered.

Berenger was not convinced of that, but there was no doubt that it was a formidable army. It reached out in an arc before them, an enormous battle of men.

'The buggers have learned from us, too,' Hawkwood commented. 'They're all on foot.'

It had been a firm principle of English fighting that it was better to dismount and fight on foot from a defensive position, rather than send cavalry against men who possessed spears and lances. A man with a spear would always be able to break a charge and threaten the knight, if he was determined enough. As Berenger watched, he could see men dismounting, their horses being taken to the rear of the French battles.

'This is going to get messy, right enough,' Dogbreath said.

There was a shout from the front of the English lines and a body of men could be seen on horseback trotting towards them from their enemy.

'Who's that?' Grandarse said.

It was Robin who answered. 'The Cardinal.'

Clip looked over and sneered. 'Perhaps he comes to say the French want to surrender?'

Berenger gave a dry chuckle, but then he was beckoned by Sir John, and he was sent with his vintaine to join the Prince. Talleyrand met them at the front of the English lines.

'Sire, will you grant me one more favour?' he asked as he stepped forward, a clerk holding his reins for him.

'No. It is too late, Cardinal. I am grateful for your efforts in saving us bloodshed, but you have overstepped the bounds of convention now.'

'I swear I have attempted to bring about peace. I have worked hard for that. I beg, just one more opportunity, please! To save all these lives, would you consider a truce for a year? Not an indefinite truce, but merely a truce for a year.'

'So he decided to reject an indefinite peace?' the Prince said. He cast a glance at Suffolk, who stood beside him, with Audley and Chandos behind. 'Very well, you can offer him this, a peace until spring, but no later.'

'But if you could—'

'Until spring, Talleyrand. Return to him and see what his answer is.'

Berenger watched the crestfallen Cardinal remount and trot back to the opposing lines of men. As Talleyrand rode, a number of men in his group broke from his entourage and rode to places in the battles.

'I know,' the Prince said when this was pointed out to him. 'The good Cardinal was keen to keep us here. He excited my suspicions last night. I believe he and his knights thought to aid the French King by keeping us here arrayed for war. After two or three days of starvation, they would attack. Although I told him we have supplies, they must know how limited our stocks are. Well, with luck the assault will come today. But we must not attack first. With all their troops, they can afford to attack us.'

Berenger went to celebrate Mass with a different attitude that morning, compared to all those other mornings before a battle.

In his youth and adult life he had attacked many towns and pillaged them. He had taken part in a number of assaults and fought in pitched battles from Crécy to Neville's Cross and beyond, but each time he had found the prayers to be routine and little more than a ritual based on the necessity of the moment: they were important because he might be killed, and the Mass could protect his soul. That was worth taking a few minutes to pray, but much of the time, while pleading his case at the feet of God, his mind had been elsewhere, thinking about the disposition of his troops, thinking about getting some food, thinking about sharpening his blades. Rarely had he, like today, considered deeply what he was about to do: kill many men.

It was a wrenching realisation, to know that he was here planning the destruction of as many men as he could achieve. And all for little reason, other than to support his Prince. It was not that he distrusted his Prince, nor that he felt the Prince's cause was not just. That had been proved to his satisfaction several times in the last weeks. However, it was strange. He had a feeling now that his presence here was not right.

He had been imbued with the desire to fight from an early age. As a loyal soldier of his King, he had thought that coming here to win back his Lord's lands was a worthwhile cause. And since then, killing had been a part of his life. Now, visions rose in his mind of the monastery, of the kindly Abbot Andry, the Infirmarer, the monks who laboured in the kitchens with their sleeves rolled up, those who toiled in the fields and the stews, those who smiled and nodded at him even when he had been sick all night after drinking too much, and their faces seemed more real to him now than the faces of his own vintaine.

'What's your trouble, Frip? You look like a frog who's eaten a dragonfly too big to swallow!' Grandarse said.

'I'm fine,' Berenger said. He could not allow his men to hear that he had any doubts. No matter what God might think, if his men realised he had doubts about the battle to come, they would lose all faith in him, and that could make some of them run. He would not do that to them.

He stood resolutely with his men at the rear of the Prince's battle and searched the landscape in pursuit of any symbol or sign from God that fighting today was a good act. Because it would be a fight today, of that he was sure.

As he left the Mass and walked back to his men, he saw Will.

His successor had a haggard look about him. Will stared at him, and there was a look of reluctant respect in the way he nodded slowly. Berenger was suddenly put in mind of Abbot Andry and the way that he would study a man with serious-ness.

'Will,' he said, and bent his steps towards the man. Owen stood in his path, his hand on his sword, but Will called him to move aside, and Berenger walked to him. 'Will, I will do you no harm this day. Today we fight for England,' Berenger said. 'We can neither of us risk the battle because of our dispute.'

'Good,' Will said. 'But after the fighting here is done?'

'I made an oath before God,' Berenger said.

'Then we will fight afterwards,' Will said. He stared out over the fields and pastures before them. 'You know, I thought that after I'd taken control, the company would move to greater and greater feats. That we'd become the strongest force in Christendom, perhaps hold our own land, and I would become a great Lord. But the men bicker and argue over every decision and never pay my views any heed.'

'Commanding a company is not easy,' Berenger said.

'I swear, I wish I'd never taken it,' Will said quietly.

'We have peace for this day,' Berenger said, and held out his hand in a sign of faith.

'We do. God preserve you, Fripper.'

'And you, Will,' Berenger said as he returned to his men.

In his mind, he wandered again amid the orchards of the abbey with the Abbot. He saw again that kind man's simple delight in the countryside and in the abbey he served. And he saw the Abbot smile as though delighted by his act of peace with Will.

After the battle, he and Will would have to fight, he thought. 'God, if I could avoid my oath, I would,' he murmured under his breath.

The idea of life as a monk had never seemed so appealing.

Returning to his men counting the rosary beads, he almost bumped into Thomas de Ladit.

'My apologies, Vintener,' Thomas said, and was about to hurry on when Berenger asked him to wait a moment.

'Yesterday, you looked like a man with an urgent message. I saw you talking to a French esquire. What was that about?'

Thomas hesitated, but then he could not restrain his glee. 'I spoke with an old friend. Martin de Rouen told me something that may help us today. You know that the King of France captured my Lord during a feast being hosted by the King's son, the Dauphin?'

'Yes.'

'The Dauphin, so I have heard, is still bitterly angry about that. He will do nothing that will honour his father, it is said, and his father will not wish to help him. In the battle, the plan is that the Dauphin will lead the first battle to let him win his spurs. If he wins, it will strengthen his position, and the King will find it harder to restrain him. But if he does not succeed, he will be withdrawn and a third of the army will go with him. That means the English will have only to hold on for the first stage, and then the forces will be more evenly balanced.'

'They will still be stronger than us,' Berenger said.

'Yes – but they will have to cross that field with your archers raining arrows on their heads the whole way. If the English army can hold fast, I think the day will be yours.'

CHAPTER FORTY-SIX

Berenger was still considering his words when the Prince appeared before the men on horseback. He progressed along the line, his bascinet in the crook of his arm, talking easily with a clear, loud voice. His household was about him as he rode on his great charger, looking at his men with his eyes bright.

'Look about you, my friends! This is a merry place for a battle, is it not? Look here, we have our men all stationed securely, with the river down there, so we cannot be outflanked. Here we have the ground, this hedge, and the ridge. Any French army trying to attack us will be broken on the lances of our men here, and on the arrows of the archers. They will try, but they will die in the attempt!'

He lowered his head and met their eyes. 'But it will not be an easy fight, my friends. When they come, they will outnumber us. It is not easy to see how we could fight so numerous an enemy, but fight we will, and defeat them we must! I am fortunate to have so many stoical and stern men in my army. You know well how difficult this will be, but you do not turn away! You acknowledge the trial to come with resolution, like hounds straining to be slipped free after the hare! Well, today I will give you such a hare as no English army has seen in many a long year.

'Some of you, my friends, were with me ten years ago. Grandarse, you were there, though you were half the man you are now! Fripper, you too. My Lords here were at my side. Sir John helped when I was almost overwhelmed. And there, that was where I won my spurs and was blooded. Crécy, they called that battle. I will give you another battle today that will ring down the ages. You will return to your homes as heroes, each one of you a Hector or Alexander. You will never want for female company after fighting here with me today! I swear that you will all be gladly serviced by all the women of England when they hear of your exploits today, hey!'

He got a cheer for that.

'But let us not be foolish. We have yet to celebrate, my friends. So, archers, hold to your orders. Do not desert your posts. Keep to strict discipline, for any man who leaves his position will be hanged. That is how important this task is. Keep to your positions. And when it comes to the mêlée, all of you must fight with all your courage and determination. Do not stop to capture a valuable prize, no matter who it is, but fight on. We must win the battle before we worry about the men captured and how much we may claim as ransom. Do you all agree?'

There was a second cheer for that, although Berenger could hear it was more muted.

So did the Prince.

'Do your duty, men. Keep your position and protect your mates on either side. Serve me well, and I will see you all rewarded. For am I not a generous Prince?'

The cheer this time was louder again, and the Prince grinned and wheeled his horse about.

Berenger watched him ride off to the easternmost battle and begin his harangue once more, but his eyes were more turned towards the French lines.

They still didn't move. Even Berenger could see that with his eyesight. Yet the English could not remain here waiting much longer. Too many of the men had not eaten for a day, and all were thirsty again. They needed provisions.

'Remember what he said, men. Don't chase after them if they appear to retreat. Listen to the orders, keep them back, hold to your lines. Is that clear enough, Imbert?'

'Aye. I'll do it.'

Archibald was tending to his fire when the messenger arrived.

'You have to pack up everything and prepare to leave.'

Archibald looked up from blowing his embers into life and glared at the man. 'Who in the name of all Heaven are you? I'm trying to keep this fire going so I can light my matches when I have to light my gonnes. I don't have time to play silly games. I've been ordered to command this place. Who told you to come here and make a jest with me? I don't have time for it!'

'The army is to move, Master,' the man said, and Archibald saw that his face was pale. He spoke quietly, but earnestly. 'We cannot wait longer for the French to decide to attack. If they won't attack us, we have to retreat and make our way to another place where we can fight them more safely.'

Archibald gaped at him. 'You can't be serious, man! If we start to pack and go, the French will attack as soon as they see us riding off! We'll be cut to pieces if we do that. No army harried in retreat has ever survived.'

'Those are your orders. You are to gather your equipment and store it ready to depart,' the man said. And in his eyes, Archibald saw the absolute certainty. He knew as well as Archibald that this could only lead to disaster.

'Can you find men to help me load my gonnes, then?'

'I will try, Master, but I cannot promise to succeed!'

Archibald turned from him and looked at the English lines running down the hill behind the hawthorn hedge. 'Dear God in Heaven, what will happen to us?'

Ed was shaking his head. 'We'll be cut to pieces.'

'We have one more trick,' Archibald said, glancing down at his little ribauldequins.

The first Berenger knew of the change in the battle plan was when he saw a number of horses brought up past him.

'What the fuck?' Dogbreath hissed, watching the beasts, and then turned to stare down the hill towards the men in the Earl of Warwick's battle. 'Frip, they're mounting! They're going!'

'They can't be,' Berenger said, and peered down the slope, his eyes screwed tight as he attempted to make sense of the scene. He was sure that there were men mounting their horses, and then he saw the flash as lance-tips were raised. Immediately his stomach lurched. 'Grandarse, what the fuck are they doing? It looks like they're riding away!'

'Ballocks, man, they wouldn't be riding away!' Grandarse glared down towards the river. 'Aye, but the buggers look like they're going. Clip, you get down there and see what they're up to, man. Be quick and get back here to tell us!'

'Grandarse, we won't have much time. Look!' Berenger said.

There was a force of riders moving from the French army. Several hundred men-at-arms were moving forward in two groups. Even Berenger could see the size of the two companies, and from their speed he knew that they had to be horsemen.

'Ach! Ballocks! Where are they going?'

'It doesn't matter, Grandarse! We'll have enough on our plate in a minute. Archers! Make ready!'

There was a clear noise of thunder in the distance now.

Berenger peered out over the fields and hedges towards the French. He could see them more clearly. The men riding to the left were heading down towards the Earl of Warwick's battle, to where the lances still gleamed, while the second company were riding more towards the Earl of Salisbury's men. There was no sign that Berenger could see, yet, that the main army was moving towards them, but that was sure to be only a matter of time. Then he thought he saw the initial ripple. It was like looking at a scene over a hot field, or watching rocks beneath a flowing river.

'They come!' Robin yelled. 'Archers, the enemy is marching to us! Prepare to receive the enemy!'

Berenger gripped his bow more firmly. Clip was only half-way to the men of the Earl of Warwick, he thought, and then he heard the roars and cries as the French began their charge.

It was a terrifying sight. He saw the destriers lengthening their stride. They were so close now, he could see them clearly. Some three hundred strong, the men-at-arms all couched lances and lowered their tips until they were pointing at the English. There were cries of alarm, at last, and trumpets blew, and Berenger saw the first of many flights of arrows fly, flat and true, at the French riders.

But these were no light horsemen with boiled leather breast-plates and thin mail. These were the heaviest soldiers in the French army. They had thick armour and plate on the horses' heads and breasts. Berenger saw only two of the horses fall, although the archers kept up their efforts. The sound of steel striking steel became a regular sound now, and at last the charge was ended as the lances ripped into the men of Warwick's battle.

Men trying to wheel their mounts about suddenly found them-selves stabbed by immense lances that pierced their armour and ripped their internal organs to pieces. The effect was instant and disastrous. The French had achieved a great shock and now they drew their swords or wielded war hammers as they set about the English.

Berenger was half-inclined to take his men and run down to support the Earl's men, but even as he called to Robin, the archer clapped his hands and pointed.

It was hard to make out. 'What?' Berenger demanded.

'Our archers in the marshes! They've moved behind the French. They're loosing into the horses from behind. Their arrows are causing havoc.'

Berenger could see some horses rearing, then he saw one crash to the ground, to roll on its back, legs flailing. Faintly over the clamour of metal on metal, he could hear the sound of screams, of wildly neighing beasts, of panicked men.

'The French are taken in flank and from behind, Frip. They're being slaughtered,' Robin began gleefully, but then he grew quieter, less gleeful. 'Some are turning back, and their mounts are trampling their own men on the ground. The brutes are pelting back to the French lines. One of them's got a spike in its rump, and it's trying to bite it free, it's going mad. It's knocked a man down, and now it's kicking and bucking like an unbroken stallion. It's a butcher's scene, Frip.'

Berenger had stopped listening to him as he felt the pound-ing on the ground again. This time the heavy horses were riding straight to the Earl of Salisbury's men. He saw the flash as lances were couched. 'Archers! With me!'

Over on the far left, Archibald had heard the noise of battle approaching even as he took up his gonne and lashed the ropes to it. With Ed and two others, he hauled on the rope. The tripod of his makeshift hoist creaked and groaned and the rope gave off ominous little crackles, but the barrel rose, swinging. Béatrice was ready to push it into position on the wagon. Archibald heard cries and shouts, and for a moment he was distracted. A man gave a yelp as the rope moved and scraped away the flesh of his hand, and Archibald grabbed the rope more tightly at once, bellowing at the men to keep hold.

'Hold hard!' he shouted as the roars and trumpet-blasts grew louder and louder. Between the ringing of metal, he heard the French cries of 'Saint-Denis' and the English returns for Saint George, but he forced them from his mind.

'Shit! We'll let it down again, quickly now. Béatrice, we will set it down on the trestle once more!'

'We were ordered to withdraw!' Ed bellowed.

'Fuck that! Do you want to die? If we try to now, we'll be killed. May as well die while fighting!' Archibald yelled back. He helped the men lower the barrel back into position while Béatrice guided it back onto its huge trestle and then he let the ropes dangle while he hurried back to hammer blocks into place to hold the gonne there.

As he did, there was a sudden commotion, and a large group of French men-at-arms appeared. They saw Archibald and his men and started to run at them, shrieking their battle cries.

Archibald grabbed his match and blew on the sparking, fizzing end, then turned the nearest three-barrelled ribauldequin around and pointed it at the men. One appeared to recognise his danger, but the rest continued without hesitation.

'Loose it, Master!' Ed cried, and Archibald touched the firehole. There was a fizzing, and then the first barrel gushed flame and fire, and he touched the next, sending a second great flare, although the third barrel fizzed and then went quiet. Suddenly it went off too, and a six-foot flame burst out, scorching the grass and sending the reek of brimstone all about.

'Reload it,' Archibald said to Ed, as he set about working on the great gonne again. He had already primed and filled the barrel with powder and was ramming a great stone ball into it with his ramrod, when the horses suddenly appeared.

Archibald threw down his ramrod and tipped a little fine powder into the vent before cupping his hand over it to stop the wind taking the grains away. Then he pursed his lips and blew on his match. The great charge of horses came down the hill, and he peered along the barrel, trying to aim, but the line was not good, and even as he held the smouldering match to the vent, and the sharp hiss of burning powder sounded, he knew he would take only a few men.

The gonne went off with a roar that shook the ground, and a flame twenty feet long reached out to the men-at-arms at their charge, seeming to lick at the horse's hoofs, closely followed by an immense cloud of smoke. He saw one horse hit above the shoulder, and there was a filthy red splash thrown beyond as the ball continued to strike a man behind, and then the smoke mercifully hid the scene.

Archibald scarcely noticed. To his horror, the trestle moved back two feet even with the bracing he had hammered into the ground. It was too damp here. The ground was so wet, the gonne leaped up and fell back half off its trestle. Archibald scurried to one side with his steel bar to force it back into position, almost tripping, and stared through the smoke, wiping smuts from his face, dreading to see a series of lance-points aiming straight at him, but to his astonishment, as he began to see the men and horses again, he saw that they had moved on, and were pelting down towards the archers, who redoubled their own efforts. Two horses and three men lay in the path of his gonne, one man feebly moving, and the nearer horse was waving his hind legs in the air, whinnying piteously.

The cavalry continued down the hillside and pushed the archers further back into the thick mud of the Miosson's marshes, but the horses couldn't follow them. Archibald saw three of the horses in the front rising and plunging in the thick mud. Two of them panicked and tried to retreat. One threw his rider and bolted, while the other riders bypassed the archers and rode into the flank of the farthest point of the English line.

Archibald yelled at Ed and the two dragged their little hand-carts round to face the French as they approached, and then the two began to set match to powder, firing one barrel at a time, carefully conserving their fire so that the flames gushed regularly. The flames and thick, oily smoke added a new terror to the horses, but then there was more screaming, and anguish from the heavy horses. The archers were now behind them, and were sending flight after flight into the less heavily armoured rears of the men and the horses alike. Men were toppling from their beasts, while the destriers were themselves rearing and plunging with every stinging barb that slammed into their flanks and bellies.

Archibald and Ed fired, cleaned and reloaded their gonnes, sending stones flying into the enemy until English men-at-arms rushed past them and began to hack and bludgeon the French.

As Clip returned to tell of the carnage at the marshes, Berenger saw the Earl of Suffolk riding up and down the battle to the right. Cries of *'Saint-Denis!'* and *'Saint George!'* rose on all sides, and Suffolk was ordering men to fill gaps, directing the aim of archers and pointing the best targets. The Earl of Salisbury had been in the thick of the fighting, and now stood panting, resting on his sword. The whole of his arm was red with blood.

'Archers!' Suffolk bawled, pointing to Berenger, and Berenger took up a handful of arrows and ran to the aid of the Earl's men. The riders were making for a gap in the thick hedge that protected the front, but the gap was only wide enough for five or six horses to ride abreast. Berenger made for it as fast as he could, aware of the panting of Imbert and Robin close behind him, and then they were in range.

'Aim at them as they enter the gap!' he shouted. If they could bring down two or three mounts there, it would give the rest of the French a difficult obstacle. He nocked, drew, aimed and loosed, then again, his arrows flying flat and true. He saw one arrow strike a horse's breast and bounce back, to land quivering in the ground. A second bounced off a knight's bascinet and whirled away out of sight.

'Archers, to me!' he bellowed, and pulled his sword free, running at the line of horsemen. The screams were deafening as he approached, and then he and his vintaine were in the thick of it. A man-at-arms was whirling his destrier, the massive iron-shod hoofs flying. An archer from the Earl of Salisbury's company drew too close, and a hoof caught his forehead. It was crushed in an instant, and the man fell. There was a shriek from Berenger's side, and he turned to see that another French knight had come from somewhere on his horse, and Baz had a poleaxe in his head. His eyes rolled up as Berenger cried out, and then Berenger hacked with all his strength at the knight's forearm, and the man tried to wrestle with his weapon to extricate it from Baz's head, but he couldn't. Berenger saw an opening and thrust hard with his sword at the knight's armpit. He felt his blade sink in, and the Frenchman gave a curse, letting go his poleaxe and slamming his armoured forearm at Berenger's head. Berenger side-stepped and yanked his sword free, swinging it at the back of the man's leg, but the horse had already moved away and his blow went wide.

He saw Robin draw his bow and loose from only a matter of feet away, and this time the arrow penetrated the armour with a solid thump. Another man tried to hit him, but that arrow flew away, spinning, after bouncing from his breastplate. A third flew, and this caught the top of his breast and bounced upwards, under his gorget, and stuck there. The knight desperately fought to grab the missile, but with his great armoured gloves, he could get no purchase. He scrabbled wildly, then released his visor, and a spray of blood came from it. Another arrow flew, and hit him beside his nose. He fell from the saddle, instantly dead. Three archers hacked at his face where he fell.

Berenger was at the hedge now. More knights and men-at-arms on heavy beasts were hacking and stabbing from their destriers, but the fight was beginning to move in favour of the English. Berenger saw with relief that a couple of the cavalrymen were turning and fleeing, while more were being dragged to the ground. He saw Imbert with a grapnel. It caught a man by the throat, and the archer and his companions hauled on it, tugging the man from his saddle, and stabbing him through his visor as he lay on the ground. Another man was slammed across the helmet with a lead maul, and tumbled out of the saddle, dazed.

And then the battle was done. The French were dead or fleeing, and Berenger leaned on his sword and rested, panting.

Pierre was by his side with Felix. 'Is that it?' the boy asked. 'Have we won?'

It was Robin who answered. 'No. That was to tickle us. Now the main battle is approaching on foot.'

'Archers!' Berenger shouted. 'To your positions, ready your bows!'

CHAPTER FORTY-SEVEN

Archibald had been busy. He had both ribauldequins loaded and pointing in the direction of the French and then, during the lull after the cavalry charge, he managed to reposition the main barrel and reload it.

As the battle progressed, fewer and fewer French fighters came down to this area so far on the flank. The archers on his left, and the bodies before him, marked those who had been foolish enough to think they could get around him.

'Where are they?' Ed asked again.

'They'll come, never you worry,' Archibald said calmly, but his coolness was a mask. Here, it was impossible to see when the French were coming. They could appear over the ground in front at any time, and when they did, he would have his work cut out. 'Make sure that the powder is in reach, Donkey, and get ready to serve those gonnes as fast as you can.'

He cast an eye over his little encampment. They had not enough men. If a main force of French came rushing down here, he would have time to fire the gonnes once before they were all overrun. He had no illusions about their position.

'Béatrice, I'd like you to go and find Berenger Fripper.'

'Why?' She had that mulish look on her face again.

'Because, wench, I can't protect you here. This isn't going to be an easy battle where we have a clear field of view at all times. And I can't fight if I'm worried about you all the time.'

'And I have nowhere else to go,' she snapped. 'I have no family but you, no friends but you. I will stay here.'

Berenger pulled Robin and Pierre back, shouting at Felix and Dogbreath to join him with the reserves. He had no idea of the passage of time now. It was impossible to tell how long it was since the first charge. Berenger was desperately thirsty, and he smacked his lips as if it could persuade him that he had taken a draught of ale or even water, but it brought no satisfaction. He shoved Felix after his father into the line, and turned to watch again as the French marched stolidly towards the English.

The Prince and other leaders had stationed archers in trenches near the gaps in the hedges, and now they began to let fly in earnest. These men were less heavily armoured than the cavalry, and every arrow that found its mark caused a grievous wound. Berenger saw three men marching abreast, and all were suddenly struck by arrows almost simultaneously. They collapsed on the spot, instantly dead. Another man he saw struck by an arrow in the breast, and he stared at it dumbly before trying to follow his colleagues, but he fell after only three paces. One man was struck with two arrows at his flank and shoulder, and it seemed to send him berserk. He picked up his sword and ran full tilt into the English line ahead of his comrades, although he was hacked down before he could strike a single blow.

The French were at the hedge now. Some tried to clamber over it, but the hawthorn hedge was so thick and deep that it was all but impenetrable. They were forced to congregate at the gaps in the hedge, and here there was a fearful killing. The men bunched and tried to force their way through, and for a long while the arrows of the archers played a terrible game of death. Men-at-arms stood with lances and swords, cutting down any who managed to pass through, but then there was a roar from the French, and a solid body of men linked arms and ran at the blockage. They pushed and shoved the bodies from the gap, and then trampled their comrades in their urgent desire to get to the English and Gascons on the other side. Berenger heard a bellow, and more men were thundering into the gap and trying to push through.

'Archers!' Berenger bellowed.

'*Saint-Denis!*' was roaring from a thousand throats and the French were making good work of it. Enough had stormed the gap to protect their comrades, and now a steady trickle of men were passing through and throwing themselves on the defenders.

Berenger nocked an arrow, and almost loosed it at a great Frenchman who had pelted up into the press of men. As he reached the gap in the hedge, this new fighter pulled off his bascinet, and long, fair hair flew in the wind. He looked like a Viking. As Berenger was about to let fly, two English fighters sprang into his line of sight. He released the tension quickly. It was too dangerous to send arrows into that crush.

'Archers, follow me!' he shouted, and sprang down the slope towards the nearest group. He heard a bull-like roar behind him, and knew that Grandarse was near. There was a moment of calm as he ran, the air clean and fresh in his throat, the taste of good soil, clean grass, and nothing evil or foul, and then he crashed into the side of a great bear of a Frenchman, and was stabbing with his sword's point, and the air was full of the smell of shit and blood and piss, and all beauty and all peace was lost forever.

He felt that he would never see it again.

He saw Will and the company as he reached the English battle. They were at the hedge's gap, but were hemmed in by a phalanx of Frenchmen, and Will already had a streak of red where his cheek had been opened. The company was being pushed back, through the hedge, and the French were beginning to pour through in pursuit. Berenger would have made his way towards them, but he couldn't. He watched as the French lines flowed forward in an unstoppable tide. There was a moment when he saw Will's face turned towards him, and he felt sure that he saw in Will's face a fresh joy, as if he had finally lost his doubts and uncertainties. Then the company rallied to him, and as Berenger watched, Will's sword was raised, and the company counter-attacked the French at the hedge. It was a sight to make an Englishman's heart surge with pride. The men rushed down the little slope, and met with the fair-haired Frenchman and his companions, and a fresh fight began, with maces swinging, axes hacking, and all weapons rising and falling with a hideous, irregular rhythm. The clatter of steel falling on steel was enough to set Berenger's teeth on edge, and he bellowed to his archers to follow him.

They ran on, through sodden mud and over the bodies and limbs of the dead and dying, slamming into the flank of the French near the company. Berenger saw Saul and Fulk at his side. They were close to three of the men from Will's own vintaine, and as they approached, there were flares of recognition, and the men seemed to gain strength from seeing that there were more on their side. The fair Frenchman had a sword in one hand and a mace in his other, and he wielded both with abandon. Berenger saw the spiked steel ball strike a man's head, crushing bone and ripping away the flesh, before swinging up and around to slam into a man's upper arm. He shrieked as his sword fell from nerveless fingers, and then his throat was opened by the sword, sending a thick gout of blood gushing over the men nearby.

And then Berenger saw Will take on the French monster. His sword darted and hammered, while he held a dagger in his other hand that he used to try to get inside the Frenchman's defences, slipping in and back with speed. Then he suddenly lunged, and Berenger saw his blade had gone wide, blocked by the Frenchman's own. It was a fatal error, Berenger thought, but just then a sword came slashing towards him, and he had to deflect it, countering with a cut that took his assailant in the side of the head. His helmet was dented with the force of Berenger's blow, and the man fell even as Berenger stabbed at his face. Then Berenger glanced back and saw that Will's manoeuvre had been a feint. Even as his sword was knocked away, his dagger had reached the Frenchman's throat and, angled upwards, stabbed up from below his jaw and into his brain.

The man was dying when Berenger saw them, but then a freak movement in the crowd showed him that the Frenchman had dropped his mace, and had put his last strength into one more blow. He had taken his sword and shoved it underneath Will's breastplate, and up into his body. Will was transfixed, but the two men struggled, each pushing his weapon further into the body of his enemy, until both fell and were hidden among the trampling legs of their men.

Berenger was engaged again as Will and his opponent fell. A sword flashed past his face, narrowly missing him, and he had to ram a man from his side – whether English or French he had no idea – then reverse his sword and stab hard at the man in front of him. He felt his blade skitter across a breastplate, catch in something else, and he shoved with all his might. A man gave a gasp of agony, and he pulled the blade free to see him fall. He didn't know whether the victim was a friend or foe, but that didn't matter in the mêlée. All that mattered was to stab and kill, and stay alive. Avoid the swords and knives that were aiming for him every moment.

He ducked under another blow aimed at his head, felt himself begin to slide in the mud, and fought to maintain his footing. A man on the ground would be stabbed by men of both sides in case he was an enemy. No one on the ground would survive – he mustn't fall – a hand caught his armpit, and he was up again, panting, a little behind the front line. Fulk eyed him gravely, nodded to himself, and threw himself back into the battle.

Berenger paused to catch his breath. Around him men were flowing forward to take part in the fight, and the French had been pushed back and back, until now they were held at the bottleneck of the gap in the hedge once more. Men's bodies were all about, on the ground, leaning against the hawthorn, piled thickly so that the fighters at the hedge itself must clamber over their dead colleagues to join in. A vintaine of archers had arrived to the right, and were pouring arrows into the flank of the French. Looking up, Berenger saw Hawkwood directing their arrows. The French advance was slowing as the arrows tore into their ranks, and then Berenger saw the flash and heard the roar of a gonne. There was a thunderous belch of evil-smelling smoke that wafted over the battlefield, and suddenly a mass of French warriors fell to the ground. A second great detonation came, and another column of fighters was flung to either side like gaming dice. The rest of the men wavered at the sight of their comrades falling, and the reek of brimstone moved more to blench and try to withdraw.

'Push them out! One more shove!' Berenger roared, and ran into the press again. The English with him took heart as he bellowed, 'The French are running!' and their efforts started to tell. The French tried to recover, but suddenly the sound of trumpets could be heard, and they began to retreat. The English cheered, and some started to pursue their vanquished opponents, but Berenger saw their danger. 'Leave them! Don't chase them, or they'll catch you!'

Even after his words, some men did try to follow the French, and were soon cut to pieces. Berenger saw a knight running after some French, battling with two men, but then he was surrounded and disarmed and hustled away. His ransom would be ruinous, Berenger considered briefly, but a ransom was better than death at the hands of the French army, which was all Berenger or his archers could expect, were they to be caught.

He was watching the men being pushed and forced back to the French lines, when he gradually became aware of cheering. He looked over to Hawkwood and saw him gesticulating wildly, while his vintaine appeared to celebrate behind him.

'What is it?' Berenger shouted.

'They're going! The French have conceded the field!'

'Come on! Let's get them!' Imbert bellowed, and ran after the nearer men. He stabbed and slashed with his weapon and a man was thrown to the ground as Imbert ran on to the next.

'Nick! Don't follow him! Felix, you too! Hold to your place!' Berenger roared.

Those in the line who had been preparing to hare off after Imbert hesitated. Two from Hawkwood's vintaine had already gone, but now Hawkwood too stood in front of his men, arms outstretched, roaring out his command to stay and hold the line.

Berenger turned to see Imbert attack another Frenchman, and Imbert's eyes caught his for an instant. An expression of dull, horrified realisation came into his face, but then he was fighting for his life as a small number of French fighters realised that he and the few English were alone. Then he disappeared beneath their blades.

Archers were soon loosing arrows into the backs of the retreating men, and Imbert was avenged, but Berenger could feel the men behind him staring accusingly.

'He was told,' Berenger said. 'I warned him.'

Gaillarde watched with horror as the French line advanced and seemed about to wash over the English line like a massive tide. She could see men falling on both sides, and in the midst she saw Berenger and her husband, only yards apart. The archers were fully in the thick of the fighting, and she clutched at her throat as she saw Denisot stumble, fearing that he had been hurt, but then he was up again, and she saw him thrust from the path of three more Frenchmen. A horse rode at him, and she gasped with horror when she saw a war-hammer strike her husband's helmet. Denisot wobbled, and stepped away, teetering like a slender birch in the wind, only to fall towards two other men. One caught him and pulled him from the worst of the battle, and Gaillarde wanted to run to help save her man, but even as she moved, Arnaud was there in front of her.

'No! You mustn't,' he said, and turned back to face the men. 'If you go there, you will die.'

Denisot could hear a roaring in his ears as he was dragged from the front of the line. A young man, barely eighteen surely, from Hawkwood's vintaine was with him, helping him, and gently deposited him near a tree to sit. Denisot realised that the ringing in his ears was subsiding, and he felt the youth clasp his arm, looking up gratefully as he said something. Denisot could make out not a word over the thunderous noise in his ears. He pulled off his helmet and stared at the dent near the crown. His skull felt as though it might have been cracked.

He was only a matter of yards from the fighting line. All about him, men were shouting encouragement and defiance. A skinny youth had a notched sword in his fist, and stood now with his mouth wide, bellowing insults to the French, building his own courage until the urge to fight overwhelmed his natural reluctance to head nearer to danger. He lifted his sword high, and ran to where a pair of Frenchmen had burst through the wall of English. Denisot saw the French move apart as he reached them, then one knocked his sword aside easily, while the other stabbed him in the throat. They left him on the ground, rolling and squirming as he drowned in his own blood.

Denisot realised that the two were heading towards him. He tried to stand, but his legs would not support him. He fell back to sit, staring at them as they approached. His rescuer ran to stop them, but as he swung his sword, one caught his sword-point in his mailed glove and easily moved it aside, then clubbed the lad in the face with his own sword's cross. The fellow collapsed, and the second man swung a hatchet. It caught the lad's face, and he hacked twice more before the two looked up at Denisot.

In that instant, Denisot's mind cleared. He was no longer a French bayle, no longer a loyal servant of King Jean II, no longer confused or in doubt; he was only a man on a battlefield who had seen a friend die. He set his helm back on his head, drew a sword, picked up a discarded axe, and walked to meet the two.

He had seen them fight. They were competent to meet any opponent who engaged the pair together. He would not. As the distance between them shortened, he began to run straight at them, but then, as the two moved apart, he lurched to the right, and now he swung his axe at the nearer of the two men. His blade slammed into the man's forearm, and while the fellow tried to reach him with the sword in his other hand, Denisot blocked with his axe-haft, and stabbed with his right, his sword-point ramming up along the man's armour and skipping off.

Denisot saw the man's companion trying to come around to attack his flank, but he slipped to the left, blocked another sword-thrust with his own sword, and flicked the axe round in a wide arc. It slammed into the man's leg, just at the knee, and while it was not strong enough to cut through the thick steel of his armour, it delivered such a shock to the joint that the man fell. Whether it was broken or not, Denisot didn't care. He hefted the axe in his hand and stepped forward warily to the second man.

This one had the hatchet in his left hand and a sword in his right, and he moved slightly crabwise towards Denisot, the sword first, the hatchet held high.

Denisot glanced over the man's shoulder and saw, lying on the ground, the fellow who had pulled him from the battle and saved his life. His head was aching and sore, and he had a roiling, hot sensation in his belly that wouldn't go away. It felt like acid, bubbling and frothing over a fire. If he stopped he would vomit, he thought.

The Frenchman took two quick steps forward. Denisot saw a stone near his foot and kicked it to his enemy. The man set his foot to one side to avoid stepping on it, and Denisot reached in to stab with his sword. His blow was parried, and as it was, he brought the axe down. It slammed into the man's shoulder, and he gave a shriek, wildly hacking with his hatchet. Denisot blocked with his sword, caught the hatchet, and then slashed with his axe. For an instant, he thought he had made a mistake. The axe moved on with no resistance, and he thought his blow had missed. All too soon he realised that he had left his breast wide open to any attack, and now the man's sword was rising as though to paunch him. But then he saw the man's eyes widen, and suddenly a great spurt of blood gushed where Denisot's axe had opened the veins of his throat. The man dropped sword and hatchet and desperately reached for his neck as if to stem the lethal tide, and Denisot swung his axe again, and his suffering was ended.

He turned to see the other Frenchman sprawled, his leg crooked and broken. Denisot walked to him. He stabbed once with his sword.

He felt nothing.

Gaillarde saw the lines begin to separate. How long had it been? An hour? Two? She could not tell. All she knew was the overwhelming relief that Denisot was not injured.

'It is a fierce battle!'

It was Arnaud. He had disappeared as Denisot was pulled from the battle, and now he returned looking strangely excited. But most of the men here looked excited, she thought. He took a cup from the bucket beside her, and splashed water over his face before taking a draught, wiping his mouth with the back of his hand.

'How goes it?' he asked.

'I thought my husband was dead for a moment there!'

'I saw,' he said. 'But you mustn't go down there. You do see that?'

'If he needed me, I—'

'If you went, he would spend his efforts to defend you, and be killed. You would distract him, and that would be terrible for him.'

'You saw him. He tried to have Bernard release me, remember?'

'But you don't love him? You will stay with me.'

517

'I have to go back to him,' she said. She could see Denisot now. He was limping a little, but he looked well enough. 'He is my husband,' she added with pride, and walked down the slope towards her man.

Behind her, she didn't see how Arnaud's face fell, twisted with jealousy. Nor how he glared at Denisot as she reached her husband.

Berenger stared up at the sun and felt the warmth soaking into his flesh. It had been a hard fight, that, and looking up at the sun he could see that it had lasted a long time. It was surely afternoon now, and the weariness in his shoulders and legs was telling. He was almost done. The effort of that last push had all but broken him.

Looking out over the plain, he could see that the French line was broken and exhausted. The men who only a few minutes before had been trying to break through the hedge and kill the English and Gascons beyond, were now little more than a faded rabble. And as they retreated, so he saw the second battle of Frenchmen marching away. They must have seen the collapse of the first battle and decided to save themselves, he thought. Surely the fight was over, he thought with elation, and was about to give a cry of relief and joy, when he saw the third battle, and the call was stopped in his throat.

And then he saw the commander's flag from the first battle being taken away with a small party of knights. That must be the Dauphin with his remaining household knights, he thought, and then he glanced at the rest of the French army.

The French had three lines of soldiers, three battles. The first under the Dauphin had marched up boldly and been beaten; the second was commanded by the Duke of Orléans, but even now Berenger could see a man riding from the Dauphin's party. It was a man with dark hair, gleaming breastplate and accoutrements, who reminded Berenger of someone. Then he recalled the esquire to whom Thomas had spoken during the negotiations yesterday. It was surely him.

The knight rode hard to the Duke's battle, and Berenger felt his breath catch as the entire force of men began to move. They all stepped forward, but then there was a curious-looking ripple down the line, and to Berenger's amazement, the battle began walking away. There was an odd silence about it, and then, on the wind, he caught the sound of catcalls and jeering. It was the final battle, accusing them all of cowardice.

Only the last command remained. But this third was fresh. It had not been tested in battle yet. It was rested and eager, having seen the bitter fighting about the hedge, and it had one great advantage. In the middle of the battle there was the great, blood-red banner of Saint Denis, the Oriflamme. It stood out proudly over the heads of the men. It was the flag of King John II of France. He would not admit defeat!

The Oriflamme was the symbol of France herself, the banner of her Kings. It was said that when the Oriflamme was raised against a foe, France must prevail. The Benedictines of St Denis guarded the banner with great care, for this was more a religious symbol than regal, but when war came, the King would go and fetch it. And now it was raised against the English.

Berenger had seen that flag once before, when the French raised it on the field of Crécy, only for them to be utterly defeated. Now he felt no trepidation to see it again. It had given the French no aid when they had needed it before. It would not help them now.

The battle advanced to the blaring of trumpets and horns, and a drum beat slowly. Gradually it straightened into a long line of men on foot, with a knot of household knights gathered about the figure of King John under the Oriflamme towards the middle. This would be a hard contest now. The English had been fighting all day, and arms and legs were already weary.

As he watched, he saw the pavisers dashing forwards with their great shields. Behind them crouched the crossbowmen. As soon as they were coming within range, English archers loosed their arrows, and Berenger saw them fall all around the shields. A few less cautious crossbowmen were hit and fell, but for the most part they huddled safely behind their defences, letting their bolts fly. Berenger saw a man-at-arms cough, falling back as though punched in the chest, and then stare at the bolt feathers protruding from his chest as he toppled over. Soon bolts were flying in a regular sequence, and men were being hit up and down the English line. However, most bolts went astray, or lost their power by penetrating the hedge, so that their speed was greatly reduced and their danger dissipated.

Grandarse appeared at his shoulder. 'Frip, ye mad bastard, you're supposed to be with the reserve, man! Get back up the hill! Take your men and get back to your position. If you see Hawkwood, tell him to go with you. I'll be up there myself soon.'

Berenger nodded and, bellowing to his men, pulled them back to the place where they had stood before. He saw Hawkwood on the way, and then two other vinteners, and all returned to their positions on the knoll overlooking the field. The battle, from here, was hard to see, but Berenger found a vantage point on some rocks near the wood's edge.

The French came closer. Berenger saw the archers on the flanks bending their bows, releasing their arrows in a regular cloud, but even as he watched, he saw archers gazing about them, ceasing to loose, and realised that they were running out of missiles. They had been fighting for hours already, and almost all their supplies were gone.

With a tremendous roar and clatter, the French reached the hedge and set upon their enemies. Berenger saw men grabbing pavises and hurling them at the hedge to give them something to clamber over, and then they were in among the English.

'Dear God,' he prayed, 'preserve us from our enemies.'

He saw archers on the flanks running down to the fight, flinging aside their bows and drawing swords. He was about to join them when he felt Grandarse's hand on his shoulder. 'Not now, Frip. We're to stay here until we're called, man. We're the reserve. We're needed here. Don't run off again.'

Archibald tried to cajole, he even tried to beg, but Béatrice refused to listen. She was going to stay and help serve the gonnes. Ed was as unhappy about it as Archibald, but there was little they could do, short of carrying her away bodily. When she decided her mind in that way, both knew that arguing was fruitless.

'In that case, you had best get working,' Archibald snapped at last.

The horns and drums were clear on the late afternoon air, and they could all sense the tension. There was a loud thundering of stamping boots, a rumble that Archibald could feel, he was sure, through his feet. The noise of thousands of men marching forward, some willingly, many unwilling but determined to do their part for their King. And the thin English line readied to repel them. Looking up at the Englishmen cradling their weapons behind the hedge, Archibald felt a pang of sadness. Most of them looked so weary already. They had the drained expressions of men who had toiled too hard, and who knew that this latest effort could be their last. Many would not live to see the sunset, he thought.

'Master!'

Ed was pointing, and there, over the lip of the land, were the first of the French.

'Dear God,' Archibald prayed, 'protect us, poor sinners though we be. Amen,' and he crossed himself and bowed his head a moment. Then: 'Turn that ribauldequin, you lazy shit for brains! Béatrice, get ready to reload!' and he blew on his match.

From his vantage point, Berenger saw the first waves pick up speed until they were running full tilt at the hedge. The English archers were there to back up the rest of the line of English fighters before the collision, but then Berenger saw the rippling of spears lowering as the French began to charge; there was a rattling crash as the two armies came together and Berenger saw the gleam of swords rising and falling, the evil metal showing oily and foul with blood, and he saw the blood spraying from a hundred vicious wounds, the men falling, a man here falling hard on his rump as if pushed, only to roll over, another running screaming from the press clutching a stump that squirted blood, another crawling with his bowels dragging a yard or more behind him, and Berenger swore to himself that he would never again come to war willingly, but would avoid it ever more.

There was a shout, and the archers prepared themselves as a small body of men appeared from the right, arguing and shouting, and the archers released the tension in their bows, letting the arrows point to the ground once more.

'Grandarse! We need your men!'

Denisot lay on his back, panting after his exertions. He was aware of a movement of men around him, and when he opened his eyes, he saw Grandarse and his vintaines trotting off towards the woods. There, he saw Gaillarde once more, and thought how beautiful she looked, almost like an angel come down from Heaven, while all about was blood and horror.

He saw her face blanch, and there was a shout from the line of the battle. Denisot turned and saw that there was a fresh eruption of French fighters. They had broken through the line of English and were attacking them from the rear.

Only a few Englishmen had realised the danger, and were falling on the French. Denisot picked up his weapons with a weary resolution. They must all work to prevent this break-through turning into a catastrophe. It wouldn't take much for the English to be persuaded to bolt, with the sudden shock of an assault from their rear. Already cries of alarm were going up, and as Denisot hefted his sword's hilt and trotted to join the others, he saw Pierre and Felix throwing themselves into the fray. A pair of Frenchmen turned to battle with them, and as Denisot reached their side, he saw Felix push a man from his father's side. Denisot's sword slid into the man's flank before he could recover and stab Felix.

It was a crushing, insane fight. Denisot was hemmed in on all sides. Before him an Englishman, at his left Felix and Pierre, to his right a lean, black-haired man, someone behind him, pushing. And a short way in front, the French.

The line was a confusion of noises. Shouting, screaming, the rattle of weapons hitting weapons or clanging off helmets, the stertorous breathing of men struggling to hold the line. The French had formed a mushroom: a stem pushed through the English line, and then turned to assail the rear of the English like a cap. But reinforcements were coming with every moment and adding to the numbers who stood with Denisot, and the French mushroom was being squeezed and forced to contract. Denisot set his shoulder at the back of the man in front, and shoved. There was a shriek somewhere in front, and Denisot looked up briefly to see a Frenchman who was being hacked about terribly by three men. Felix was one, and he swung a short sword with abandon, until the Frenchman fell underfoot. The next man was there, and Denisot saw Felix lift his sword and bring it down, lift it again, and then there was a cry, and when Denisot glanced to his side, he saw Pierre. Felix had brought his blade back too far, and the point had entered his father's neck, slicing through to the bone. Even as Denisot watched, Pierre fell to his knees.

Felix was unaware of the accident. He cut again and again, and his latest opponent fell; he stepped forward, and then he must have become aware that his father was no longer behind him. He glanced around, and saw his father lying on the floor. In that moment Denisot saw the raw misery on his face. Felix dropped his sword and was about to fall to his knees to help his father, when an axe cut into his neck. He toppled, already dead before his body hid his father's from view.

Denisot felt little at that moment. His world was a sweating area of grim, relentless toil. He pushed, the man in front of him moved forward. There were more bellowed orders, and he pushed once more. There was a slippery sensation underfoot, and the unmistakable odour of blood and piss, and he was pushing again, when suddenly everything seemed to move about him. Like a drunken man in a world that was spinning around him, Denisot was vaguely aware of the men all about him, but all his concentration was focused on remaining upright. To fall in that mêlée could spell instant death.

The man before him was stabbed. He toppled and collapsed, and Denisot was just able to keep to his feet, but the haziness was all but engulfing him, and he could feel his legs wobbling. He had to keep on his feet.

He must stay upright!

CHAPTER FORTY-EIGHT

At his gonne, Archibald let fly with another trio of blasts and the smoke mercifully concealed the devastation wrought as his stones struck men, breaking into two or three shards of lethal, whining and spinning fragments. He had seen the effects before: the pieces of stone and scraps of snapped armour from his targets moving on and ripping into the men behind.

Béatrice mechanically sat before his gonne with her little rod covered in wet lamb's wool. She was washing the barrels, and then she would pour powder into each and tamp it, set the fresh stone ball on top and ram that in too, just tight enough to make it fix in place.

He blew on his match and waited until she was away from the line of fire. She was squatting now before Ed's gonne. A fresh group of Frenchmen were running to the front, and Archibald set off the first barrel. He saw the flames leap, and saw the front man's face disappear, throwing the man backwards to join the bodies slaughtered by Archibald's gonne. A moment later, the second barrel erupted and a pair of men went down. The third barrel – but there was no explosion.

'Stop!' he bellowed, but Béatrice was already in front of his gonne. And then with a spitting hiss, the barrel poured flame and smoke and its deadly missile into her.

Berenger waited but Grandarse waved an arm. 'Here, quick, Frip!'

Before he knew what was happening, Berenger was being taken down to where the horses had been kept all that long day.

'We charge with the Captal de Buch,' Grandarse gasped after his unaccustomed rush. 'Follow him if I fall, Frip, Hawk. You and your men must charge with him. You understand?'

'You won't fall,' Berenger said.

Grandarse grinned, but Berenger could see his anxiety.

'Aye, we'll all get killed. You watch and see. We'll all die,' Clip said cheerfully.

'Shut the fuck up!' Saul snapped. 'This is no time for jokes, man!'

'Oh, aye?' Clip said. 'What are you going to do, you lanky piece of piss? Kill me? Too late! The Frenchies will do that for you!'

'Shut up, Clip!' Berenger shouted. 'Archers? Keep tight. We're going to ride around behind them and give them the shock of their lives. Ready?'

The Captal was already on his destrier, sixty men-at-arms trotting behind him, and he rode up now with his sword in his hand. He lifted it and set off at a fast trot, and Grandarse's centaine followed behind the men in armour, up beyond the main plain and around the nearer hill, out of sight of anyone on the battlefield.

There was a wind in Berenger's face and he was suddenly struck with the peacefulness of the land here. He saw a bird rising from the field on his right, and the smell in his nose was fresh and clean and wholesome. It was as if the battle had never taken place, as if the last hours had not truly existed, except as a malign dream on the edge of consciousness, but then the vision of peace and joy was destroyed as they rode around the hill and saw the battlefield before them. Berenger heard a shout, and they were riding more quickly, and then there was a sudden blast from a horn, and the English formation clapped spurs to their mounts and began to hurtle across the plain at full speed.

As the Captal bellowed his battle cry and galloped towards the French, the man at his side lifted the standard of St George, and it flew in the wind of their passage. Then, when they came closer, Berenger saw that a second charge had come about the bottom of the English line, and leading that charge he recognised the banner of Sir James Audley.

There was no time to register more. Berenger and the men were suddenly in among the French, scattering the men in the heavier armour so that they were sent sprawling in the mud and filth, while the foot soldiers were beaten about the head and slain where they stood, many of them not knowing where the blow had come from. Berenger brought down his sword on a youth, and felt the grim sadness at killing once more. At his side, he saw Clip attacking a Frenchman, but then another man sprang up behind Clip with a long billhook. Before he could shout to warn Clip, Grandarse rode alongside him and lopped the arm from the man. Grandarse turned to Clip with a look of satisfaction, but then Berenger saw that his Centener jerked and glared about him. A Frenchman had taken a spear and thrust it up, under the old man's plate. Now the Frenchman shoved again, and Grandarse coughed blood. He tried to hack at his enemy, but the effort made him fall from his horse. All at once two men were stabbing at his face. Clip shouted something inarticulate, and turned his horse towards Grandarse's killer, but even as he rode up, Berenger saw

527

a man behind him cut the hamstrings of his horse, and Clip was tumbled to the ground. Before Berenger could move to help him, his throat was cut.

'*NO!*'

Berenger roared with horror, with dismay and fierce hatred, and slashed wildly. He knew nothing from that moment but a red, irrational hatred. He missed both men, but saw Dogbreath and Fulk kill them both. It was not enough. In his rage, Berenger set his horse at the thickest group of French fighters, and urged his horse towards it. He still gripped his sword, and now he beat with it at the first men he came to. There was a knot of knights battling, and he rode to them, slamming his sword at them with a desperate fury, trying to break through their armour, then stabbing where the metal plates joined, trying to reach the man beneath, but without luck. He saw a French fighter without armour and rode to him, his blade sinking into the man's shoulder, and saw another man who fought with a pair of archers. Berenger brought his pommel on the man's head and felt the bones shatter under the blow. He was about to ride back, when Fulk appeared and caught his bridle.

'Frip, you've done enough.'

The blood lust had not left him. 'You saw what they did to Grandarse? They killed *Clip*, too!' And that was when he felt the fury leave him, and his soul was taken instead with an inconsolable grief. Clip, the cheery predictor of all their deaths. In all the years Berenger had known him, that whining voice had assured him that they would all die, and yet no one would have believed that it would be Clip himself who would be killed. All knew that somehow he was impregnable. Yet now he was dead.

He felt the tears start.

But the battle was not yet over.

*

As the men-at-arms rode past Archibald, he paid them no attention. All he knew was an overwhelming emptiness.

He had known Béatrice for ten years, ever since Berenger
had asked him to protect her, and she had been an invaluable
companion. Her knowledge of powders, her dedication, and her
easy manner with him and Ed had endeared her to him. He felt
as if his own daughter had been taken from him.

He picked up her shattered body and carried her gently to
the wagon. There, he set her down amid the powder kegs and
covered her face with a shred of cloth. It was filthy, but it would
serve. She would feel humiliated to be left with her face exposed,
he knew.

'Archibald ...' Ed began, but Archibald busied himself
making Béatrice comfortable. It was important, he knew. He had
to leave her comfortable.

'Master?' Ed said.

Archibald was consumed with a rage that passed through
him like a fire. He felt cleansed by the purity of his hatred for all
the French. He took up his axe from the wagon and began walking to the battle, Ed anxiously scurrying in his wake.

A French man-at-arms saw him and lifted his sword, but
Archibald batted it aside and brought his axe down two-handed
on his head. The axe embedded itself in the steel and when he
jerked it away, the helmet came with the axe-head, the man-at-
arms falling dead with a huge gash in his padded coif through
which the blood leaked.

Archibald didn't notice. He didn't care. He stalked forward,
ignoring the men on horseback and the huddles of men rolling on
the ground, until he came to the main battle, and there he pulled
the helmet from his axe and gripped it in his left hand like a
great metal glove. He saw a pair of archers battling with a French
esquire, and slammed the helmet into the back of the man's

head. He fell, and Archibald found himself facing two Genoese bowmen with long swords. He slammed his axe-head down on one and stepped on it, smashing his steel glove into the man's face, before facing the second man and aiming it at his face too. The man held up an arm to defend himself, but the steel of the ruined helmet was heavier than his arm, and there was an audible snap as the bones of his arm were shattered, and then Archibald swung the axe again and the man was down. Archibald walked on and a man blocked his path, a tall man with the build of a giant. He lifted a sword and Archibald stepped up, inside his reach, batting his sword-hand away, moving his grip on the axe, and shoving it hard into the man's throat. There was no spike, but the sudden slamming effect of two pounds of steel with all Archibald's weight behind it broke his windpipe, crushing it against his spine, and the man collapsed retching, desperately fighting for air.

But Archibald cared nothing for his suffering, for his tormented death. He walked on until he came to a pair of French fighters. One took one look at him and bolted, but the other crouched, a long knife held at the ready.

Archibald swung his helmet, but the boy was faster. He ducked, and Archibald gave a bellow of rage as he felt the knife pierce his thigh. He brought the helmet down on the boy's head and saw him tumble to the ground, and then raised it again, slamming it into the fellow's face four times, oblivious to the world about him, he was so entirely taken up with his personal fight.

But there was a keening sound. It gradually managed to break through the red mist of rage that had entirely absorbed him, and Archibald glanced about him. That was when he saw the other lad, the one who had bolted. He stood now, with tears streaming, shivering and watching with mingled horror

and terror as Archibald beat at the face of his companion. And
Archibald looked down and realised that the dead man beneath
him was little more than a child, and he climbed to his feet, still
staring down at the body. He looked at the other, who stared with
utter incomprehension at the ravaged remains of his friend, his
brother, his comrade, whatever he might be, and Archibald felt
the full weight of God's contempt and anger land on his shoulders. He dropped his bloody, broken helmet, and stepped away
from the body, appalled and shocked at his own actions.

The other lad ran at him, and Archibald waited for the blow,
but before the fellow was within reach, Ed reached out and casually grabbed him by the chin, exposing his throat. He slashed
once, quickly, like a butcher bleeding a hog. There was a flash of
blood and the youngster fell to the ground.

It was enough. The blood lust had left him. Archibald stared
at the young body before him, then back to the ruined boy he had
killed, at the helmet, and then the weapon in his hand, and was
filled with a profound despair.

'Master? Come, Master,' Ed said, and when he grabbed his
arm, Archibald obediently turned from the field and walked with
his companion, past the bodies and down to where they had left
Béatrice's body.

As soon as the men-at-arms slammed into the flank of the French
battle, the French were thrown into a turmoil. Their strong force
was shattered into a hundred small groups of men fighting on all
sides as the English surrounded them. Some were forced away
from the main battle, and continued their defence further away,
while some few took to their heels and ran straight into Berenger
and his men. Berenger fought with a stern ferocity marring his
features. He hacked and hacked, and the men before him were
despatched with every blow. Hawkwood and his men worked as

hard, but it was Berenger who passed through the French on the heels of the Captal de Buch, and who sent many of the enemy flying away, down the hill, and straight onto the knives and daggers of the waiting archers. A few had arrows, and the groups of Frenchmen were broken up until only a few remained. Some of these intended to fight on, but they were soon overwhelmed as English archers ran among them, stealing spurs, swords, equipment, and catching all those who would later merit a valuable ransom.

Berenger was content. That day he had seen too many friends die already. He felt that he had taken his fill of death. But then he and the others were called by the blast of a trumpet, and Berenger wearily turned back to a fresh battle.

The last battle of France.

Berenger walked up to where the fight continued and he felt the horrible scenes as a fist clenching about his heart. No man should die like this. No man should see a field so sprinkled with death.

For men were dead or dying all about. As he passed, Berenger saw a man spitting out shards of teeth from his broken mouth; men slipped on mud created from their own blood, and collapsed; he saw a man who tripped and stumbled, white-faced, as he clutched his shoulder, the arm dangling loose and the blood pulsing steadily through his fingers; another, his eyes as wide as a tortured cat, dragged himself along, both legs gone below his knees; others wept and begged for their mother, their wife, their lover, while others wriggled and squirmed in the mire. It was a scene from Hell. Berenger looked all about him at the slaughterhouse horror and felt sure that the scene would never leave him. If he went to join a monastery and prayed every hour of every day for the rest of his life, he could never eradicate the foul deeds done here on God's good, clean earth. It was polluted.

The standard of the French still fluttered in the midst of a circle of English fighters. Berenger went to join them with reluctance in his heart, but he saw Sir John de Sully, and went to his side. A man swung his sword and Berenger saw it flying towards his face, but he lifted his own sword and let it slip to the cross of his own before turning his blade. The leverage in his weapon allowed him to push the man's away, and Berenger was about to punch him in the face and make him surrender, when Sir John thrust with his sword and the man fell with the blade in his eye. Berenger stepped forward, and the ring of English contracted. A man fell, knocked down by a blow to his head, and Berenger saw two more stabbed who fell on top. The man was going to be smothered until he was suffocated. Another man wielding a lance near the French King stabbed with all his strength, and the man to Berenger's right took the blow in his cheek. The force turned his head, so the blade came out through his other cheek, and Berenger was momentarily blinded by chips of tooth and splashes of blood. He dashed it away from his face as the man fell back.

All this long while, the French King and his household continued to fight. His standard flew over his head, a lasting picture of beauty and colour in that hideous patch of gore and grass.

And then Berenger saw the standard shudder like a tree as the final axe blows strike. It wobbled, and then crashed down, and Berenger felt a curious, detached sadness. While men took prisoners, he watched with dull lack of interest.

These were the last few men to surrender, the men of King John's entourage. The King himself refused to submit. He continued to bellow defiance and swing his sword until at last a knight of Artois called upon him to surrender and promised his safety. The

King agreed at last, demanding to know whether his opponent was actually a knight, before he agreed to give up his sword, and Berenger felt relief to think that the main battle was done at last, but then a rowdy group of Guyennois soldiers took him and dragged him from the field.

Berenger nudged Sir John. The men were all exhausted from their exertions, and worse, they were deafened by the commotion of battle. Berenger had to bellow to Sir John to persuade him that the Guyenne men were taking the King away, but when Sir John realised, he nodded and he and Berenger straightway took as many men with them as they could, and ran to the French King. He was furious to have been grabbed and manhandled away, and Berenger found it almost amusing to see how he roared and raged at being snatched away by a group of 'Treacherous, thieving, felonious lying dogs and their lackeys!'

'*Hold!*' Sir John shouted at the top of his voice. Some of the men in the party turned, but for the most part they continued onwards, whether because they were deaf or because they were past obedience now, Berenger could not see.

Berenger ran on in front of the men and held both hands aloft to slow the Guyennois. The leading men looked as though they might contest his right to stop them, but gradually the group slowed and halted. In their midst an argument was raging over their shares in the King's capture.

'You cannot take him!' Berenger bellowed.

'You want him, you'd better take him,' said one of the men at the front.

Berenger lowered his head. 'You want to fight some more? I'll fight you, tarse-breath, and then I'll fight any others of you! You want to see more men dead about here? Fine! Let's do it! You want to fight? I'll fight you!'

Sir John was already pushing his way through the mass of

Guyennois even as the man in front of Berenger squared up and took a pace forward. But before he could draw his knife, Berenger ran forward and butted him in the face with the full weight of his bascinet. He felt the man's nose shatter, and the fellow staggered back, momentarily blinded.

Berenger could think of nothing but Grandarse and Clip, their bodies up on the hill above them. The man tried to rise, but now his companions held him back, glaring at Berenger, and soon he realised why. Behind him stood the Earl of Warwick and Reginald Cobham with a large force of men-at-arms. The Earl shouldered the Guyennois from his path, declaring, 'We are taking His Royal Highness. Any of you who try to prevent us will die here.'

He and Cobham pushed their way through to the French King, and before him both bowed low. The Earl said, 'Your Majesty, I have a horse here, if you would honour me by using it, I will take you to Prince Edward, who is most keen to meet you.'

Berenger watched the party as the King deigned to mount the Earl's horse and was taken away. So that, Berenger thought, was that.

Sir John had walked to his side and stood there now, eyeing the Guyennois. The man with the broken nose and bloody face had been led away by his companions, and the men remaining seemed less keen to continue fighting, especially now that their prize had been removed. Sir John nudged Berenger. 'That was a dangerous act.'

'I don't think I cared for his attitude,' Berenger said, trying to make light of it, but when he looked at his hands, they were shaking.

'Are you injured?'

'No, Sir John. But Grandarse is dead. And Clip.'

And untold hundreds of others, he could have added. His vintaine was sorely depleted, he knew. But it was much worse for the French.

Sir John nodded. 'I am right sad to hear that. Grandarse was a good man.'

'As was Clip.' A burst of honesty made him add, 'Mostly.'

CHAPTER FORTY-NINE

That night there was great celebration in the English camp. Archers, gynours and all the tradesmen rested where they could, most moving to find a place upwind of the battlefield and the bodies. Men moved about the field, searching the bodies for anything to steal, but most found that they were too late. Some, having found stores of wine, were raucously merry, but most were so exhausted by the excitement and effort of the day that they tumbled to the ground where they could and were soon asleep.

Berenger wanted nothing to do with any of the festivities immediately after the battle. He heard about the Prince going down on one knee to serve the King of France, and he heard how Audley, who had led the last charge, was found dying on the field and brought to the King on a shield, but Berenger was not there. Those were events for the great and important. He was neither. Berenger was only a fighter in the Prince's army, nothing more. He knew that, and he didn't aspire to any form of greatness. All he wanted was to hear Grandarse's rough voice, or Clip's irritating whine. To have lost those two was appalling.

He found a cart, and with the help of Fulk, Saul and Dog-breath, he collected the dead of his vintaine. Robin was suffering from a gash in his arm, but he joined the four and watched as they picked up Clip and placed him in the bed of the cart. Hoisting Grandarse proved a struggle, but in the end they succeeded. Over in the corner of the field they found Pierre and Felix, and added them too, before taking the cart back to their camp.

It was on the way that they saw Ed.

'Have you seen Archibald?' he asked.

Berenger looked up. His head felt heavy with grief, but he could hear something in Ed's voice that caught his attention. 'No. Why?'

'Béatrice is dead. He was in the thick of the battle, but after that he walked away. I haven't seen him.'

Berenger nodded. He felt dull-witted, but he knew he must find Archibald. 'Which direction did go in?'

Ed pointed towards the road that led to Poitiers. 'I think he went along there, but it was at the end of the battle. You know what it's like.'

He did. The hurried men trying to grab a knight or a count to make their fortunes, the opportunists searching among the dead and wounded for valuables, and the others who moved about looking for those who were too far gone to be saved and who were given the kindness of the *misericorde*, the long dagger. With so much movement, it would be easy to lose sight of one man.

'Go back to your gonnes, Ed. We will find him.'

'He was so upset, Frip. He was more like a bear than a man. I was scared for him, and I'm his friend, but . . .'

'There was nothing you could have done. Go back to your gonnes and wait there.'

Berenger was sure he knew where Archibald would have

gone. He set off with the men and the cart, up to the roadway, and thence around the top of the forest of Nouaillé. He was sure that the old gynour would not have elected for the seven or more miles he would have to walk to Poitiers, and if he had, he would know that he could be cut to pieces on the way, either by French troops escaping the battle, or by English troops mistaking him for an enemy. It would be greatly preferable to head in the opposite direction, towards Nouaillé, where there was the great church. Besides, the vintaine had all their own fallen comrades to bury.

The church at Nouaillé was Benedictine, but when he reached the gates, he found them already open. The men pulled and pushed the cart across the little bridge that crossed the moat and stopped outside the church. The door was ajar, and Berenger entered.

Inside, the church was painted a glorious white that was blinding to a man used to the grimness of that day. Pictures of the saints decorated the walls, but Berenger was immune to the charms of the colour. Instead he strode quietly to the altar and knelt at it beside the silently weeping gynour.

'I am sorry indeed for your loss,' he said.

Archibald appeared not to hear him. He was kneeling, with Béatrice's body lying across his knees, and every so often he wiped her face, as though to comfort her.

A nervous priest stood nearby, and Berenger went to him, giving him enough coins to buy wax for a king's funeral, and had the men bring in the bloody and broken bodies of his men. He watched as they were collected by lay-brothers and taken out to a separate chamber to be washed and cleaned, but when he went to Archibald, the old gynour refused to allow any of them to clean her. 'This is for you and me, Fripper,' he said. 'It's the last thing we can do for her.'

'I don't know how to.'

'It's a damp cloth. That's all we need. And a clean tunic to clothe her.'

They set her on a table and removed her clothes. The wound at her belly was appalling. The ball had ripped through her intestines and out through her spine. Fragments of bone and faeces erupted from her back, while her belly was black with burning powder. Berenger worked automatically, wiping with the cloth until it was black and red and foul, and then he rinsed it in the bucket provided by a lay-brother. The two worked until Archibald was happy, and then he stood back and wiped his face. He motioned to Berenger to help, and both lifted her body upright. Berenger held her there while Archibald wrapped clean linen about her middle to stop her blood from marring her winding-sheet, and then they enfolded her in the sheet.

'She always loved you, you know,' Archibald said.

'I know. But we never had the words to say so.'

Archibald nodded, as if it was the most natural comment in the world, and the two finished their task, carrying her body out to the altar. They bowed and knelt in prayer, but Berenger's mind was blank. He could only peer down at the face of Béatrice hidden in the folds of the linen, and wonder whether she was, at last, happy and in peace.

Before long the rest of the vintaine walked in carrying the great body of Grandarse between them, before fetching the others and setting them down beside Béatrice. Berenger stood staring down at the bodies of his friend and the woman for whom he had felt such great affection, if not love. He suddenly pulled the crucifix and rosary from his neck and looked at it, before setting it down softly upon Grandarse's breast. 'There, old friend. You have need of His compassion more than I,' he said, his voice breaking.

Berenger rose, and with Archibald behind him the two slowly made their way to the door.

A Benedictine was there as they reached it, and he frowned at them. 'I do not have space for mercenaries and soldiers of the Devil in my graveyard,' he began, but then Berenger's forearm was at his throat and he was thrust back against the wall, Berenger's bloodshot face an inch from his own.

The vintener hissed, 'You will find space, and you will install them on consecrated ground, or as I am an Englishman, I swear I will return and destroy this entire monastery!'

'Have you not done enough harm here without threatening a monk?' the man snapped. 'Look at you! Covered in blood, with weapons still at your belt, and you come here to make demands here in God's house?'

Berenger took his arm away. 'Brother, I apologise. We have seen too many of our friends dead.'

'So have we all,' the monk said. He glanced down at the bodies. 'A woman?'

'Yes. She was a countryman of yours, who suffered at the hands of both sides. I beg that you give her absolution.'

'I have a duty to serve all the poor souls who die, no matter who they are, if they are Christian.'

'I thank you.'

It was not a long journey to the English camp, but none of them was in a hurry, and they took their time, each at peace with his own thoughts, until they came to their own huddle of belongings. That was where they found Denisot.

'I've lost her, Fripper,' he said, and wept.

When the battle was over, Gaillarde's first thought was for Denisot and how he had fared. There were men leaving the field in dribs and drabs, and she searched among their faces hopefully, but without luck. Before she could go and search for her husband, Arnaud was back.

Arnaud was smiling at her with that sly, childlike expression that she had always liked. It made him look like a naughty child, and at first she had thought it was merely proof of his simplicity. But now she knew it was his cruelty that made him look like that. He enjoyed making her worry. He liked to see fear in others.

'Your husband is injured.'

She felt her breath catch. 'Denisot? Where is he?'

'You promised me,' he hissed. 'You promised to stay with me, but now at the first chance you'd leave me for him, wouldn't you?'

'He's my husband, Arnaud!'

'I *heard* you! You spoke to him yesterday, didn't you? You told him you'd go back to him, you told him you loved him!'

Gaillarde felt the breath catch in her throat. 'You were listening?'

'But if he's dead, you can't go to him, can you?' he said, half-turning away from her as if cradling her horror close to his breast.

'You think he will die?'

'I am sure of it,' he said, and suddenly he span so that he could watch her.

She saw the glee in his eyes then, and she was convinced he had killed Denisot. After all this time, after his searching for her and trying to find her, only for her abductor to learn of him and kill him. The thought made her feel that her heart had died and shrivelled within her. 'You killed him?'

'Not yet,' he said smugly.

'Where is he?'

'Why should I take you to him? So you can desert me and

make a life with him again, when you promised to stay with me? No, I don't think so,' he said.

She fell to her knees then, snatching at his tunic. 'Please, Arnaud, please! He is my husband. I have to see him if he is dying. Please take me to him!'

He appeared to go through an internal struggle, but finally gave in with a bad grace. 'If you're sure. Very well.'

She followed him into the forest behind the English camp. Arnaud must have brought him here, she thought. Perhaps he told poor Denisot that she was in here, and that she was injured and was calling for him? No, more likely it was Denisot who saw Arnaud and decided to follow him to injure him as a sub-stitute for Bernard, for taking away his wife. He could be so hot-blooded sometimes. Not that she had seen that during their marriage, but then their marriage had been such a strange, miser-able affair after the death of their children.

Brambles snagged at her skirts and a deep trench made her fall to her hands. Arnaud was leading her down the hill, parallel to the English fighting line, as though he was taking her to the ford again, but then he took her away, deeper into the trees.

'Where is he?' she said as Arnaud stopped her at an old, dilapidated cottage.

'He's in there, if you want him,' Arnaud said, and stood aside dismissively. He picked up a stick and began to cut into it with his knife as though he was disgusted with the whole matter, and her in particular.

She stepped inside, her hand on the door's jamb. It was a single-roomed building which had been left to decompose like a human's body. The trees, beetles and worms were gradually pulling it apart. Soon the roof would collapse entirely, and then the trees would have their land back. Cobwebs abounded, and through the rotten roof she could see the trees overhead. She took a nervous step inside, and a rotten branch snapped under her foot. She curled her lip at the feel and withdrew her foot. 'Denisot?'

Suddenly she was shoved. A hand or boot in the small of her back sent her tumbling with a little squeak. A splinter stabbed into her knee, and she felt her jaw strike a broken spar. Blood spurted into her mouth and she gagged. She put a hand to her face as she felt the loose tooth, and she whimpered with the pain.

'Bitch! You thought you could fool me? I can see through your little lies and great fabrications! You never loved me. You just pretended to because you thought I could guard and protect you. Well, now I will do as I want!'

'What have I done?' she asked.

'You slept with my brother as if you were repelled by me.'

'I had to! I thought he would hurt you if I showed him I preferred you. You know how jealous he was!'

'Him? Jealous?'

For a moment Arnaud stood staring at her in dumbfounded amazement. 'Is that what you thought? He took you to protect you from *me*, woman. He didn't want me to show you my skills.'

He had pulled a pair of thongs from under his shirt and now he stepped to her. She tried to slap his hands away, but he gave her a backhanded blow across the mouth that sent her reeling. Almost senseless, she was aware of him tying her wrist to something, and when she tried to pull her hand away, he hit her again. Harder. This time he had her other wrist and soon she was bound to something.

'Poor Bernard, he was always so sad when I told him. In Bordeaux he crouched before the little slut I killed there, and wept. It took him so long, I had time to drink a quart of ale while I waited.' He pulled on a rope, and she realised that he had tied her to a long board of wood. 'Then, at some little farm near Uzerche, when we were scouting out the land, I heard him bawling again before he stabbed her to death. He always killed quickly. Bernard hated to see people suffering. He never understood it was necessary for them. It was His divine revenge for their guilt.'

His rope was over a solid roof beam and now, as he hauled on the rope, she was raised to her feet. When she was on her toes, he tied his rope off and sat comfortably before her.

'I don't like to kill, you know,' he said conversationally. 'But I have to. When people like you have been bad, you have to be punished. You are married, and yet you permitted my brother to push his prick into you. That makes you an adulterer, and God hates adulterers. You have to be punished for that.'

'So you will rape me?'

He giggled. 'Yes! That is my reward. And then, in a little while, I will kill you.'

Berenger and the men strode quickly down to where Will's company were camped. Peter of Reading stood as soon as Berenger appeared.

'Fripper. I hope you aren't here to get revenge on Will. You're too late.'

'I know. I saw him die,' Berenger said. 'This is different. We hanged a man a few days ago. He and his brother were here with you. They had a marching wife with them.'

'Yes, Bernard and Arnaud. What of them?'

'Their woman was this man's wife. But she is not around now.'

'I haven't seen her,' Peter said. He turned to his men. 'Anyone seen Arnaud and Gaillarde?'

A man who was nursing a long cut on his upper arm nodded.

'Arnaud was here after the battle. I didn't see him during it, but he went with the woman into the woods there.'

'Thanks,' Berenger said.

Peter nodded to him. 'If you're going to kill him, carry on. He gives me the shivers. There's something wrong in him. I think he has a demon inside him.'

Berenger nodded and crossed the battlefield. The hawthorn hedge was ragged where the fighting had been hardest, and they had to climb over bodies, most of them already stripped, to reach the trees.

'They are in there, you think?' Denisot said.

'That's what Peter said. We need to find her.'

He walked along the line of the trees, peering in. 'These woods are too thick. We'll never see in there.'

'If he took her in there, Frip,' Saul said, 'it would be because he knew something there, perhaps. A trail he could use, or a building, perhaps. If he didn't just run away at the first noise of battle, it must be somewhere close to the edge of the trees.'

'So?'

'I was thinking, if we go into the woods from the bottom and walk up, we'll cross over his path if he's in there and has taken Gaillarde. The two together must have flattened bushes and undergrowth, especially if he had found a place beforehand and was taking her back to it.'

Berenger nodded slowly. Then he nodded to Fulk and Robin. 'In case he went the other way, nearer the top of the woods, you two start at the top. Go into the woods about fifty yards from the treeline here, and see if you can find a distinct path made by two. We'll go to the bottom and work our way up.'

Leading the way to the bottom, near the ford, Berenger stared in among the trees. It would be growing dark soon, and it would be difficult to see anything in the murk between the tree trunks.

It was worse than he thought. They walked in and fought their way through the first yards, but then they found themselves confronted with a broken, trampled mess.

'The soldiers came in to find firewood. Make it further,' Denisot said. 'If we move back to a hundred yards, we will be less likely to find the marks of the English soldiers.'

Berenger thought him hopeful, but they moved into the woods until they were beyond the main thoroughfares used by soldiers hunting more wood. They found one path that was heavily trampled, but that looked as though there had been twenty or thirty men. They continued up through the bushes and undergrowth until Denisot gave an exclamation. 'What is that?'

He had seen a path that appeared to travel parallel to their own, and had noticed a flattened section. He stepped towards it cautiously, and picked up a shred of stained material. 'This is like the linen she wore in her skirts.'

'Are you sure?' Berenger said doubtfully. 'It could be anyone's shirt material or—'

'How many soldiers would wear such a fine material? And how many women would be in here, this far in the woods?' Denisot demanded.

Berenger glanced at Saul, who gave a shrug.

'Very well,' Berenger said. He started to cross to the indistinct path through the bushes. By crouching, he could make out an indirect route through the plants, as though one person had tried to follow another, but without any clear view of where to go. It grew boggy, and a couple of times he nearly fell, once grasping a thick, thorny plant that ripped into his palm. Sucking it, he went on more carefully.

The light was fading quickly. The birdsong was stopped, and the only sounds were of their boots crashing through the undergrowth, breaking twigs and rotten branches, and their panting.

'What is that?' Denisot said. He had caught sight of a building.

'I don't know,' Berenger said, unwilling as always to admit how poor was his eyesight.

They continued more cautiously, Berenger glancing down every now and again to see if others had used this same path recently. In one muddy clearing, he saw what looked like a man's boot and, overlapping slightly, a much smaller shoe print. He said nothing, but looked around at the others, before pointing at the building. Saul nodded, and Denisot stared at him, chewing his lip fretfully.

Berenger stepped out into another clearing, and as he did, they all heard Gaillarde's voice: 'No! Please, no!'

Denisot was over the intervening space before Berenger could hold him back, and Saul and he followed as quickly as they could. Inside the cottage, they found Gaillarde hanging, exhausted, her head held back, and behind her was Arnaud with a knife at her throat. 'Keep away, or we'll see how much blood she has in her cold, cold veins!' he said, and chuckled amiably.

'Let my wife free,' Denisot said through gritted teeth.

'I think I want her to stay with me.'

'He's going to kill me,' Gaillarde said. 'He told me he would rape me, then kill me. But he wanted to watch me as I hung here. He likes to hurt people.'

'No! It was your punishment for your incontinence,' Arnaud said with heat. 'If you hadn't thrown yourself at my brother—'

'I didn't throw myself at him! He beat and raped me!'

'He wanted to remind you that you were foul.'

Berenger said, 'Is that why he didn't tell us you were the murderer? He didn't let on at all, did he, not at the trial, not at the rope. He took all responsibility for your murders.'

'They aren't murder, Vintener. They are punishments. You know how evil women are. The priests all tell us about Original

Sin, the failing that is in all women. I was trying to show how all those women were tempting men.'

'The little girls you killed?'

'They're all the same!'

'But Ed thought he saw your brother in Bordeaux. He said your brother killed the girl there.'

'Yes.' For a moment Arnaud's face darkened. 'He kept doing that, going and killing them before it was time. If he found them, he put his knife in them to end their suffering. He didn't realise: making them suffer was for their own good. It meant that they would go to Heaven shriven.'

'And this woman?' Berenger asked. He was weary. After fighting all day, all he wanted was to have a chance to lie down, to rest. There was a strange sense that he had experienced this before. A negotiation for a life. It teased at his mind for a moment or two, and then he realised: it was the day that Will wrested power from him, the day when his man held first Alazaïs in his hands, then her child. That day he had allowed Will to take control, just as this time Arnaud wanted to. It had led to the death of Alazaïs and her children. He would not allow such an evil act again.

'Her? She's just a whore. She's married, but she threw herself at my brother and tried to pull him from me. She tried to break up the love between him and me. Can you imagine that? It's why she ought to suffer longer. I don't want to kill her now, but I suppose . . .' he smiled, gesturing with his hands, as though holding the palms of both uppermost. The knife moved with his hand, pointing away from her neck.

In that moment, Berenger drew his knife and flung it. It missed Gaillarde's head by an inch, and cut into Arnaud's cheek. He screamed and dropped his knife, and as he did, Berenger was on him, slamming his fist as hard as he could into the lad's nose, feeling the satisfying crackle of breaking bone and cartilage, and then he lifted his knee with all the force he could, smashing it into Arnaud's groin, before stamping with all his weight on Arnaud's foot. The lad fell over, and Berenger retrieved his own blade from the mess on the floor, making sure that he had Arnaud's knife as well.

With his own knife he cut the thongs holding Gaillarde to the cross, and she slumped to the ground, moaning. Denisot went to her and threw his arms about her, and she gave a sigh of relief, but then her eyes were open and on her tormentor.

Arnaud was rocking back and forth on his knees, holding his cods with both hands, his mouth open but silent. Anguish was in his eyes.

Berenger shook his head. Then he took the thongs and bound Arnaud's arms.

CHAPTER FIFTY

They hauled the man through the door of the cottage.

'I should kill him here, now,' Denisot said, holding tightly to his wife.

Voices were approaching. Berenger recognised the other men from his vintaine. 'No. If we kill him out of hand, we're no better than outlaws. He deserves death, and he will have it, but at the hands of our knight.'

'He won't want to hurt me. I am working for God. You can't hurt me.' Arnaud's voice was muffled. He smiled through the blood. 'You can't do anything to me.'

'Really?' Denisot said.

The others appeared in the gloom. 'Is that you, Frip?' Robin called.

'Aye. Don't worry. We have the bastard here.'

But as Berenger walked on, he saw again Sir John de Sully's face as the idea of seeking a murderer in the army was suggested. He saw the doubt in the face of the good Abbot of St Jacques, and he wondered whether Arnaud would truly find his punishment here. It seemed less than likely. Perhaps a dagger to the back of the neck, here in the woods, would be a better solution for all.

Except for the Abbot's expression. He saw again that kindly old man, and heard his calm voice telling him he should go, rather than stay. Now he seemed to hear the Abbot speaking to him again, but this time it was to say that he should deliver Arnaud to justice. He should preserve his own soul, rather than worrying about Arnaud. Perhaps after this war, now that the French King himself was captured, it would be possible for Berenger to find a place in a quiet monastery. He could discover the peace he had craved for so long.

They had reached the farther limit of the trees now, and Berenger pushed their prisoner onwards. The main English camp was at the far edge of the battlefield now, on the plain, and Berenger headed towards the bright glows of campfires.

'Frip, is that you?'

Berenger heard the voice of Peter from Will's company, and he called out quickly in case he and the vintaine could be mistaken for a French counter-attack. 'It's me, Peter, yes.'

'Did you find the man?'

'Yes.'

There was a sudden clatter of weapons. In the darkness, Berenger realised that his little group was surrounded. He saw Fulk lowering his head as though to charge and held up his hand, 'Wait, Fulk! Saul, you too. What is it you want, Peter?'

'Only one thing. We want Arnaud.'

Berenger felt a quickening of his blood. After all the effort to find the murderer, after the guilt he now felt for executing Bernard, the man's commander was going to try to rescue him! 'Your loyalty to your man does you credit, Peter. I hadn't thought you would be keen to help a rapist and murderer who takes his pleasure by inflicting pain on women and children.'

'You think so?'

'I had you marked as an honourable man. You should want to help see this piece of garbage swinging on a gibbet.'

Peter stepped forward now. He had a thin smile on his face as he stood opposite Berenger. He beckoned with a finger and two of his men pushed past Berenger to get Arnaud. 'You understand very little, Fripper.'

Berenger heard a blow and a gasp. Turning, he saw Arnaud collapse.

Peter continued, 'Our company was marked as a group of murderers and heretics because wherever we went, a man with us tortured women and children unnecessarily. It did not serve to enhance our reputation.'

'What would you have me do? If you take him, I must let Sir John know.'

'Fear not, Frip. This is a matter of martial law. I am commander of the company now. He will have a trial, and then the punishment will be meted out in accordance with the law.'

Denisot tugged at Berenger's sleeve. 'You cannot let them take him! He should be punished!'

'I don't think you quite understand, Denisot,' Berenger said, watching as Arnaud was marched away, back down the hill towards the Miosson. 'This is the army's punishment. And he will not survive.'

CHAPTER FIFTY-ONE

Tuesday 20 September

Berenger woke to the sound of clattering. When he opened his eyes fully and stared over the field of the dead, he saw a hand-cart. Dogbreath and Nick were there with the archer's cart, collecting all the spare arrows, but also taking any remnants of iron or steel that other men had missed. Sprinkled over the field were other men, similarly engaged.

He started a fire and mixed himself a small oatcake with a handful of his remaining bag of oats. It was light now, and he weighed the remains of it in his palm, thinking of all the men he had known. He remembered the men from the Crécy campaign: Jack, Geoff and the others, and now this. No more Grandarse, no more of Clip's irrepressible 'Ye'll all get killed!' and he felt a deep sadness to think that they were gone.

'How bad was the carnage up here, Frip?'

He looked up to see Ed. The Donkey had hollows at his cheeks, and the dark bruises under his eyes spoke of the lack of sleep he had enjoyed.

'See for yourself. You were uninjured?'

He touched the back of his head wryly. 'A pommel caught my head and put me out of the fight. I was lucky not to have worse. Archibald pulled me to safety.'

'I am sorry about Béatrice.'

'It was horrible. I think I don't want to serve gonnes again. Seeing what it did to her ...' He broke off, staring at the field of bodies. 'I don't think I could loose one again.'

Berenger said nothing. After some moments, he held out the bag of oats to Ed. He took it, and slowly mixed a patty, adding water from his bottle. 'What will you do?'

'I don't know. I really don't know,' Ed said. 'I mean, I've always been in the army. And now we have their King, so there won't be any more wars. What *can* I do? Without Béatrice, without the army ...'

He looked at Berenger, and in his face there was real fear.

'Frip, what is there for me?'

Others in the camp were being struck by the same thought.

Over with his vintaine, Hawkwood eyed his men. They were not the most effective of fighters, but they had done more than many. He had a grudging sense of pride in them.

'What will you bastards do now?' he asked. Robin had been walking past and stopped to listen.

'Us?' an older warrior asked. He bared his two teeth in what Hawkwood hoped was intended to be a smile. 'We'll drink, eat, and shag as many women as our money will buy!'

'Is that all? What about when your money is gone?' Hawkwood said.

'That's far enough off,' the man said, to general applause.

'Just think, lads,' Hawkwood said. 'You've won a lot today, but now the whole of France is in a turmoil. The whole country, boys.

All the way from Galicia to Brittany is without a king. It seems to me that for a while there will be money for a bold man and a brave bunch of men. The Prince doesn't need us any more. He's off back to Guyenne and thence to London to show off his captives, but we could do a lot worse than stay here. Fripper took a town or two and lived like a Lord. Why shouldn't we do the same?'

'You reckon we could do that?' another man said. He looked thoughtful.

'I reckon we could do better than him. There's good lands down south, so I've heard. The Pope didn't go live at Avignon because it was cold, wet and miserable. There are lands down there that a man could take and enjoy for years.'

'With just eighteen men?' Robin said.

Hawkwood smiled wolfishly, and cast an eye at Robin. 'No, master. But with the men of Fripper's old company, we'd be nearer a hundred, and I'll bet we could collect more as we went. So, what do you men say?'

Berenger found Gaillarde and Denisot later in the morning.

Gaillarde had made some effort to clean her hair and wash her clothing, and now it was still hanging from her in sodden bags, but Berenger could not miss the alteration in the faces of her and Denisot. They looked like newlyweds, or a youth and his first lover. He had no need to guess how they had occupied themselves that morning.

'I hope I see you well, Denisot,' he said.

'We are very well, Vintener.'

'Do you have any plans?'

Gaillarde nodded. 'We have to return to Domps. It was only a tiny town, but it was our home. Our friends would want us to return.'

'There are likely to be all too few living there,' Berenger said.

'We know that. But if nothing else, we can bury our friends,' Denisot said. 'They deserve that.'

'So you will go?'

'Yes, if you give us your permission,' Denisot said.

'As to that, you owe me no allegiance,' Berenger said. 'You joined my vintaine for a period, but I never asked for your oath to me or to the Prince. As far as I am concerned, you are free to leave whenever you wish.'

He took Denisot's hand, and the two men embraced a last time before Denisot took his wife's hand. The two had blankets rolled and tied, and Denisot had a costrel at his waist; his scrip looked as though it was full of bread or meat. Berenger watched as the two made their way down the path to the river, and then out of sight.

'They've gone then?'

It was Peter of Reading. He stood chewing a piece of dried meat, and he cut off a slice for Berenger and held it out to him on his knife's blade.

'It's good.'

Peter gave a grin. 'And I didn't steal it! I paid a brother at the abbey in Montaillou for it. I think they have a good recipe for their dried and cured meats.'

'Monks have the best recipes for anything like that,' Berenger said.

He felt weary, but now he was realising that he felt more an emptiness inside. His life for the last month or more had been driven to seeking out and killing Will and the murderer of Alazaïs and her children, and now that Will was dead, the focus of his life was taken from him.

'It's odd, isn't it? To think that we've caught the King of France! The King himself!'

Berenger nodded. 'Aye. It means our presence is no longer needed here.'

'There are a number of men here who'll leave here with full purses and reach their homes with little left,' Peter said. 'An English soldier with money is easy prey.'

'It was ever the way,' Berenger agreed.

'Would you come back to our company?'

'What?' Berenger burst out, startled. 'Me? After some of the men tried to kill me?'

'Your speedy defence and killing of them would be enough to prevent a repetition of that,' Peter said. 'Besides, you'd have me and the other vinteners working for you. Even Hawkwood. He's keen to come with us. I thought we could become a great army, a Grand Company. We could have our own gynours, farriers, armourers, cooks and all else needful.'

Berenger laughed. 'You think so? No. I am done with war. I will retreat a last time, this time into obscurity. I will join a monastery, if there is one which will have me.'

'The offer remains open.'

'I thank you for that. Tell me, what happened to Arnaud?'

Peter's face hardened like boiled leather. 'He was executed. His body still dangles. I won't cut him down. He went to his death gloating over all the women he killed, saying God will be glad to take him.'

'*His* god is the Devil.'

EPILOGUE

December 1356

It was a good day when he reached the town, but cold. The track had a bluish tinge with white crystals of hoar frost, and his face was pinched from the chill when he turned and saw the massive building at the other side of the river. Smoke rose from two hundred fires, and he stood resting on his staff for a moment, drinking in the view.

Berenger's was not normally a face that a man could easily forget. The livid scar that slashed across, and twisted his mouth into a sardonic grin as though he was laughing at the world, was white in the wintry air. He carried his small pack on one side, and on the other he carried his battered sword.

The bridge was stone, and he stood staring at it for a moment, before stepping onto it and crossing a river yet again. The sound of the river was musical in his ears, but it could not detract from his quick discomfort, thinking of other rivers, other bridges. He had crossed enough rivers in his life. No more, he thought. No more.

Built of granite, the gatehouse was large, grey and imposing. A wicker gate was shut, but there was a grille of iron set at a man's face-height. He tapped on the gate with his staff.

'Yes?'

'I am cold and weary, Porter. May I come and warm myself at your fire for an hour or two?'

'Friend, you look frozen! Please enter.'

'I thank you.'

He walked in with the feeling that his journeys were at last coming to an end. This would, he hoped, soon be his home. And at last he hoped to find peace, here at Tavistock Abbey, where Sir John de Sully had paid for him to live the remainder of his life.

Berenger had served. That last battle at Poitiers was noted as a great victory. The King of France, John, was the King of England's guest, and appeared to have taken to his new life in captivity, until his ransom could be organised, with a good spirit. Sir John said that so long as the man had access to horses, hounds and hawks, he was very content. And meanwhile his son in France continued to make the right noises about supporting his father, while apparently machinating to try to gain ever more authority and power.

That last fight, so Berenger had heard, had been quite winnable by the French. Yet the Duke of Orléans had taken his second battle away from the fight without permission. He later would say that he thought it was already lost, and some said that a messenger came to order him to leave the field. Berenger remembered how Thomas had spoken of the battle beforehand, as though the Duke's action was inevitable, and that the Dauphin wanted to leave his father there. It was surely incredible to think that.

It didn't matter. The battle was done. The fight was over.

Berenger Fripper's wars were over.

AUTHOR'S NOTE

This is a sad note to write, because it is the last in my *Vintener* trilogy.

I had the idea for this book while reading George MacDonald Fraser's excellent *Quartered Safe Out Here*, in which he tells the story of the Burma campaign at the end of the Second World War under Bill Slim. It was clearly a formative time for the author, but the aspect that glowed from every page was the memory of his comrades. The book was a memorial to his platoon, and I wanted to write a trilogy about English soldiers in medieval times.

The stories always had a simple outline: first, the Battle of Crécy; second, the siege of Calais; third, Poitiers. But the battle of Poitiers was a difficult one. It was a whole ten years after the period of the first book, it meant the men would have survived (or not) the Plague, and a number of battles. That aspect always appealed to me, because I thought it would give me scope to look at the lives of the men and how they had changed since the capture of Calais.

MICHAEL JECKS

I have to admit, when I began planning the book, it didn't occur to me how tough the lives of certain men would be!

In the summer of 2014 I was lucky enough to be able to visit the site of the battlefield of Poitiers and the surrounding lands. It was a wonderful experience, and standing and driving about that battlefield helped enormously to let me see and assess how the battle progressed.

While there, I saw the great stone memorial installed by the French. It is dedicated to the dead of France, Guyenne and – to my surprise – England. It was deeply touching to stand there, where so many men had fought and died, and to see that they were all respected, no matter where they came from.

It struck me very forcibly that the English would have been unlikely to have installed, say, a memorial at Hastings to the dead of the Norman invasion, which also made mention of the good men of Normandy who gave their lives.

The battlefield was one highlight; another was our visit to the town of Poitiers.

We were walking about the town with a rather unhappy small boy who was overheating, when we found ourselves outside a lovely medieval church. Thinking it would be less warm inside, we persuaded him to enter, and while he and my wife sat to cool down, I meandered about the place, admiring the carvings and the art. It really was very delightful. However, at one point I noticed a fellow who was equally fascinated by the artwork. He was staring at the ceiling when I realised it was my friend, neighbour and fellow medievalist Ian Mortimer, the author of the superb *Time Traveller's Guide* books. He was visiting Poitiers on one stage of his family holiday, and his appearance that day was pure chance, as was my own!

We had a wonderful time in France, but life for an author rarely runs smoothly, as the following story will illustrate.

On our return, I stored all my photos, plans and outlines on my main computer. Because I used to work in the computer industry, I know the advantage of retaining backups. I have always invested in the most efficient backup systems. However, one evening in February I noticed that there was a glitch with some operations on my computer. Being sensible, all my work was daily backed up to a separate disk and all my photos backed up to a remote server too. However, some photos weren't backed up yet, owing to a problem on the internet service. Still, no matter. Everything was safe on the backup drive. I told my computer to recover from that and thought nothing of it.

Next morning I thought a lot more about it when I discovered the backup disk had a fault. In trying to recover my system, it had successfully wiped my entire disk. My photos from the day of meeting Ian and his family to the present were all lost. All my photos of the battlefield, the pictures of the memorial, the landscape, the French noticeboards explaining the battle and aftermath – all were lost. And still are.

That computer was finally recovered, and I wrote the first draft of this story. And yet my life was not yet to be sweet and easy. After setting up the computer as necessary, I wrote solidly for weeks, only to see that the computer's screen had developed a fault. Pink hieroglyphics scrolled slowly across it, which was interesting. It was caused by a hardware fault that was irreparable. I had to throw that computer away and replace it with a new one. This one.

So, after losing some seven weeks to computer issues and the inevitable time needed to reset them to the standard I need, I was glad to be able to finish the final edit of this book, content in the knowledge that I left the computer industry for good reasons.